FULL CRY

Books by Rita Mae Brown
with Sneaky Pie Brown

WISH YOU WERE HERE
REST IN PIECES
MURDER AT MONTICELLO
PAY DIRT
MURDER, SHE MEOWED
MURDER ON THE PROWL
CAT ON THE SCENT
SNEAKY PIE'S COOKBOOK FOR MYSTERY LOVERS
PAWING THROUGH THE PAST
CLAWS AND EFFECTS
CATCH AS CAT CAN

Books by Rita Mae Brown

THE HAND THAT CRADLES THE ROCK
SONGS TO A HANDSOME WOMAN
THE PLAIN BROWN RAPPER
RUBYFRUIT JUNGLE
IN HER DAY
SIX OF ONE
SOUTHERN DISCOMFORT
SUDDEN DEATH
HIGH HEARTS
STARTING FROM SCRATCH:
A DIFFERENT KIND OF WRITERS' MANUAL
BINGO
VENUS ENVY
DOLLEY: A NOVEL OF
DOLLEY MADISON IN LOVE AND WAR
RIDING SHOTGUN
RITA WILL: MEMOIR OF A LITERARY RABBLE-ROUSER
LOOSE LIPS
OUTFOXED
ALMA MATER
HOTSPUR
FULL CRY

FULL CRY

RITA MAE BROWN

BALLANTINE BOOKS · NEW YORK

A Ballantine Book
Published by The Random House Publishing Group

www.ballantinebooks.com

Library of Congress Cataloging-in-Publication Data
is available from the publisher upon request.

ISBN 0-345-46519-9

Manufactured in the United States of America

First Edition: November 2003

1 3 5 7 9 10 8 6 4 2

Dedicated to Marion Maggiolo
of Horse Country. Foxhunters
would be naked without her.
Now that would scare the foxes!

FULL CRY

CHAPTER 1

A bloodred cardinal sparkled against the snow-covered ground. He'd dropped from his perch to snatch a few bits of millet still visible by the red chokeberry shrubs scattered at the edge of the field. The snow base, six inches, obscured most of the seeds that the flaming bird liked to eat, but light winds kept a few delicacies dropping, including some still-succulent chokeberry seeds.

Low gunmetal gray clouds, dense as fog in some spots, hung over the fresh white snow. In the center of this lovely thirty-acre hayfield on Orchard Hill Farm stood a lone sentinel, a 130-foot sugar maple. Surrounding the hayfield were forests of hardwoods and pine.

Two whitetail deer bolted over the three-board fence. Deer season ran from mid-November to January 2 in this part of Virginia. Those benighted humans who had yet to reach their legal bag limit might be found squatting in the snow on this December 27, a cold Saturday.

Bolting across the field in the direction opposite the deer came two sleek foxhounds. At first the cardinal, now joined by his mate, did not notice the hounds. The millet was too tasty. But when the birds heard the ruckus, they raised their crests and fluttered up to the oak branches as the hounds sped by.

Before the birds could drop back to their feast, four more hounds raced past, snow whirling up behind their paws like iridescent confetti.

In the distance, a hunting horn blew three long blasts, the signal for hounds to return.

Jane Arnold, Master of Foxhounds for the Jefferson Hunt Club, checked her advance just inside the forest at the westernmost border of the hayfield. The snowfall increased, huge flakes sticking to the horse's coat for a moment, to her eyelashes. She felt the cool, moist pat of flakes on her red cheeks. As she exhaled, a stream of breath also came from her mount, a lovely bold thoroughbred, Rickyroo.

Behind her, steam rising from their mounts' hindquarters and flanks, were fifty-four riders. Ahead was the huntsman, Shaker Crown, a wiry man in his middle forties, again lifting the hunting horn to his lips. The bulk of the pack, twenty couple—hounds are always counted in twos or couples—obediently awaited their next order.

Sister cast her bright eyes over the treetops. Chickadees, wrens, and one woodpecker peered down at her. No foxes had just charged through here. Different birds had different responses to a predator like a fox. These creatures would have been disturbed, moved about. Crows, ravens, and starlings, on the other hand, would have lifted up in a flock and screamed bloody murder. They loathed being disturbed and despised foxes to the marrow of their light bones.

On Sister's left, a lone figure remained poised at the fence line. If Shaker moved forward, then the whipper-in, Betty Franklin, would take the old tiger trap jump and keep well to the left. Betty, a wise hunter, knew not to press on too far ahead. The splinter of the pack, which had broken now, veered to the right, and the second whipper-in, Sybil Hawkes, was already in pursuit well away across the hayfield.

Whether Sybil could turn the three couple of hounds troubled Sister. A pack should stay together—easier said than done. Sister blamed herself for this incident. It takes years and years, decades really, to build a level pack of hounds. She had included too many first-year entry—the hound equivalent of a first grader—in to-day's hunt.

First-year entry sat in the kennels for Christmas Hunt, which had been last Saturday. Christmas Hunt, the third of the High Holy Days of hunting, overflows with people and excitement. Both she and her huntsman, whom Sister adored, felt the Christmas Hunt would have been too much for the youngsters. Today she should have taken only one couple, not the four included in this pack. Shaker had mentioned this to her, but she had waved him off, say-ing that the field wouldn't be that large today, as many riders would still be recuperating from the rigors of Christmas. There had been over one hundred people for Christmas Hunt, but she had half that today, still a good number of folks.

The hounds loved hunting in the snow. For the young entry this was their first big snow, and they just couldn't contain themselves.

She sat on Rickyroo who sensed her irritation. Sister felt a per-fect ass. She'd hunted all her life, and, at seventy-two, it was a full life. How could she now be so damned stupid?

Luckily, most people behind her knew little about the art of foxhunting, and it was an art not a science. They loved the pageantry, the danger, the running and jumping, its music. A few even loved the hounds themselves. Out of that field of fifty-four people, perhaps eight or nine really understood foxhunting. And that was fine by Sister. As long as people respected nature, pro-tected the environment, and paid homage to the fox—a genius wrapped in fur—she was happy. Foxhunting was like baseball: a person needn't know the difference between a sinker and a slider when it crossed home plate in order to enjoy the game. So long as people knew the basics and behaved themselves on horseback, she was pleased. She knew better than to expect anyone to behave when off a horse.

She observed Shaker. Every sense that man possessed was working overtime, as were hers. She drew in a cold draught of air, hoping for a hint of information. She listened intently and could hear, a third of a mile off, the three couple of hounds speaking for all they were worth. Perhaps they hit a fresh line of scent. In this snow, the scent would have to be fresh, just laid from the fox's paws. The rest of the pack watched Shaker. If scent were burning, surely Cora or Diana, Dasher or Ardent would have told them. But then the youngsters had broken off back in the woods. Had the pack missed the line? With an anchor hound like the four-year-old Diana, now in her third season, this was unlikely. Young though she was, this particular hound was following in the paw prints of one of the greatest anchor hounds Sister had ever known, Archie, gone to his reward and remembered with love every single day.

Odd how talent appears in certain hounds, horses, and humans. Diana definitely had it. She now faced the sound of the splinter group, stern level, head lifted, nose in the air. Something was up.

Behind Sister, Dr. Walter Lungrun gratefully caught his breath. The run up to this point had been longer than he realized, and he needed a break. Wealthy Crawford Howard, convivial as well as scheming, passed his flask around. It was accepted with broad smiles from friend and foe alike. Crawford subscribed to the policy that a man should keep his friends close and his enemies closer still. His wife, Marty, an attractive and intelligent woman, also passed around her flask. Crawford's potion was a mixture of blended scotch, Cointreau, a dash of bitters, with a few drops of fresh lemon juice. Liberally consumed, it hit like a sledgehammer.

Tedi and Edward Bancroft, impeccably turned out and true

foxhunters, both in their seventh decade, listened keenly. Their daughter, Sybil, in her midforties, was the second whipper-in. She had her work cut out for her. They knew she was a bold rider, so they had no worries there. But Sybil, in her second year as an honorary whipper-in (as opposed to a professional) fretted over every mistake. Sybil's parents and two sons would buoy her up after each hunt since she was terribly hard on herself.

Betty Franklin loved whipping-in, but she knew there were moments when Great God Almighty couldn't control a hound with a notion. She was considerably more relaxed about her duties than Sybil.

Also passing around handblown glass flasks, silver caps engraved with their initials, were Henry Xavier (called Xavier or X), Clay Berry, and Ronnie Haslip—men in their middle forties. These high-spirited fellows had been childhood friends of Ray Arnold Jr. Sister's son, born in 1960, had been killed in 1974 in a harvesting accident. The boys had been close, the Four Musketeers.

Sister had watched her son's best friends grow up, graduate from college. Two had married, all succeeded in business. They were very dear to her.

After about five minutes, Shaker tapped his hat with his horn, leaned down, and spoke encouragingly to Cora, his strike hound. She rose up on her hind legs to get closer to this man she worshipped. Then he said, "Come long," and his pack obediently followed as he rode out of the forest, taking the second tiger trap jump as Betty Franklin took the first. If the pack and the huntsman were a clock, the strike hound being at twelve, Betty stayed at ten o'clock, Sybil at two, the huntsman at six.

Sister, thirty yards behind Shaker, sailed over the tiger trap. Most of the other riders easily followed, but a few horses balked at the sight of the upright logs, leaning together just like a trap. The snow didn't help the nervous; resting along the crevices, it created an obstacle that appeared new and different.

As riders passed the sugar maple, Cora began waving her stern. The other hounds became interested.

Dragon, a hotheaded but talented third-year hound and the brother to Diana, bellowed, *"It's her! It's her!"*

The thick odor of a vixen lifted off the snow.

Cora, older, and steady even though she was the strike hound, paused a moment. *"Yes, it is a vixen, but something's not quite right."*

Diana, her older brother, Dasher, and Asa and Ardent also paused. At nine, the oldest hound in the pack, Delia, mother of the D litters, usually brought up the rear. While her youthful speed had diminished, her knowledge was invaluable. Delia, too, put her nose to the snow.

The other hounds looked at her, even her brash son, Dragon. *"It's a vixen all right, but it is extremely peculiar,"* Delia advised.

"Well, maybe she ate something strange," Dragon impatiently spoke. *"Our job is to chase foxes, and it doesn't matter if they're peculiar or not. I say we give this field another run for their money."*

Cora lifted her head to again look at Shaker. *"Well, it is a vixen and whatever is wrong with line, I guess we'll find out."*

With the hounds opening, their vibrant voices filled the air with a music as lush to the ear of a foxhunter as the Brandenburg Concertos are to a musician.

No matter how many times she heard her pack in full cry, it always made the hair stand up on the back of Sister's neck.

They glided across the hayfield, soared over the stone jumps on the other side, plunged into the woods as they headed for a deep creek that fed the apple orchards for which Orchard Hill was known.

The cardinal once again left off the millet and flew back up into the oak tree.

"Bother," he grumbled to his mate.

"Maybe they'll turn up more seed," his shrewd helpmate answered.

The hounds, running close together, passed under the oak, followed by Shaker, then Sister and the field.

They ran flat out for twenty minutes, everyone sweating despite the cold. The baying of the pack now joined the baying of the splinter group.

It sounded queer.

Shaker squeezed Showboat. A true huntsman's horse, Showboat would die before he'd join the rest of the field. He would be first and that was that.

"What in the goddamned hell!" Shaker shouted. He put his horn to his lips, blowing three long blasts. "Leave him! Leave him!"

The hounds stared up at Shaker. The vixen scent was so strong it made their eyes water, but they weren't crawling over a vixen.

Betty rode up as did Sybil, each staying back a bit so as to contain the pack just in case. Each woman's face registered disbelief. Betty put her gloved hand to her mouth to stifle a whoop of hilarity.

Sister rode up. There, curled into a ball, was deer hunter Donnie Sweigert. His expensive rifle with the one-thousand-dollar scope was clutched to his chest. His camouflage overalls and coat were encrusted with snow, slobber, and a drop or two of hound markings. She wondered where Donnie found the money for his expensive gear. He was a driver for Berry Storage.

Shaker kept calling back his pack, but they didn't want to separate from the terrified Donnie.

"What'll I do?" the cowering man hollered.

Shaker gruffly replied, "Put your head between your legs and kiss your ass good-bye, you blistering idiot!" He spoke sharply to his hounds now. "Leave him! Leave him!"

Shaker turned Showboat back toward the hayfield. The hounds, reluctant at first to leave this human drenched in vixen scent, did part from their odd treasure.

Dragon couldn't resist a parting shot at Donnie. "*And you think we're dumb animals.*"

Sister, as master, couldn't tell Donnie that she thought covering his human scent with fox scent remarkably stupid. She needed to be a diplomat. "Don, are you in one piece?"

"Yes." He unsteadily rose to his feet.

The fox scent, like a sweet skunk, was so overpowering even the members of the field could smell Donnie.

"Would you like help getting back to your truck?" She winked at Walter Lungrun. "Walter will take you back. And he's a doctor, so if anything should be wrong, he'll fix you right up."

"I'm fine." Donnie was still recovering from his fright.

"No one bit you. They would never bite anyone, Don, but, well, you have to admit, the situation is unique."

"Yes, ma'am." He sighed.

"Tell you what." She smiled, and what an incandescent welcoming smile it was. "If you want to, come hunt Monday morning at my place back by the peach orchard. Maybe that will make up for our spoiling your sport today."

He brightened. "Thank you, Sister."

"And Don, don't cover your scent with vixen, hear? Just stay on the backside of the wind. I'm sure you'll get a big one."

"Uh, yes, ma'am."

With that, Sister followed Shaker and the hounds back to the hayfield, back to the tiger trap jumps.

"Edward, take the field a moment, will you?"

Tall, elegant Edward Bancroft touched the top of his hunt cap with his crop.

Sister rode up to Shaker, tears in his eyes from laughing.

"Oh, God, that man is dumb as a sack of hammers."

She laughed, too. "Donnie Sweigert isn't the brightest bulb on the Christmas tree, but to make amends I'm letting him hunt the peach orchard Monday morning. He'll forgo *eau de vulpus*."

At this they both laughed so loudly a few of the hounds laughed out loud, too. That only made the humans laugh harder. The hounds took this as a cue to sing.

"All right, all right." Shaker wiped his eyes as the hounds ended their impromptu carol.

"We've had a pretty good day, all things considered. Let's lift these hounds and go home."

"Yes, boss." He touched his cap with his horn.

Later at the breakfast held at Orchard Hill's lovely 1809 white clapboard house, the mirth increased with each person's retelling of the situation.

Clay Berry told everyone that come Monday morning he'd present Donnie with a bottle of cologne. He'd also give Donnie a fixture card so he could stay away from fox hunts.

"Do you really think humans can disguise their scent? Would a deer have been fooled?" Jennifer Franklin, Betty's teenage daughter, asked Walter. She had a crush on Walter, as did every woman in the hunt club.

"I don't know." Walter smiled. "You'll have to ask Sister that one."

He motioned for Sister to join them. Walter was a well-built man; he'd played halfback at Cornell, and even during the grueling hours of medical school and his internship, he had worked out religiously. Sister stood next to him. At six feet, she was almost as tall as he. She'd lost an inch or so with age.

Those meeting Jane Arnold for the first time assumed she was in her middle fifties. Lean, strong, her silver hair close cropped because she couldn't stand "hat head" from her hunt cap, she had an imposing yet feminine presence.

Walter repeated the question. She thought a moment, then replied as she touched Jennifer's shoulder. "I expect a deer or any of us can be fooled for a little while, but sooner or later your real odor will rise on up, and then you'll be standing like truth before Jesus."

On weekends Jennifer Franklin, a senior in high school, and her best friend, Sari Rasmussen, cleaned and tacked up the horses for Sister, Shaker, and Betty. When the hunt was over, the girls would cool down the horses, wash them if necessary, clean all the tack. When the horses were completely dry, they'd put on their blankets and turn them out, an eagerly anticipated moment for the horses.

The two attractive girls would then attack five pairs of boots, which included their own two. However, this Saturday their high school was having a special late-afternoon basketball tournament, so Sister had given the two girls time off.

During weekday hunts, Betty saw to the horses while Sister and Shaker fed the hounds after a hard hunt. This gave them time to check each hound, making sure no one was too sore or had gotten torn by thorns or hateful barbed wire. If anyone sustained an injury, he or she would be taken to the small medical room, lifted on the stainless steel table and washed, stitched if necessary, or medicated. The hardy hounds rarely suffered diseases, but they did bruise footpads, rip ears, cut flanks.

When Betty finished with the horses, Sister would usually be finished with the hounds. Then the two women would stand in the stable aisle cleaning their tack, the bucket of warm water loosening stiffened, cold fingers as well as softening up the orange glycerin soap.

While the ladies performed this convivial task, Shaker used a power washer on the kennels. Sister would clean his boots when she cleaned hers during the weekdays.

The familiar routine was comforting, but the hunt club really did need at least one more employee. While wealthy members like Crawford would build show grounds because it was flashy, they didn't throw their money in the till for a worker. An employee lacked the social cachet of a building, and the slender budget left no room for another pair of hands. Since Sister and Shaker performed most all of the work, their days were long: sunup to past sundown.

Sister and Betty stood side by side, cleaning their bridles. They were almost finished.

"Read the paper this morning?" Betty asked.

"I don't get to it until supper. What have I missed?"

"Oh, those antique furniture and silver gangs are at it again. The *Richmond Times-Dispatch* had an article about how they're moving through the west end."

"Every couple of years that happens in Richmond. Smart thieves," Sister said.

"Well, what I found interesting was these rings work full-time. They move through Richmond, Charlotte, Washington, even the smaller cities like Staunton or ritzy places like Middleburg. Apart from knowing real George II silver from silver plate or a Sheraton from a Biedermeier, they're obviously well organized."

"I get the Sotheby's catalogues. Some of those pieces sell for the gross national product of Namibia."

Betty laughed. "I've always wondered why people become criminals. Seems to me if they put all that energy into a legitimate career, they'd make enough money."

"I wonder. I can understand a thirteen-year-old kid in the slums not wanting to work for McDonald's when he or she can realize a couple of thousand a month dealing and delivering drugs. But a furniture gang? I know what you mean. The same effort could just as well produce profit in an honest trade."

"Well, maybe there's more profit than we realize. Guess there's a chain of people to make it all work, too, like crooked antique dealers."

"Hmm. It's one thing to steal money, but family silver, furniture—so much emotion tied up in those things. Like all those little silver plates and big trays we won in horse shows when we were young."

"Or my great-grandmother's tea service."

"Are you going to lock your doors?"

"Oh, they won't come out here."

"Hope not, but still, glad I've got my Doberman," Sister said.

The phone rang. As Sister hung up her tack on the red bridle hook, she picked it up. Betty reached up next to her, putting up her hunting bridle with the flat brow and nosebands, its simple eggbutt-jointed snaffle gleaming from rubbing.

"Hello, Ronnie, I'd thought you'd had enough of me today."

He laughed. "It's all over town, hell, all over the county about Donnie Sweigert being, uh, quarry. Guess his nearest and dearest will take to calling him fox urine."

"Bet they shorten that."

"Bet they do, too." He laughed harder.

Ronnie, a man who, besides being fashionable, needed to be the first to know everything, enlivened every hunt. Usually discreet, he could let it rip and surprise everyone.

"What can I do for you? I hope you aren't calling about the board meeting. It's not for three more weeks, and I haven't even thought of my agenda. Well, except for more money."

"Oh, that." His voice registered sympathy. "I say we get each hunt club member to buy a lottery ticket for a dollar each week. If they win, they give half to the hunt club."

"Ronnie, that's a great idea!" Betty leaned close to the earpiece of the phone upon hearing Sister's enthusiasm. Sister put her arm around Betty's waist. A fabulous thing about being a woman was touching, hugging, being close to other women without worrying about repercussions. Men misunderstood affection for sexual interest, and it caused no end of difficulty.

"I was joking."

"But it's a great idea, I mean it. Oh, please propose it at the board meeting. And Betty's right here next to me. I'll tell her all about it so you have two passionate supporters."

"Really? I mean, really?" His tone rose.

"I mean it. You are so creative."

"Actually, that's not why I called." He breathed in, a moment of anticipation and preparation. "You are not going to believe this. I just heard it from Marty Howard at the Subaru dealership. She was picking up her Outback, and I was dropping mine off for its sixty-thousand-mile service."

"I'm waiting. . . ."

"I'm setting the stage." He loved to tease a story. "Anyway, we chatted. I so like Marty, and I will never know why she puts up with that man, but that's another story, so—waiting with bated breath?"

"Yes. So is Betty, whose ear is also jammed to the phone."

"Ah, a larger audience. Well, here it is. Ta da!" He sang the "ta da." "Ready?"

"Ronnie, I'll slap you the minute I next see you."

"I might like it. Well, my dear master, Crawford Howard has hired Sam Lorillard to train his steeplechasers." The silence was so long Ronnie raised his voice. "Sister, did you hear me?"

"I'm trying to fathom the information."

"Can you believe it?"

"No."

Betty shook her head. "Me, neither," she said into the mouthpiece.

"Isn't this gossip too good to be true?"

"I'll say." Sister released her hold on Betty's waist.

Betty reached for the phone. "May I?"

"Of course." Sister then pressed her ear to the earpiece as the women reversed positions, Betty's arm around Sister's thin waist. "Ronnie, it's the Big Betts here."

"Cleavage."

"As if you cared."

"I do care. I'm a highly attuned aesthetic being." He was proud of Betty losing twenty-five pounds last season, and she was working hard on the last ten. "Knowing you, you'll pepper me with questions."

"Right. Since I haven't heard a breath of this, and I know you didn't either or I'd already know, shall I assume Crawford didn't talk to any of the gang?"

"Yes."

"Did Marty say how he hired Sam?"

"She did. We must have talked twenty minutes. The landscape business always slows down to nothing in winter, so she had all kinds of time. Anyway, madam, what she said was, and I quote, 'Crawford called trainers in Maryland, Pennsylvania, and South Carolina, all the big names. They swore that Sam had oo-scoobs of talent.' "

"Did she really say 'oo-scoobs'?"

"Yes."

Betty replied, "I thought only Southerners used that expression."

"She's acclimating. Anyway, I asked her if she knew about Sam's history." He paused. "She said she knew he's fought his battles, hit the bottom, but he's recovered."

"Recovered?" Sister spoke into the phone.

"His brother, Gray, who made all that money in Washington, D.C., put him in a drying-out center. He was there for a month."

"So that's why we haven't seen him passed out on a luggage cart down at the train station?" Betty mentioned one of the favorite hangouts of the county's incorrigible alcoholics. The downtown mall was another.

"How long has he been dry?" Sister again spoke into the mouthpiece.

"Do you want the phone back?" Betty asked.

"Actually, you ask better questions than I do."

"According to Marty, Sam has been sober four months. She said that they extensively interviewed him. They also spent two hours with Gray, and they're satisfied that Sam's the man for the job. Crawford intends to get into chasing in a big, big way."

Betty took a long time. "Well, I hope it all works out."

"But you don't think for a skinny minute that it will, do you?" Ronnie sounded almost eager.

"Uh, no."

Sister took the phone back, "What do you think?"

"I think there's going to be hell to pay."

Sister sighed, then brightened. "In that case, let's hope Crawford's bank account is as big as we think it is."

After they hung up the phone, Sister and Betty just looked at each other for a moment.

Betty finally said, "He *is* good with a horse, that Sam."

"And with a woman."

They said in unison: "Jesus."

CHAPTER 2

Heavy snow forced Sister to drive slowly to the Augusta Cooperative, usually just called the co-op. Since the Weather Channel predicted this storm was going to hang around for two days, she figured she'd better stock up on pet food, laying mash, and kerosene for the lamps, in case the power cut. She also took the precaution of putting the generator in the cellar. Shaker did likewise for the kennel, as well as for his attractive cottage, also on the property of Sister's Roughneck Farm. In these parts, such a structure was called a dependency.

Last year, Sister broke down and bought a new truck for her personal use. The truck used to haul the horses and hounds, an F350 Dually, could pull a house off its foundation, but those Dually wheels proved clunky for everyday use. Installed in her new red half-ton truck was a cell phone with a speaker so she didn't have to use her hands.

"Shaker."

"Yes, boss."

"I'm on my way to the co-op. Need anything?"

"Mmm, late thirties, early forties maybe, good sense of humor, must like hounds and horses and be in good shape."

"Get out." She laughed.

"Mmm, pick up some Espilac if they have any," he said, referring to a milk replacer for nursing puppies. "And if you want extra corn oil for kibble, might could use some."

"Okay. I'll drop it in the feed room at the kennel. Oh, hair color preference?"

"Bay or chestnut."

"I'll keep my eyes wide open, brother."

Ending the call, she maintained a steady fifty miles an hour. The snowplows kept the main arteries clear, and even the secondary roads remained in good shape. If the storm kept up, the volume of snow would overwhelm the state plows, the dirt roads would become difficult to negotiate, and even the major highways would be treacherous. Sister knew that as soon as he hung up the phone, Shaker would pull on his down jacket, tighten the scarf around his throat, jam that old lumberjack hat on his head, and crank up the huge old tractor with the snowplow. He'd keep their farm road open, not an easy task; it was a mile from the state road back to the farm, and there were the kennels and the farm roads to clear out, plus the road through the orchard. Apart from being a fine huntsman, Shaker was a hard worker who could think for himself.

She pulled into the co-op's macadam parking lot, trucks lined up, backs to ramp. The ramps, raised two feet above the bed of a pickup, made it easy for the co-op workers to toss in heavy bags of feed, seed, whatever people needed. Huge delivery trucks fit the ramps perfectly. A man could take a dolly and roll straight into the cavernous storage area.

Each section of the co-op had its own building. The fertilizer section off to the side even housed a shed for delivery and spreading trucks. The special seed section was to the right of the fertilizer building. Catty-corner to both these buildings stood the main brick building, which contained animal food, gardening supplies, and work clothes.

As Sister pushed open the door to the main section, she saw many people she knew, all doing the same thing as she.

Alice Ramy, owner of a farm not far from Sister's, rolled her cart over. "Heard you chased an interested quarry today. I always did think Donnie Sweigert's elevator didn't go all the way to the top."

"Poor fellow. He was stiff with fear." Sister laughed. "He thought the hounds would tear him apart."

"Would we miss him?" Alice tartly remarked.

"I reckon we would. Now Alice, all souls are equal before God."

They both laughed, then rolled down separate aisles to wrap up their shopping before the storm worsened.

As Sister reached for milk replacer, another cart whizzed by her before stopping.

"Jane Arnold," a deep voice called.

She turned to look into the liquid brown eyes of Gray Lorillard, a man of African American descent. Gray was the name of his maternal family, and everyone had always teased him about it when he was a kid. Few teased him these days; he was a powerful, wealthy tax lawyer and partner in a top-notch Washington, D.C., firm.

"Gray, how good to see you. We hardly ever do see you. Home for Christmas?"

He leaned on his cart. "I retired."

"I hadn't heard that. How wonderful."

"Well, I turned sixty-five last August, and I said, 'I don't want to do this for the rest of my life.' I want to farm. Took me this long to wrap things up. Kept the apartment in D. C., still do consulting, but Sister, I am so glad to be back."

"Will you be at the old home place?" She referred to the Lorillard farm, which abutted the eastern side of After All, the Bancrofts' enormous estate.

He looked her directly in the eyes. "Have you seen it?"

"I drive by." She tactfully did not mention its state of disrepair.

"Sam didn't even change the lightbulbs when they blew out." He breathed in, lowering his voice. "I won't be living there with him, though I think he's beat the bottle this time. God, I hope so."

"I'm amazed he's still alive," Sister honestly replied.

"Me, too." He smiled, his features softening. "I expect this storm will have us all holed up. But it has to end sometime." He hesitated a moment. "When it does, may I take you to lunch at the club? We can catch up."

"I hope it ends tomorrow." She smiled.

All the way home, Sister thought about the Lorillards: Sam, Gray, and Elizabeth, each with different destinies. Elizabeth, the middle child, married well, a Chicago magazine magnate. She sat on the city council of the expensive suburb in which she lived, Lake Forest. She evidenced no interest in the home place, Virginia, or, more pointedly, Sam. Gray, a good athlete and horseman, won an academic scholarship to Syracuse, going on to New York University Law School. Sam, also a good athlete and horseman, won a scholarship to Michigan, finished up, then returned to attend the University of Virginia's Darden School of Business. He couldn't stay away from the horses, which everyone understood, but he couldn't stay away from women either. These disruptions and his ever-escalating drinking seemed intertwined.

Sister had ridden with Gray and Sam when they were young. It baffled her how someone like Sam could throw away his life as he did. Not being an addictive personality, she failed to understand willful self-destruction.

The Lorillards' tidy and tight farmhouse had fallen down about Sam's ears. Until four months ago, one often found him down at the old train station, sitting on the baggage carts knocking back Thunderbird with the other drunks.

It pained Sister to see those men. One, Anthony Tolliver, had been the first boy she ever danced with and loved. They remained friends until he lost the battle with the bottle. Anthony, well born, lost everything. On those times when she did see him, he would smile, happy for her presence. The fumes from him made her eyes water. She alternated among disgust, anger, and pity. Bad as he was, Anthony could bring back wonderful childhood memories. She couldn't understand why he couldn't get control of his drinking.

Sister had lived long enough to know you couldn't save someone from himself. You can open a door, but he still must walk through it. It sounded as though Sam had at long last walked through the door his brother opened for him.

At the kennels, she unloaded the corn oil. Shaker walked in. As he took off his cap, snow fell to the floor in white clumps.

"Thanks for plowing the road."

"I'll give it another sweep before the sun goes down."

"Four-thirty. We're just on the other side of the solstice. I miss the light." Sister stacked the Espilac on the shelf.

"Me, too." He shook the remaining snow from his cap as he stamped his boots.

"Ran into Gray Lorillard. Said he's retired and just moved back."

"Ah, that will be a good thing. Maybe he'll start hunting again."

"Hope so. I think he went out with Middleburg Hunt when he worked in D.C. Anyway, we're having lunch once the storm is over. I'll get the scoop."

"Where's my girlfriend?"

She snapped her fingers. "I knew I forgot something. Next trip."

CHAPTER 3

Early Sunday morning, the snow continued to fall. With a six-inch base of snow remaining on the ground from the week before, its depth now measured nearly two feet. Branches of walnuts, black gums, and the gnarled apple trees, coated with snow, took on a soft appearance. The younger pine boughs were bent low with its weight. The older pines appeared wrapped in shawls.

The silence pleased Inky, snuggled in her den at the edge of the old cornfield. This, the easternmost part of Sister Jane's big farm, provided a safe haven for the two-year-old gray fox in her prime. Some grays are quite dark, but not many. Inky was black and uncommonly intelligent. Of course, being a fox meant she was extraordinarily intelligent compared to other mammals.

Even red foxes, haughty about the grays, conceded that Inky was special. She could connect with most mammals, even humans, and had a rare understanding of their emotions. The other foxes readily outsmarted hounds, humans, horses, even bobcats—trickier and tougher than the three "H's," as the foxes thought of the fox-hunting crew. Foxes, reds and grays, thanks to their sense of smell, could pick up fear, sickness, even sexual attraction among other species. But Inky delved deeper. Young though she was, even reds listened when she spoke.

Her den, disguised under the ancient walnut tree, was also hidden by rocky outcroppings, some of the rocks as big as boulders. On high ground with many entrances and exits, not far from Broad Creek—which divided Roughneck Farm from After All Farm—this location offered quick access to fresh running water and all the left-over corn bits Inky could glean. Even better, the field mice haunted the cornfield. There was nothing like a fresh field mouse for a hot, tasty meal.

Inky's littermate, Comet, had stupidly taken over a gopher den on Foxglove Farm across Soldier Road, about three and a half miles from Inky's. Set smack in the middle of a wildflower field, at first this looked like a good thing. However, last fall Cindy Chandler, the owner of Foxglove, had decided to plow under the stalks, fertilize and then reseed with more wildflowers, as well as plant one side of the field with three rows of Italian sunflowers to bring in the birds. Comet, appalled that his den had been exposed, moved to the woods. He should have listened to his sister, who told him not to nest in an open field.

At fourteen inches high, thirty inches long, and weighing a sleek ten pounds, Inky was the picture of health. Her tail, a source of pride, was especially luxurious now that she was enrobed in her rich dense winter coat.

A low rumble alerted her to a human visitor. She stuck her black nose out of the den, a snowflake falling on it. Sister Jane, on her four-wheel drive all-terrain vehicle, pulled up the low farm road, following Shaker's plowing.

The ATV negotiated the snow and most anything else. Sister cut the motor and flipped up one bungee cord, which held a flake of straw. Putting that under her left arm, with her right hand she un-hooked a second bungee cord, which held down a small plastic container of dog food.

She trudged up the rise to the walnut tree. The cold and snow stung her rosy cheeks.

An old cowboy hat kept the snow out of her eyes. As she approached Inky's den, she whistled. She didn't want to frighten the fox, who, if asleep, might not have heard her.

Inky, who had popped back into her den, stuck her head out.

"Good morning, Inky." Sister dearly loved her foxes, but none so much at this one.

"Morning." Inky chortled, a low sound in her throat.

"Here's some straw in case you need to sweeten your bedding. I'm going to put the kibble right by your main entrance here. It's in this plastic canister, which will keep some of the snow away, and Inky, I liberally drenched it in corn oil. You love that."

A round hole, paw sized, had been cut from the bottom of the canister so Inky could pull out food.

"Thank you."

Sometimes when Sister walked alone, no hounds, no house dogs, Inky would walk with her, ten or fifteen yards to the side. They'd reached an accord, these two females, one born of affection and solitude.

Inky didn't much mind the Doberman, Raleigh, but that damned Rooster, the harrier, felt compelled to put his nose to the ground and follow her scent, talking all the while. As a hound, Rooster couldn't help but show off. Much as he irritated Inky, she knew old Rooster had suffered sadness in his life. His master, Peter Wheeler, a handsome, vital man in his eighties, had died two years ago, bequeathing Rooster to Jane—once his lover—and his entire estate to the Jefferson Hunt Club. Sister lavished care on Rooster, but he still missed his "Pappy," as he thought of Peter.

The one Inky really detested was Golliwog, the calico cat,

whose airs plucked Inky's last nerve. As a rule, felines feel they are the crown of creation. Golly took this hauteur to extremes. Sometimes when Inky would visit the kennels to chat with Diana, a particular favorite, Golliwog would saunter by, nose in the air, always no hello. Then she'd buzz around the corner toward Shaker's dependency and emit an earsplitting shriek, "*Fox at the kennels!*" This would rouse the entire pack, who would then rouse Shaker. Inky would skedaddle out of there. Golly was a royal pain.

Sister breathed in, the air heavy, the sky darkest pewter. Inky put her entire head out of her den. Corn oil smelled wonderful. She wasn't going to emerge totally though.

"You know, New Year's Hunt is Thursday." Wanting to reach down and pet the glossy head, Sister restrained herself. "Oh, what a hunt that always is. It's the last of the High Holy Days, so everyone will be decked out in their finest, regardless of the temperature. The horses will be braided. Some of the field will be so hung over they'll glow green." She laughed. "But if they don't make it, they are tormented until the next New Year's Hunt by everyone else who pulled themselves together to brave all. Inky, I don't know why people drink like they do. A glass of champagne or a good single malt scotch now and then, just one, mind you, but anything more," she shook her head, "damned foolishness. Course, if people want to destroy their bodies, that's their business, so long as they don't destroy mine. I look at you and Athena," she mentioned the huge horned owl who showed little fear of humans because she inspired fear in them, "and our other friends, and you all don't wreck your bodies. I can't decide if the human is genetically flawed or has created a society where the pressures are so fierce many folks can't endure them without a little chemical help. Or maybe it's both."

"*You all worry about death too much,*" the prescient creature said, but it sounded like a soft yap.

Sister couldn't understand, but she was a country girl, acutely attuned to animals. "Well, sugar, I'm off to feed the reds down by

Broad Creek. And I am hunting on New Year's, weather be damned. The snow will be over by tonight, the roads will be passable, and Tedi and Edward will plow out a field so everyone can park. The ground will stay frozen, too. That can be difficult." She smiled at the beautiful orange–light hazel eyes looking up at her. "We'll cast down by the covered bridge, so I don't know which way we'll go. Anyway, I don't think you'll be much bothered. And then, dear Inky, the dilettantes will hang up their spurs, winter will deepen, and the balls-to-the-wall gang will stay out. Or should I say the ovaries-to-the-wall? Oh, how I love those January, February, and early March hunts."

"*Sister, you're looking well, and I wish you a Happy New Year.*"

"Bye-bye, babydoll." Sister turned, her tracks already half covered in snow, and returned to her bright red ATV.

Inky hopped out, reaching her paw in the canister hole to retrieve the delicious treat.

Sister drove back to the other end of the cornfield, where a rutted road ran into the farm road. It wasn't plowed out. She would have a long walk to the red fox den. She shouldered a large canister. The two reds, Charlene and Target, lived together and produced many wonderful cubs, most of whom survived, thanks to the care bestowed upon them by Sister and Shaker.

She wormed the foxes on her fixtures once they were old enough—about four months—to ingest wormer. She would stuff freshly killed chickens or sprinkle it over kibble. She and Shaker wormed their foxes on the same schedule as the hounds, once a month, on the first except for whelping season.

When possible, the foxes were trapped and administered a rabies shot—no easy task. Trapping the same fox later for the booster wasn't easy either, but they tried.

Sister and other Masters of Foxhounds did all in their power to ensure a healthy fox population, but most especially they struggled to break the rabies cycles, which spiked about every seven years. Luckily, foxes didn't prove to be the vast reservoir of the rabies virus that skunks, silver-haired bats, and raccoons were, but they still came down with this horrible disease. Thanks to Sister's efforts, the rabies incidence in foxes dropped. Townspeople never thanked fox-hunters for their battle against rabies, a battle that benefited them and their pets, but then again, they didn't know about it. It wasn't in the nature of foxhunters to advertise.

The French had invented an oral rabies vaccine not yet available in the United States. Sister hoped it would come to the States soon because it would greatly help her and other foxhunters protect foxes. Trapping took skill and some sense. A fox will bite. If she could instead put a pill in chicken or ground meat, it would make Sister's mission much easier.

The mile walk to Target's den in the woods winded her. Pushing through the snow sucked up a lot of energy. She placed the canister by the den. Most likely neither Target nor Charlene would pop out and show themselves, but nevertheless they had a decent relationship with their human.

Rarely do a female fox and her mate cohabit. The male may help raise cubs, but he usually has his own place. Still, for whatever reason, these two got along famously, and Target lived with Charlene.

Sister mused on this. When one reads books about foxes or other wildlife, the information is usually correct. But in nature, as in human society, there are always exceptions that prove the rule. In truth, humans knew much less about foxes than about other animals. Considered vermin by state governments, they weren't studied. The sheer adaptability of foxes—their high intelligence and omnivorous appetite—meant the fox could change quickly, do whatever it had to do to survive. Then, too, foxes didn't read books about their supposed behavior. They were free to do as they pleased without fretting over breaking the norm.

"All right, you two," Sister called to the reds, "this will get you through the next week. I'll be coming your way Thursday. You might consider showing yourselves."

"*Maybe*," Target, huge at sixteen pounds, barked.

Sister turned back. The snow was even thicker now, heavier, and she'd have to stick to the last cut cornrow to find her way.

Sister's senses, sharper and deeper, connected her to her quarry as well as her horses and hounds; in a profound sense, she was closer to certain species of animals, closer than she was to most people.

Some believed that those who exhibited this unusual closeness had experienced a childhood trauma, and that such animal lovers are unable to love or trust other people. But Jane Arnold grew up in a loving home in central Virginia. Her friends were the bedrock of her life. In 1974, when her son died at fourteen, and, in 1991, when Big Ray, her husband, died of emphysema, her many friends and the animals pulled her through.

Her son, Ray Jr., also called "Rayray" by the Musketeers, would have been in his forties now. Odd to think of him as middle-aged. His friends had grown older, but Ray Jr. stayed a teenager. She thought of her son every day. Sorrow had long ago burned off. What remained was a love that lifted her up. She did not talk about this. After all, most people are wrapped up in their own lives. She didn't begrudge anyone his or her self-interest. And to speak of love beyond the grave, how might one discuss such a thing?

A grave claims the body, but love will triumph over it. Love is the force of life, and of life after life.

Sister brushed off the ATV's seat, climbed on, turned the key, and headed back to the farm. She'd fed the foxes closest to the farm on the eastern side. Shaker was feeding those on the western side. The people who lived on hunt fixtures, those locations where the club chased foxes, would be out today or tomorrow with food for their foxes. Even the people who didn't ride took care of their foxes. If someone couldn't do it, all they need do was call Sister and she'd make arrangements for the welfare of those foxes.

She parked her ATV in the equipment shed. Smoke hung low over Shaker's chimney. She walked over and knocked on the door.

"'Mon in," he called.

She stepped inside. "What do you think?"

They'd worked together for two decades. He knew what she was asking.

"I think we'll have a good New Year's Day. But you might want to cancel Tuesday and make it up later."

"I've been turning that over in my mind. I'll put it on the hunt-line," she said, referring to the club's phone number, which people call to get messages about the day's activities.

"I don't think the back roads will be plowed out, and Tuesday's hunt is over at Chapel Cross. That's a haul under the best of circumstances. Guess I'll call the Vajays."

The Vajays, a wealthy family originally from northern India, were enthusiastic supporters of the Jefferson Hunt. They owned Chapel Cross and would need to be informed of the change in plans.

"Take off your coat, boss. I'll make coffee."

"Oh Shaker, thanks, but I'd prefer a hot chocolate. You and I haven't had a minute to catch up. Christmas makes us all nuts. Thank God we don't do Boxing Day."

Boxing Day, December 26, was a big hunt day for some American clubs and for all the clubs in Great Britain.

"Got a white Christmas this year, though. Made everyone happy."

"Yes." She hung her coat on a wall peg, opened the outside front door, and shook off her cowboy hat. After she closed the door, she stamped her boots, untying and removing them. Her stocking feet felt the coolness of the uneven-width heart pine floorboards.

"Someone needs to darn her socks." Shaker pointed to a hole in her left sock.

She sighed. "I haven't bought new clothes in years. Jeans, hunt clothing, but no real clothes. I don't know what's the matter with me. I actually like clothes."

"No time to shop." He put on a pot of hot water. She joined him in the small kitchen.

Shaker, a tidy person, liked to entertain. His wife, who had left him four years earlier, had always pulled social events together. When they were together, the dependency was regularly filled with people and laughter. But Mindy, much as she admired her husband, found the long hours of a huntsman and his total dedication to the hounds displeasing. She needed more attention and more money. She left him for a well-off man in Fauquier County. By all reports, she was happy. She was also driving a BMW 540i.

Shaker put out a box of cookies. They sat down.

Sister reached for a sugar cookie. "Before I forget, neither Alice nor Lorraine is particularly a strong woman. Once the snow stops, we ought to go over there tomorrow and see what needs to be done. You can fire up Alice's tractor and plow. I'll feed the chickens and dig out the house."

Alice Ramy studied at Virginia Tech three days a week. She rented and shared her farm with Lorraine Rasmussen and her daughter, Sari—a good arrangement for all.

"Sure. Call and see if they need anything. We can bring it over."

"Okay." She drank her chocolate, happy that Shaker hadn't figured out her hidden agenda concerning Lorraine Rasmussen.

She loved the concreteness of men, particularly Shaker. However, they often missed subtle emotional signs. He was lonely. A good man, he would never be rich or even middle class. But Shaker loved what he did, and he was good at it. That counted for a lot in life.

With the right kind of setting and a little help from friends, Shaker might discover Lorraine Rasmussen and vice versa.

CHAPTER 4

The snow still fell in the Sunday twilight, shrouding the imposing stone pillars to Beasley Hall. The tusks of the two exquisitely rendered bronze boars, now covered in white, glowed even fiercer in the bluish light.

These boars had cost $25,000 apiece when Crawford Howard purchased them eleven years ago. An arrival from Indiana, Crawford made a fortune building strip malls throughout his home state. Upon visiting Monticello in his early thirties, he'd fallen in love with central Virginia. Once he made enough to feel truly secure, he moved to the area and promptly became a member of the Jefferson Hunt. This was complicated somewhat by the fact that he couldn't ride the hair of a horse. Determination and ego kept him taking lessons for years until he finally edged up from the Hilltoppers to First Flight. Not everyone in First Flight welcomed his graduation, for, although he could usually keep the horse between his legs, he knew precious little about foxhunting.

A man of many vanities, he endured liposuction, a face-lift, and hair plugs. Yet, Crawford had good qualities. Highly intelligent, he was not bound by the Virginia Code: a complex ritual of behavior rivaling the eighteenth-century courts of Europe. Upon reflection, Virginia was still in the eighteenth century. Of all the southern states, Virginia and South Carolina were the strongest in their labyrinthine codes. Crawford thought outside the code, and sometimes even his good ideas and insights ruffled feathers. Sister Jane, herself a product of the code, squelched her distaste and listened to him. Being a good leader, Sister knew you used the material at hand.

At first Crawford couldn't stand Jane Arnold. She could ride like a demon. He hated being physically shown up by a woman, especially one nearly twenty-five years older than himself. She circled around problems and people instead of striking straight to the heart of the issue, which drove him crazy. Unless she was dealing with someone extremely close to her, Sister took her time, stepped lightly, and tried to help antagonists save face. In time, he learned to respect her methods just as she learned to respect his.

This gave rise to Crawford's greatest vanity; he desperately wanted to be joint-master. It was apparent to all that Sister must take on a joint-master to train for the day when she would be riding with the Lord. She was dragging her heels.

Crawford thought Jane Arnold did not wish to share power. Well, yes and no. She needed the right person, one whom the other members—all of them strong people and opinionated—would respect. She also wanted a true hunting master.

Putting MFH behind a man or woman's name could turn him or her into an insufferable grandee. Crawford could be plenty insufferable as it was.

His wealth was a crowbar. Sooner or later he would pry open the old girl. He was counting on it. It fed his drive, shored up his patience, propelled him to build an expensive showgrounds with a grandstand on acres donated by the Bancrofts, who had even more money than Crawford, which irked him. In a flash of brilliance, he named the grandstand in honor of Raymond Sr., and the ring—a beautiful thing with perfect footing—after Ray Jr.

He didn't think of this himself. His wife, Marty, helped him. The idle town gossips said she was with him because of his money. Anyone who doesn't comprehend the importance of money is a born fool, but Marty, during a public affair of Crawford's and their separation, had acted with dignity. In the end, this meant more to Crawford than anything else. She could have stuck him up, kept them in court for years, and curdled whatever joy might be possible with someone else. She did not upbraid him for his affair. In fact, she never mentioned it. The Virginians, in their overweening pride, felt that Marty Howard acted as "a lady of quality"—which is to say, as a Virginian. Marty *was* a lady of quality. Apparently, they breed them in Indiana as well as Virginia.

Marty actually loved Crawford. She knew underneath his terrible need for show and power, and his fear of losing his sex appeal, beat the heart of a good man. His ways might offend, but he truly was on the side of the angels. She had loved him from the day they met at the University of Indiana in Bloomington.

Without recognizing it, Crawford gave clues to his inner life. When Sister Jane first beheld the imposing, ferocious boars atop the equally imposing pillars, she said to Crawford, "The Duke of Gloucester, later Richard III, had just such boars as his emblem."

Before she could continue, Crawford jumped in, "1483 to 1485. Yes, he's a bit of a hero of mine because I believe he was faithful to the crown. When his brother, King Edward, died, the Woodvilles tried to take over England. They were commoners—grasping, greedy—but, well, Edward had to have her. And by God, she was queen. Civil war seemed unavoidable, even though Richard was named protector until the eldest son, just a boy, could inherit. He was an able administrator, a good warlord. From his estate at

Middleham in Yorkshire, he was forever driving back the Scots. He was a strong king, but so many suspicions were planted against him, many by the Woodvilles and their supporters."

Sister, upon hearing this, was not surprised that Crawford knew history. She smiled. "I always thought his biggest mistake was not in killing the princes in the Tower, if indeed he did, but in dispensing with the Earl of Warwick, his cousin. Richard Neville was more than a cousin, he was Richard III's right arm."

This discussion and recognition built the first bridge between Sister and Crawford. Impressed that she read history and had a real sense of the swing of power, he wondered whether perhaps there was more to her than a hard-riding, handsome old broad.

For her part, Sister sensed that Crawford was a kind of Richard III, a man of tremendous ability and loyalty whose ambition was not naturally destructive. Like Richard, Crawford lacked the outward conviviality of Edward IV, whom Richard succeeded and mourned.

As years rolled by, Sister made a point now and then to invite Crawford for coffee, just the two of them. She would also have Crawford and Marty to small dinners, carefully selecting her guests, never more than eight.

In time, older hunt club members did their best to get along with Crawford because of Sister's example. And he did siphon money into the treasury, for which every single member was grateful, even Bobby Franklin, the president, and Bobby couldn't abide the man.

Bobby Franklin would say, sotto voce, that one of the happiest days of his life was when Crawford moved up from the Hilltoppers to First Flight. Poor Bobby. As Master of Hilltoppers, he had to handle green horses, green riders, or, the worst of the worst: a green horse dealing with a green rider. Bobby's sympathies rested with the horse. By the time people made it to First Flight, Bobby, a font of hunting lore, had drummed the basics into their heads.

Crawford looked out the window from his beautiful living room decorated by Colefax and Fowler. The decorating bill for the living room alone amounted to $275,000. Naturally, his estate had been featured in decorating magazines on both sides of the Atlantic.

In Virginia, money whispers. For Crawford, it shouted. He couldn't help it. Marty tempered him a bit, but his need for display usually won out.

"Well, the goddamned Weather Channel has it wrong yet again." He tapped his manicured forefinger against the cold windowpane.

Marty walked over. "Here."

He gratefully took the brandy snifter and sipped the warming, delicious cognac. "Rituals of pleasure."

She smiled. "Perfect coffee in the morning; a strong cup of tea at four in the afternoon; and brandy at twilight in the winter, a cool Tom Collins in the summer."

"Hot kisses at bedtime." He wrapped one arm around her waist. "Bet Tuesday's hunt will be canceled. I was sorry that Sorrel Buruss canceled tonight's cocktail party, but only you and I could have gotten there."

He had recently bought a Hummer II and thought he could drive up Everest with it. His daily driver was a metallic red Mercedes S500. Crawford eschewed the other Mercedes: M's, C's, and E's. A real Mercedes was an S or an SL, and that was that. Marty sensibly drove a Subaru Outback and was quite happy with it, even though Crawford wanted to buy her a Toyota Land Cruiser.

"Hot kisses? I'll drink to that." Marty touched her glass to his and took a sip.

"Hard to believe it's almost the New Year. Honey, I've been thinking. I swore when we moved here I would retire—"

"Managing your investments is a full-time job."

"It's not enough for me."

"Darling, you're on the Board of Governors of the Jefferson Hunt Club, the board for Mercy Hospital, the national board for

Save Our Farmland. You do so much even I lose track, and I'm pretty good with details." She flattered him. "And let's not forget that you are treasurer for the Republican Party in this county and, I expect, sweetie, will be tapped for that job for the state."

"I don't think they'll put a non-Richmonder in that slot," he replied.

"Oh, yes, they will. You're smarter than all of them, and you have great connections out of the state. But," she sighed a mock sigh, "I know you. What are you planning now? What world will you conquer?"

"First things first: I will be joint-master this year. The hunt selects the master on Valentine's Day. A funny little tradition. Most hunts do it May first, unless they're private packs, of course. February's Board of Governors meeting is February eighteenth, so Sister Jane will have to make her decision by January's board meeting, the twenty-first."

"You'll be a wonderful master." Marty kept to herself that she thought immediate chances of this honor were slim.

He stared out the window. The snow, a white curtain, obscured even the English boxwoods lining the curving front walkway to the columned portico.

"This has been some kind of winter." He took another sip. "Let's sit by the fire. I like to look at you in the firelight."

She kissed his cheek. They walked to the overstuffed sofa, squeezing side by side as the flames, orange, red, a hint of blue, cast warmth.

"Honey, how do you think Sam Lorillard is working out?"

He put his snifter down, stretched his hands. His joints hurt. "So far, so good. Too early to really tell."

"Fairy thinks there will be trouble in the hunt field with Sam."

Fairy Partlow kept the Howards' foxhunters in tune. In her late twenties, she had proven surprisingly capable and reliable.

He exhaled through his nostrils. "Reminds me. I forgot to give the club money for Sam to ride as a groom. I'll check with Sister."

"Fairy hasn't been out in two weeks. Hunting, I mean," she said.

Fairy rode as a groom, a policy most hunt clubs use to include stable help employed by wealthier members. As a rule, the grooms rode better than their employers and were helpful in the field, as they rode in the rear.

"Well, now that Sam's here, and I've hired Roger Davis to help out with the horses, maybe she can hunt more. But this damned weather has got us all holed up." He put his arm around his wife's shoulders. "Hunt field is the best place to bring young 'chasers. Sam needs to hunt, too."

Crawford, having talked to old-timers in the steeplechase world, thought he'd stick to the tried-and-true ways of the past, although many a modern owner and trainer no longer did.

Eager to make a bigger mark, he was purchasing young steeplechase and hunter prospects, hence his recent hiring of Sam.

"Fairy says over the years Sam has worked for members of the club and fallen foul of some of them."

"Oh, these damned Virginians never forget a thing. That's ancient history."

"If someone sleeps with your wife, I doubt it ever becomes ancient history," she quietly said.

His eyebrows rose. "Oh. Who did Sam sleep with?"

"Henry Xavier's Dee. Ronnie Haslip told me in confidence. That Ronnie knows everyone and everything."

"Really?"

"And the list goes on, of women I mean."

"Hmm." He dropped his chin for a moment, thought, then raised it. "He's gone through rehab. He goes to AA meetings at least five nights a week. There has to be some forgiveness in the world." Crawford did believe in forgive but never forget.

"Hopefully."

"Can't understand how those women fell for him. He's a bandy-legged, skinny little thing. Nice color though."

Café au lait was Sam's coloring.

"He was younger then. Alcohol ravages even the most beautiful. Think of Errol Flynn or William Holden."

"Mmm. Too far back for me."

She lightly punched him. "You'll pay for that."

"How about now?" He pulled her to him, kissing her.

"What a good idea."

CHAPTER 5

Are you doing this to irritate me?" Delia, mother of the D litters, crossly said to Trudy, a racy second-year entry.

"*No,*" the young hound replied as they walked through the snow. The humans accompanied them on foot this Tuesday morning.

Sister, Shaker, Betty, and Sybil Bancroft—she'd taken back her maiden name—each wearing warm boots, marveled at the beauty of this crisp morning.

The snow did not stop Sunday night as predicted, but floated down throughout Monday, finally ending late Monday night. The road crews in Virginia, more accustomed to dealing with flooding conditions or old macadam roads bubbling up in fierce heat, worked twenty-four hours even in the storm to keep the interstates open. Given that Virginia generally gets far less snow than upstate New York, the state budget allowed for the purchase of only a small number of snowplows. Close to the mountains it snowed more regularly, so the state, and it was a good plan, sold the work out to local people. Anyone with a snowplow attachment to a heavy-duty truck, a bulldozer, or even a big old dump truck could earn some extra money during the storms. The dump trucks followed the plows. As the snow would be scraped up and piled to the side, the dump truck driver would slowly release a load of sand. Sometimes salt would be mixed in with the sand, wreaking havoc on the underbodies of older cars and trucks.

Unless more snow fell, or, worse, the temperature climbed and it rained, the New Year's Hunt would go off without a hitch. And it would be beautiful, given the snow.

All the hounds that were not in season or were puppies came out on hound walk today. Sister and Shaker wanted to see if anyone was footsore or not moving properly. Both master and huntsman bordered on the fanatical concerning hound care. The Jefferson Hunt pack of American foxhounds enjoyed robust health, shining coats, and clean teeth. Their monthly expenses ran at about $1,500, give or take a few hundred, depending on special events such as a whelping difficulty, which would entail a veterinary bill.

Sister Jane's kennel standards were so high she was often cited as a model by other hunts. Individuals hoping to start a pack of foxhounds made the journey to see her kennels and hounds. They came from as far as California.

The pack knew they were splendid. Even on hound walk they moved in long fluid strides, brimming with confidence, bright eyes, and cheerful demeanors. This was a happy pack.

However, at this exact moment, Delia wasn't happy. She feared being left in the kennel for New Year's Hunt due to her age. While indeed the territory was demanding, her conformation was so good, her lung capacity and heart girth perfect, that she showed no signs of breaking down. Still, she had slowed a little, and Dragon, Dasher, and Diana, her third-year litter, pushed up front. Last year's litter— now in their first year, Darby, Doughboy, Dreamboat, Dana, Delight, and Diddy—also possessed speed, as well as their mother's power of endurance.

Trudy, also quite fast, was walking next to Delia. She bumped the older hound by accident, turning around to see what Betty Franklin was laughing about. A young hound didn't bump into an older hound without repercussion; the older hound took this as a challenge to authority. Kennel fights could be started with less provocation. Fortunately this pack had few of those.

"*You mind your manners,*" Delia growled.

The other hounds knew not to respond, even Dragon, a real smartass. While Delia was not the head bitch, she was older, and the other hounds knew their place. Cora, the head bitch, lorded it over everyone. She used her power wisely, but no one except for the first-year entry, who weren't born yet, would forget the hunt when Dragon disobeyed her: she bumped him so hard he fell on his side, and then she sat right on him. When he struggled to get up, she threw him down again, this time with her jaws on his throat. Dragon deserved it, and he might challenge other hounds, but he had yet to challenge Cora again. That reminder of who was boss kept the rest of the season running smoothly.

Above Cora on the ladder of authority were Shaker and Sister. The hounds respected the two whippers-in, but didn't necessarily think those two humans were pack leaders. Sometimes it was hard for the pack to remember that Sister and Shaker were humans. To the hounds, they were flawed hounds on two legs, yet possessing special gifts such as better sight during daylight.

The going would be tough on Thursday, so Sister and Shaker closely watched hounds. No one with even a slight crack in his or her pad could go out since they would be crossing icy creeks. Better not to take a chance of cutting open a crack. Any hound who was a bit weedy wouldn't be going out. On a day like Thursday might be, some slim hounds ran off every bit of extra fat they had, and Sister didn't want that. If a hound ran off too much weight during the season, it was hard to put it back on until the off-season. She monitored weight daily. All her hounds enjoyed good lung capacity, but Delia, well built, was older, as was Asa and a few others. Steady and true as they were, and therefore worth their weight in gold, Sister was indeed considering keeping them in the kennel on this particular High Holy Day.

A good hound cries, whines, howls when it sees the rest of the pack go to the draw pen. It's like a quarterback being benched.

Each branch and bough, the sunken lane, the top of the ridge, sparkled with a million tiny rainbows as the sun rose. First the snows were blue, then pink, then orange to scarlet, and finally white, with the rainbows dazzling everyone.

Athena, wings close to her body, dozed in a blue spruce. Her nest wasn't far, but she didn't feel like going inside just yet. She opened one golden eye, peering down at the hounds and humans, then she closed it. Athena, over two feet high, occasionally worked with the foxes. As they flushed game on the ground, she'd swoop down and snatch up a mouse. She would sometimes tell the groundlings where mice, rabbits, and other creatures moved about. She didn't make a habit of it, though. She preferred working alone.

Sometimes Bitsy, the little screech owl, now residing in Sister's barn, flew alongside her. Athena could tolerate Bitsy only until she let out one of her hideous screeches, which the little bird thought so melodious. Tin ear.

Cora caught a whiff of Athena. No point mentioning it. Owl wasn't game. And it wouldn't do to get on the bad side of Athena.

They walked a mile west, then turned back. The return was easier since they didn't have to break snow.

Asa moved up alongside Delia. *"What do you think?"*

"They need us," she answered. *"If Sister and Shaker put in too many of the T litter, they'll be toast. Those young'uns haven't settled yet."*

On hearing this, Trident couldn't help but protest. *"We've done really, really good."*

"Oh? I recall during cubbing that you wanted to track a skunk." Asa chuckled.

"No fair. My first real hunt." Trident, handsome, with unusually light eyes, didn't appreciate the reminder.

The other hounds giggled.

"They love the snow," Betty said, smiling, upon hearing the low chatter among the pack.

"That they do. Much rather be out in this than those hot September mornings," Sybil agreed.

"I start at seven, and it's boiling by eight." Sister, on the front left corner, chimed in.

"Summer in Virginia can stretch into November sometimes," Shaker said.

"Not this year." Betty laughed. "I can't remember this much snow. In 1969 we had a lot, or maybe we didn't. Maybe I just remember it because it snowed like blazes on Easter."

"No one could get to church." Sybil, too, remembered. She had been in grade school.

"We've been lucky this year." Sister paid a lot of attention to the weather. "This was our fourth year of drought. Without the wet fall and snow to date, I think we'd all be cooked this summer. My well has never run dry and Broad Creek has never run dry, but I think it would have happened this summer without this rain and snow."

"I remember the first time I traveled out west," said Sybil. "Mom and Dad sent Nola and me to a dude ranch in Sheridan, Wyoming. Loved it. But that's where I learned the history of the West is the history of the battle for water. They killed one another for it in the nineteenth century. Drought is a part of their history. Pretty rare here."

"Westerners kill one another with SUVs instead of six-guns." Betty laughed.

"That's California." Sybil smiled. "Wyoming, they drive trucks just like us."

"Beautiful place, parts of it." Sister, like Sybil, loved the West, including the Canadian West. She bore a deep respect for Canadians.

They turned into the kennels. Sister, Betty, and Sybil watched as the hounds bounded into the draw yard, to be separated there into the bitch yards and the dog yards.

"Well?" Betty's light eyebrows quizzically shot upward.

"Given conditions, I think I'd better leave first entry in the kennels. It's a lot to handle: all those people. I really shouldn't have taken out those two couple for Christmas Hunt. I mean, even though the field is behind the hounds—God willing." They laughed because dumb stuff does happen. "All the excitement is pretty overwhelming for a young hound."

"Our hounds are high. No doubt about that." Sybil said this with pride. While a high pack is harder to handle, Sybil believed they showed much better sport, as did everyone else on staff.

This was not a belief shared by every foxhunter. The four types of foxhound—American, English, Crossbred (a cross between the American and English hound), and the Penn-Marydel hound—reflected different philosophies of hunting, as well as adaptation to different climates and terrain.

American hounds possessed high drive, sensitive temperaments, and good noses. They were often racy-looking, although the old American bloodlines might have heavy bones.

Added to the hounds used for mounted hunting were foxhounds for foot hunting or night hunting: Walkers, Triggs, even Redbones and Blueticks could do the job if trained for fox scent. These, too, were wonderful canines, each displaying special characteristics.

Such a wealth of canines created passionate discussions about which hounds are best for what. Foxhunters and all Southerners learned as children that you can criticize a man's wife and children before you can say word one about his hounds.

Although loath to admit it, Sister, too, fell into that slightly fanatical category. She kept her mouth shut about it, but she was devoted, passionate, even rapturous about the American foxhound, especially those carrying the Bywaters bloodline. This didn't mean she wouldn't listen to other hound people, and she had ridden behind packs of other breeds that would have made any master proud. But she loved the American foxhound with her heart and soul.

"Okay, boss," Shaker called from the draw yard.

The hounds, bellies full, retired to their respective runs for sleep or conversation.

Sister, Betty, and Sybil joined Shaker in the small toasty kennel office. Sister sat on the edge of the desk, Shaker leaned against the refrigerator, Sybil and Betty perched on the old office chairs.

"Coffee?" Shaker offered.

"God, yes." Betty rose and poured herself a cup from the eternally percolating pot. She blinked, realized she'd forgotten her manners, and handed the cup to Sybil, who laughed at her.

"Okay, this is what I think. First year in the kennels. We can take all the second-year entry, and I'm still debating about our oldest hounds." Sister thought a moment, then spoke a bit more rapidly. "Unless there's a big change in the weather or injury, let's take Delia, Asa, and the few older citizens. I don't think we're going to have a four-hour hunt in the snow on Thursday. I really don't. And this will be their last High Holy Day; they need to retire after this season."

"I have dibs on Asa." Sybil held up her hand.

"After cubbing. I'll need them with me to start our next year's entry, but he'd be happy to grace your hearth."

"He'll hunt," Shaker mentioned.

"Oh, well, he can hunt to his heart's content. All the foxes at the farm will hear him coming."

They would indeed, for Asa had the voice of a basso profundo.

"Do you want me to come over to the kennels?" Sybil inquired.

"No. We're hunting from your farm. Might as well stay there. We'll meet you at the party wagon." Sister called the hound trailer— a refitted horse trailer—the party wagon.

"Hope it's a good go." Sybil's eyes brightened.

"Hope it's a good year." Betty laughed.

"If we're all together, we're healthy, the hounds are healthy, it's going to be a banner year."

"I'll drink to that." Shaker held up his coffee mug.

The others followed suit, touching one another's mugs.

CHAPTER 6

Thursday morning, New Year's Day, when Sister awoke at her accustomed five-thirty, a low cloud cover hinted more snow was on the way. Darkness enveloped the farm. The thermometer outside Sister's bedroom window read thirty-six degrees Fahrenheit.

When the sun rose two hours later, the cloud cover remained. This was going to be an interesting day: the ground was hard, icy in spots, and the snow hard packed to about a foot and a half. Sister could smell more moisture coming.

In the winter most Virginia hunts meet at ten. As the earth tipped her axis and more light floods the rolling pastures and woodlands, that time is pushed up to nine, often by mid-February.

New Year's Hunt, however, begins at eleven: a concession to the rigors of braiding and the struggle to sober up for many. The later time also allowed the earth to warm a bit more, though today's cloud cover held in some warmth.

Later that morning, parked to the right of the covered bridge at Tedi and Edward Bancroft's After All Farm, the hounds peered out of the party wagon. They saw some people blowing on fingers as they slipped on polished bridles, while others repaired unruly horse braids or tried for the umpteenth time to force their stock tie pin level across their bright white or ecru stock ties.

The most fashionable of hunters, and this was unrelated to wealth, wore a fourfold tie on formal hunting days. Occasionally, they might wear a shaped tie, but on the High Holy Days, one wouldn't dream of anything but the fourfold tie. For one thing, it looked better. For another, it kept one's neck warmer. These good features did not make the tie any easier to work with. Many a fox-hunter expanded his or her vocabulary of abuse while fumbling.

The High Holy Days required members and horses to look their best. In the old days of hunting when agricultural labor, in-deed all labor, was less costly, people came to every formal hunt with their horses' manes braided. They usually came with two horses. Their groom kept the second horse at the ready to be switched halfway through the hunt. Then, also, many hunts enjoyed a brief repast while members switched horses. Those days had vanished.

Most foxhunters worked for a living. They prepared their horses themselves, and braiding sucked up time as well as patience. At the Jefferson Hunt Club, braiding was now required only for Opening Hunt, Thanksgiving Hunt, Christmas Hunt, and New Year's Hunt. Many older hunt clubs wished their members to braid for a meet with another hunt, but few could enforce this. It was seen as a tip of the cap to the visiting hunt, a form of respect and welcome.

With the exception of Tedi, Edward, Sybil, Crawford, Marty, Sister, Betty, and Shaker, everyone present had braided their own horses. As master and huntsman, Sister and Shaker had Lafayette and Hojo braided by Jennifer Franklin, who also did her mother's horse, Outlaw. Of course she held it over her mother. At seventeen Jennifer could be forgiven.

On New Year's Hunt, Sister Jane wore her shadbelly: a black swallowtail coat, exactly as one sees in the nineteenth-century prints. The canary points of her vest peeked out underneath the front, perfectly proportioned. Her top hat glistened, the black cord fastened to the hook inside the coat collar in back. Her breeches, a thin buckskin, were much like what Washington himself wore when he hunted. Over the years they had softened to a warm patina: once canary, they were now almost buff.

For years, people could no longer find buckskin. Then Marion Maggiolo, proprietor of Horse Country in Warrenton, found someone in Europe to make them. One pair of breeches could last a lifetime, justifying the stiff price of six hundred and some odd dollars.

For Christmas, the members had all chipped in and bought Sister a new pair of buckskin breeches. Betty drove up with her to Warrenton to be properly fitted, and Sister couldn't wait for their arrival.

Crawford, of course, flashed about in his impeccably cut scarlet weaselbelly. His properly scarlet hat cord, a devil to find these days, hung from his top hat, the crown of which was about a half inch higher than that worn by a lady. Both top hats slightly and gracefully curved into the brim. Like a red hat cord for a man, a lady's proper top hat was a deuce to find. Given the difficulty in finding the real thing—it could take years—many women gave up, donning dressage top hats. No one was critical, and although they didn't look quite as lovely, they still looked good.

Leather gloves were soft canary or butter. Along with leather gloves, a pair of string gloves were under the horse's girth. These warm gloves helped riders keep the reins from slipping through their fingers if it rained or snowed. Then, if necessary, riders would tuck their leather gloves in their pocket or under their girth and pull out the string gloves, which were brilliant white or cream.

Men with colors wore boots with a tan top. The ladies with colors wore boots with a patent leather black top. Everyone else wore butcher boots, usually with the Spanish cut—meaning the outside part of the boot covering the calf was longer than the inside portion. Butcher boots had no tops. All boots were polished to such a feverish degree that one could see one's reflection.

The spurs, hammerheads or Prince of Wales, also sparkled, even with cloud cover.

Fabulous as people looked—some wearing hunt caps, a few others in derbies, which were proper with frock coats—the horses trumped them all. Chestnuts gleamed like flame, and bays glowed with a rich patina. Seal brown horses and blood bays, not often seen, caught everyone's eye. A blood bay is a deep red with black mane and tail. It's a beautiful color, as is a flea-bitten gray or a dappled gray. A few of these were present, as well as some of those dark brown horses that appear black to the human eye.

Henry Xavier had mounted his paint, Picasso—a large warmblood—to account for his increasing weight. Dr. Walter Lungrun was so resplendent in his tails, black rather than scarlet, that women swooned when they beheld the blond doctor. He was on a new horse he'd purchased in the summer, Rocketman, a big-boned, old-fashioned thoroughbred bay with a zigzag streak down his nose. Clemson, Walter's tried and true, went out with him on informal days.

The horses were bursting with excitement, for the morning was cool and they liked that. In many ways, they reflected their owners' skill, status in the hunt field, and, in some cases, dreams. Hunt fields always have those members who are overmounted, members who want desperately to be dashing on a gorgeous horse. Usually they're dashed to the ground. Sooner or later, such folks realize what kind of horse they truly need. Pretty is as pretty does. If not, they stalk away from foxhunting with grumbles about how dangerous it is and how stupid their horse is. It's not the horse that's stupid.

Hunting is dangerous. However, the adrenaline rush, the challenge, the overwhelming majesty of the sport, the sheer beauty of it get in a rider's blood. Those who foxhunt can't imagine living without it; even the danger adds spice.

Life itself is dangerous, but millions of Americans in the twenty-first century are so fearful of it that they retreat into cocoons of imagined safety. Small wonder obesity is a problem and psychologists are thriving.

Humans need some danger, need to get their blood up.

It was up at eleven. The field was large even with the cold. Seventy-one riders faced the master.

"Ladies and gentlemen, the hounds and I wish you a Happy New Year. We wish you health, prosperity, and laughter. May you take all your fences in style, may your foxes be straight-necked, and may your horse be one of your best friends.

"Shaker, Betty, Sybil, and I are grateful that so many of you have turned out, looking as though you've stepped out of a Snaffles' drawing, on this cold day. The footing will be dicey, but you've ridden through worse.

"Tedi and Edward invite us all to breakfast at the main house after the hunt. Do remember to thank them for continuing the wonderful tradition of New Year's Hunt here at After All Farm.

"Let's see what the fox has in store for us." She looked to Shaker, cap in hand. "Hounds, please."

He clapped his cap on his head, tails down (for he was staff). Whistling to the pack, he turned along Snake Creek, which flowed under the covered bridge.

Huntsman and hounds rode up the rise, passed the gravesite of Nola Bancroft, Tedi and Edward's daughter, who had perished in her twenties. She was buried alongside her favorite mount, Peppermint, who, by contrast, lived to thirty-four. This peaceful setting, bound by a stonewall, seemed especially poignant covered in the snow.

Betty, first whipper-in, rode on the left at ten o'clock. Sybil, second whipper-in, rode at two o'clock. The side on which they rode did not reflect their status so much as it reflected where Shaker wanted them on that particular day at the particular fixture. He usually put Betty on the left though.

Sam Lorillard and Gray also rode out today. How exciting to have Gray back in the field. Crawford had requested Sam to ride as a groom, and Sister had given permission.

The edges of Snake Creek were encrusted with ice, offering scant scent unless a fox had just trotted over. Shaker moved along the low ridge parallel to the creek. An eastern meadow about a quarter of a mile down the bridle path held promise of scent. The sun, despite being hidden behind the clouds, might have warmed the eastern meadows and slopes.

Once into the meadow, a large expanse of white beckoned.

Delia advised her friends, *"Take care, especially on the meadow's edge. Our best chance is there because the rabbits will have come out on the edge of the wood and meadows. All foxes like rabbits. Our other chance for scent today is if we get into a cutover cornfield. Fox will come in for the gleanings."*

Asa, also wise in his years, agreed. *"Indeed, and foxes will be hungry. I think we'll have a pretty good day."*

Trudy, in the middle of the pack and still learning the ropes in her second year, inquired, *"But Shaker's been complaining about the temperature and the snow. He says snow doesn't hold scent."*

"Shaker is a human, honey. His nose is only good to perch spectacles on. If there's even a whiff of fox, we'll find it." Asa's voice resonated with such confidence that Trudy put her nose down and went to work.

The hounds diligently worked the meadow for twenty minutes, moving forward, ever forward, but to no avail.

Trudy's, Trident's, Tinsel's, and Trinity's brows all furrowed.

Delia encouraged them. *"Nobody said it would be easy today, but be patient. I promise you: the foxes have been out and about."* She said "out and about" with the Tidewater region's long "o."

"Yes, ma'am," the T's responded.

Cora, as strike hound, moved ten yards ahead. Her mind raced. She'd picked up an old trail, but discarded it. No point yapping about a fading line. Her knowledge and nose were so good Cora could tell when a line would pay off, when it would heat up. She never opened unless she had a good line. Some hounds blabbed if they even *imagined* fox scent. Those hounds were not found in the Jefferson Hunt pack. Cora couldn't abide a hound that boo-hooed every time it caught a little scent.

"Mmm." She wagged her stern.

Dragon noticed. He hurried right over, but dared not push Cora. She'd lay him out right there in front of everybody, and then she'd get him again on the way home in the party wagon. He tempered his aggressiveness. Now he, too, felt his nostrils fill with the faint but intensifying scent of gray dog fox.

Diana trotted up, swinging the pack with her as she intently watched Cora. She could bank on Cora, her mentor.

The hounds, excited but still mute, moved faster, their sterns moving faster as well.

Sister checked her girth.

"Ah, ha, I knew it!" Cora triumphantly said. *"A suitor."*

She and the others usually recognized the scent of the fox they chased, but this was a stranger, a gray fox courting a little early, but then foxes display their own logic. The common wisdom is that grays begin mating in mid-January, reds at the end of January. But Cora remembered a time when grays mated in mid-December. Just why, she didn't know. No great storms followed, which could have boxed them up, nor a drought, which would have affected the food supply then and later. All these events could affect mating.

Perhaps this gray simply fell in love.

Whatever, the scent warmed up.

"Showtime!" Cora spoke.

Dragon spoke, then Asa and Delia. Diana steadied the T's when she, too, sang out and told them to just stick with the pack, stick together.

The whole pack opened. A chill ran down Sister's spine; Lafayette's too, his beautiful gray head turned as he watched the hounds.

Those members with a hangover knew they'd need to hang on: when the pack opened like that, they were about to fly.

A thin strip of woods separated the eastern meadow from a plowed cornfield, the stubble visible through the windblown patches. A slight slope rested on the far side of the cornfield. The hounds had gotten away so fast they were already there.

Sister and Lafayette sped to catch them. She tried to stay about twenty yards behind Shaker, depending on the territory. She didn't want to crowd the pack, but she wanted members to see the hounds work. To Sister, that was the whole reason to hunt: hound work!

The footing in the cornfield kept horses lurching as the furrows had frozen, buried under the snow.

All were glad once that was behind them. A simple three-foot coop rested in the fence line between the cornfield and the hayfield. The bottom half of the coop, where snow piled up, was white.

"*Whoopee.*" Lafayette pricked his ears forward as he leapt over.

Lafayette so loved jumping and hunting that Sister rarely had to squeeze her legs.

Everyone cleared the coop.

Hounds could hear their claws crack the thin crust of ice on the snow. In a few places they'd sink in to their elbows, throw snow around, and keep going, paying no heed.

Within minutes, the pack clambered over another coop, rushing into a pine stand, part of Edward's timber operation. The scent grew stronger.

The silence, noticeable in the pines, only accentuated the music of the hounds. As the field moved in, a few boughs, shaken by the thunder of hooves, dusted the riders underneath with snow.

Sam Lorillard felt a handful slide down his neck.

Crawford tried to push up front, but Czpaka wasn't that fast a horse. Crawford hated being in the middle of the pack, and he *really* hated seeing Walter Lungrun shoot past him on Rocketman.

Jennifer Franklin and Sari Rasmussen giggled as the dustings from the trees covered their faces. Both girls loved hunting, their only complaint being that not enough boys their own age foxhunted.

On and on the hounds roared, turning sharply left, negotiating a fallen tree, then charging through the pines northward, emerging onto the sunken farm road, three feet down, the road used to service an old stone barn in the eighteenth century. The building's crumbling walls remained. The field abruptly pulled up as hounds tumbled pell-mell over one another to get inside the ruins.

"He's gone to ground!" Dragon shouted. *"Let's dig him out."*

"Dream on, you nitwit." A high-pitched voice called out from inside.

"Uncle Yancy, what are you doing here? Where's the gray?" Cora recognized the small red fox's voice. He was not pleased with the visitation.

"You could be on a little red Volkswagen for all I know, Cora, but you haven't been chasing me."

Shaker dismounted and blew "Gone to ground."

The hounds loved hearing that series of notes, but Cora, disgruntled to have been so badly fooled, sat down. Where had that gray gone?

"There's nothing we can do about it," Dasher advised.

"Oh, yes, there is," Cora determinedly replied. *"I know the difference between Uncle Yancy and a stranger. Somehow we got our wires crossed back there in the pines, and we were all so excited we didn't pay proper attention."*

Diana said, *"Cora, if you'd switched to Uncle Yancy, you would have known."* She walked over and poked her head into the den. *"Uncle Yancy, is he in there with you?"*

A dry chuckle floated out of the main entrance. *"He left by the back door not ten minutes ago."*

"Damn you, Yancy!" Dragon frantically began searching for the back door of the den, which happened to be outside the walls of the old barn.

The sound of Dragon's travails made Yancy laugh even harder. Infuriated, Dragon could hear the fox's mirth. He ran for the opening where a door used to be to get outside the ruins.

"Dragon, come back here and pretend you're thrilled about this," Cora commanded as Shaker finished the notes on his horn. *"We can put up the gray once we're out of here."*

And that they did. As soon as Shaker mounted back up, the hounds moved around the outside of the structure.

"Got 'im!" Asa called as he'd found the correct exit. With that he ran north, ever northward, as the scent was now *hot, hot, hot* on the cold snow.

Asa lost the line for a moment when they reached a small frozen tributary of Snake Creek, a silver ribbon of ice. Young Trident put them all right when he crashed across the ice, the water running hard underneath, and picked up the scent on the far bank.

The fox zigzagged west. After fifteen minutes of flat-out flying, the pack, the staff, and the field soared over the stone fence, leading into After All's westernmost pasture. Within minutes, they'd be on Sister's farm.

Again the fox turned; grays tend to do that. He was running a big figure eight, but the scent stayed hot. The pack, in full cry, ran so close together they were beautiful to behold.

Back over the stone fence, across a narrow strip, over the old hog's back jump, which looked formidable in the snow. Lost a few people on that one. On and on, then finally Cora skidded to a halt beneath a pin oak, its brown leaves still clinging to the snow-coated tree. Those leaves wouldn't be released until spring buds finally pushed them off their seal.

Snow spun out from paws as the hounds abruptly put on their brakes.

"Got you!" Cora stood on her hind legs, her forepaws as high on the tree as she could reach.

"He climbed the tree! He climbed the tree!" Trinity was so excited she

leapt up and down as though on a pogo stick. *"I never saw a fox do that!"*

Asa, thrilled but in control, said, *"If we get too close, those grays will climb up neat as a cat. Can you see him up there?"*

"Yes!" Trinity spotted a pair of angry eyes staring down.

"Go away," the gray yelled, just as the snow again began to fall, the clouds now dark gray.

"Who are you?" Diana asked.

"Mickey. You should all just go away. Look at it this way, you need me to come courting, don't you? Means more foxes next year," he said raffishly.

Shaker handed Showboat's reins to Betty. He walked up under the tree. "Hey there, fella. Hell of a run."

"Yeah, well, you can find your pleasures elsewhere," Mickey barked.

Shaker lavishly praised his hounds for their excellent work, then mounted back up and called them along. He beamed.

The pack, in high gear, cavorted as they turned back east.

"I'll find another fox!" Dragon bragged.

"You are so full of it," Ardent, Asa's brother, growled. *"You aren't the only hound with a nose, and furthermore, I suspect we're going back."*

"Doesn't mean we can't run another fox if we find one," Dragon sassed.

"True." Cora would have liked another hard run. *"But we've been out an hour and a half, the footing is deep—slippery in spots—and some of the horses are tiring. Sister's smart. She'll end the day on a high note, and we'll be back at the trailers in twenty minutes. Plus, it's snowing again."*

"Ever notice how more people get hurt at the end of a hunt than at the beginning?" young Trudy wondered out loud.

"They're tired, horses and riders, and sometimes they get so excited they don't realize it. It's those last stiff jumps that will get them if it's going to happen. It's New Year, we've got until mid-March to hunt. This is a wise decision." Asa spoke to Trudy.

"Yancy is a cheat." Dragon switched subjects.

"No, he's not." Cora laughed. *"If another fox ducks into his den for*

cover, Yancy can hide him. But I'm surprised that Uncle Yancy is at those stone barn ruins. He lives closer in."

"Oh, Uncle Yancy moves about." Ardent knew the fox, same age as himself. *"Changes his hunting territory and gets away from Aunt Netty."*

Aunt Netty, Yancy's mate, harbored strong opinions and was not averse to expressing them. Yancy, a dreamy sort, liked to watch Shaker through the cottage windows or simply curl up under the persimmon tree. After the first frost when the persimmon fruit sweetened, Yancy would nibble on the small orange globes.

When the hounds returned to the covered bridge, cars, trucks, and SUVs lined the drive for a half-mile up to the house. Some cautious few parked nose out in case they couldn't get enough traction. This way they could be pulled with one of Edward's heavy tractors.

New Year's breakfast attracted nonriders, too. Upon the riders' return, After All was already filled with people. The event was hosted by social director Sorrel Buruss, who merrily bubbled with laughter and talk. Having Sorrel run the breakfast meant both Tedi and Edward could hunt.

"Well done." Shaker patted each hound's head as the animal hopped into the party wagon. Inside this trailer at the rear, a two-tiered wooden platform had been built. A second platform on a level with the lower one on the rear ran alongside the sidewall. This way hounds would climb up or snuggle under a platform and relax. Like humans, they preferred one hound's company to another's, so there were cliques. This platform arrangement allowed them to indulge their friendships. No one wanted to be next to someone who bored him or her silly.

Cora hung back. She liked to go in last, partly because she always wanted to keep hunting and partly because she liked seeing the humans back at their trailers. Some would dismount and be so exhausted their legs shook. Others would nimbly slide off, flip the reins over their horse's head, and loosen the girth a hole or two. They'd remove the bridle, put on a nice leather halter, and then tie the horse to the side of the trailer, careful not to allow the rope to be over long. That caused mischief. The horse would step over the rope or pull back and pop it. Wool blankets, in stable colors, would be put on the horses. The different colors looked pretty against the snow.

Cora liked horses, although, as they were not predators, she sometimes had to think carefully to appreciate what was on a horse's mind. She was always grateful when a staff horse informed her what was behind her; their range of vision was almost, but not quite, 360 degrees.

"Cora."

"Oh, all right." She grumbled as Shaker tapped her hindquarter.

The other hounds fell silent when the lead bitch entered the trailer.

Asa said, *"Happy New Year, Cora. You were wonderful today."*

The others spoke in assent.

Henry Xavier, in his trailer tack room, exchanging his scarlet weaselbelly for a tweed coat, commented to Ronnie Haslip, who had already changed and was standing at the open door, "The hounds are singing 'The Messiah.' "

Ronnie, always dapper, smiled. "Damn good work today. I didn't think we'd do squat out there in that snow, did you?"

"No." Xavier shook his head.

"Tell you what, I'd put this pack of hounds against any other pack out there."

"Me, too. I wish Sister pushed herself more. You know, would go to the hound shows and publicize our club more. People don't know how good Jefferson Hunt is until they cap with us."

Ronnie nodded in agreement. "When Ray was alive, she did go. She needs the push, and she needs more hands. Remember, she used to have Big Ray, Ray Jr., and then until last year she had Doug Kinzer. It's probably a little lonesome for her, you know."

Doug Kinzer, a talented professional whipper-in, had moved up to carrying the horn at Shenandoah Hunt over the Blue Ridge

Mountains. In the past, particularly during the days of slavery, many an African American carried the horn. After the War Between the States, people couldn't feed themselves, much less a pack of hounds. When hunting with a large pack again became feasible, about twenty years after the end of the war, it was often feasible because of Yankee money. For whatever reason, having black hunt staff made the Yankees uncomfortable. Doug, an African American, carried on a long, complex, even contradictory tradition. The last great black huntsman whom folks could remember in these parts was the convivial, talkative Cash Blue. He had hunted hounds for Casanova Hunt Club way back when today's older members were children.

"If only I didn't have to pull those long hours, I'd love to go to the shows, wash hounds, stand them up." Xavier straightened his stock tie.

"Yeah, but not having to pay that extra salary has put the club in the black." Ronnie, tight and treasurer, appreciated the bottom line.

"Listen, Crawford Howard hemorrhages money when he walks to the john." Xavier disdained him. "If Sister asked him, he'd come up with the salary. I heard through the grapevine that he offered to do so last year."

"He did. He made sure we all knew that, but not from his lips." Ronnie half smiled: Crawford was beginning to learn some of the round-about Virginia way. "He did, but his condition was that he be made joint-master."

"She has to pick someone soon." Ronnie folded his arms over his chest.

"Wouldn't want to be in her boots. She's between a rock and a hard place." Xavier had known Jane Arnold all his life. Although he didn't know it, he loved her. He was devastated when Ray Jr., his best friend, had been killed. Sister was part of his past, present, and future, as she was for Ronnie.

"You said a mouthful. Crawford's got the money, but he'll alienate the club or at least most of us."

Xavier stepped down from the tack room, closing the door. "I heard that Shaker said he'd leave. He wouldn't serve under Crawford even if she kept that blowhard out of the kennels."

"Heard that, too." Ronnie straightened the blanket on Xavier's Picasso.

"Thanks."

"As I see it, the choices are Crawford, Edward, possibly Sybil, or maybe even Bobby Franklin. Each has pluses and minuses. Clay Berry could do it, he's making a lot of money these days, but I don't think Izzy would go along with that. She covets social events, traveling. Being master would take up too much time for her taste. And there's you, Xavier; there's you. As head of that nice big old insurance company, you know everybody, and everybody knows you. Some of us even like you." He slapped his childhood friend on the back.

"Well," Xavier put his arm around the smaller man's shoulders, "I would love to be joint-master. Really, I would, but right now the business is demanding. Insurance has been in a slump since September eleven. You can imagine the hit the huge carriers have been taking. Rates are changing, and that impacts even a small guy like me who deals with those carriers. I try to find my people the best rates, and even I'm appalled. I don't know where this is headed, but I do know these next couple of years, I've got to keep my nose to the grindstone."

"Sorry to hear that. You'd be good."

"And Dee would love it." He mentioned his wife by her nickname. "Saw our Explorer, so she's already here and wondering why I'm not at the house. Come on."

They walked through the snow, following the line of other hunters.

"Crawford would rile everyone but Jesus, X." Ronnie called Xavier "X," as did other old friends. "The pressure financially would be off. Of course, it would be off if Edward or Sybil logged on."

"Edward is in his midseventies, and he's glad to pitch in, but he doesn't want the full-time responsibility. Same for his daughter. Sybil would be good, I think, but her boys are in grade school, and, truth be told, I don't think she's recovered from that whole gruesome mess with her ex-husband."

"She still loves him." Ronnie, for all his paying attention to money, did have a romantic streak.

"Jesus Christ, I hope not. What a rotter."

"Yep. That leaves Bobby Franklin."

They neared the front door, festooned with a sumptuous wreath, bright red berries dotting the dark evergreens.

Xavier whispered since people were close, "Bobby's got some money. Their business has been really good this year. He knows hunting. Wife and daughter know hunting. Great family, except for the daughter in prison, but hey, she's not the first person in America to go haywire on drugs."

"True." Ronnie felt quite sorry for the Franklins. Cody, their oldest girl, once showed such promise.

"He and Betty work like dogs down at the press. That's why they're successful, but I don't see how he'd have the time to be a master."

The Franklins had weathered the challenge from home printing off computers only because their work was of such high quality. They had invested in a Webb printing press back in the early nineties, which expanded their capabilities, bringing in business throughout the mid-Atlantic region.

"So we're back to Crawford?" Ronnie thought Crawford would tone down, and he thought Shaker would come around.

"Sister will pull a rabbit out of the hat. You just wait," Xavier predicted.

"Time's a flyin'."

"You just wait." Xavier smiled, then focused on Sam Lorillard, holding a glass, whom he could see as the front door swung open. "That sorry sack of shit."

Ronnie's gaze fell on Sam. "He was in the hunt field behind us. Riding groom."

"Yeah, well, I don't have to like that either, but you know the rules: you hunt with whoever is out there. Doesn't mean I have to drink with the son of a bitch."

"He's dry now."

"Oh, bullshit. He'll be back on the sauce before Valentine's," Xavier predicted.

"Well, I hope not."

"I don't give a rat's ass. That piece of excrement cost me thousands of dollars; you know that."

"I know that, Xavier, I do. What he did was terrible, but the past is past. Maybe he can be useful and productive. And maybe he can make amends. He didn't do right by me either when he worked in my stable. Not that I had it as bad as you did. He cheated you, and he betrayed you."

"If he dies, that will make amends." Xavier pressed his full lips together.

Ronnie stood up on his toes to whisper into Xavier's ear as they walked past the cloakroom. Why didn't you say something when Crawford hired him?"

"Because I don't give a good goddamn what happens to Crawford. In fact, I figured I'd sit back, watch the show, and eat popcorn."

Inside the Brancrofts' house, the two men brushed through the crowd as they moved toward the bar.

Dee, who kept her shape even as her husband lost his, spied him. She pushed through the throng. "Honey, I was starting to worry that perhaps you'd bought some real estate." She used the phrase for hitting the ground.

"Dee, he rides Picasso very, very well," Ronnie defended his friend. "Now I wish you'd come out. We need a little pulchritude."

"Liar!" She poked Ronnie in the ribs. Since he was gay, she figured he was teasing about pretty women.

"I love looking at beautiful women. I just don't want to marry one." He kissed her on the check.

"Hey, you're my best friend," Xavier said, shaking his head good-naturedly, "but I tell you, that's the one thing about you I don't understand."

Ronnie flattered him. "When I look at Dee and the life you've made together, I don't know that I understand it, either."

"Oh, Ronnie, you are sweet." Dee threw her arms around him, giving him a big hug.

"I saw that!" Betty Franklin yelled from the crowd. "Another Jefferson Hunt affair."

"Ronnie, take a number and get in line," said Walter, walking up behind the three, and towering over them.

"Walter, you don't need a ticket. I'll take you right now," Ronnie fired right back at him.

"Three points." Walter laughed. "Dee, can I freshen your drink?"

"No, I'm going to drag my husband to the bar. I want to hear every detail of the hunt, and hopefully a few misdeeds as well."

"Crackerjack day." Walter smiled.

As husband and wife left, Ronnie said, "There's something about hunting in the snow."

"Indescribably beautiful," Walter agreed. "Say, Ron, how about a drink for you? Hi, Sorrel." Sorrel, in her middle forties and a recent widow, walked over.

"Gentlemen, they've gone through two cases of champagne, a case of scotch, two and a half of vodka, and we're running low on the roasted boar. You'd better hurry to the table."

"The muffin hounds have struck again." Ronnie called nonriders muffin hounds, as did everyone else who rode.

"Let's go." Walter led the way. The men chatted, touching hands or shoulders of others they met along the way.

Lorraine Rasmussen, slight and shy, stood with her daughter, Sari. The two closely resembled each other.

"Mom, everyone is friendly. Come on."

"Oh, honey, I don't ride. I feel——"

"Lorraine!" Sister emerged from the kitchen. It was the only place she could grab a bite. Once people saw her, she never got the food to her mouth.

"Sister, this is so grand." Lorraine smiled. Her light brown hair, well cut, fell to her shoulders.

"Tedi and Edward never do anything halfway. And, of course, Sorrel is the best social director we've ever had. Now come meet people, Lorraine. Most of the people here didn't hunt today. You can tell. Their shoes are clean, and there's no blood on their faces."

"And they're fat." Sari giggled.

Sister saw Shaker squeeze through the crowd. Shaker had to attend to the hounds, but today was a High Holy Day. Staff were allowed a spot of socializing before driving hounds and horses back to the kennels and stables.

Today, while not particularly long, had been hard, thanks to heavy footing. Shaker didn't like hounds or horses standing around too long after a hard hunt.

"Shaker, let's all get a drink, shall we?" Sister suggested, intercepting Shaker's escape from socializing.

"Why don't I get a plate for you, sir?" Sari, polite, knew how hard Shaker worked.

"Thanks, Sari." He liked the young girl and could see some of her mother in her. Though he knew little of Lorraine, he thought her a polite woman. Looking at her now, he realized she was pretty, too.

"Sari said today was just one of the best," commented Lorraine. "She said when the hounds ran into the stone ruins, she got goose bumps."

He smiled at Lorraine. "We got lucky."

"Nonsense," said Sister. "You're a fantastic huntsman." She kissed him on the check. "Excuse me."

"Sister," Marty Howard called to her.

As Sister reached Marty, she brushed against Gray Lorillard. A flicker of electricity shot through her.

"The weather fouled our lunch date," Gray said. "How does January third at the club sound to you?"

"Do I have to wear lipstick?" She laughed.

"Sister, you don't have to wear anything at all." Gray smiled. "Twelve."

"Twelve."

"Sister," Marty breathlessly grabbed the master's hand, "Sam has found me the most exquisite horse. I am so excited. A gelding. I like geldings, and he's right out of a Stubbs painting."

"To hunt?"

"Oh, no. Sorry, I'm so excited. No. To run. A timber horse. Oh, I've always wanted a timber horse. He's been calling around, and he just now told me. I've been on cloud nine. I'm calling him Cloud Nine!"

"Where is Sam? I can't wait to hear the details," she replied.

"Last I saw him was by the fireplace in the living room. But it will take you half an hour to reach him. We're packed like sardines."

Twenty minutes later Sister reached the living room. Sam looked better than he had in years but still had the gaunt thinness of a lifelong alcoholic who forgets to eat. He smiled when he saw the master.

"Happy New Year, Master."

"Sam, glad to see you in the hunt field. Gray, too. I hope you'll be out with us more often."

"Depends on the man."

Sister smiled. "In your case, it just might depend on the woman. She's levitating over the timber horse you've found." She paused a moment as she nodded to friends in the crowd. "How's it going?" Sister asked.

"Pretty good."

She placed her hand on Sam's shoulder. "Well, I hope the job works out. Crawford's a demanding man but, ultimately, a fair one. And I'm happy to have you in the hunt field."

"Take it no one much likes Crawford," Sam whispered.

"People who are against something or someone are always more expressive than those who think things are just fine. He has his detractors, but over the years I've learned to appreciate his good points. If you need anything, Sam, call or drop by."

"Thank you. That's white of you."

She laughed. "You are bad, Sam Lorillard."

Sliding back through the crowd, Sister squeezed up behind Clay Berry. His wife, Isabelle, hair shoulder length and honey blonde, didn't see Sister behind Clay's broad shoulders. She might have changed her tune had she known Sister was there.

"Not another horse, Clay. You have two perfectly good field horses, and I never see you as it is."

"Sugar, that's not true." His light tenor hit a consoling note.

"The hell it's not. You disappear during hunt season. I have one month with you when it's over, and then you're off to the golf course. I might as well be a widow."

"Izzy," he called her by her nickname, "you're being overly dramatic."

"I'm starting to think of you as my insignificant other." She pouted. "And how you can think of another horse when you know I am dying, dying for that new 500SL convertible. I want it in brilliant silver with the ash interior."

"That car costs a hundred and six thousand dollars with the options you want."

"I'm worth it," she coolly replied.

He shifted gears. "How could any man put a price on such a beautiful woman? Of course you're worth it, baby. However, it is a big hit at this time."

"Oh, pooh." She suddenly became flirtatious. "You're making money hand over fist. My birthday is coming up and," she rubbed the back of his neck, her lips now very close to his, "you will never regret it. I'll do anything you want whenever you want it."

He swallowed. "Honey, let's talk about this later."

Sister tried to get beyond these two, but the crush of people was so great, the din of conversation so loud, she was pinned.

Izzy stood on her tiptoes to kiss her husband. She bit his lower lip. In doing so, she saw the master.

"Sister!" She quickly reached around Clay to grab Sister's hand. "I need you to weaken Clay."

More power to you, Sister thought to herself. At least you aren't denying what you are. She then spoke out loud. "Isabelle, I think you can weaken Clay all by yourself."

"But I'd love to be between two beautiful women." Clay rolled his eyes heavenward.

Izzy, in a studied breathless voice, crooned, "I must have that 500SL. I mean I am *dying* for that car. It's the sexiest thing on the road. Sexier than a Ferrari or Porsche Turbo or the redone Maserati. I'm nearing forty. I need a boost." She now held both of Sister's hands as the crowd pressed them bosom to bosom, and both ladies were well stacked.

Sister found the situation comical. "It is a spectacular car, and you'd make it even more spectacular. Mercedes-Benz ought to pay you to drive one."

"You say the sweetest things. I want to grow up to be just like you. You're so beautiful." Izzy waxed enthusiastic.

"She's right." Clay seconded his wife. "Except for your silver hair, you look just like you did when I was in Pony Club. I don't know how you do it."

"She has a painting in her attic," Izzy recalled the famous plot from Oscar Wilde's *The Portrait of Dorian Gray*.

"Thank you. You're both outrageous flatterers, but it does my heart good to hear it."

Clay leaned down, his face serious. "I do mean it. You're

beautiful, Sister." He smiled then. "And your arms are more muscular than mine, and I work out like a demon."

She cocked her head a bit sideways while looking up at him. "I don't know about that, but I do know farm work sure burns the fat off your body."

"Oh, Clay, guess you'd better buy another hunter, and I'll take care of it." Izzy laughed, a pleasing musical laugh.

Walter spied Sister pressed between Clay and Izzy. He pushed his way toward her.

"You can't have her all to yourselves. It's my turn." Walter kissed Izzy on the cheek, which she rather liked, then used his body to make a path for them through the people.

"You're a hero."

"You say that to all the boys," Walter teased her.

Once out of the worst of the press, she took a deep breath. "Well, Walter, it's been my privilege to watch how a woman works a man for her gain. Whew. I never could do it."

"You never needed to do it." His slight grin enhanced his rugged handsomeness.

"Walter, you are a true Virginia gentleman."

"I mean it. Guile, throwing yourself at a man, deceit, and that sort of thing. It's not you. You could never do that."

"Maybe that's why Ray found other women attractive. I didn't play the game."

"Ray found other women attractive because he needed conquests to feel like a man." Walter, Ray's natural son, said this with authority.

Both Walter and Sister had learned of this old secret a year ago. Everyone knew but them, and Walter was the spitting image of Ray Arnold Sr.

"It's all water over the damn, honey. We're still here, and life is wonderful."

"Life is wonderful because I have you in my life." He kissed her tenderly on the cheek. "You've given me foxhunting, understanding, and more than I can express."

"Walter, you'll make me cry."

He hugged her. "That would shock everyone here."

"Have you been drinking?"

He laughed. "No. One cold beer. No, my New Year's resolution is to tell the people I care about how I feel. I'm overcoming WASP restraint."

"Is there a class for this? I need to sign up."

They laughed together, then Walter said, "Did you hear on the news? Found one of the alcoholics dead down at the train station."

Walter could have said winos, but, being a physician, he looked at alcoholism with a scientist's eye.

"What a dreadful way to squander a life." Sister shook her head.

"Yes," Walter replied. "It's an insidious disease in that it's both chemical yet voluntary. In my darker moments I wonder if they aren't better off dead. Medicine can't reach them. Perhaps God can reach them."

Sister considered this sentiment. She truly believed that people could be redeemed.

Xavier bumped into her, back to back. "Pardon me. Oh, Sister, if I'd known it was you, I'd have bumped you harder."

Walter kissed her again on the cheek and moved away.

"Any New Year's resolutions?"

"Lose forty pounds." He grimaced. "Damn, I don't have a spare tire, I've got enough to put four Goodyears on a Camaro."

"It's all that sitting at work."

"If only I had your discipline," he moaned.

"Not sure it's discipline. I don't sit at a desk. I'm in the stables, in the kennels, out on the land. I burn it right off. Humans weren't meant to sit still for hours. Apart from the pounds, think what it does to your back."

"Damn straight." He leaned over to her, speaking softly into her ear. "Is Sam Lorillard going to be hunting with us a lot?"

"I don't know. It's up to Crawford."

"I'm not the only one with a big grudge against Sam. Edward's not overwhelmed with him. Jerry Featherstone either. Ron. Clay. Actually, if you went down the hunt roster, there are a lot of us who gave him a chance over the years. He either seduced our wives, stole money, lied about horses, or smashed up trucks."

"I know, Xavier, I know. But in the hunt field, all that is left back at the trailers. What you all do or say when we're not hunting is your business."

"I'm not going to make a scene in the hunt field, but I might rearrange his face if he looks at me cross-eyed."

"You don't think people can change?"

"Hell, yes, they can change. I'm gonna be forty pounds changed. But inside? Their character? No. Sam was born weak, and he'll die weak. He'll probably die dead drunk, forgive the pun."

"I hope not, but I appreciate your feelings. If he'd lightened my wallet, I think I'd turn my back on him, too. I'd like to think I wouldn't, but I reckon I would."

The swirl of gossip and laughter and the running feet of the children filled the Bancroft house. A group of men and women, standing in the corner of the dining room, were discussing why the state of Ohio produced great college football teams but rotten pro teams. The discussion was raising the rafters.

Everything Tedi and Edward did, they accomplished with great style. Before leaving with Betty Franklin, Sister thanked her host and hostess as well as Sorrel Buruss.

"Great day. The snow has picked up." Outside Betty squinted at the deep gray sky.

"If you want to go home with Bobby, go on. You can pick up your car tomorrow or whenever."

"I don't mind driving home in the snow. Gives us a chance to be together." Betty happily stepped into Sister's red GMC half-ton. "How do you like your other truck now that you've had it a year?"

"Like it fine. Nothing pulls like the Ford F350 Dually. But I like this for everyday."

"You had that truck since the earth was cooling."

Sister turned on the motor, flipped on the windshield wipers, and waited a moment while the blades flicked off the new-fallen snow. "Nothing about this on the weather report."

"Why listen? We're right at the foot of the Blue Ridge Mountains. We have our own weather system." Betty shivered. The heat would kick on once the motor warmed up.

"Got that right." Putting the truck into four-wheel drive, they carefully rolled down the long driveway. "What did you think today?" asked Sister.

"Hounds worked well together, and you were smart not to bring out the young entry. Even though we finally hit a good line, the patience it took to find it might have been too much, what with all the people."

"Thanks. I'm pleased. Thought the T kids came right along. They've matured early," Sister said proudly.

"Good voices."

"Yes." She changed the subject. "Betty, Xavier and others sure are upset about Sam Lorillard hunting with us today."

"He's not high on my list, but he's no problem out in the field. I just hope the guy can stay the course. His brother spent good money on him. A one-month stay at a detox center complete with counseling dents the budget. The horrible thing is, half the time the people slide right back to their old ways. Look at how hard Bobby and I tried to keep Cody off drugs," she said, referring to her oldest daughter. "She couldn't or wouldn't do it, and by God, she's paying the price, but so are we."

"Can she get drugs in jail?"

"Of course she can." Betty sighed. "She says she isn't using, but

I don't believe it. She puts on her good face when Bobby or I visit. She tells her sister more than she tells either of us. And you know what, I have cried all the tears about it I can cry. You birth them, raise them, bleed for them, cry for them, and pray for them, but they're on their own."

"Yes."

"I'm sorry. Sometimes I forget that you might be glad to have Ray Jr. here even if he did drugs." Betty exhaled through her nostrils. "I don't think Rayray would have gone that route. Kid always had sense. Some do, some don't."

Sister slowed for a curve, "Oh, they'll all try whatever is out there: marijuana, cocaine, ecstasy, the date rape drug. I can't even keep up with the proliferation of mood-altering substances. I think all kids try it once. I worry more about alcohol than drugs. Our whole society pushes booze and drugs at you. The stuff I like to sniff is the odor of tack, horse sweat, and oats. Don't even mind the manure. And I like the sweet scent of my hounds, too."

"Heaven." Betty put her hands up to the heating vent. "Doesn't matter what any authority decrees in any century, people will take whatever makes them feel good. You and I have one kind of body chemistry, Cody and Sam have another. And who knows why?"

"Big Ray drank, but he controlled it. He could go months without a drink and then maybe knock back four at a party one night."

"He was tall though. He could handle it better than a pipsqueak." She turned to observe Broad Creek, swollen and flowing swiftly under the state bridge on Soldier Road. "Another day of this, and that water will jump the banks."

"We were lucky we didn't run into trouble today."

"I thought of that, too." Betty turned to look at Sister. "Want to hear something crazy?"

"You're talking to the right woman."

"I feel younger, stronger, and better now than I have for years—years. Cruel as this sounds, I think it's because Cody is put away. She can't come home and drag me down. She can't call from Los Angeles or Middleburg or Roger's Corner." Betty mentioned the convenience store located at the intersection of Soldier Road and White Cat Road. "I'm free. She's in jail, but I'm free. My energy is my own."

"I understand that."

"I didn't at first. I thought I was a terrible mother. Bobby set me right." A glow infused her voice. "How did I have the sense to marry that man? He's not the best-looking guy in the world. When I was young, I thought I was going to marry someone handsome, rich, all that. But he persevered. The more he did, the more I got a look at his good character. He's a wonderful man, a loving husband, and a loving father. I am one lucky woman."

"He's lucky, too." Sister pulled off Soldier Road onto the dirt state road, considered a tertiary road by the highway department. Snow was deeper here.

"Thank you, Jane. You're a good-looking woman. I hope you find someone again."

"I thought about it for a time after Big Ray'd been dead two years or so, but then it faded away." She turned onto the farm road, snow falling harder now. "I thought I was past that until Walter returned to the hunt club two years ago. Last time I saw Walter, he was on his way to college. Once Walter was hunting with us, I felt so drawn to him. It was physical. Shaker finally told me, bless his heart. Wasn't easy for Shaker. Maybe I knew without knowing."

"Everyone knew but you and Walter."

"That he's Ray's natural son?"

"Uh-huh."

"Stirred me up. Not that Walter is going to sleep with me. The man is in his middle thirties and I'll be seventy-two this August. Or is it seventy-three?" She giggled for a moment. "Can't believe it, no matter what the number is. Christ, the years fly by so damned fast I can't keep track. But I woke up, or my body woke up, or something.

You're sweet to tell me I look good, but Betty, how many men are going to look at me unless they're eighty? The game's over for me."

"It's New Year's Day. Want to make a bet?"

"How much?"

"One hundred dollars."

"Betty!"

"I bet you one hundred dollars that a man does come into your life before December thirty-first. Deal?"

"Easiest one hundred dollars I'll ever make." Sister laughed as she pulled into the stable yard.

In the stable, the two women checked their horses. Having left the breakfast early, Sari and Jennifer had gotten all the chores done. The radio hummed, on low for the horses. The news was reported on the hour.

"Hey, did you hear that?" Betty, standing next to the radio, called over to Sister, who was checking water buckets.

"Not paying attention."

"The first guy, the one they found dead the night of the twenty-seventh, Saturday? Well, he was full of alcohol to the gills, but hemlock as well."

"What?" Sister paused for a moment.

"He drank hemlock, just like Socrates."

"On purpose?" Sister was incredulous.

"And this morning they found another one frozen down at the train station. Dead."

The two women looked at each other. Sister said, "What on earth is going on?"

CHAPTER 7

Clay and Isabelle Berry loved to entertain. Their modern house, built on a ridge, enjoyed sweeping views of the Blue Ridge Mountains. Because each of their rooms opened into other rooms or onto a patio, people rarely became bottled up in narrow door openings at their parties.

The floors, polished and gleaming, were hard walnut, stained black. Izzy, as Isabelle preferred to be called since she was named after her mother, Big Isabelle, fell under the spell of minimalism. Every piece of furniture in the house had been built to fit that house. Each piece, a warm beige, complemented the lighter beige walls.

The occasion for this party, January 2, Friday, was Izzy's thirty-eighth birthday. A few guests, possessed of remarkable stamina, hadn't stopped drinking since New Year's Eve.

Tedi, scotch and water in hand, whispered to Sister that these were blonde colors. As Izzy was a determined blonde, she shone to great effect.

The kitchen, stainless steel, gleamed. Overhead pinpricks of high-intensity light shone down on guests.

The downstairs boasted a regulation-size pool table, itself starkly modern.

Donnie Sweigert, along with three other men, manned the two bars, one in the living room, one downstairs.

A flat-screen TV, built into the wall of the library, glowed. The one in the poolroom did likewise. Both TVs had men and women watching snatches of football reportage. They'd get a pigskin fix, then quickly rejoin the party, only to return periodically or ask another sports fan what he or she thought about the countdown to the Super Bowl.

Sister and Tedi both stared as a commentator narrated clips from the most recent pro football games. The playoffs kept excitement mounting across America.

"Do you think these men are mutants?" Tedi asked.

"How?"

"Look at their necks." Tedi clinked the cubes in her glass as a close-up of a well-paid fullback beamed from the wall.

Wearing a fabulous electric blue dress, Sister stared. "And that's just someone for the backfield. Imagine what the defensive guard looks like."

Clay, who was moving by, a drink held over his head thanks to the press of people, overheard.

"Better nutrition, better dentistry. Remember, a lot of bacteria come in through the mouth. Better workouts, better methods for reducing injuries or healing them when they occur. Better drugs."

Tedi smiled at her attractive host. "When you played football in high school, you made All State, Clay, and you never looked like that. You had a good college career, too."

Clay, middle linebacker for the local high school, had been outstanding at the position. He'd won a scholarship to Wake Forest and been a star.

He laughed. "Tedi, you're very kind. Think how long ago that was. I'll be forty-four this year. I don't think I would do half so well at Wake now as I did then. It's a different game. The training alone is so different."

"But you never looked like a bull on two legs."

"Steroids." He shrugged genially. "Just wasn't much of an option then. Even if I had taken them, I was too small to make it to the pros. I don't mind. I came home, built a business, and discovered golf."

Sister touched his arm. "What is it they say about golf: a good walk ruined?"

He laughed. "The devil plays golf. He'll give you just enough great drives, good putts, to keep you coming back."

"So pretty out there, a verdant paradise." Tedi adored golf, carried a respectable twelve handicap.

"Clay!" Izzy called from the living room.

"The birthday girl." Clay smiled. "Good hunt yesterday, Sister. Despite the weather, we're having a terrific season."

"Thank you, Clay." She was glad to hear the praise as he left to join Izzy, who was surrounded by women from her college sorority.

Kappa Kappa Gamma songs filled the house.

"Janie, were you in a sorority?" Tedi asked. "I don't remember. They didn't have them at Sweet Briar, did they? Didn't have them at Holyoke." Tedi didn't wait for her question to be answered since they both realized Tedi figured out the answer for herself. "Loved Holyoke. Loved it. But you know, I missed you so much. Think of the fun we would have had if we'd gone to the same school."

"We'd have gotten ourselves thrown out." Sister grinned.

"Well—true." Tedi tipped back her head and laughed. "And I never would have met Edward. Imagine going all the way to Massachusetts to meet your future husband, himself a Virginian, who had gone all the way to Amherst. Course I was wretched when neither Nola nor Sybil elected to go to Holyoke. Still can't believe they did that."

"That's the thing about children. Damn if they don't turn out to have minds of their own."

The corners of Tedi's mouth curled up for an instant. "Shocking. But really, Janie, University of Colorado for Nola, and then Sybil, well, she did go to Radcliffe. She applied herself, probably to make up for Nola. God, how many schools did that kid roar through? I miss her. Even now." Tedi stopped for a moment. "Stop me. Really, what is it about a new year? One casts one's mind over the years, but the past is the past. You can't change a thing about it."

"Historical revisionists certainly are trying."

"Yes, well, that's not exactly about the past. That's about a bid for political power now. Rubbish. Every single bit of it." Tedi knocked back her scotch. "Sometimes I think I've lived too long. I've seen it all, done it all, and now am colossally bored by the ignorance and pretensions of the generations behind us. If anything, Nola and Sybil's generation is tedious, hypocritical, and lacking in fire."

"Tedi, they've only known peace and plenty. That's like a hound who has only slept on the porch. If they have to run, they'll be slow at first, but I promise you, they'll run."

"You're always hopeful."

"I'm an American. They're Americans. When the you-know-what hits the fan, we do what has to be done, and it doesn't matter when or where we were born. Doesn't matter what color we are, what religion or none, what sex or how about having sex. Anyway, you get my drift."

"I do. I'm still cynical." She turned her head. "And speaking of that generation, here comes an extremely handsome member of it." She smiled, holding out her hand as Walter took it, pressing it to his lips, then leaned over to kiss Sister's cheek.

"You two look radiant." Walter knew how to talk to women; beautiful would have been very nice but radiant showed imagination. "Sister, that color brings out your eyes." He stopped, then lowered his voice. "Can't get out of this." He smiled big as a dark, intense, attractive man, early forties at most, pushed over to him. "Mrs. Bancroft, Mrs. Arnold, allow me to introduce Dr. Dalton Hill from Toronto. He's come up from Williamsburg, where he gave a lecture this morning."

Tedi, who'd looked him over, inquired, "How good of you to make the trip. What is your specialty, Dr. Hill?"

"Endocrinology." He exuded a self-important air but had good manners, nonetheless. "However, my lecture was on the development of ornamentation in furniture during the eighteenth century."

"A passion?" Tedi's eyebrows lifted.

"Indeed." He inclined his head.

"English and French furniture from the eighteenth century is beautiful," Sister joined in. "Is there anyone who can make such pieces today?"

"Yes." His voice was measured. "A few, precious few. It's not talent, you see, it's temperament."

Both women smiled.

Walter said, "I never thought of that, Dr. Hill."

"Call me Dalton, please."

"Dalton, you hunt in Canada, don't you?" asked Walter.

"If you're going to be here for any time at all, please hunt with us." Sister extended an invitation.

"You are the master, I believe?" Dalton had been informed of Sister's status when he asked Bobby Franklin who the tall, striking-looking gray-haired woman was.

"I am, and I'm a lucky woman."

Ronnie Haslip came by, Xavier and Dee behind him. They swept Walter and Dalton along with them after a few more comments.

"Has an air about him." Tedi sniffed.

"Winding, are you, Tedi?"

They laughed and headed back to the bar. Tedi ordered another scotch on the rocks, and Sister asked for a tonic water on the rocks with a twist of lime.

Donnie, who had been nipping a little here and there behind the bar, quickly made the drinks. "Ladies."

"I couldn't help but notice your rifle and the scope the other day. What a beautiful piece of equipment." Sister took her drink from him, fished a dollar bill out of the unobtrusive slit in her dress, dropped it in the tip glass.

"Thank you." He nodded, then said, "I saved and saved. Cost me over two thousand five hundred dollars." He paused for effect. "I'll go without food to get the best. Makes a huge difference."

"Yes, it does," Sister replied.

"Clay Berry is tight as a tick with his employees."

Tedi piped up. "I know you went without food."

They moved back into the crowd, after a few more words with Donnie.

"I suppose I ought to find my husband. It's ten, and the roads will be dreadful."

"I ought to move on, too. Thought maybe Gray Lorillard would be here."

"Do you know he's rented the dependency over at Chapel Cross, the Vajay's place? Haven't they just brought that farm back to life?" Tedi paused. "Alex is here," she mentioned the husband. "Solange should be here, too. Well, there're so many people packed in here, I think I've missed half of them."

Tedi put her drink down on a silver tray, half-finished. She'd had enough. "I study how different civilizations deal with wealth. How different people deal with it." She could say anything to Sister. "The truth is, few people can handle it, whether it was China in the seventeenth century, a great industrial fortune in Germany in the nineteenth, or today, dotcom, that sort of thing."

"You've managed."

"I was trained since birth, Janie. When you make it in your lifetime, it's quite savage really. You're a stranger from your own children who never had to fight for it. I was fortunate in that our money was made with Fulton, with the steamboat fortune. It has been prudently invested and managed ever since. I grew up in a milieu that understood resources and understood restraint. Edward, of course, has more recent wealth. His grandfather developed refrigeration for food processing, transporting foods. But the Bancrofts were and are people of common sense. They kept working, kept producing. But we were all born and raised before the Second World War. Times have changed."

"Yes, but they always have."

"Then let's hope there's a pendulum. I was flipping through the channels last night before falling asleep, and I caught, for the barest second, a show where people had eaten a lot of food, consumed different colors of food dyes, then threw it all up to see who vomited the best color. That's just unimaginable to me."

"Me, too." Sister leaned on Tedi, so petite. "If you've been watching the gross shows, then what do you think of the sex channels? Not that they're gross, just hard-core."

"Oh," Tedi brightened, "I like them."

They both laughed uproariously as the Kappas sang more lustily.

As Sister, Tedi, and a captured Edward stood outside the house, its windows ablaze, and casting a golden glow over the snow, sounds of merriment seeped from inside.

"Well, dear, win anything?" Tedi figured Edward had played pool.

"Forty dollars. Five bucks a game. Took five dollars from Ronnie. We needed smelling salts to revive him. I swear Ronnie has the first dollar he ever made, probably sewn over his heart."

"Maybe that's why he doesn't have a boyfriend," Tedi said forthrightly as they walked to their vehicles.

"Now why do you say that?" Sister listened to the crunch of packed snow under her heels.

She hated heels, but she looked so good in them, and they could jack up her six feet to six three if she wanted. She liked that.

"Too damn cheap. If a man dates another man, doesn't he pay

for dinner just as one would with a woman? And then if Ronnie found a partner, I bet he'd watch every penny and drive the other man insane."

"Well, I think many men keep their finances separate," Edward remarked. "Not quite like marriage or our version, I should say, because now even middle-class people sign prenuptials."

"I think of the money at stake when we married, it's a wonder we didn't spend a year on prenuptials."

"I know it's wise, but it seems so calculating. Doesn't seem like a good way to start a marriage," Sister said.

Edward thought a moment. "You and Ray had no agreement concerning finances?"

As she opened the truck door, she answered, "No prenuptial. I didn't have much. I mean, we were comfortable, but nothing extravagant. Ray was about the same. Everything we had, we made together, and we didn't think divorce was an option. Look at our generation. How many divorced people do you know?"

"That's true." Edward waited as Sister, door open, changed into a pair of L. L. Bean boots.

"I can't drive in these damned things." She tossed her heels onto the seat. "Oh, who else did you clean out down there at the pool table?"

Edward puffed out his chest. "That Toronto doctor. Bragged about what a good pool player he was, so I let him have the first one, then I cleaned his clock. A bit of a pill, that one."

"We thought so, too." Tedi giggled.

"You drive safely now." Edward pecked Sister on the cheek.

Tedi playfully kissed Sister, too, then said in her beguiling voice, "Minimalism is for the young."

Cruising out the driveway, thinking of Tedi's comment and all the money Izzy had spent to achieve the pared-down look, Sister laughed. She also noted a brilliant silver Mercedes 500SL, which passed her at the entrance gate. Bill Little, one of the men at Brown

Mercedes on the Richmond road, carefully navigated the treacherous road. An enormous yellow ribbon and bow rested on the driver's seat next to him.

She waved to Bill. He waved back.

On the way home she wondered just what Izzy did to get such a fabulous birthday gift. Then she laughed out loud, imagining she had a pretty good idea. Even as an adolescent, Clay exhibited an intense interest in sex.

Come to think of it, Sister thought to herself, Izzy earned that Mercedes.

CHAPTER 8

"Those High Holy Days take it right out of me." Sister leaned over the counter at her equine vet's office. "Wish you'd come on out sometime."

The assistant, Val, a trail rider, shook her head. "You all are crazy."

"It helps." She rolled her fingertips on top of the counter—one, two, three, four—a habit of hers when she was trying to set something in her mind. "If the weather holds, how about if I bring that mare down next Wednesday?"

Val checked the computer screen. "That's fine. I'll tell Anne."

Anne Bonda, the vet, had a flourishing practice, although her clinic was located a little out of the way in Monroe, Virginia.

Sister had delivered many a foal in her time, but Anne had delivered thousands. If something were to go wrong, having the vet attending was far preferable to calling in the middle of a snowy night and asking for help. Yes, it might add a thousand dollars to the vet bill, but a healthy baby was worth it.

Sister bred for stamina, bone, and brain. She pored over thoroughbred pedigrees, studied stallions and their get. She needed the old, staying blood, blood now woefully out of fashion.

Rally, this particular mare, carried Stage Door Johnnie blood, blood for the long haul, and she'd been bred to an extremely beautiful son of Polish Navy, called Prussian Blue, standing in Maryland.

This year she'd bred three mares. Secretary's Shorthand didn't catch, a bitter disappointment since she was an old granddaughter of Secretariat. When an ultrasound was done on Shorthand, an embryo couldn't be observed. Curtains Up, Sister's other mare, was bred to an interesting, tough horse named Arroamanches. She took. You just never knew with mares.

Driving home, she noticed a line of Princess trees bordering a pasture. The dried fruits hung on the tree along with spring's fat buds. The force of life may be sleeping, but is ever present. Four months from now, on some warm April day, huge clusters of lavender flowers would cover the tree, bringing a smile to all who beheld such beauty.

Thanks to traffic on Route 29, a highway she hated, she arrived at the Augusta Cooperative an hour later.

She pushed open the glass doors and called to Georgia at the cash register, "Forgot birdseed last week."

"You just wanted an excuse to see me," Georgia drolly replied.

"There's truth to that. This is Gossip Central."

"We have hot competition in the country club and Roger's Corner," Georgia fired back.

"Different kind of gossip," Sister replied.

Georgia wrinkled her nose. "Not as wild."

"All those Episcopalians." She hoisted a twenty-five-pound bag of birdseed on the counter. "I say that being one."

"You're the exception that proves the rule." Georgia, whose lipstick snuck up into the cracks of her upper lip, winked.

"An exceptional exception." Sheriff Ben Sidell emerged from an aisle. He pushed a big wire cart, filled with a plumbing snake, bags of dog and cat food, a fifty-pound salt block, plus other items tucked between and behind the big ones.

"I didn't recognize you there for a minute without your uniform and out of your riding clothes," Sister said.

"Did you notice me with the Hilltoppers yesterday?"

"I did, and I'm so glad you're sticking to your riding lessons."

He leaned over the handle of the cart. "I had no idea there was so much to foxhunting. People see riders in their scarlet coats, 'What a bunch of snobs,' they think. Not like that at all. I'm trying to hang on my horse, my wonderful Nonni, but every now and then, I'll notice something, like when the temperature changes, everything changes with it."

"You're observant. Professional training," Sister complimented him. "Strange things happen. For instance, the prevailing wisdom is that only gray foxes climb trees, and yet I have seen a red do it. That isn't supposed to happen." She played with the signet ring on her little finger. "Fortunately, for us, foxes don't read books about how they're supposed to behave."

Ben smirked. "Be better off if people threw the books out as well. Everyone spouts watered-down psychology, another form of excusing bad behavior. Every criminal was abused. Well, I'd better stop before I—"

"Don't. I'm interested. You know more about this than we do. I've always thought that some people were born bad. We can't rehabilitate them." Georgia looked at him.

Ben ran a hand through his close-cropped black hair. "There is not one doubt in my mind that there is such a thing as a criminal mind. Some people are born psychopaths, sociopaths, or just plain liars. Men born with an extra Y chromosome usually wind up in prison, usually can't control their violent impulses."

"Ben," Sister's deep, pleasing voice contained a hopeful note, "surely some men in prison really are there because of circumstances, something as mundane as falling in with the wrong crowd as a kid."

Turning his brown eyes to look into hers, she was startled for a moment at their clarity and depth. "There are. Things happen. People can be in the wrong place at the wrong time or make a stupid decision, but I'm ready to go to bat and say that ninety percent of the men in prison are either of low normal intelligence or truly criminal. You can't fix them. Can't fix a child molester."

"I got a fix for them." Georgia pushed her eyeglasses on top of her abundant, colored hair.

"Yeah, well, I'm with you, Georgia," Ben said, "but the laws don't allow that."

"What about rapists?" Sister was curious since she had so little contact with or knowledge about criminals or the prison system.

"Much more difficult." Ben moved his cart back so another customer could pass. "There is an awful lot of debate in law enforcement concerning when rape becomes rape."

"If she says no, it's rape." This seemed perfectly clear to Georgia.

Sister nodded. "But men are raised to believe that when a woman says maybe, it means yes, and when she says no, she means maybe. Whether we like it or not, there are an awful lot of women out there who use sex as a weapon. Sooner or later, some of them pay for that."

"Yes, but it's often the wrong woman." Georgia nailed that one.

"This culture is still so dishonest and foolish about sex," mused Sister. "I'm surprised we don't have more damage than we do in the form of rapes and murders. It's twisted."

Ben blinked. He hadn't expected to hear that from Sister, even though he knew she wasn't a narrow-minded woman. "Twisted?"

"Ben, sex is used to sell everything except caskets. Every single day Americans are fed images of sexual content allied to commercial purpose. Popular music is one long note of masturbation; excuse me for being blunt. At the same time, young people are counseled not to engage in sex. Women are told no, no, no, and young men are given a mixed message. Twisted like a pretzel."

"Hmm." Georgia turned this over in her mind. "What you said

about criminals, that people are born that way, Sheriff, do you think that's true about alcoholics?"

"Yes." Ben replied without hesitation.

Sister joined in. "I say yes, too, but what makes that dicey is no one puts a gun to your head and says 'Drink.' There is a matter of choice."

"Make mine a margarita." Georgia started whistling a Jimmy Buffet song.

"Interesting question." Ben watched a customer load up his Volvo. "About drunks."

"Runs in my family," Georgia stated flatly.

Sister smiled at Georgia. "I expect it runs in most everyone's family."

"The Sidells have contributed their share of alcoholics to the nation," Ben said ruefully.

Georgia put her pencil back behind her ear. "What do you think about those two guys poisoned down at the train station?"

Ben sighed. "They'll drink anything. Sterno, rubbing alcohol. I doubt they tasted anything in their bottle—if it was murder, I mean. At this point, we don't know if their deaths were a mistake or intentional. Those fellas won't stay at the Salvation Army. And the nights when both men died, it was bitterly cold, down in the teens. They don't feel the cold. If they don't die of alcohol poisoning, they freeze to death. We'll round them up and throw them in jail, but you'll recall the weather was filthy. I had on duty every officer because of wrecks. That was a real department test."

"You know, I never heard the names of the men who died," Sister said.

"We're trying to find next of kin."

"Sam Lorillard might know. He used to be one of them," Sister suggested.

"You can tell us, Sheriff. My folks have been here since the earth was cooling and Sister, too. We might know."

"Anthony Tolliver and Mitchell Banachek."

"Dear God," Sister exclaimed, "what a sad end for Anthony. I can't believe it."

As they stared at her, she added, "We went from grade school through high school together. I adored him."

"Awful." Georgia frowned.

"An awful waste." Sister sighed, remembering a high-spirited, green-eyed kid with gangly limbs.

"Do you know his people?" Ben inquired.

"They've all passed away. He was an only child. If there's distant kin in other parts, I never heard of them."

"Mmm, well—" Ben folded his arms across his chest. "—another expense for the county."

Georgia's eyes widened. "You mean to bury him?" When Ben nodded in affirmation, she blurted out, "Can't the medical school use his body?"

"I'll inquire," Ben replied.

"Don't. I'll take care of this. Let me know when I can claim the body."

"Sister, that's extremely generous."

"Let's hope he's in a better place now." She paused, then said, "There but for the grace of God. We're lucky. Anthony wasn't." She shook her head in disbelief. "I look over schoolmates and friends, as I'm sure you all do, and most people stayed on track. Some surprise you by becoming a great success, and others, like Anthony, surprise you by becoming a great failure. He had everything going for him. I'm sorry you didn't know him then."

"I'll get everything squared away for you." Ben glanced at the floor, then up into her luminous eyes.

"Sister, could he have cured himself? I mean, do you believe in rehabilitation?" Georgia asked earnestly.

"Actually, I don't." She paused for a moment. "But I do believe in redemption."

"What's the difference?" Georgia asked as she checked out work gloves, lead ropes, and a big can of Hooflex for a customer.

"Rehabilitation comes from outside the person. That's why it doesn't work," Sister clarified. "People are forced into programs whether they're alcoholic or in a crumbling marriage or whatever. You know what I mean. There's a huge industry in America now for the purpose of getting people to improve themselves or stop destructive habits. Redemption comes from within. If you want to save yourself, you can and you will. Of course, prayer helps."

"Put that way, I see your point." Ben inclined his head slightly.

"To change the subject—" Sister waited until the customer had left the store. "—if you find that Mitch, too, drank or ate poison, then we might have someone who thinks they're cleaning up the town by killing the drunks."

"That's terrible!" Georgia's hand flew to her mouth.

Ben quietly replied, "The thought had occurred to me."

"Well, if it turns out that way, I give you fair warning. If I find that sorry son of a bitch, I'll kill him myself."

Georgia and Ben were surprised at the comment, the steely tone in Sister's voice.

She even surprised herself.

CHAPTER 9

Bitsy, the soul of extroversion, flew out of the turreted stable at Beveridge Hundred, an estate first farmed in the mid–eighteenth century. Like all Piedmont estates back in those early days, the folks bending their backs to the task of clearing and plowing lived in a log cabin. Even then, many were second- or third-generation Americans, although they thought of themselves as English. Few owned slaves. That trade exploded in the colonies at the turn of the seventeenth to eighteenth century.

Colonists, even in Puritan Massachusetts, needed hands, strong backs, stout legs. And so the Boston traders constructed the unholy triangle of rum, tobacco, and slaves, picking up one at one port, selling it at the next. The Africans suffered in those New England winters. Pennywise New Englanders quickly discerned that owning slaves wasn't profitable. However, this did not prevent the sea captains disembarking from New London, Boston, or Newport from doing business with the Portuguese, then dumping their human cargo only in southern ports. A bargain with the devil had been struck, enriching the captain, his investors, and the planter. As years passed, those morally upright people living in the great mansions built with slave money along the cobblestone streets of Boston contracted a specific form of amnesia: they forgot where that money originated.

The Cullhains kept good records. By 1781, the end of the Revolutionary War, the sons and daughters of the first owners of Beveridge Hundred had done so well they could afford twenty-five slaves: wealth indeed. By 1820, during a boom cycle, the number swelled to 159 souls. By the standards of the day, they treated their people—as they thought of them—well.

Thanks to God's beneficence, by 1865, Beveridge Hundred had not been burned to the ground by Yankees. Half of the slaves, now freed, left. Half remained. Their descendants lived around Beveridge Hundred, taking Cullhain as their surname. The white Cullhains remained as well, their daughters marrying into some of the great Virginia families and some of the not-so-great Virginia families.

Xavier had married a descendant of the Cullhains, Dee, descended on her maternal side. When the insurance business grew, X bought the old place from Dee's great aunt and uncle, who could no longer keep it up.

Year after year, X poured money into the plantation, gradually lifting it up, if not all the way back to its former glory. Some years he had more money than others, but it was a sure bet the funds would be spent on Beveridge Hundred.

Bitsy found this place a rich trove of gossip as well as mice. The little owl would fly over from Sister Jane's barn, ready to hear all from the resident owl: a chatty barn owl.

Xavier liked Bitsy and the resident barn owl, who was much larger than Bitsy. He'd put out sweet corn for her and watch her while she ate it.

The first trailer, the party wagon, rolled down the snow-packed lane.

"Ah, time to pull me boots on." He chucked her some more corn.

"You've got another forty-five minutes."

Xavier smiled as Bitsy chirped and burped—at least that's what he heard. He hoped she would not emit one of her famous shrieks. The barn owl clucked: an endurable sound.

The hunt promptly took off at ten, with a field of forty-five people.

Bitsy shadowed it for a time on her way back home. The foxes gave short runs and then returned to their dens. Treacherous footing kept the foxes close to their dens and kept Sister, Shaker, and the hounds moving slowly, too. Freezing and thawing had coated the fencerows in ice.

After two hours of this torture, Sister called it a day.

Still on horseback they carefully walked back to the trailers; Sister fell in with Edward, Tedi, Xavier, Crawford, Walter, and Marty.

". . . recovered completely." Walter beamed.

He hadn't been talking about a patient, but rather Bessie, a young vixen he and Sister had rescued last year. She'd had to have her front paw amputated after an infection had destroyed much of the bone. She'd become a quiet house pet, even learning to go outside to go to the bathroom. Walter was devoted to Bessie, though her habit of burying food tried his patience.

"Can you breed her?" Xavier asked.

"That's up to Sister." Walter turned to the master.

"If we ever run short of foxes, I suppose we could, but right now the supply is good, and they're healthy. I don't remember seeing such shiny coats."

"Walter, would you like me to send over Fannie and Kristal next Saturday?" She named her cook and head maid. Marty lived well.

"Thank you, Marty, that is so kind of you, but I hired Chef Ted once I knew I was having the big breakfast."

"Oh, that's right. The photographer Jim Meads is flying over from Wales. Guess we have to braid." Crawford sounded as though it would be his fingers that cramped up, not Fairy's joints. "You'll be glad to see your old friend, I know."

"Up to you," Sister replied. "And I can't wait to see Jim. He'll be in the lap of luxury, staying at Beasley Hall." She wanted Jim to herself, but she knew Marty and Crawford would knock themselves out to entertain him plus buy numerous photographs. She'd host him some other time.

"His photographs are shown all over the world. I mean, even the Prince of Wales sees them. He's been in some of them, wearing, I can't remember which hunt's colors, whether it was the Quorn or the Duke of Beaufort." Crawford couldn't wait to be snapped by Mr. Meads.

Edward and Tedi remained silent. Of course they would braid. Why ask?

"My field always looks proper and rises to any occasion," said Sister. "Jim Meads will be impressed as always when he sees the Jefferson Hunt."

"And Mill Ruins is a romantic fixture," Tedi said.

"As is Beveridge Hundred." Sister smiled at Xavier.

Xavier laughed. "Beveridge Hundred would be a lot more photogenic if I'd paint the outbuildings. Even though it doesn't last."

"Nothing lasts anymore since they took the lead out of the damned paint," Crawford grumbled.

Showoff that he was, every fence on his property was four board—not three board but four board—white. Men toiled, painting throughout each summer. With a half million dollars worth of fencing at Beasley Hall, Crawford aspired to perfection.

Most everyone else used Fence Coat Black, a special mixture from a paint supply in Lexington, Kentucky. Sister shipped it in fifty-five-gallon barrels. The stuff lasted almost eight years if one put on two coats.

However one looked at it, fencing was a necessary expense.

"Where's Clay today? Or Ron?" Tedi inquired.

"Some kind of Heart Fund do," Sister said. Both sat on the board for the County Heart Fund.

They rode up on the Hilltoppers.

Bobby Franklin, face ruddy from the cold, said, "Filthy, filthy footing."

"You've still got the horse between your legs," Sister told him.

"And everything else, too, I hope," Walter teased.

"Bunch of perverts." Bobby shook his head.

Ben Sidell, on Nonni, chimed in, "You just figured that out? That's why I moved here from Ohio. I thought being sheriff in a county full of perverts would be, well, a challenge."

"And are we disappointing you?" Tedi sweetly inquired.

He laughed. "Mostly there's good people, but there's just enough of the other kind to keep me busy."

"Nonni's a packer, isn't she?" Bobby admired the tough mare; being a packer meant she could take care of a green rider.

Nonni knew more than the human atop her, which made her special.

"Thank God," Ben agreed. "Oh, Sister, you were right, by the way. Sam Lorillard did know Mitch Banachek. The other men down at the railroad station were either too drunk or too afraid to tell us. Whenever they see a squad car, if they can, they walk."

Crawford, on hearing his trainer's name, spoke a little too rapidly. "Not in trouble, is he?"

"Not at all, Mr. Howard." Ben swiveled to look behind him. "Sam was very helpful in locating next of kin to the two men who died down at the train station."

"Good, good." Crawford cleared his throat.

No one said anything because Gray Lorillard rode behind them. He'd been at the back of the First Flight, and Crawford hadn't realized that when he asked Ben about Sam. Of course, he might have asked it anyway, while other riders, had it been their question, would have waited.

Sister slowed for other riders. "Go on—" She then smiled. "—you can ride in front of the master."

She waited for Gray to come alongside. "Gray, would you mind terribly coming back to my farm for lunch? The girls are with me today, Jennifer and Sari. They can clean your horse and tack. They'll put your horse in a stall, and, when you're ready, you can load him right back up again. If we each go home, see to our horses, clean up, we won't get to the club until three or four. Let's just eat a relaxed lunch in my kitchen. You can take me to the club on a non-hunting day."

His teeth shone bright white when he smiled, his military mustache drawing attention to his teeth. "What a good idea. Are you sure the girls won't mind?"

"No. They are two wonderful kids."

She checked the hounds at the party wagon, thanked her whippers-in, and quietly told Betty she'd be having a tête-à-tête with Gray. She then handed her horse over to Jennifer. As she walked by Ben, he motioned her to come over.

"Sister, the results came back on Mitch. Hemlock. Same as Tony."

She grimaced, imagining their last moments. "Hope it's some kind of fluke. My throat constricts just thinking about them drinking that poison."

"You can claim Anthony tomorrow if that suits." He lowered his voice.

"I'll have Carl Haslip," she named one of the local funeral homes run by one of Ronnie's relatives, "go to the morgue tomorrow. If nothing else, Anthony will have a Christian burial."

She gingerly walked back to her truck, thinking about the total loss of self-respect those men at the station exhibited. She had noticed how oddly some walked, their legs wide apart in a strange kind of lurching shuffle. She'd realized they had peed themselves so many times that the skin on their legs was burned. Their pants, encrusted, rubbed them raw. When a human sank that low, maybe he wouldn't even notice hemlock, or maybe he had tired of the slow suicide of alcoholism and had elected a swifter route. Then she also recalled their raucous laughter at times when she'd seen them at the downtown mall. Suicide didn't ring true. Nor could she imagine Anthony Tolliver wanting to kill himself. He'd hang on for one last drink.

CHAPTER 10

Thou unravished bride of quietness," Gray quoted Keats. "However, once she was ravished, she babbled incessantly and usually it was a litany of my shortcomings."

Sister laughed as she poured the Mumm de Cramant. They sat in front of the huge kitchen fireplace.

The coffeepot gurgled. She put the bottle of Cramant back in the ice bucket shaped like a sitting fox, a beautiful Christmas gift from Walter. Back at the counter Sister poured her favorite coffee, Shenandoah Eye Opener. "Cream? Sugar? Honey? I have crumbly brown sugar."

"Barefoot."

She brought him a steaming cup of black coffee, putting cream and honey in hers. "Gray, I'd forgotten how funny you can be."

The deep creases around his eyes lengthened as he smiled. "Well, I might as well laugh at my own expense. Doesn't cost a cent."

"I imagine the divorce did, though."

"Women extract their revenge for love lost, but here I am talking to one. You know, Sister, everyone has his or her story, and everyone can make excuses. It seems to me you can make a life or you can make excuses, but you can't do both."

She clicked her champagne glass to his. "Exactly."

"Actually, I learned a lot. Theresa and I grew apart. Living with another person is like visiting another country; you have to learn a new language, and so does she. It's obvious, but it wasn't at the time." He paused. "You and Raymond managed."

"We practically killed each other, but we never did stop talking. And Gray, it's no secret that he had his affairs, and, well, it's more of a secret, I suppose, because women are better at glossing over these things, but I had mine."

He perked right up. "Did you now?"

"I did, and I don't regret a single one."

"But you still loved Ray?"

"You can love more than one person at a time, and I don't give a damn what the self-help books say, or the marriage mafia. If I hear the words 'family values' one more time, I may explode. All this business of how monogamy creates stability. Perhaps for some it does, but what creates stability is the balance of opposing forces or energies. And that's Life According to Jane Arnold."

"You'd forgotten how funny I could be—" He sipped more champagne. "—I'd forgotten how you cut right to the bone, right to the core of an issue. Most people don't have the guts."

She smiled. "Thank you, but I don't know as it's guts. I live on a farm. I work with animals every day of my life, as well as working in the soil. I believe all these ideas, overblown ideologies—religious or political—serve to drive a wedge between us and nature, between us and what we really are, which is a higher vertebrae, but an animal just the same."

"Might I conclude that you are not enamored of democracy?"

"Democracy is running the zoo from the monkey cage."

"What's the alternative?" he asked.

"An enlightened despot, whether by birth as a king or queen or someone strong enough to accrue power to themselves. That's the most efficient system, but we live in times that make that impossible. Democracy has become the Holy Grail of the West, of industrialization, and you know why. Because the real worship is not one man, one vote, it's one man, one dollar. Commerce drives democracy, not vice versa."

"I'll have to think about that." The firelight accentuated his high cheekbones.

"To change the subject, how long have you been divorced? The women in our club are dying to know."

A boyish grin made him attractive. "Three years. My two children are grown. Mandy, whom we named for Nelson Mandela, back when he was incarcerated, is thirty-one. She's a tax lawyer in my firm. I never thought she'd follow in her father's footsteps. Mandy was the cheerleader/prom queen type, but she is a brilliant tax lawyer." He stopped himself for a second. "I'm bragging."

"Please do."

"Brian, now, he is a maverick if ever there was one. He graduated from the University of Missouri, majored in animal husbandry; his specialty is cattle. He went on and got his doctor of veterinary medicine and now has a practice in Grand Junction, Nebraska. I swear he's the only black cattle vet in the U.S." Gray laughed. "Thriving practice. He loves his work."

"Did you love yours?"

He reached for his coffee and took a sip. "This is delicious. Yes, I did, still do. The tax code will never be simplified in our lifetime because it's not about taxes; it's about congressmen distributing the pork. If a congressman from Florida can slip a provision into the code that gives some stone crab producers a big break, he will, and he'll get reelected. The hypocrisy of our taxes is outrageous. People focus on the IRS, the symptom of their pain, instead of focusing on

Congress, the source of the sickness. There will never be a good tax lawyer out of work. I like it: it's war without the guns. I go in to win."

"I never thought of that."

"I could tell you stories until sunup."

"I wouldn't mind." She smiled.

He smiled back. "When did Raymond pass?"

"In 1991."

"That long ago? I remember Sam calling to tell me in a sober moment."

"You wrote a lovely condolence."

"I liked Ray."

"Everyone did. He was a big outgoing man who made everyone feel important. And he wasn't acting. He loved people."

"He was good to us. I never felt an ounce of racism from Big Ray."

She stroked her chin for a second. "Not consciously, but by virtue of when we were born and where we were raised, which is to say the United States, damaging concepts crept into our minds. One has to root them out, stay vigilant. Still, Ray trusted people. What I find among most people concerning race is terrible mistrust. It's a poison. He never had that poison." She thought for a flash of Mitch and Tony.

"Yes, it is, but how do you wipe out three hundred years of it?"

"You don't. At least not in a generation or two. But don't you think if one dwells on it, then one is trapped?" She hesitated. "Hope I haven't offended you. I know none of us can escape our gender, our age, our race, and those things affect one. The whole world can be against you, but if you view yourself as your enemies view you, you've lost. Grab mane and kick on!"

He leaned forward, the warm cup of coffee in his hands. "You know that's why I admire you. You tell the truth. Even if it's painful, you call it as you see it. You said people liked Ray. People like you, Sister, because you're honest and strong. And you're not hard to look at either."

She laughed again. "Gray!"

He laughed, too. "I know what you mean. The question for me as a political animal has always been: How do I address my oppression without being obsessed by it? I made the right decision for me. I became proficient at my profession, and I supported those leaders and causes that I thought would help our people. I also supported causes that have nothing to do with race. I love the symphony and never minded writing a check each year to the Opera Guild. In fact, how lucky am I to be able to give?"

"I feel the same way, although most of my giving is directed toward the hunt club and the No Kill Animal Shelter. Those are my passions. Well, if there's a woman candidate who looks good, I'll support her, but so many of them are more liberal than I am. You know, antiguns and all that." She threw up her hands. "How can you live out in the country without guns?"

"You can't." He leaned back in his chair just as Golliwog sauntered through the kitchen.

"Time for treats." She hopped on the counter to lick the plates.

"Golly, you get off of there," Sister commanded.

"Make me." Golly didn't jump down until Sister came after her.

"All cats are anarchists." Gray watched the imposing feline give Sister a baleful glance, as though she were the wronged party and not the other way around.

"Maybe I'd better start flying the black flag over the house."

"Ever read that stuff? Bakunin?"

"No. I read *Das Kapital* in 1968, hoping it would help me understand the riots here and in Paris. Torture. Anyone who is a communist has a far greater capacity for tedium and repression than I do, tedium being the worst of the two." She freshened his coffee. "Would you like more Cramant?"

"No, thank you. I have to drive Vagabond and myself back to the barn."

"Good-looking horse."

"Jumps the moon. I enjoyed hunting with him in Middleburg."

"Troy Taylor is a fine huntsman, and Jeff Blue and Penny De-nege are good masters. And they've got Fred Duncan, former hunts-man at Warrenton there, too."

"We'd hunt with Orange Hunt and Piedmont on occasion, and the last year I was there, I capped the limit at Old Dominion. You know, I had fallen into northern Virginia myopia, thinking that hunting stops south with Casanova Hunt and Warrenton. I'd forgot-ten just how much fun and how challenging hunting with Jefferson Hunt can be."

"You couldn't have said anything that would make me happier! We don't have as much good galloping territory, obviously. We're sinking down into ravines and clambering up foothills or mountain sides, especially at our westernmost fixtures, but if you can sit tight, there's good sport."

"May I ask you a personal question?"

"You can try."

"Why didn't you remarry?"

She took a long sip of coffee. "The truth?" When he nodded, she said, "For the first year after Big Ray's death, I was numb. The second year I could feel, but it was a dull ache. When Ray died, I was fifty-nine. By the time I started to feel that I could be happy again, I was sixty-two. I thought, 'I'm too old and no one will want me.' "

"Not true, of course."

"You're very kind, Gray, and then, then Peter Wheeler began to slow down. Peter and I had had an affair stretching throughout my forties. I stuck close to him. No affair. I mean, that was over, but I sup-pose I wasn't emotionally available, even if someone had wanted me."

"Actually, I think you scare the hell out of most men."

"I do?"

"You're six feet tall, probably taller when you were young, as I recall. You ride like a bat out of hell. You go through snow, rain, hail, sun, bogs, over stonewalls and big-ass coops. You come back smiling. You don't have an ounce of fat on you, at least not that I can see. And you're the master."

Her eyes opened wide. "That's fine with me. I wouldn't want a man who wanted a weak woman."

He laughed. "Touchdown."

"Now may I ask you a personal question?"

"Yes, ma'am."

"What do you think Sam's chances are of staying clean?"

"Good. No, better than good. The deaths of Tony and Mitch have scared him. That could have been him. He was that out of control."

"The thieving?"

"He stole to feed his habit. I believe he'll stay straight. If he doesn't—" Gray threw up his hands. "—I have done all I can do. No more."

"I see."

"What do you think Sam's chances are?" he asked her.

"I don't know. I haven't been close to him for years. I hope he pulls it together. He's a good horseman, and those are hard to find. And, before he fell by the wayside, he was a good man as well."

As Gray rose to go, being a Virginian, he knew not to ask if he could help do the dishes. Although that is considered helpful outside the South, especially among those who are not wealthy, in the South, you don't ask unless you're at a Yankee's house. What you do, knowing hardly anyone has the money for servants anymore, while preserving the fiction, is to later send to your hostess flowers or something else she likes. Or you can ask her to dinner.

"Your cat has returned to her evil ways." He laughed at Golly.

Sister clapped her hands. "You get down from there."

"Ha, ha." Golly laughed, giving up her post just as Raleigh and Rooster hurried in, hearing Sister clap her hands.

"What's up! We're ready." The Doberman's ears lifted up.

"Yeah, I'd like a ride in the truck." Rooster lived for rides, and he knew the county better than most humans who drove it.

"All right, boys. Just a bad cat."

Disappointed, they sat down as Golly, bursting with pride, rubbed right up on Raleigh's chest. The Doberman looked the other way.

When Gray drove out of the stableyard, Sister sat down for a moment before doing the dishes.

"Whooee." Golly added her two cents.

The two dogs stared at their human. She looked into their beautiful eyes. "Boys, he makes me feel—" She shrugged. "—can't explain it."

"Yahoo!" Golly sat and purred. *"Time for the beauty parlor, a facial, and hey, maybe a boob lift."*

"Golly, you are insufferable," Rooster moaned.

"Yeah, just think if you had a boob lift, the doctor would have to hoist up eight of them," Raleigh teased.

The calico swatted Raleigh, rubbed against Sister's leg as she stood up, then sauntered off.

Sister watched her. "What gets into her?"

"You don't want to know," the dogs replied.

C H A P T E R 1 1

Picking her way through the sodden earth, Inky had ample time to consider the fabled January thaw. Without fail, this warm-up occurred soon after the New Year, unlocking ice on the ponds and at the edges of creek beds. Frozen pipes and hoses suddenly spouted leaks, which meant plumbers raked in the bucks.

Shrubs bent low under snow would pop up, releasing dried berries still on the bough. And, of course, the footing was awful.

Inky had den fever, so she crossed Soldier Road to visit Grace, a small red fox living at Foxglove Farm.

Cindy Chandler, owner of this lovely place, had created two ponds, each at a different level, with a water wheel turning water from the upper pond to the lower. Underneath, buried below the frost line, was a pipe that carried the water back to the upper pond. The small insulated pump house served as a winter nest for one groundhog and many field mice, so both Grace and Inky found it most enticing. The field mice screamed bloody murder the second they smelled Inky and Grace. The groundhog, slovenly creature that he was and dreadfully fat, just rolled over and snored more loudly.

The two friends wearied of terrorizing the mice, so they trotted up the low long hill to the stable, a tidy affair with a prominent weathervane in the shape of a running fox.

The girls cleaned out the gleanings, some with molasses coating. Then they visited the Holstein cow and her calf, now as big as she was. These two, Clytemnestra and Orestes, wreaked havoc on Cindy's fences and occasionally the gardens, too. Cly, as she was called, bored easily. As she had a pea brain, she craved excitement as well as clover. She'd lower her head, smashing through any fence in her path. Orestes, a tiny bell around his neck, would follow.

Finally, Cindy gave up, opened gates, and let her roam. The gardens, off limits, were patrolled by Cindy herself, with a cattle prod or her German shepherd.

Winter curtailed the naughty cow's depredations. She and Orestes elected to remain close to their shed since it was filled with fresh hay and some special flakes of alfalfa, too. Cly was spoiled rotten. Humans chastised Cindy for babying the huge animal, but Cindy justified this by saying Cly behaved better if she had alfalfa and sweets.

Even the other animals told Cly she was so bad she ought to be hamburger. She'd lower her head, toss it about, let out a "Moo," and then go about her business.

The foxes slipped under the shed overhang. The cow had bedded down in the straw, Orestes next to her.

"How are you, Cly? I haven't seen you in some time," Inky politely inquired.

"Good. What about you?"

"Pretty good, thank you. There's been so much snow, I don't imagine too much has been going on around here."

"Cindy's planning a potting shed. That's the news." She flicked her long tail, which happened to hit her son in the nose.

"Mother," he grumbled.

"Well, don't sleep so close to me."

After more desultory conversation, the two foxes left for Sister's stable. Sister left out fruit candies, which Inky craved. Moving in a straight line, as the crow flies, Sister's stable was only three and a half miles from Cindy's stable.

"Little shapes like the fruit. Grape is a tiny bunch of grapes, and it's purple. Cherry is a little red cherry. They fit exactly right in your mouth." Inky anticipated her treats.

"Wish I could get Cindy to put out candy. She puts out corn, and I do like it, but I have a sweet tooth." Grace also liked to fish. She would sit motionless at the edge of one of the ponds for hours. Quick as a flash, she'd nab one.

The two foxes ducked under fences, finally coming into the large floodplain along Broad Creek. Built up along this floodplain was Soldier Road. The road, used since before the Revolutionary War, had originally been an Indian footpath leading to the Tidewater. Back during the Depression, when the federal government created work, the state built up the road through the floodplain. Even being twenty feet above, with culverts underneath, the road would flood at least once a decade. Modern-day people had to wait for floodwaters to recede, just as their ancestors had.

The two foxes moved four feet in from the creek itself.

"That's strange." Grace stopped at a spot that had been dug: small holes, not more than seven inches deep.

Inky peered into the shallow holes. *"Cowbane. Wasn't this where the cowbane was?"*

"Still is. There're roots all over here. Smells like parsnip." Grace could only smell the odor of thawing earth as the scent from the tubers had vanished. *"This is where Agamemnon died."*

Agamemnon, Clytemnestra's mate, had died two and a half years ago.

"Bet that was a mess." Inky wasn't out and about yet at that time since it had been spring and she had still been a cub.

"*Yes, had to get the tractor, the big eighty-horsepower one, put the chains on him and drag him out. Couldn't bury him here because of the flooding. What I don't understand is how could he miss it? I mean, the stems were up, the little umbrella clusters ready to open. We all know what cowbane looks and smells like.*"

"*Cows just pull up hunks by the roots. Maybe he didn't know until it was too late,*" Inky said thoughtfully.

"*Every part of that plant is poisonous but the roots are the most lethal. Even a big bull like Agamemnon takes only a few little bites of a tuber and that's it. Gone.*" Grace's voice carried the note of finality.

"*Kill you in fifteen minutes. If you eat a big enough dose. It can kill any of us. I guess that's why all this is fenced off, and even Clytemnestra is smart enough not to come down here and eat.*"

"*That Cly,*" Grace shook her head, "*she is so dumb. I know she can't help it, but I wouldn't be surprised if she forgot. You know when Cindy started to plow the roads in the snow, Cly ran out and stood in the road, then she charged the tractor. She's got a screw loose.*"

"*Yeah, but she's not dumb enough to eat what killed Agamemnon,*" Inky replied. "*I'm surprised Cindy hasn't put plant poison on this stuff.*"

"*She does, but it comes back. It's all over. I guess most humans know what it looks like. It's pretty when it flowers, you know. All these city people and suburban people moving into the country, they don't know. They think the white flowers are pretty.*"

"*They use 'country' as a put-down, those folks. They don't realize how much you have to know to live in the country, to hunt, to farm.*" Inky shrugged. "*I try to look on the bright side. I mean, they can learn, I guess.*"

"*Inky, who would dig this up?*" Grace's slender, elegant ears with the black tips swept forward.

"*Not an animal. We all know better.*"

"*Well, someone dug up the cowbane roots.*" Grace again examined the shallow holes, moist with the melting snow.

"*Had to have done it before the snow. Maybe some human wanted it. You know, some herbalist. Better hope they wore gloves. Cowbane can make you sick just from the stuff that rubs off on your hands.*"

The two walked through the culvert to the other side of the road and were now on Roughneck Farm, the high Hangman's Ridge to their right. They wondered about the little holes a bit more, but soon forgot it as they hurried to the stable where, sure enough, those little sweet fruit candies awaited.

Cowbane is the country term for *Conium maculatum*: hemlock.

CHAPTER 1 2

The hard freeze forced the graveyard manager, Burke Ismond, to bring out the heavy equipment early in the morning to dig a grave for Anthony Tolliver.

As he'd known Anthony, he mused that, even in death, the town drunk was a pain in the ass.

The Episcopal service was attended by Sister Jane, Tedi and Edward Bancroft, Betty and Bobby Franklin, and Donnie Sweigert and Clay Berry, the latter two feeling they ought to show up because Anthony did, from time to time, work for Berry Storage.

The sky, a hauntingly brilliant blue, only intensified the cold at the gravesite. The temperature, at nineteen degrees Fahrenheit, underscored the coldness of death.

After the simple, dignified service, the mourners walked together back to their respective cars.

"He had a good sense of humor, even when his whole life fell apart," Bobby spoke. "These things take over a person." Bobby knew whereof he spoke because of his eldest daughter, Cody.

"Some are born strong; some are born weak. That's as near as I can figure." Sister inhaled the bitingly cold air. "Once upon a time he was handsome, full of energy, and a good dancer."

"Janie, I expect you and I are the only ones left who remember Anthony like that. By the time Edward and I married and we moved back here, Anthony was a lost cause."

"Must be terrible to die alone and unloved." Betty thought of his fate.

"Millions do. What was it Hobbes wrote, 'The life of man is brutish, nasty and short,' " Bobby quoted. "Not that I like the idea, mind you. But Anthony didn't live in Beirut or Sarajevo. He lived right here in central Virginia. I can't help but think he had more chances than millions of others in devastated places. We'll never understand what goes on in a brain like his."

"Just as well." Donnie Sweigert finally said something.

"Why?" Betty asked.

" 'Cause if you know how they think, maybe you start to think like they do." He put his ungloved hands in his pockets. "He was okay. I didn't have any problems with him. He knew if he was on the job that day, he was sober that day. What he did at night with his paycheck was his business."

"What surprises me is how long he lived, considering how much he drank. He probably didn't have any liver left." Clay remembered how rail thin Anthony was in the last years of his life. "Man must have had an iron constitution to keep going."

"Guess he did," Bobby replied.

Clay shook his head. "This sounds awful, but maybe it's just as well he drank what he drank. He would have died of cirrhosis, no doubt, and it's an awful death. At least he didn't linger, and we might take comfort in that."

"I'd take comfort in it if it had been his idea." Sister's voice was firm. "Yes, he was a falling-down drunk much of the time, but he still had a spark of life in him. I know he didn't commit suicide."

"Maybe he just grabbed the wrong bottle." Donnie shrugged. "I feel sorry for him."

"We all do, and I thank you all for coming here. At least he had a few people to mark his passing." Sister met each person's eyes. "Thank you."

As people gratefully slipped into their vehicles to start their motors and the heaters, Clay remained behind. "Sister, allow me to pay for this. I should have thought of it in the first place, and I apologize."

"He was an old friend."

"Well, he worked for me when he could work. Why don't we split it? I really should do something. I've had too much on my mind. I apologize again for not seeing to this when he died."

"All right. We'll share."

Clay bent down and kissed her on the cheek. "You're the best."

"Best what?" Her eyes brightened.

"Best master, best person. Best."

"I don't know about that, but every now and then the Good Lord gives you a chance to do something for someone else. I wish I could have done for him while he lived but . . ." Her voice trailed off.

"Yeah. Thing with the Anthonys of this world is you've got to cut them loose before they take you down."

"That's true."

"I'll call Carl Haslip, send half the cost directly to them." He kissed her again and opened the door of her truck. "Crazy world, isn't it?"

She smiled. "Sometimes. Mostly, I think it's us who are crazy. The foxes seem to do all right. Never heard of a fox, drunk or at a psychiatrist's office."

Clay laughed, shut her door, and then headed for his SUV.

CHAPTER 13

Failure haunted Sam Lorillard. Turning around, he'd constantly bump into ghosts from his past. Hauling a mare up to Middleburg to be bred, he'd pass through graceful brick gates, drive to the breeding shed, and unload the mare. He'd notice that the stable colors were green and yellow, and that would remind him of a stable at the track. Or he'd drive down to the feed store to pick up a small item, passing estates along the way where he'd once worked, disgraced himself, and been canned.

At first the rehab center had felt like prison. When he finally faced himself, he had felt like hell. After weeks of intensive therapy, he began to believe he could do it, he could stay dry, he could fight this curse in the blood. The center then felt less like prison and more like a school to teach survival.

Alcoholism stalked the Lorillards, selecting its victims with savage relish. Rarely did the more phlegmatic succumb to the siren call of gin, bourbon, or vodka, or perhaps those more modern allures, heroin and cocaine. The victims were bright, personable, possessed of talent. Sam's mother, at the end, had looked like a stick figure. She died not even knowing who she was. Her uncle drank himself to death in his little house. When they finally found his body on the sofa and picked him up to remove him, he'd languished there so long his skin sloughed off.

Generation after generation, one or two more Lorillards battled the bottle, drugs, or pills. Most smoked.

As near as anyone could tell, this proclivity arrived from France with the first Lorillard in 1679. It flourished among both black and white Lorillards. Some overcame it even before the days of clinics, Alcoholics Anonymous, and drug rehab. They learned never to take one drink, not one drop, nor to fiddle with any other substance that made their bodies soar with pleasure, only to be smashed to earth. Those Lorillards showed great strength of purpose. Nowadays when Sam felt that terrible thirst come over him, that parching of the throat coupled with the memory of sweet bourbon and the warm buzz it gave him, he'd remember the family curse.

In Sam's generation, Timothy Lorillard, white, had owned a large company that produced picture frames. He'd lost everything. Another cousin, Nina Davis, black, went cold turkey after the birth of her first child. She never looked back. Maybe working as a nurse in the local hospital snapped her awake, too.

Sam knew it could be done, and he prayed constantly: "Dear Lord, give me the strength to do some good in this life, what's left to me."

Anyone who had known Sam from his drinking days would burst out laughing at the thought of the rebellious man praying. He prayed grooming horses. He prayed while drinking a cup of coffee. He prayed each time he saw his brother; he most especially prayed then because he thought he would kill himself before letting his older brother down. When Gray had endured his divorce, Sam couldn't help him because he couldn't help himself. When Gray had broken down and cried because he did love his wife, and because he couldn't believe the condition of his brother, what did Sam do? He took another drink.

When he felt himself ravaged by guilt, he'd tell himself, "I can't change the past. The past is past. I can only live in this minute and do the best I can. I can forgive myself. I forgive myself."

He walked along the railroad track, rails gleaming in the night, ribbons of steel reflecting the sparse streetlights from the raised road above, a chill squiggled down his spine. This is where his brother had finally found him, hauled him up by the collar, threw him in the SUV, driven his drunken ass all the way to Greensboro, North Carolina, to the special place there for people like Sam, people who ran Fortune 500 companies as well as filthy people who sprawled on baggage carts at the station.

The temperature dipped to twenty-nine degrees, signaling the end of the thaw. Ahead, the Chinaman's hat light hung over the door into the station. The drunks couldn't go in here; the station master chased them out. The stench of the men offended customers.

Addled as he had been when he used to end up here, Sam remembered the pleasant odd hum of the rails when a train was coming. The vibrations started a mile off. He could hear the hum as the train drew closer. Many times on an unruly horse, his senses had saved his butt. They had saved him even when he hit bottom. He had pulled Rory Ackerman off the track when he fell asleep and a train was coming. Drunk as he'd been, Sam possessed a sixth sense.

That sixth sense now brought him back.

Rory, huddled behind a cart, back to the wind, looked up, blinked. "Sam."

"How you doin', man?"

"Doin'," the large man, coal black hair, heavy beard, shrugged. His eyes, black as his hair, were cloudy. Cleaned up, shaved, Rory would be good-looking, although it was hard to imagine it now.

"Where're the rest of the boys?"

Rory snorted, "Salvation Army, bunch of goddamned pussies."

"Been cold. Got to warm up sometime."

"I'd rather be cold than have the Bible rubbed off on me. They're down there cleaning up 'cause there's a service for Tony and Mitch."

"Hadn't heard about a service."

Rory stared up at him. "Why would you? You ain't one of us no more."

"I'll always be one of you," Sam said with a simple dignity. "I'm not better; I just decided I wanted to live. Wish you would, too."

"For what?" Rory said this without bitterness or self-pity. "I'm good for nothin'."

"We're all good for something."

"You. You good for horses. You got something. I didn't even get out of junior high."

"Some of the dumbest people I know have an education." Sam laughed.

Rory laughed, too. "Hey, got a smoke?"

"Yeah." Sam handed him a weed. As Rory fumbled in his pocket for a match, Sam lit the cigarette for him with a two-dollar blue disposable lighter.

"Least you haven't gone totally pure."

"I can only give up one vice at a time. Calms my nerves."

"Yeah." Rory inhaled, closing his eyes. "What you doin' here, man?"

"Wondering what really happened to Tony and Mitch. Don't guess anyone told Ben Sidell but so much."

"Mmm, he's okay, but still, he's a cop." Rory shifted, turning up the collar of his shirt, an old muffler, caked with dirt around his neck, an ancient down jacket over that.

"You warm enough?"

"Yeah. Worse time is just before sunup."

"I remember."

"Mitch and Tony drank some bad shit; that's all I know. I think they drank it at the same time. Took longer to find Mitch, who was frozen stiff. Like a board."

"Did you see anyone give them a bottle?"

"No."

"Were they working? Enough for the next bottle?"

"Yeah. They'd go down to the S.A.—" He used the initials of the Salvation Army. "—shower, shave, get some clothes that didn't stink, get a job for a day or a week or however long they could hang on."

"Where?"

Rory shrugged. "Tony was a pretty big guy. I know he delivered feed for some guy over in Stuart's Draft. He'd catch a ride over. Never said who was driving. He'd stay over there sometimes. Unload furniture for Clay Berry sometimes. Tony mucked stalls with Mitch, too. Mitch knew all the horse people. They're all the time needin' someone. 'Cause they get hurt a lot, I guess." Rory half smiled. "Not you."

"I've bought my share of dirt." Sam hunkered down to be eye level. "Rory, if you want to change, I can help."

Rory's eyes flashed for an instant. "Change for what? Who's gonna hire me iffin' I do?"

"If you're willing to work, I'll help you there."

"You saved my white ass once. I never did squat for you."

"We had some laughs."

"Yeah, yeah, we did." Rory softened. "How'd you do it, man?"

"I ran out of excuses."

"Well, I got a few left."

"When you run out, let me know." Sam handed him a folded sheet of paper with his phone number on it at home and at work. Inside the paper was a five-dollar bill. He figured Rory would buy a bottle or two of vile cheap stuff with the money on Monday, but, well, he couldn't walk away without giving him something.

"Thanks." Rory saw the money inside the folded paper.

"Oh, yeah, if you think of anything else about Mitch or Tony, let me know."

"I will. Weird." Rory stubbed out his cigarette, which he'd smoked down to his nicotine-stained fingers. "Your brother living with you?"

"No. The home place is so bad he can't stand it."

"Gray always was the kind of guy who buffed his nails." Rory laughed uproariously. "Expensive suits. Expensive women."

"He's rented a cottage at Chapel Cross. He's looking for a place. If you do want some help, I got a room for you after."

A mixture of gratitude and even a flicker of hope crossed Rory's once attractive features. "You're okay, Sam. You're okay."

"Here." Sam handed him the rest of a pack of Dunhills, red box.

"Shit, man, you must be living good."

"My boss has more money than God. He doesn't mind that I smoke, but he says he can't stand the smell of cheap cigarettes, so every Monday morning, he puts a carton of Dunhill reds in the tack room. Funny guy. He's a real hardass son of a bitch, but he has a kind of sweet streak."

"Who?"

"Crawford Howard."

"Heard of him. Owns Beasley Hall. Beastly Hall." He laughed sarcastically. "Guess he does have more money than God." Rory examined the beautiful pack, a rich red edged in gold. "No filters. Anyone who smokes filtered cigarettes or lights, you know, man, no balls. No balls. I don't even respect women who smoke that shit. All they get is additives. Worse for them than real tobacco." Rory said this with some enthusiasm.

Sam smiled. "Yep. You know, if you were a few shades darker, Rory, you'd be a real bro'."

Rory laughed, a genuine laugh. "Sam, you always were full of it." Then he stopped and said slowly, "You look good, Sam; you look good. I'm proud of you."

As Sam walked back to the ancient Toyota, parked up on Main Street, he sent up a little prayer that the good Lord would help Rory find his way. And he prayed for Tony and Mitch. Something wasn't right, his sixth sense warned.

CHAPTER 14

The mist rose off the earth like silver dragon's breath. Eighty-two people quietly rode past the old Mill Ruins. Its two-story water wheel slowly turning, the lap of water comforting. Tiny ice crystals clung to the millrace, the straight chute of water feeding the mill.

Thanks to the presence of British photographer Jim Meads, Saturday's hunt brought out every Jefferson Hunt member not flattened with a cold or flu, as well as cappers from surrounding hunts. Vanity, a spur even to those who deny it, ensured the assemblage dazzled in their best.

To Sister's surprise, Dr. Dalton Hill was there, well turned out, riding a handsome Cleveland bay that suited him.

Artemis must have had a fond spot for the indefatigable Mr. Meads, because she granted perfect hunting conditions. Light frost glittered on grass, stones, pin oak limbs, and the old vines hanging from trees. As the sun rose, this silvery coating turned to pink, then salmon, then scarlet in early-morning light.

Sister upset people by casting hounds at sunup, but the sun rose at seven-fifteen on January 17, and it would afford Jim spectacular photographs. As Jim had flown in all the way from Wales, she could certainly get everyone's nether regions in the saddle just as the pulsating rim of the sun crested the horizon.

Sister beheld each sunrise with hope. Today's promise hovered with the slightly rising temperature, the light frost, the sweet faint breeze out of the west.

As hounds moved past the old mill, the mercury registered thirty degrees. Shaker would cast on the east side of the slopes, hoping for enough warmth that scent might lift off the fields. The temperature felt as though it would climb into the midforties by noon; scent should improve by the hour. The Weather Channel's radar screen had shown a large band of rain clouds, circling counterclockwise. The first streaky clouds might sneak in from the west by nine o'clock. As further clouds moved in, the scent would—with luck—stay down.

Sister kept a detailed hunting journal. She noted the temperature when starting, the wind, its direction, the first cast and draw, the couple of hounds hunting, her mount, the number of people. She religiously wrote in her journal as soon as she got into the house. She tried to be accurate, to remember each sweep of the hounds. She saved decades of journals. Perhaps years hence, some future master would profit from her attention to detail.

Crawford spared no effort in his turnout. Sam Lorillard, although in an old habit, looked fine. His coat had been cut for him, as had his still serviceable boots.

Walter wore his black swallowtail coat. Other members, ladies with colors, wore derbies with their frock coats. Sister liked that look. Because a shadbelly or a weaselbelly isn't worn as often as a frock coat, many people didn't own them, even though they might be entitled to wear them. Shelling out eight hundred dollars for the High Holy Day hunts or those special days with other hunts proved tough on the pocketbook, or too much for those inclined to be tight. So a well-cut bespoke frock, or one off the rack that had been modified by a hunting tailor, always created a smart appearance. The entire Vajay family wore perfectly cut frock coats of darkest navy, which was as correct as black. What a good-looking group they were.

Jim, at six feet four inches and rail lean, had gotten the photographs he wanted as the field filed past the water wheel. He wore sturdy shoes, tough pants to repel thorns, and a much-loved waterproof jacket. Running kept him warm, so he wasn't bundled up. He was already up ahead, skirting along the side of the farm road. He eagerly snapped away as Shaker, twenty-four couple of sleek hounds, and the two handsomely mounted whippers-in rode by him.

Originally Sister had planned on entertaining the outgoing Jim, but Crawford begged to have him at Beasley Hall. Crawford reasoned that with his servants, and an extra car, Jim would luxuriate in amenities after his long journey. And Sister could always catch up with her favorite former British airman at tea. She gave in. Because she had a political agenda for Crawford, she wanted to make him happy. Crawford took this as a sign that he truly was on track to be named joint-master.

Ronnie and Xavier smiled as they rode past Jim. Even Xavier's weaselbelly didn't help him look slimmer. He was disgusted with himself and Ronnie didn't help matters by asking him when the blessed event would occur.

Ronnie, always in shape, sat his horse smugly, his weaselbelly faded to the best shade of scarlet, his cream colored vest points protruding at the correct length, his fourfold stock tie, so white it hurt the eyes, tied with such aplomb that Ronnie was the envy of all who aspired to such splendor. Ronnie, like many gay men, had a way with clothes.

Try as Crawford might, he looked too flash, though he was perfectly correct in his turnout. Ronnie, however, had pegged it just right.

Clay looked good, too, although not as polished as Ronnie. He had a satisfied smile on his face since Izzy continued to thank him for the 500SL. Nothing like wake-up loving to put a man in a great mood. Izzy had already joined the Hilltoppers.

Sister turned in the saddle, inspecting the long line behind her, snaking through the mist lifting off the millrace. Keepsake, gleaming, felt her turn. He kept his eyes and ears on the pack thirty yards ahead. His powers of smell, not as profound as a hound's, were good, far better than any human's. He detected a number of scents and wished Sister could as well. Both human and horse were passionate hunters, but Keepsake felt sorry that his rider's nose was woefully underdeveloped. Humans couldn't help it. They had fewer olfactory receptors, and with those pitiful little nostrils, how could anyone suck up scent?

He flared his wide nostrils, being rewarded with the clear but fading odor of bobcat. Bobcats, if hounds get on a line, will give a rough chase. They'll shoot through the meanest, lowest ground cover. Hounds get shredded with thorns. It usually doesn't take long for the bobcat to have his fill of it. Since the bobcat is not a sporting animal by nature, he or she then will climb a tree, viewing those below with thick disdain.

Hounds lifted their heads, winding.

Sister noticed, but no sterns moved. She inhaled deeply, smelling the beguiling odor from the pines, the distinctive moist scent of the millrace.

"Why aren't you going over there?" Rassle, a precocious first-year entry, asked Dasher.

"Bobcat."

"Ooh." Rassle lifted his head higher. This was the first time he'd smelled such a varmint. Had he seen this particular customer, respect would have been his response. The male bobcat, a tight forty pounds, had padded down to the mill to snatch a little dog food. Walter put dog food and corn there and at other spots for the red foxes. For whatever reason, only reds lived at Mill Ruins.

While he could and would run, a bobcat wouldn't shy from a fight. His fangs, his lightning reflexes, and his frightening claws could reduce animals far larger than himself to a bloody mess.

"Can we chase bobcat?" Ruthie, Rassle's littermate, inquired.

"If there's no fox, we can, but," Asa warned, *"you don't get too close, and you'd better be prepared to go through hateful briars."*

"How about bear?" Ruthie was curious.

"Well, again, if there's no fox, but it's not recommended." Dasher spoke low.

"And never forget, young 'un, it was a bear that killed the great Archie," Cora called back from the front. *"Before you were born. I say we leave bear to Plott hounds."* Plott hounds, larger and heavier than fox-hounds, were used to track bear. They were slower than foxhounds, possessed deep voices, and never ever surrendered the line once they found scent.

"Hear, hear." Delia, Nellie, Ardent, Trident, and Tinsel agreed.

"Any more of this talk and we'll be accused of babbling. Sister will get really upset with Mr. Meads here," Diana wisely noted.

Even though they were not yet at the first cast, they were expected to move along quietly, focused on business. Shaker, hearing the chat, glowered at them, saying nothing. He wasn't a huntsman to chide his hounds unless he felt they were doing wrong and would do so again. The invigorating early morning lifted the pack's spirits. If they had a few words to say, he'd overlook it, but not encourage it.

They reached a small pocket meadow, perhaps ten acres. The slope eastward glistened as a light vapor lifted off the warming frost.

Shaker put horn to lips and blew "Draw the Cover"—one long blast and three short ones.

"Lieu in there! Lieu in there," Shaker called, his voice light and high, as hounds associated higher notes with happiness and excitement. Low notes among themselves, a growl, generally signaled discipline or disagreement.

"I'll get him first," Dragon bragged.

Cora ignored him, nose to the swept-down grass. The coldness tingled. The competing scents of rabbits, the bobcat, and deer all lifted into her amazing nose. The other hounds, noses down, read the pocket meadow. A gaggle of turkey hens had pecked their way through not an hour ago, then flew off as the bobcat came too close. The deer, a large herd, an old doe in charge, moved west to east. A few dots here and there signaled crows had touched down, but for what reason neither Cora nor the other hounds could discern. In warmer weather, the hounds could identify other scents, even insects. No insects in this weather, no pungent earthworm trails. A lone beaver had waddled along the edge of the meadow before turning back to the creek, which fed the millrace.

The hounds carefully moved over the pocket meadow.

Rassle was so enchanted with the bobcat scent that he wandered a little too far to the east, where the meadow sloped downward. He stopped in his tracks. His stern flipped back and forth furiously: fox! Indeed, a fresh fox track, too. Rassle had never before found a line on his own, and he was just first year, but he'd been to the fox pen enough, and he had watched the big kids do their job. With astonishing confidence, the young tricolor let out a rip.

"Red! Big red!"

Cora flew to him. She put her nose down. *"He's right."*

The others quickly came to Cora, and Asa called, *"Showtime!"*

Marty leaned over to Crawford. "I just love that hound's voice," she whispered.

He nodded, having no time to reply because the hounds shot out of the meadow. Sister, never one to get left behind, shot with them.

Shaker tried to stay up with his lead hounds, Cora and Dragon, but as they'd gone into heavy woods, he skirted the thick part, emerging on an old deer trail. He squeezed Gunpowder, moving as fast as he could.

Betty on Magellan today—a big rangy thoroughbred given to her by Sorrel Buruss—rocked in his long fluid stride. She covered the left side, the creek side. Shaker, trusting her, figured if there was going to be rough or tough duty, it would be there.

"Ride to cry," Shaker told his whippers-in if they couldn't see the pack.

Sybil was getting it, though, and the more she whipped-in, the more she appreciated what a difficult, exhilarating task it was. She felt as though she had the best seat in the house.

"Tallyho!" Betty sang out as a big bushy-tailed red dog fox burst from the heavy woods into a cutover track that Walter hoped to turn into pasture this spring. Betty didn't recognize the thick-coated fellow. She reasoned he wasn't a local, so to speak, and she was correct.

No fool, the fox knew the cutover would make for heavy going for the horses and slow down the hounds, since they were sixty to seventy pounds heavier than he.

Betty, appreciating his guile, galloped to the old logging road, hoping to keep him in sight. He dashed through the cutover, twenty-five acres of slash, nimbly leapt over the old coop in the fence to the next, large meadow.

Magellan loved to jump and he took off farther back than Outlaw, Betty's quarter horse mount. She got left behind, her hands popped up.

"Sorry, Magellan."

"*You'll get the hang of me,*" he kindly assured her. He was delighted to have her on his back. His former owner, a hard-riding man, possessed okay hands, but he was a squeeze and jerk rider, which upset Magellan. In fact, the less you interfered with the rangy thoroughbred, the better he performed.

The red fox, knowing Betty was there and alone, gave her a show. He had a perverse sense of humor. Also, he'd just visited a vixen, and he felt terrific. He pulled up sharp, sat down on the moss-covered rock outcropping in the meadow. A thin veneer of frost covered the bright green moss.

Betty and Magellan pulled up, too.

"*The only reason men wear scarlet is to imitate foxes,*" the fellow said. "*All humans secretly want to be foxes.*"

"*Arrogant twit,*" Magellan snorted.

To Betty it sounded like barking, but his insouciance made her laugh. She heard hounds in full cry perhaps half a mile back.

To her complete astonishment, Jim Meads appeared at the edge of the meadow, stopped, and took photographs of the fox, Betty, and Magellan.

"My left side is my best." The fox slowly turned to Jim. The silver-haired man, big smile on his face, snapped what he knew would be some of the best hunt pictures he'd ever taken, and he'd taken thousands.

The hounds drew closer. The fox paid not a bit of mind. Only when Cora soared over the old coop, her form flawless and floating, did he bestir himself.

"Ta-ta," he called to Betty and Jim.

Sister saw only Magellan's tail and hindquarters as the horse took the stout log jump at the southwestern end of the field.

Hounds streamed over the frost turning to dew, the subdued winter green of the grasses underneath shining through.

Although it was only in the high thirties, Sister sweated underneath her shadbelly. Silk long johns stuck to her skin, a trickle of sweat zigzagged down her left temple. She was running hard. She was going to run harder.

Keepsake, in his glory, would have been only too thrilled to pass Gunpowder. However, he knew to stay behind as huntsman and mount flew over the logs. It irked him all the more since he thought he could outrun Gunpowder. He tired of hearing the gray thoroughbred, a former steeplechaser, deride Keepsake because he was a thoroughbred/quarter horse cross. Keepsake knew he had the stuff. Not all thoroughbreds were snobs, but Gunpowder was.

The field stayed well together, a testimony to their riding abilities; it would have been easy to get strung out on such a day. The footing started out tight but was getting sweaty in spots.

Ahead, another fence line hooked into the old three-board fence at a right angle. Sister took the log jump, then turned sharply left to soar over a stiff coop. You had to hit that second jump just right, which meant you had to put your right leg on your horse's the instant his or her hooves touched the earth from the first jump.

Sister knew she'd lose a few people at this obstacle, or they'd go past the second jump and wait for the rest of the field to clear before taking it. If a person misses a jump or his or her horse refuses, hunting etiquette demands he or she go to the end of the line. The exception to this is staff. Should a staff horse refuse a jump, which can happen, the staff person, who always has the right of way, may try again. If he or she can't get the animal over, a person in the field, usually Sister, gives them a lead. Now and then, even the best of staff horses will take a notion to refuse.

The red flew straight as an arrow, not doubling back, ducking into a den, or even cutting right, then left. He seemed intent on providing the best sport of the last two months. Before Sister knew it, they had run clean through Alice Ramy's farm. Alice waved from the window. They flew on to the next farm.

Down a large oval depression twenty feet below, with rock outcroppings and roughly forty yards around, the hounds suddenly stopped. This low land rested above a narrow, strong-running creek, part of a mostly underground creek. The somewhat higher ground in this shrubby area was defended by an outraged badger.

Badgers aren't supposed to be living in central Virginia, but here he was, and he was not happy. The first thing that fanned all twenty-five pounds of his bad mood was a damned coyote who had earlier watched him as he dug into a tempting rat hole. When the rat had popped out the other side, the coyote nabbed him, broke his back, and walked off. Didn't even bother to run. The badger, not fast, gave chase, hopeless though it was. So he had to settle for a morning meal of mice while he dreamed the gray squirrel chattering above would fall out of the enormous naked willow. Squirrels delighted his taste buds. But that wasn't bad enough. Not an hour later, an extremely rude fox ducked into his den, beheld the badger with no small surprise, turned around, and blasted right out again.

Now, a pack of hounds, and, worse—people on horseback—were at his front door. Well, he'd tell them a thing or two at the lip of his den, of course. This day had been too much, plucked his last nerve.

"Get out!"

The speechless hounds stood stiff-legged as the badger continued his stream of uncomplimentary conversation.

"What is that?" Tinsel inhaled an unusual odor.

"Only ever seen one other one." Delia wished Shaker would give them an order. *"Badger. They're powerful. Mostly live farther north, but they're moving in, I guess."*

Dragon lifted his head: the coyote scent proved stronger, heavier than the fox scent, even though the fox had so recently been there. Dragon wasn't known for his patience. He walked away from the badger and put his nose down the rat hole.

"Let's go." He bellowed, taking off, half the pack taking off with him.

Diana shouted after her brother. *"Wait!"*

Diana and Cora hurried to the spot. Cora shook her head. *"Coyote."*

Shaker knew his hounds. Cora did not follow the half that shot off with Dragon. Instead, she, Diana, Asa, Dasher, and others patiently moved a bit away from the still-fuming badger, casting themselves as good hounds do.

"Here he is. Here he is, that devil!" Asa got a nose full of fox scent first.

He opened, and the other half of the pack went with him, including Tinsel, who'd had the great good sense not to follow the impetuous, arrogant Dragon.

Shaker hesitated a second. Should he blow the errant half back and risk blowing back the hounds he knew to be right, or should he just blow the rapid series of notes—three short notes in succession—three or four times to try and bring the others back to Cora and Asa? He elected the latter, clapped his leg to Gunpowder, blowing as he galloped.

The splinter half bolted on Sybil's side. She heard the horn moving farther away in the opposite direction, so she knew what her

job was. Mounted on Colophon, a purchase in the summer to aug-
ment her hunter string, she hit the afterburners. She'd have to draw
alongside Dragon, a little in front, and reprimand him. If that didn't
work, harsher measures would.

Luckily, the hounds chased over a meadow, so she wasn't ducking trees in the woods. Colophon, sixteen hands, a bay thoroughbred and fast, streaked, his lovely head stretched out. Height in
horses is measured in hands; one hand equals four inches.

"Dragon, leave it!" Sybil commanded.

"Make me!" he challenged her.

She cracked her whip, which brought the other hounds to a
halt, but not Dragon. She again drew alongside the speedy hound,
pulled out her .22 pistol with ratshot, and fired a blast on his rear
end that he would never forget.

"Leave it!"

"Ow! Ow! Ow!" he shrieked.

His cries of pain at the tiny birdshot pellets—foxhunters called
them ratshot—scared the other hounds. If they'd had a mind to dis-
obey after pulling up for the crack of the whip, the thought now
vanished.

"Come along." Sybil said this with authority. They obediently
turned, following her.

A mile later, moving at a canter, she heard Shaker again blow
the rapid series of three notes, three or four times, on his horn. Of
course, the hounds with her had heard long before that.

"Go to him," she ordered. Those hounds couldn't get away fast
enough. It would be a cold day in hell before anyone in that group
elected to listen to Dragon again. Whether Dragon had learned his
lesson remained to be seen. His many gifts were sullied by a hard head.

Sister heard the ratshot blast after the whip crack as she thundered along. The crack of the whip, the tip moving faster than the
speed of sound, sounded like a sharp rifle report. Depending on the
humidity, it could be heard for miles.

Within ten minutes the coyote hunters swept past her, joining the main pack up ahead.

All on, Sister thought to herself. Thank God.

As Keepsake trotted through a wide creek, she noted spice-bush all along the banks and realized she was now at Chapel Cross, an estate four miles southwest of her place. They were still running hard.

A dirt crossroads, a small stone chapel on its northeast corner, came into view. The red, now in plain sight, reached his den, snug under the foundation of the church.

The hounds started to dig, but Shaker pulled them off with Betty's help. Walter and Ronnie rode up to hold their horses at Sister's bidding. Much as Shaker liked to reward hounds with a bit of digging, it wouldn't do to have the small Methodist church disgraced.

He blew "Gone to Ground," praised his hounds extravagantly while noting the tiny red dots on Dragon's rear end.

"You'll learn, buddy, or you'll be drafted out of here," Shaker said in a low voice to Dragon, and then in a higher one, "Good hounds! Good hounds!"

He slipped his left foot in the stirrup, swinging up in one graceful motion. Betty swung up a little less gracefully, as Magellan was taller than Outlaw. Patiently the thoroughbred waited for her to wiggle herself settled in the seat.

"Be glad she's lost weight," Gunpowder said. *"Used to be twenty-five pounds heavier."*

"She's not bad." Magellan liked Betty. *"I'd put up with twenty-five more pounds. She's a hell of a lot better than Fontaine ever was."* He mentioned his former owner.

The field stood; people breathed hard, as did a few horses. And there was Jim Meads, who had shadowed them on foot. Alice Ramy came out of the house when she saw him running. She offered him a ride in her car since the field showed no sign of slowing at that point. The instant he closed the door of her car, they chatted as if they'd known each other all their lives.

Sister thanked her hounds, thanked Shaker, thanked Alice, then turned to face the field.

"Ladies and gentlemen, I believe we have just put to ground a religious fox, and a Methodist at that. I suppose that means he doesn't dance or drink.

"I myself am not a Methodist, and if any of you are, time to cover your eyes." She held up her flask. "Lays the dust."

The field laughed. People pulled out their flasks. The men fastened theirs on the left side of their saddle. Ladies' flasks nestled in a small square sandwich box on the right rear of the saddle, usually. The ladies' flasks contained less liquor than the men's, so the gentlemen gallantly offered their flasks to the ladies first. It never hurts to get on the good side of a woman.

Sister offered her flask first to Betty, then to Walter, who had come up behind her.

"Thank you, Sister." Walter took a sip, then offered his flask, which contained a mixture of scotch, orange juice, a dash Cointreau, and a secret ingredient he wouldn't divulge. It hinted of bitters.

Hattie Baker Parrish offered Sam Lorillard her flask, then realized he couldn't drink it. Sam, by chance, was just behind Xavier.

"Sam, I forgot."

He smiled. "I brought iced tea." He lifted his flask to his lips and, as he did so, loosened the reins. A movement behind the church made his horse turn his head, and, in so doing, the flecked foam from his mouth splattered Xavier.

Xavier turned, beheld Sam. His face turned beet red. He took his crop, scraped a white line of sweat off his own mount, flicking it right in Sam's face. "Yours, I believe, sir."

"You're an ass, Henry Xavier," Sam shot back.

That fast, Xavier—as big as he was—was off his horse, pulling Sam from his. The two started whaling the living shit out of each other; Xavier, bigger, landed more telling blows. Sam, small and slight, bobbed and weaved as best he could, but he was too mad to care about getting hurt, and he landed a few.

Gray dismounted, as did Walter, Ronnie, and Clay Berry. It took Clay and Walter to pull off Xavier. Gray managed to grab his brother's upper arms and drag him backwards.

"I will have satisfaction!" Xavier struggled.

"Chill," Walter advised, his voice calm. "Dueling days are over."

Meanwhile, Meads caught it all on film.

Gray put his hand over his brother's mouth because Sam had a mean tongue when he felt like it. Anything coming out of his mouth would only make a bad situation worse.

The humans, hounds, and horses observed this drama with great interest, none more so than Sister. As the master, she couldn't let it slide.

She rode to Xavier. "X, I know there's bad blood, but I can't allow this kind of behavior in the hunt field. You are excused. I will speak to you later when we are both in a better frame of mind."

Shocked, as he had never once been reprimanded, and still angry but beginning to recognize he had done a really dumb thing, Xavier wordlessly remounted. He turned for the long ride back to Mill Ruins. Ronnie, a friend always, turned with him after saying, as was proper, "Good night, Master. Thank you for a glorious day."

"Good night, Ronnie."

Sam, head down, Gray still holding his upper arms, now looked up at Sister. "I'm sorry."

"He provoked it, I know that; but Sam, you, too, are excused. I advise you to ride a good distance behind Xavier and Ronnie or, if you prefer, to ride at a distance from the field because we're going in. I will speak with you later."

"Yes, Master." He bowed his head again. "Good night, Master."

She nodded to him as Gray looked up at her. "Good night, Master."

"Night, Gray."

The brothers waited for the field to move off, then slowly walked behind them.

Walter, abreast with Sister, finally said, "Unforgettable day."

She smiled. "The phone lines will be burning up tonight."

Cranking on members wasn't natural to Sister, but like so many people before her, she had learned that if you are going to lead, you must be fair, firm, and decisive. If a master tolerates bad behavior once, she or he will be certain to see it twice. And if a Board of Governors or the field senses a weak master, mischief multiplies like fleas in summer.

Humans, like hounds, need a strong leader. Sister was strong. She hoped she was fair.

"Thank you for your help, Walter. It could have been worse."

"You know, I am always glad to help you or the hunt any way I can," he said, meaning every word.

"If your schedule isn't too busy this week, let me take you to breakfast, lunch, or dinner, whatever you prefer. I'd like to have your undivided attention." She smiled, not wanting him to think it would be a difficult meeting. Actually, she hoped it would be positive.

"Tuesday, lunch."

"At the club or will you be in scrubs? I can meet you close to the hospital."

"The club. I look forward to it."

Tedi and Edward winked at Sybil as she rode on the right side of the pack. She'd glanced back at them. They were proud that she had performed so well in a difficult situation.

Shaker complimented her, and did Betty. No one threw compliments around idly on staff. If you heard one, you knew you did a good job.

Cora growled at Dragon, *"You are nine miles of bad road."*

He didn't reply.

"Well, at least we know there's a coyote here," young Rassle said.

"I'm not arguing that, Rassle, but you'd better damn well know the difference between coyote scent and fox scent, and you must try for fox first. We were right behind our fox. You could have thrown a blanket over us all. We

threw up at the badger den, but he had to be close, scent had to be hot. It de-
manded a bit of patience to cast a wide net and pick him up. Obviously, he
walked into the creek, but he came out, now, didn't he?" Cora sounded
like a schoolteacher.

"Yes, ma'am." Rassle listened.

Asa couldn't resist. He hissed at Dragon, *"Pizza butt."*

Humiliated and furious, Dragon kept his mouth shut, a surprise to all.

Cora then raised her voice for a moment, for the benefit of the
pack, but especially for the education of the young hounds. *"Hounds,*
we don't have to think alike. We do have to think together."

CHAPTER 15

Three different types of grits, succulent ham, roast turkey, and a joint of beef crowded on the long hunt table, along with salads, breads, hot buttered carrots, squash, and the ubiquitous deviled eggs. The special dessert consisted of a hot glazed donut with a huge scoop of vanilla ice cream plopped in the middle, fudge sauce drizzled over that. This concoction, so much a part of the region, and so delicious, seduced even the most disciplined to cast calories to the wind. Every now and then a body has to go for it.

The breakfast, stupendous even by Jefferson Hunt standards, threw a jolt of sugar, protein, and carbs into hunters depleted by hard riding—apparent on the long walk back to Mill Ruins. More than one set of legs wobbled when the rider dismounted.

The bar, commanded by Donnie Sweigert, much in demand for these affairs, carried standard good liquor as well as a few exotic bottles such as Talisker's peaty-tasting scotch. There was also the lovely Chartreuse liquor, which a few people poured over their desserts along with the fudge. The Absolut vodka and the Johnny Walker Black disappeared at a fast clip.

The excitement of the hunt and the drama of the fight sent blood sugar and conversation sky high.

The fox Bessie had the run of the house. She moved quite well despite her amputated front paw. But this was all too much. She re-treated to the basement, but not before nabbing a tasty bit of ham. She ate half and buried the rest. Walter, realizing he couldn't con-trol her cache digging, had put down a load of dirt. Every other day while Bessie walked outside for a breath of fresh air, he'd sneak down, dig up her treasures and put them in the garbage. If the vixen minded, she didn't say.

Even Tonto, the Welsh terrier puppy, now six months old, felt overwhelmed by the crowd. He joined Bessie.

The two canine relatives listened to the revelers upstairs. *"Bet there's no leftovers."* Tonto's merry little eyes clouded over.

"Has to be some. Chef Ted drove up with an entire truckful of food." Bessie remained hopeful.

"I don't know. I didn't know humans could eat so much at one time. I thought only dogs gorged."

Bessie's special house, wooden with a big overhang, reeked of her special scent. Tonto, accustomed to it, paid it little mind. He himself gave off faint odor compared to other breeds of dog. And terrier though he was, and prone to digging, he was fastidious in his personal habits, which helped keep whatever odor he possessed low.

"Bessie, do you think if the hounds saw you, they'd kill you?"

"Yes," she said matter-of-factly, *"if the pack did. Maybe if just one hound saw me or came upon me, it wouldn't happen, but a pack gets in a frenzy. Although Walter says he has seen Shaker call hounds off a quarry and it was impressive, I sure wouldn't want to take the chance."*

The footsteps upstairs sounded heavier.

"Glad this old house has beams the size of tree trunks." Little Tonto grinned.

"They are tree trunks. Peeled the bark off."

Tonto peered upward. His eyes weren't as good as a cat's, nor even a human's, but they weren't awful. He could see better in the dark than a human. *"Oh. Old, huh?"*

"This section, mmm. 1792. Heard Walter say so." Bessie tilted her head, ear upward. *"Now they're singing."*

The assemblage, euphoric, gathered around the piano, Tedi Bancroft at the keys, belting out, "Do Ye Keen, John Peel?"

Those who weren't singing stayed back in the dining room where, as Tonto feared, pickings were slim. Even Chef Ted himself had never seen people eat so much, and he'd catered many a hunt breakfast.

Sister, drinking a cup of tea, listened to Edward Bancroft expound on the conflict between Xavier and Sam.

". . . in the bud. You did the right thing."

"Now I have to make those calls." Sister looked up at her dear old friend.

"You're a good master, Janie. Better than good, one of the best."

"Edward, you flatter me, and I thank you." She sipped. "Were you surprised at X?"

He nodded his silver head. "We've all known him since he was in diapers. He's not a rash man. He wasn't even that wild as an adolescent. For Xavier to lose his temper like that, I wonder if there's more to his past dealings with Sam Lorillard than we know. Ronnie would know."

"I wonder, too." She inhaled the bracing fragrance of the tea, a strong Ceylon type. "I'm grateful neither man came to the breakfast. It was tense enough."

"Do you have a plan?"

"I want to hear X's reasons. As for Sam, I can't very well fault the man for defending himself. I am not going to suspend either man, but each will receive a fair warning. If X can't put a lid on it or if Sam carries on an obvious grudge after this event, then I will ask the board to suspend them for the season. I really don't think I'll have to use such drastic measures."

He shrugged. "I certainly hope not."

"And I know a tornado of gossip will swirl upwards, ah yes, talk so quickly turns into a gaseous state." She ruefully smiled. "There will be those who think I should let them settle it without the hunt club's intrusion, those who think I should throw their asses—excuse me—out now. So it goes."

"Actually, I don't think there will be that much second-guessing." He motioned with his head to those singing in the next room. "They trust you. It takes years to build that trust."

She laughed. "Well, why are they always fussing then? 'You go too fast.' 'You go too slow.' 'Why did you take us over that jump?' "

"Who says that? Only the ones who aren't tight in the tack. If you can ride, Janie, you ride."

"That's the God's honest truth. But you and I grew up when riding was one of the social graces. In the South you learned to ride, shoot, play cards, and hopefully speak a foreign language—French was the one always shoved at us girls. That's gone. Middle-class people had high social expectations of their children. Now both parents work, and expectations aren't uniform. Maybe in some ways that's good, Edward, because if a little girl wants to play soccer instead of learning to ride, she has the choice. I never had much of a choice, although if I wanted to go to the symphony or something cultural, Mother took me."

"Our culture has fragmented. Part of it is the pushing upwards of people who aren't WASPs. Maybe part of it is just the change that occurs at any time in history, but I believe, sooner or later, some kind of cultural consensus will emerge. We'll see more cohesion. I hope so." Edward, a man of his time, thought long and hard about large issues.

"Just as long as foxhunting is part of it." She put down her cup and saucer, an attendant smoothly picking it up.

"More, Sister?"

"Oh, thank you, no." As the white-coated server left, she turned her attention back to Edward. "We're old, Edward. Our memories encompass things the young can't even imagine, such as being expected to dance, shoot, ride. And yet . . . and yet—" She burst into the biggest infectious smile. "—I feel young. I feel better than I have felt in years."

He put his arm around her shoulder. "Honey, you're a twelve cylinder engine that's been running on six cylinders since 1991."

Startled, she said, "What?"

He kissed her forehead. "How long have we known each other?"

"Good God, Edward." She thought. "Forty years. More."

"More. Time is jet-propelled. I saw how you handled Ray Jr.'s death in 1974. You grieved, then in time you came back to us in spirit. You had Big Ray and the two of you pulled each other along. But when Big Ray died in 1991, who was there to pull you along? Who was there to say, 'Sugar, it will be all right. We'll get through this'?" She started to say something, but Edward held up his hand. "I'm not saying you moped around. You carried on. That's your nature. And Archie's and Peter's deaths were blows. But remember, I knew you before all those losses, just as you knew me before Nola died," he said, referring to his beloved daughter. "Such blows take something out of us even as they give us depth and heart, more heart."

Quietly, she replied, "Yes."

"For whatever reason, your other cylinders have fired up again. I'm happy for you."

"And I'm happy to have such a good friend." She hugged him.

As she looked for Walter to thank him for the breakfast, Jim Meads touched her arm.

She turned around. "Jim. I hope you're having a good time."

"Wonderful, Master. I'll have proofs for you to look at tomorrow."

"That fast?"

"Now, I don't know how I should take a lady calling me fast."
He winked.

Clay Berry, back to Jim, twisted slightly. "Fast. Is it beautiful
horses and fast women, or fast horses and beautiful women?"

"Clay, you should know." Sister laughed, as Clay was known to
stray off the reservation.

"Oh, I took your silver fox fur out of storage. You forgot to pick
it up this winter, and I know you'll want it. In fact, I put it in your
truck."

"Thanks. I did forget. This hunt season has been jam-packed,
and I think I'd forget my head if it weren't attached to my body."
She then said to Jim, "I'll come by tomorrow morning if that's a
good time."

"Perfect."

An animated group of people blocked the front door. As Sister
picked up her fleece-lined Barbour coat from the low coatroom, she
turned around, bumping into Dr. Dalton Hill, who was searching
for his coat.

"Splendid day, Master."

"I'm happy you could join us. That Cleveland bay you were riding is a handsome fellow."

"Yes. One of Mr. Wessler's breedings. A friend over in Green
Springs, Louisa, lent me the horse. I think I'll rent him for the
season."

"You'll be here then?"

"Yes." He wasn't a warm man, but he was proper. "I'm teaching
at the university for a semester. My partner is keeping up the practice in Toronto. We take turns when opportunities like this arise."

"How do you like the university?" Locals always referred to the
University of Virginia as "the university."

"Quite, quite beautiful."

"Dr. Hill, do you hunt with any of the hunts in Ontario?"

He drew himself up to his full height, five foot eleven inches, good shape. "Toronto and North York, founded in 1843. Oldest hunt in Canada. And it's my good fortune to go out with Ottawa Valley, founded 1873, and London Hunt, founded in 1885. Did you know there are eight hunts just in Ontario Province?"

She did know, but elected to murmur, "It's in the blood."

"Ah . . . yes." Took him a moment.

"While it is not to say we are the same . . . just that we share many of the same disciplines and pleasures. If I didn't live in Virginia, I would certainly consider myself lucky to be in Canada." She wasn't indulging in flattery.

"Thank you."

"As I recall, your specialty is endocrinology. You must treat unusual cases."

"Yes, and the medicines and technology are changing at warp speed." He didn't use medical terms, which was thoughtful. "If I can get a patient in time, in childhood, often a humiliating condition like dwarfism can be cured or tempered. Mrs. Arnold, in the next ten years, you and I will see breakthroughs that are miraculous."

"I see you love your work."

"I do. I always liked science, but science in the service of healing, of improving the human condition."

She paused before returning to the subject of hunting. "You can reach so many hunt clubs within an hour and a half or so of Charlottesville. You're in a perfect spot."

"I can see that. I've rather struck up a friendship with Walter. I'd like to continue with Jefferson, if that can be arranged, and cap with the others. And I assume there will be joint meets."

"Of course. Are you a member of a recognized hunt?"

"Yes."

"Well, we have a buddy program—that's my term. If you're a full hunting member, say of London Hunt, you can join us for half price. Many hunts in central Virginia have instituted this type of program. The bells and whistles might be slightly different, but the point is to pull together. Who can afford full memberships at all these hunts, and one can only cap three times in a season. It's working quite well."

"Virginia has more foxhunting clubs than anywhere in the world, I believe."

"For a single province—" She used the Canadian term. "—we do. To live here as a foxhunter is to be in nirvana." She smiled broadly.

"I would like to avail myself of your program. To whom do I write the check?" Dr. Hill didn't waste time as he slipped his checkbook out of his Filson tin cloth packer coat.

Surprised, Sister replied, "I'll give it to Ron Haslip, our treasurer."

"Very light rider."

Sister realized Dr. Hill knew a little something about riding. "Yes, he is, was, light on a horse since childhood. I notice you have a Filson tin coat. Ever notice how foxhunters usually wear Barbour coats or the Australian coats? Every now and then, I'll see one of these."

"Indestructible. I wear the tin cloth pants, too, during pheasant season. I bought this coat twenty-five years ago when I visited Seattle the first time. I had just finished my residency, and the trip was my present to myself."

"You have an eye for quality."

He smiled slightly. "Well, I hate squandering money. Buy the best then, you weep only once."

She laughed appreciatively. "I'm looking forward to seeing you in the hunt field."

"I'll arrange my schedule to come out as much as possible."

As she left Mill Ruins, she wondered if Dalton Hill had a wife. He hadn't said anything. The ladies of Jefferson Hunt would ferret out this information in no time.

She also reflected on the persistence of hunting in the English-speaking world. Piedmont Hunt, outside of Upperville, Virginia, was founded in 1840, the oldest organized hunt in the United States. But colonists had hunted from 1607 on. And they did so in Canada, in Australia, in New Zealand, and in India under the raj. She thought the English language and hounds were intertwined, from Beowulf and beyond to today. Curious yet somehow comforting, satisfying.

Later, as she checked the hounds, the horses already snug, thanks to Jennifer and Sari, she watched Darby, Doughboy, and Dreamboat, first-year entry.

Shaker came out of the feed room. "What do you think?"

"Well done, thou good and faithful servant! I haven't had a second to catch up with you. I hope you ate something at the breakfast. What a show Walter put on."

"Stuck my head in. That turkey with the herbed dressing was something."

"Sybil did a good job today."

"She did. I asked her how she rated the hounds. She said she first called out Dragon's name since he was in the lead. He ignored her. She then used her whip. He ignored her, so she hauled out the ratshot. Gave the other mutineers something to thing about."

"They weren't a hundred percent wrong."

"No, they weren't, but when I blow them back, they'd better come." He spoke with conviction.

"Let's take Dreamboat and Darby on Tuesday. Oh, Doughboy, too. They ought to be all right. We can take Dana, Delight, and Diddy on Thursday." She mentioned the girls from the same litter.

"Those girls are high, boss. Let's just take two."

"All right. Thursday put in Diddy and Dana, and then we'll see if Delight can handle a Saturday. She'll have steady eddies all around her."

"You sure did the right thing back there at Chapel Cross."

"Thanks."

He nodded, she thought, then said, "Shaker, how bad was I after Big Ray died?"

Surprised, he answered, "You held up."

"Mmm, well, I said to Edward that I feel fabulous, that I feel young again, and then he said that I've returned to myself."

Shaker kept watching the gyps. "He's right."

"The funny thing is, I don't know why. But I think you're kind of coming back, too."

"Me?"

"It's good."

"Yep." He did feel different.

Neither one mentioned why they thought they were happier. Perhaps they didn't yet know why.

CHAPTER 16

Atrocious. Can you believe it? Fifty million Americans can't read or understand anything above the eighth-grade level." Marty Howard, chair of the Committee to Promote Literacy, warmed to her subject as Sister and Jim examined his photographs.

Crawford had flown to New York on business, which meant Marty had center stage, an unusual and pleasant experience for her.

Jim, although living in Wales, was an Englishman to the bone. He said, "How can someone get through school without learning to read and write?"

Marty, admiring his photos with Sister, replied, "That's just it, twenty-nine percent of American students drop out of high school. Drop out. Do you know what the drop-out rate is in Japan?" When he indicated that he did not, she jumped right in. "Five percent. And in Russia, poor torn-up Russia, the drop-out rate is two percent. Something is dreadfully wrong with our schools."

Jim, without looking up from the dramatic photograph of Xavier taking a swing at Sam, said wryly, "Maybe Americans should go back to teaching reading, writing, and arithmetic instead of self-esteem, right?"

Sister, not terribly interested in education, politely listened as this conversation raged on. Her attitude was that if you wanted to learn, you would. If you didn't, you pretty well deserved what happened. If 29 percent of Americans wanted to drop out of school, they could push brooms, dig ditches, or suck up welfare. After performing these exciting tasks, if they had a lick of sense, they might want to learn to read.

She didn't feel it was her job to be nanny to the nation. People made their own decisions. If they made bad decisions, they had to live with them, and sometimes so did she. We all bump up against one another. But in her heart of hearts, Sister really believed that some people are born stupid. One couldn't introduce a new idea or a provocative thought into those thick skulls even with a crowbar.

Marty, on the other hand, truly believed that with ameliorative agencies, plus her own good works, life could be made better for some. Imbued with a Protestant drive for self-improvement, and a perfect society, it was her duty to do these things. She did them well.

"Sister, what do you think?" Marty inquired.

"The photographs are wonderful."

"No, about illiteracy."

"Marty, you are a dynamo of organization. That group is fortunate to have you, and I would be most happy to write a check. You know how much I admire your good works." While not wanting to lie, Sister, being a Virginian, did not feel compelled to tell Marty what she really thought about the issue. Find the positive, and, in this case, it was Marty herself.

Jim left Marty with a fat book of proofs for club members. They could order those photographs they wanted.

Sister, her checkbook fetched from her worn Bottega Veneta purse—a favorite given to her by Ray before he died—wrote a check for five hundred dollars to the Committee to Promote Literacy. Another check to Jim for the photographs she'd selected.

He'd fly back across the ocean tonight, and she already missed him. They had managed a bit of time to visit, and she had laughed herself silly. Jim was a tonic to her. His deadpan sense of humor never failed to lift her spirits.

"Marty, I know it's working hours, but do I have your permission to have a word with Sam before I leave?"

"Of course." Marty fretted a moment. "I feel terrible about what happened yesterday, but it wasn't his fault."

"Not yesterday, but there are years of bad blood—not just with Xavier, but with many people in the club."

Jim folded his hands. "One thing to straighten yourself out, another to pay back the damage."

"He can't." Sister held up her hands, palm upwards. "That's the hardest part of life, I think."

Marty, ever eager for a discussion of substance, sat down as she pushed more scones toward her guests. "Meaning one cannot make amends, achieve closure?"

Sister stifled a laugh. "Marty, there is no closure. That's a made-up word. Whatever happens to you, whatever you've done to others, yourself, to the wide world, in general, sticks with you like chiggers."

"Oh, Sister, you can't mean that!"

"I do. The past doesn't go away. It's in your head; it's in your heart. What's hard is finding the balance. Recognizing that you can't, say, in Sam's case, pay back the money, restore the damage to the sullied marriages. All you can do is ask forgiveness. A few people truly will forgive you; most won't. They'll turn their backs and try to forget it and you."

"Or strike back." Jim drank his tea with pleasure. Marty, for an American, brewed a decent cup of tea.

"Yes."

"But that solves nothing!" Marty exclaimed. "That just keeps the pain alive."

"Marty, I respect that opinion, but I don't agree. Hurting someone who has hurt you is deeply satisfying," Sister responded. Then

— 147 —

she thought to herself that hurting whoever killed Anthony Tolliver would satisfy her.

"Sister, that is unlike you. I've never seen you hurt anyone."

"Oh, I have. I hurt my husband. In the main, I haven't tried to hurt people. That doesn't blind me to the fact that revenge is sweet. There's no longer justice through the court system—perhaps there never was. Whoever has the most money and can keep the case going all the way to the Supreme Court, if need be, has the advantage. If you take justice into your own hands, it is sweet. Someone makes you bleed, you make him or her bleed. Even steven."

"Brutal." Marty shook her head.

"But real." Jim had a clear idea about things like this. In his worldview, nations behaved as childishly as individuals. Airmen like he had once climbed into jets and risked their lives to try to redress the latest cycle of revenge, greed, territorial expansion.

"Can't we improve? I have to believe we can."

Sister inhaled the buttery scent of the scones, the tang of the hot tea in its expensive old Dresden china pot, covered with a knitted cozy. "In fits and starts. I mean, Marty, in the Western nations we no longer employ child labor from sunup to sundown six days a week. That's improvement, but what are children doing in Asia or Latin America or parts of Africa? In Africa, they cut off women's clitorises. Pardon me, Jim. I hope I haven't ruined your appetite."

"Nothing ruins my appetite, Master. You wouldn't believe the things I've seen," he answered jovially.

"What I'm saying, Marty, is that one place moves ahead, say, with respect to child abuse, but perhaps slides back in literacy; another place works their children to death, but everyone can read. It's a jumble of contradictions, pain, and outrageous injustice, yet there is beauty in the world. I can't make sense of it, and I no longer try. I just live the day I'm in."

Marty cupped her chin in her right hand as she sat at the table. While such a posture would upset anyone who had suffered the rigors of cotillion, it was her table, and it was more comfortable than always having her hands in her lap.

Jim spoke up. "In many ways I think life was better at other times than it is now. Not in terms of medicine, but people were closer to one another."

"Give me an example." Marty's eyes opened wider.

"England from 1815 to 1914. I don't think it was good for those people chewed up by industrialization, but for farmers, the middle classes and above, life was pleasant. Now you turn on the telly and see body parts."

Sister, mindful of the time, gently said, "If there is an answer, I know you will find it, Marty. And I know that Crawford will support your efforts. He is a generous man. And I hope you do find the answer because I'd like to know it." She smiled. "But, honey, I've been on earth longer than you. Maybe it's made me a touch cynical."

"You could never be cynical," Jim said gallantly. "I'm the same age as you. We have seen a lot in our time, and I, for one, just look at people and governments and wonder what dumb thing they will do next. Sometimes it's funny, most times it's not. At least in your country, you don't have class warfare. What do you think the Labor Party is all about? It's class warfare. So bloody stupid."

"You're right, Jim, we don't understand. I'm not sure an American can understand, but just because we don't have class warfare doesn't mean we can't be as bloody stupid as the Brits." Sister laughed.

"You two!" Marty sighed.

"Birds of a feather." Jim laughed.

"Flock together," Sister finished. "Marty, don't take it all so seriously. A little levity might not add years to your life, but you'll certainly enjoy them more. I'm not saying you shouldn't be involved in your projects. It's wonderful that you care so much but, well, *don't care too much*. And you know why? Because none of those people you are trying to help cares about you. If one or two got to meet you, they might, but you need to take care of yourself. You know what I think about? When you're in an airplane and the stewardess runs through her number about seat belts and exit doors, remember the part when she talks about air, about losing oxygen? Okay, the yellow umbilical cord drops out of the overhang with a plastic oxygen mask on it. The stewardess tells you to put on your mask before you put on your child's mask, right?"

"Right." Marty nodded.

"That's what I'm saying. Put on your oxygen mask first. And now, after that piece of unsolicited and probably unnecessary advice, I'm going down to your stable."

Marty watched Sister walk through the slush down to the extravagant stable. Sister didn't seem like a selfish person. She had always thought of the tall older woman as generous and kind, but what Sister had said to her seemed selfish. She would need to think more on these things. Instead of diminishing her feelings for her master, their conversation only made the older woman more intriguing. It occurred to Marty that there was a great deal to Sister that she didn't know.

As Sister reached the racing barn, she marveled at its organization. The hunting barn was well run, too. Fairy Partlow was no slouch. Sam had transformed the beautiful racing barn into a true horseman's stable. The twenty-four-stall stable was built with a cross-center aisle in the middle, two wash stalls on each side, and a huge feed room. In the cross aisle, Sam had a long scale; each day he would have his assistant, Roger Davis, weigh each horse on the scale, recording its weight in his logbook. Also in the book was each horse's food for the day, turn out, work notes if they were breezed or jumped. Medical notations were there, too, as well as in an extensive color-coded file for each horse in the big oak file cabinets in the cavernous tack room. This information was also entered daily into the computer. Crawford adored technology: buying the latest, the fastest, the most expensive stuff. Sam took no chances. He used the computer, but everything was duplicated in the hard-copy files.

He found it a lot easier to grab a color-coded file than to sit down and punch it up on the computer. Sam was middle-aged.

He smiled when he saw the master.

"Sam, this place runs like a clock." She glanced at the large railroad clock on the tack room wall.

Sam had just been double-checking the files on Cloud Nine, the timber horse he had purchased for Marty.

The paneled pecan-wood walls—unusual for Virginia—bore gilt-framed photographs of past great chasers. As Crawford was only now entering the game, no photographs existed of his winners, but he had felt the walls needed something. In time, his winners would grace these walls. Encased in Lucite on one wall were his racing colors: red silks with two blue hoops on the chest and three on the sleeves, and a red cap with a blue button.

"Please sit down." Sam stood as he motioned to the leather club chair.

The tack room was so large that the big sofa, two club chairs, and a large coffee table took up only one corner. The carpet, red and blue stripes, mirrored the silk colors.

Sam sat opposite Sister.

He offered refreshments, but she'd already drunk so much tea she was afraid her kidneys would float away. As this barn's bathroom had a big shower, makeup mirror, and toilet, she didn't worry too much about her kidneys. In many barns, if you had to go, you used a stall, same as the horses.

"Sam, I know you didn't provoke the fight yesterday; I'm here to tell you that, and to tell you I am genuinely happy you are back in the hunt field. This is a good place for you."

"Thank you."

"As you know, you've made enemies, you've disappointed many people. Some of them, like Xavier, boil over. It's not really like him, and, of course, I'll talk to him, but I was wondering if you could help me?"

"How?"

"Exactly what did happen back there in, was it 1987?"

"Yes." Sam looked away, out the big picture window, then looked back. "I was out of my mind on booze and drugs, and I stole from him."

"He says you cost him a lot of money."

"I did. I made purchases at the feed store in his name and used stuff myself or sold it. I sold tack out from under him and lied that it was being repaired. I stole money from the kitty and said it had been lost. I wrecked his new F350 Dually and said it had a bad U-joint."

"And?" Shrewdly, she pressed on.

"I slept with his wife." Sam exhaled. "That was worse than the money." He leaned forward. "When someone works as hard as Xavier, it's easy to jive him, jam him. He's tired when he comes home. If everything looks good, he doesn't dig up the dirt for months and sometimes even years, but Xavier kept his own books. He figured it out sooner rather than later."

"But that wasn't really what set him off, was it?"

"No, it was his Dee." The lines around his dark brown eyes deepened. "I guess they went into couples therapy or something, because they're still together. By that time I was down the road at the next place. They handled it better than most. The other women I slept with screamed about being played or their husbands beat me up, and the whole county watched the show." He stared at her. "I have never told anyone about Dee, but you asked, and I know I can trust you. I expect one or two other people know, though. People can't keep their mouths shut."

"Thank you."

He tipped back in the deep chair. "You'd be amazed at how many bored women there are out there. They feel ignored by their husbands. Translates into feeling unloved. It was just all too easy all those years."

"I'm not surprised."

He blinked, his shoulders rising. "I guess not. People confide in you."

"Well, I have my eyes wide open. And I don't rush to judgment."

"I know." He compressed his lips. "Would it be easier for you if I didn't hunt? I can put Roger on some of these guys—Fairy, too—although she's got her hands full with the hunters. I like chasers to hunt a bit, the greenies."

"It might make it easier, Sam, but it wouldn't make it right. The hunt field is open to all who pay their dues and respect the ethics of hunting. That means hounds have the right of way, you do not turn a fox, *ever, ever, ever,* and you do as the landowners bid you. When you swing up in the tack, your mind should be on hunting. Whatever else is going on in your life is left behind. You don't have to like everyone in the hunt field, but you can't express it while hunting."

He nodded, knowing the ethics as well as any true foxhunter. "Yes, ma'am."

"Xavier knows the rules of the road as well as you or I. I can only surmise that years of pent-up emotion affected his reason. As I said, I will speak to him." She drew in a deep breath. "Sam, I don't want to remove anyone from our club, and I do think this can be ironed out. Hunting is such a joy, a religion in a way. Nothing should tarnish that. If you drop down to nuts and bolts, people pay a lot of money for horses, trailers, trucks, tack, you name it. They should have a peaceful experience, if not an exciting one. Depends on the fox." She smiled.

"Good one yesterday."

"Yes, I didn't know that fox. Usually I do."

"Sister, you study the game trails. You know where the fox is, the turkeys, the deer. People don't realize how much thought and knowledge goes into your job. Of course, there are masters who don't know these things."

"All serve, even those who stand and wait." She slightly misquoted Milton.

"Would you like to see the new timber horse?"

"Love to."

They walked outside into the cold air, down the long aisleway, stopping in front of a freshly painted stall. The nameplate read "Cloud Nine."

"Nine's her barn name." Sam leaned over the opened top of the Dutch stall door. "16.2 hands, incredible stride once she gets into it. Tucks those front knees right under her, just folds 'em." He imitated her form over fences.

"When she retires, she'll be the perfect field hunter, right? I always think the timber horses are more careful than the brush ones."

"And look at that engine!" He pointed to her hindquarters. "The ones that have heart, you can teach them. They'll respect those solid jumps in the hunt field, even if they've been sliding through the brush ones. Bet we win, then in a few years you can hunt her." He laughed. "No way can Marty or Crawford handle Nine. Too hot. Too forward."

The brush fences for national steeplechase races at one time actually were brush, but now the manufactured fences had artificial brush set in. The horses jumped over or through it. If their hooves touched the brush, judges heard a *swish, swish* sound. The problem with the brush horses is they could get accustomed to dragging their hooves, not picking them up neatly like the timber horses. Can't be dragging hooves over a three-foot-six coop or a stone wall.

"When's her first race?"

"Maybe end of March in Aiken; I'll need to work with her some more. If I don't think she's ready for South Carolina, then I'll run her at My Lady's Manor in Monkton, Maryland, in mid-April."

"She looks the part." Sister walked back to the truck, Sam accompanying her. "I see a lot of empty stalls. Knowing Crawford, they'll be filled within a year, and you'll have three more people working for you."

"That's the plan."

"It's exciting." Sam opened her door for her, and she stepped up into the driver's seat.

"Heard my big brother had lunch with you and talked himself silly."

Sister blushed. "Did he tell you that?"

"He did."

She drove into town, whistling the whole way. Then she realized she hadn't spoken to Jim about his photographs. She dialed Marty's number and luckily got Jim.

"Mr. Meads."

"Master," he said, a smile in his voice.

"Those photographs you took where X and Sam are flailing away—our own Taylor and Holyfield—could you not make those public?" She paused. "Although, I expect people would buy them."

"I understand."

"Well, I will buy every shot of same."

"There's no need of that." His clipped accent and warm voice were reassuring.

"Oh, Jim, I know that. But I do want them for my files. And just in case I need to lord it over those boys."

"You'll have them next week. Five-by-seven or eight-by-ten?"

"Mmm. Eight-by-ten."

"Good then."

CHAPTER 17

Monday—catch-up day—found Sister cruising along roads she'd known since childhood, yet she always found something to capture her imagination.

She crossed the railroad tracks, smack in the middle of the working-class section of the small town. The men who built the railroads lived in neat clapboard cottages, constructed by the railroad. They'd hop a hand-pumped car to move themselves down the tracks. This particular line ran through the Blue Ridge Mountains and then the Alleghenies as it headed west into West Virginia and Kentucky, with branches cutting north into Ohio.

Squatting alongside the tracks were the redbrick buildings of Berry Storage. Smaller square brick structures were attached to the original four-story building.

The first structure, built in 1851, was a woolen mill. During the War Between the States, the mill ran at full capacity. After 1865, nothing was running. Twenty years passed. Although abandoned, structures were built to last for generations, centuries.

The mill cranked up again, thanks to an influx of outside money. The fortunes of the woolen mill reflected the roller coaster of capitalism.

By the time Clay Berry purchased the mill in 1987, it had again been abandoned. Because no one wanted the old place, Clay bought it for a song—a good thing since that was about all he had in the world.

Clay's father was a lineman for the phone company; his mother worked at the old Miller and Rhoads store. He envied Ray Jr. and Ronnie their position. Xavier, from a solidly middle-class family, had less than young Ray or Ronnie's people, but more than Clay. Both ambitious, Xavier and Clay became close over the years.

Clay worked like a dog, securing a loan on the building and turning it into a storage warehouse. Over the years he added cold storage, cleaning of expensive furs, shipping households overseas. He added more buildings to accommodate the different demands of his business. Sister was proud of Clay. He was a good business-man, sensitive to the fact that he was dealing with people's precious possessions even if he, himself, thought they were junk. Over time he developed a sharp eye for quality in furniture, rugs, and furs, al-though he preferred stark modern things.

The cell phone rang in the truck. Sister pushed the green button.

"Yo."

"Boss, that damn Rassle dug out of the yard, taking all the first-year entry boys with him."

"I'll be right home." She paused a second. "Tell me where you'll be."

"I think they headed toward Hangman's Ridge."

"Great," she replied sarcastically. "I'll go slow on Soldier Road just in case. And then I'll park at the kennels and find you."

"Better you find them. I am pissed."

"Me, too, but we'll get them. See you soon." She pressed the End button, picked up speed for home.

When she and Big Ray built the kennel, they cut a two-foot ditch, laying in a thin wall of concrete so the hounds couldn't dig out. But that was close to forty years ago. She wondered if part of that deep inner core had crumbled. This might be a long day and night.

It had already been a long day. When she called on Xavier, she was surprised at how emotional he became, which exhausted her.

"That man put me through hell." Xavier's voice trembled as he thought of Sam.

While she sympathized, and she did, she reminded him of the rules of hunting.

He agreed, promising to keep a lid on it. He did say one unnerving thing, which was that when Sam had lain about the train station, among the flotsam and jetsam of broken lives, Xavier had wished the son of a bitch had died there. Too bad he didn't get run over by a train or fall in front of a car or drink whatever crap Mitch and Anthony swallowed.

"He doesn't deserve to live." Xavier finished his line of thinking.

"Xavier, that's not like you," she said calmly.

"I'm not as good a person as you think I am."

A wound that deep—to the heart and to the pride of a man— leaves a scar if it heals.

When she left, she hoped he could keep his anger in check. She loved him. He deserved every consideration. Some masters would understandably be tempted to ease Sam Lorillard out. People who are dear to the master or who write big checks to hunt clubs or who work hard usually receive special consideration. But in the field, no. She firmly believed in the principles of the hunt. On the back of a horse, you leave your troubles behind. On the back of a horse, your hunting knowledge and riding ability count, not your pocketbook.

She hardly adored every single person in the field, although she liked most. When Big Ray was joint-master, she had to ride next to some of the very women he was seducing. But when the hounds opened, thoughts of Ray's sexual peccadilloes scooted out of her brain. The ride back to the trailers would get her, though. She'd notice the color in the latest flame's cheeks, the size of her bosom under a well-cut hunting coat, the length of her leg, the turn of her nose. Sister had to hand it to Big Ray, he had never picked a bad-looking woman. But then, he also had to ride back with her paramours, although like most women, she had been clever at hiding her extracurricular activities.

These days she had to laugh at herself. A young person hunting with her, such as Jennifer or Sari, saw an older woman. They could never imagine that fires scorched through anyone over forty. She still had some fire left, as did Xavier; although his, at the moment, fanned out in rage.

Some people never had that fire, not even in their twenties. They never slept with the wrong person or with too many people, never did anything silly, dangerous, or ill advised. To hear tell, every man and woman running for office in the United States had lived life as a blooming saint.

How else do you learn except by being foolish?

She pondered these things while hurrying along the outskirts of town, passing a trailer park, before breaking free into the open country, true home. The fields, sodden, cast a gray pallor. The trees stood out black and silver, green if a conifer, against the deep blue sky. She noticed a thin outline over the Blue Ridge, powder blue since the snow hadn't melted that high up. The line looked as though drawn by a metallic gray pencil. Snow clouds would soon enough be sliding down the Blue Ridge, catching a little updraft from the valley below to move ever eastward. These clouds weren't moving fast.

Sister turned on the truck radio. The weather report on NPR said snow would be starting in the valley in the early afternoon, turning to rain by the time it reached Richmond. The precip, as they dubbed it, would last a day, possibly longer, as it was a stalled front.

Sister believed national characteristics had been formed by weather. An Italian couldn't be more different from a Swede.

Her character had been formed by the four distinct, ravishing seasons of central Virginia. Expect the unexpected, the weather had taught her. She'd also learned to plan ahead; violent snowstorms or those exotic green-black thunderstorms could knock power out for days.

She pulled in at the kennels, then drove back out, following Shaker's tracks. They turned down the farm lane, past the orchard, then headed to the wide-open fields that lapped up on Hangman's Ridge, already swathed in low clouds. A sprinkle of snow dotted her windshield.

She cut the motor, pulled on her heavy jacket, and stepped outside.

The tiny *click, click, click* of icy little bits struck the windshield.

Little snows turn into big snows, meaning little ice bits, tiny flakes, often turn into big flakes, big storms. She peered upwards. Oh, yes, this was going to hang around.

She listened intently. She heard the three long blasts on the horn. The air, heavy, changed sound. He was probably a half-mile off to her right, near the ridge.

She heard a splatter, and three hounds appeared.

"Darby, Doughboy, and Dreamboat. *Good* hounds. Were you going back to the kennel?" If she punished these young ones, it would do more harm than good. When one young entry digs out, it's sure the others will follow, thinking the whole thing is a romp.

"We saw a bear!" Darby, wide-eyed, reported.

"Big!" Doughboy repented leaving the kennel without the humans and without the pack.

"All right, kennel up." She dropped the tailgate, and the three gracefully leapt up. She marveled at the power of their hindquarters. In her territory, a hound with a weak rear end wouldn't last three seasons.

She shut the tailgate, hearing the latch catch, then climbed back in the cab and opened the sliding-glass window so she could talk to the three hounds. This kept them interested. She didn't want anyone jumping out.

Back at the kennel Raleigh and Rooster greeted them, having come out through the dog door in the house.

"*Hi,*" the two house pets called.

"Boys, you can help," she called the two to her. "Walk along with me and be my whippers-in."

Raleigh loved this task. He accompanied most hound walks. He quickly moved to the right side of the three, leaving Rooster the left, an easier side since it bordered the kennels.

Rooster sternly said, "*You creeps shouldn't leave the kennels.*"

"*Rassle dug out. No one said stop.*" Dreamboat defended them.

"*You're supposed to know better.*" Raleigh lowered his head, now eye to eye with Dreamboat. "*You'll never make the grade acting like a dumb puppy. Do you want to be part of this pack or not?*"

"*We do!*" The three whimpered as Sister opened the gate into the draw yard.

"*Then you'd better behave,*" Rooster warned.

Sister shut the gate behind them. She put out a bucket of warm water. It would be a few hours before it would freeze. She didn't want to put the hounds back in their first-year boys' yard. They'd go back out the hole.

She, Raleigh, and Rooster walked back to the truck to head out and find Shaker when she heard the horn closer now, then, faintly, his light voice, "Come along, lads, come along."

She trotted out to the farm lane, her boots squishing with each step, the snow turning from bits to tiny flakes. She could just make out Shaker down by the orchard.

"Got three 'Ds.' "

"Good. I've got Rassle and Ribot."

Within minutes, they had joined up. Rassle and Ribot got a tongue-lashing from Rooster and Raleigh.

Shaker put the two boys in the draw yard with the others, then he and Sister walked back into their yard.

She bent over. "Wall's fine. Not crushed."

"Dug under it. That's a lot of work. You know, we've had enough of a thaw that they could do it." He stood up, peering upwards. "Well, from the looks of it, that's over. Ground's tightening up as we stand here. I'll fix this with stone." He sighed. "They get bored sometimes, but boy, they really had to work to get under your concrete barrier."

Sister folded her arms across her chest. "Well, I hate to say it, but we're going to have to hot-wire the bottom here. Keep it hot for a week or two and see if that does the trick. If it does, then we can turn it off."

"Yeah."

Neither Sister nor Shaker liked using a hot wire with such young hounds, but Rassle, full of piss and vinegar, was going to have to learn the hard way. If he didn't learn fast, the others would start digging. Monkey see, monkey do.

"Why don't I fill this back up while you get on down to the hardware store?"

"I can fill it up. Easy if I use the front-end loader."

"Shaker, I think you're a better judge of what kind of wire we need than I am, but I don't think we need one of those boxes that works off the sun. Not much sun in the winter."

"Have to, boss. Can't run a wire into the kennels. The boys will chew it right up, and you'll have Virginia-fried foxhound."

"Ah, I forgot about that."

"They've got better solar collectors than they used to." He headed back out of the kennels over to the equipment shed. There were always two dump truck loads of crushed rock, plus one load of number-five stone behind the equipment shed. If potholes in the road were promptly filled, the road lasted a lot longer.

Shaker filled the front-end loader with stone, drove back to the boys' yard, and dumped it in the hole. Sister stomped it tight with a heavy tamper.

"Boss, this is no job for a lady."

"Who said I was a lady?"

C H A P T E R 1 8

Only a handful of riders followed hounds on Tuesday, January 20, at the old fixture called Mud Fence, so named because in the eighteenth century, the enclosures were red clay and mud.

The snow continued, light and powdery—which was unusual since snow in this part of the country is generally heavy and sticky. This dreadful viscous snow then stuck to horses' hooves, turned slick as an eel under tire wheels. This snow felt like a bracing morning in the Rockies. The cold, however, could cut right to the bone.

The moon, one day shy of full, often presaged how much game would be moving around. According to the moon cycle, this should have been a decent enough morning.

However, the foxes at Mud Fence proved lazy as sin.

Shaker cast hounds into the westerly stiff breeze. Hounds worked diligently. Doughboy, Darby, and Dreamboat settled with the pack, and Sister kept her eye on the youngsters. Shamed by their great escape, they yearned to redeem themselves.

Behind her, Walter, Xavier, Clay, Ronnie, Marty Howard, and Dalton Hill composed the field. Most days, when the weather turned bitter, Tedi and Edward valiantly rode forth, age be damned, but this morning Edward had felt as if he were coming down with the flu, so Tedi stayed home to tend to him. The last thing anyone needed was the flu bug making the rounds.

Bobby led the Hilltoppers on weekends and Thursdays. Tuesday, often a big fence day, kept many people at home, regardless of the weather. No Hilltoppers showed up today.

Since Betty was now whipping-in full-time, Bobby ran Franklin Printing on Tuesdays. Thursdays they didn't open until one, but they stayed open until nine. In return for Bobby's support of her whipping-in, Betty covered Mondays and Wednesdays so he could go to meetings, run errands, or even play nine holes of golf. Because they now had seven other employees, managing people was almost as important as the printing work itself.

As the snow fell, Betty, again on the left side, wasn't thinking of the shop. She saw a shape ahead. Outlaw snorted. Hounds, to her right, remained silent. As she drew nearer, she observed a large doe still alive although shot, most likely at the end of deer season, which was the day after New Year's. The animal's leg dangled uselessly; gangrene had set in. Betty, a hunter herself, knew game could get away from even an experienced hunter. If it left no blood trail and did not crash through woods, a clever deer could elude a good hunter, though the good hunter would keep pushing. No responsible person wanted an animal to suffer.

One of the problems in central Virginia during deer season was that so many men came in from Washington, D.C., or other cities. Dressed in cammies, toting expensive rifles, black smudged under their eyes, they usually didn't know as much as they thought they knew. They might be able to shoot, but their tracking skills left much to be desired.

Betty quietly pulled out her .38 and crept closer to the doe, whose poor head was hanging. When the deer turned to look at her, Betty fired. She hit the doe right between the eyes. The suffering animal's legs folded up like a lawn chair, and she went down with an exhalation of air.

Outlaw jumped sideways, not from the report of the gun, but from the fall of the doe.

Betty patted her best friend's neck and whispered, "Outlaw, if I'm ever that bad off, do me in. It's the coup de grâce."

Sister heard the shot, peered to see if any of her hounds had broken. They had not.

Shaker pulled the pack to the right, away from where he had heard the shot. They drifted down a low rolling bank, then dipped into a steep, narrow ravine. There might be a chance at scent here. The hounds eagerly worked the area but again nothing. As young entry had not yet developed the patience of the male hound and, therefore, could be more easily tempted by the heavy scent of the other game or a bad day, Shaker paid special attention to the D boys.

Though the signs had been promising, this was a blank day. Sister waited for a check, then rode to Shaker.

"Let's not frustrate hounds or ourselves, Shaker. We've been out two hours, and there's not a hope in hell the temperature is going to rise enough to help us." She squinted in the snow. "Funny, we often get our best hunts in the snow."

"That's what makes foxhunting, foxhunting. You never know." He raised the horn to his lips, the rim icy cold, and blew three long notes.

When he removed the horn, a bit of skin came with it.

"Smarts, doesn't it?" Sister smiled.

"If I smear on Chapstick, I can't blow this blessed thing." He stared at the offending instrument as the hounds came back to him. "All right, come along."

Sybil hove into sight at the right edge of the narrow ravine. She turned her horse, Colophon, to follow back, as did Betty, now a ghostly figure wrapped in white, standing on the left.

Back at the trailers, Betty told them what had happened. All country, they understood, though no one liked it.

Sister knew swift death was a good death. The longer she lived, the more adamantly opposed she was to keeping people alive, breathing cadavers. When her time came, she prayed the gods would be gracious. Then again, she hoped her time receded at least until she clocked one hundred. Life was too glorious.

Xavier's voice, rising, drew her attention to the trailers where he, Ronnie, Clay, and Dalton passed around a thermos of hot coffee.

"You have to say that. You're a doctor." X swallowed the warming coffee.

"I say it because I believe it," Dalton coolly replied.

"Well, I don't." X bordered on belligerent. "Once a drunk, always a drunk. Sooner or later, they all slide back. They're worthless."

Clay spoke up. "Not entirely worthless."

"Why?" X turned to Clay.

"They can serve as a horrible example." Clay's answer eased the tension.

"I heard you and Sister buried Anthony Tolliver." Ronnie finished his coffee, using a mug with the Jefferson Hunt logo on it.

"Oh, that." Clay shrugged.

"You wasted your money on Anthony Tolliver?" X was incredulous.

"He didn't waste it," Dalton quickly replied.

"The hell he didn't. The county would have put that old souse in the ground. Actually, he was probably pickled. They could have dumped Anthony back at the train station, and no one would have noticed a thing." X laughed.

"He occasionally did the odd job for the company." Clay's face reddened; X was irritating him. "And Sister would have paid for the entire thing. Not right. I owed him something, I guess. Or her."

"Why would Sister Jane care about an old alcoholic?" Dalton asked.

"School." X exhaled, then realized Dalton needed more information. "They'd gone to grade school together and through high school. I reckon she's one of the few people left in the county who knew him before he became a drunk."

"Loyal," Dalton simply said.

"That she is," Clay added. "Dalton, we all grew up with Sister and her son. In fact, X, Ronnie, and I were Rayray's best friends. We know Sister right well."

"She wasted her money, too." X twisted the cap back on the thermos, now empty.

"You're kind of a hard-ass today." Ronnie looked straight into X's eyes.

"I have no use for drunks."

Clay slapped his old friend on the back. "Lighten up. Everyone has a use."

Once hounds were chowing down in the feed room, Sister excused herself. Shaker and Betty handled the chores today. Sister rushed to the house to clean up so she could meet Walter Lungrun at the club.

Steam from the shower soaked into her bones, where the cold had settled. Once her fingers moved better, she scrubbed her short gray hair, put on a conditioner for shine, and then rinsed it all out. She toweled down with an audience: Golly, perched in the sink, her fluffy tail hanging over the edge. Raleigh and Rooster sat side by side on the deep pile bathroom rug. She stood on the bath mat, vigorously rubbing her hair, which stood up in little spikes.

Looking in the mirror, she laughed. "All I need is giant hoop earrings."

"She's a star." Golly flicked her tail, half closed her eyes.

The old house had horsehair stuffed in the walls for insulation. The bedroom had a fireplace, much needed as it was on the northwest corner of the house, cold in winter, cool in summer. She and Big Ray broke down and installed new plumbing back in 1989, paying special attention to all the bathrooms, especially this one, while they also insulated with modern insulation. That had set them back forty-five thousand dollars.

As she wrapped the towel around her waist, she gave thanks that they had done it back then. Were she to pay for the materials and labor now, the cost would be about seventy-five thousand.

They had also installed a second set of two eighty-gallon hot water tanks for this side of the house, with a special pump to create a lot of water pressure. She didn't mind paying the electric bill on the four big tanks. The house had two separate systems, which she liked. She always had hot water the minute she turned on the tap.

She combed her hair and applied face cream. The indoor heat had dried her skin out. She whipped on a little mascara, no eyeliner. She slapped on skin-tightening cream around her eyes and on her upper lip. It worked. Then she smudged faint violet powder on her eyelids, finishing off with a peachy blusher on her cheeks. She liked being clean and well turned out. She wasn't vain, not even when she was young and people told her she was beautiful. She had never thought she was beautiful. She had angular features and big light brown eyes, but she was not beautiful. She was, however, sensationally athletic. Nor did she underestimate the lovely breasts that capped the whole affair. These days those mounds of pleasure sagged, but not as much as most women her age, thanks in no small part to a life of intense physical activity. Her pecs held them up as best they could.

She critically appraised herself, then leaned down and spoke to Golly, who looked up, whiskers swept forward. "Not bad for an old broad."

"Not bad at all," Golly agreed.

Raleigh added, *"I love you. You are the most beautiful woman in the world."*

Rooster, pink tongue curling out, seconded that. *"True."*

"You two are so slavish." Golly snuggled farther down in the sink as Sister stood up straight again. Her cosmetics, lined up on the counter, included three different colors of blusher and an array of lipsticks, tossed in a big glass brandy snifter. This was self-defense; when cross, Golly would knock the cosmetics off the counter. A second line of attack for the cat was to pull toilet paper all over the bathroom and shred it.

The second sink, Big Ray's, no longer held his implements. Golly might have hunkered down there, but then she wouldn't have been close enough to be a bother.

As Sister's hair dried, she ran her fingers through it. "All right, that's it."

She sprinted into the closet, yanked out a long plaid skirt, whipped on a pair of high Gucci boots—thirty years old and still fabulous. She slipped a thin belt with small gold stirrups for a clasp through the skirt loops. Then she pulled a cashmere turtleneck over her head and tucked it into the skirt.

She came out, inspecting herself in the long mirror. Checking the time, Sister hurried down the back stairs, grabbed her shearling three-quarter-length coat, heavy but so warm. Outside, she hopped into the truck.

Even with the snow, she was at the club five minutes before Walter.

Under a tall window with a graceful curve at the top, the two caught up. While she had already written him a note thanking him for the fine hunt breakfast, she again told him how wonderful it was.

Finally, after turtle pie dessert, her tea and his coffee steaming, she reached for the handsome young man's right hand. "Walter, you're a natural foxhunter."

Beaming, he squeezed her hand. "That's the nicest thing you've ever said to me."

She laughed. "I don't know about that, but you love the sport, and you pay attention. That means so much to me. Oh, I know most people are out there to run and jump. Makes them happy. I have no quarrel with that, so long as they respect the hounds. After all, we each take away from our pastimes what we most need. But the natural foxhunter, the true foxhunter, loves the hounds and loves the quarry. And he knows that if he lived one hundred years, well, he'd still be outfoxed."

Walter smiled, his large even teeth an attractive feature. "I expect even Tom Firr didn't know it all." He referred to an English huntsman from the nineteenth century, reported to be the greatest huntsman of his time.

"You've already contributed so much to our club. There are times, Walter, when I turn around and catch sight of you, and I think it's Ray. If you had the military mustache, you'd be his twin."

A quiet note crept into his voice. "You know, I often think about Big Ray, how I wished I had known he was my natural father. How strange that neither of us knew until last season, but everyone around us knew."

"That's Virginia." She smiled, glad that something of Big Ray remained and simultaneously sorry that her genes would be washed away. Still, you take what life gives you.

"Dad didn't know; I'm sure of that." Walter referred to the man he knew as his father: a hardworking man bested in business many times over, the last time by Crawford Howard. It had destroyed him.

"I'm sure, too. We can both be glad of that, for your father did not live a happy life." She paused slightly, changing the subject. "My mother used to say, 'Eventually all things are known, and none of it matters.' She was a foxhunter. They all were. Lucky me." She smiled.

"Everyone needs a passion. If it were rational, it wouldn't be a passion, would it?" He smiled back. "We're both lucky."

The waiter put the check on the table. As both were members, he did the correct thing, placing the bill midway between them, rather than assuming the man would pay.

Walter reached for it to sign it, but Sister was quicker and grabbed it. "I asked you to lunch."

"Sister, let me. You do so much for all of us. I don't know how to repay you. Allow me."

"No. Speaking of passion, I'm here because of that passion." She scribbled her name, club number, then added a tip. "When I look at you, Walter, I am reminded of love. I'm reminded of being young. I'm reminded of how life is one surprise after another, a jumble of emotions, events, but, ultimately, joy." He sat stock-still as she spoke, her low voice resonant. "I am reminded that I must tend to my passion, for I want others to experience the same sharp grace that I have experienced in the hunt field." She took a deep breath, reaching for his hand once more. "Walter, I want you to be my joint-master."

CHAPTER 19

At eight o'clock Tuesday evening, the skies turned crystal clear. The last wisp of noctilucent cloud scudded toward the east. The mercury plunged to twenty-two degrees.

Like most horsemen, Sam Lorillard obsessively listened to the radio weather reports. Before he left Crawford's, he double-checked each horse's blanket. For those with a thin coat, typical of many thoroughbreds, he took the precaution of putting a loosely woven cotton blanket under the durable turnout sheet.

Like Sister, Sam believed horses needed to be horses. He kept them outside as much as possible, bringing them in to groom, feed, weigh, and carry on a conversation. Sam liked to talk to the horses. Roger Davis, his assistant, also took up the habit.

Crawford's thoroughbreds knew a great deal about Super Bowl picks, college basketball, and socks—quite a bit more about socks because Sam's feet remained cold until the middle of May.

The Lorillard home place, improving now that Sam was back

on his feet, had a huge cast-iron wood-burning stove in the middle of the kitchen.

Sam was also trying to improve his eating habits. He hunched at the kitchen table, a heavy leather-piercing needle in his right hand, a workday bridle in his left. The small keepers, which kept the cheek straps from flapping, had broken. He patiently stitched them.

Jabbing a needle through leather hurt his fingers, which ached in the cold. Sitting by the wood-burning stove helped.

His cell phone rang. He no longer bothered with a line to the house, using the cell for everything.

"Hello."

"Sam," Rory croaked, "come get me. I'm ready."

"Where are you?"

"Salvation Army. Thought I'd clean up."

"Hang on. I'll be right there."

Sam hurried to his battered 1979 Toyota truck, which, despite age, ran like a top.

One half-hour later, after a fulsome discussion with the sergeant in charge, Rory left with Sam.

"It's a three-hour ride. Can you make it?"

A haggard Rory slumped on his seat. "Yes." He produced a pint of Old Grand-Dad. "This is the last booze I'll ever drink. If I don't, I'll get the shakes. You don't need that." Rory took a swig.

A pint was nothing to Rory Ackerman's system. Sam said nothing about the whiskey, was surprised that he didn't crave it himself.

The long ride to Greensboro, North Carolina, was punctuated by sporadic bursts of talk.

"Expensive?"

"The clinic?" Sam kept his eyes on the road.

"Uh-huh."

"Not as bad as some."

"How am I gonna pay for it?"

"Don't fret about that now. Just get through it."

Rory licked his lips after another pull. "You got some secret source of money?"

Sam smiled, the lights from the dials on the dash illuminating his face with a low light. "If I did, I wouldn't tell you."

"Am I gonna work this off for the rest of my life?"

"I told you, don't worry about that. You and I can work that out later. Your job is to dry out, clean up, sober up, wake up."

"Yeah, yeah," Rory responded with little enthusiasm.

As they crossed the Dan River, then over the North Carolina line, Rory spoke up again.

"Heater works good."

"Truck's a keeper." Sam smiled.

"Pisses me off that the Japs make better cars than we do."

"Nah," Sam disagreed, "not anymore. But if I get enough money together, I'll buy another Toyota Tacoma. Easy on the gas. And red. I always wanted a red truck."

"Sure I got a bed?"

Sam nodded. Rory stretched out his feet, not far since the cabs of Japanese vehicles are made for people smaller than Americans. "Been thinkin'."

"I figured."

"No. Been thinking about Mitch and Tony."

"Oh."

"Day jobs." Rory glanced out the window at the flat landscape. "They knew something."

"Like something illegal?"

"I reckon. You know how it is. We work a farm for two days, paint a fence, however long we can hold it together. Anyone who needs someone fast doesn't mind scraping the bottom of the barrel, rides on down to the train station."

"Yeah."

"Loading docks. Once when storms dropped trees over the tracks, we even worked for the C and O, cutting them up. If you talked to all of us, we've about covered every odd job in the county. You notice things even if you're hung over."

"Mitch and Tony notice anything out of the way?"

Rory closed his eyes. "Brain's no good. I remember sometimes they'd be flush."

"You'll remember when you're back to yourself."

He paused, then whistled. "If I can figure it out, I might be drinking the next bottle of Thunderbird enhanced with poison." He cackled for a second. "Like those wine snobs would say, 'a floral top note,' or maybe in this case, a hemlock finish."

As Sam drove to Greensboro, only to turn around and drive back to get to work by six-thirty in the morning, Sister sat up in bed, wood crackling in the big fireplace. Propped on her knees was a yellow legal pad, much scribbled upon.

Each time Sister would write something else with her Number 1 lead pencil, Golly would bat at the pencil.

"*Gotcha.*"

"You're a frustrated writer." Sister batted back at the cat, who loved this game.

Rooster got up from his bed, walked over, and put his head on the bed, eyes imploring.

"No."

"*Why does she get to sleep up there?*"

"Rooster, go to bed, honey."

"*I want to get on the bed.*"

Raleigh, disturbed, joined the harrier. "*It's not fair. It's not fair that that snot cat gets to be up there and we sleep in dog beds. We're man's best friend. What's she?*"

"*The Queen of All She Surveys,*" Golly replied.

"I can't think. Boys, go to sleep. The dog door isn't locked downstairs, so you can go out if that's what this is about."

Sister usually locked the door at night so Rooster, particularly, wouldn't hunt. But on a cold night, Rooster had no desire to chase fox, rabbit, or bobcat, hence the unlocked dog door.

"*Disobedient dogs don't get treats.*" Golly rolled over to display her stomach, adding further insult to the barb. She fetchingly turned her head, too.

"*Smart-ass cats get tossed over our heads,*" Rooster threatened.

"*I am so scared I think I'll pee on the comforter,*" Golly purred.

"*Then she'll throw you off the bed,*" Raleigh said.

"I can't hear myself think." Sister scratched Golly's tummy while the cat peered down at the dogs. They sighed, gave up, and padded back to their beds.

"*One of these days that fat cat will go too far,*" Rooster grumbled.

"*No sense of restraint, obligation, or duty.*" Raleigh put his sleek black head on his tan-tipped paws. "*She does nothing to earn her keep.*"

Golly righted herself. "*Oh, yes I do, you two sanctimonious toads. Dogs are so, so—*" She pondered. "*—goody. Makes me want to cough up a fur ball. I kill mice. It's why we have a mouse-free barn and house.*"

"*Ha! Inky comes in and gets the mice and what she doesn't want, Bitsy gets. The last time you caught a mouse was an eclipse of the sun.*" Raleigh kept his eyes open in case she shot off the bed to attack him.

"*You just thought there was an eclipse of the sun. You had your head up your ass.*" Golly giggled.

That made Rooster laugh, so Raleigh now growled at him instead.

"I am going to throw everyone out of this bedroom and shut the door. I need to concentrate." Sister's voice took on that *listen-to-me* edge.

Golly moved to sit behind Sister on the pillow. She peered down at the tablet, covered with names, squares beside some, X's beside others, question marks by a few.

"*Looks complicated.*" Golly exhaled through her tiny nostrils.

Squares rested in front of the names of those on the Board of Governors who would oppose her plan. X's meant agreement. A question mark was just that.

Tomorrow was the board meeting. She would announce her

decision concerning a joint-master. After initial shock and some good questions about just what she expected from him, Walter had happily said yes.

Now she had to get this through the board. She had spoken to the people with an X by their name. Bobby Franklin, stepping down as president, was the first person she talked to after Walter. She'd been politicking. She wondered how elected officials did this morning, noon, and night. Guess they liked it.

She had not spoken to the few people with squares by their name, Crawford being one. She knew she'd face opposition. Why give the two people she knew would oppose this plan time to pressure the question-mark people? Better to lay this out tomorrow night and hope the X's could help her swing the question-mark people right there at the meeting.

As for Crawford, she had a plan so he would be kissed and socked at the same time.

Not for nothing had Jane Arnold been Master of the Foxhounds for over forty years.

As she scribbled, she stopped and then spoke to the dogs.

"I think this will work. I'm excited about having a joint-master. Oh, I know there will be bumps in the road. I've had my own way here, captain of the ship and all that, but Walter and I will be a good team. Oh, la!" She threw up her hands. "I might be seventy-two, but, I'm telling you, I feel thirty-five!"

"*Sometimes she gets simple.*" Golly yawned.

"*Humans worry about their age. The whole cosmetics industry would collapse, plastic surgery would tank if people accepted themselves as they are,*" Raleigh shrewdly thought out loud.

"*I figure if you can't bring down a rabbit, it's time to sit on the porch,*" Rooster added his two bits.

Thrilled with her plan, Sister checked the clock on the nightstand, picked up the phone, and called Tedi Bancroft to again discuss bringing in Walter.

The two dear friends laughed and chatted. Tedi and Edward thought electing Walter as joint-master was inspired. Sister told Tedi how young she felt, light, elated.

Just before hanging up, Tedi said, "You know, Janie, I think aging is a return to your true self."

CHAPTER 20

B ut look how much money the showgrounds have already gen-
erated." Clay Berry, first year on the Board of Governors,
glanced down at his notes. "Surely by next year there will be enough
to hire a part-time manager, at the least."

The board meeting was held the third Wednesday of each
month except July. Every member took a turn hosting, a practice
that drew them together. Although they hunted together, board
members didn't necessarily socialize. This was not because of personality conflicts, but the group's interests varied widely. There wasn't
as much time to sit around in one another's homes as there had
been for Sister's parents' generation. People worked long hours,
even those with money. They ferried their children to and fro, their
kids as overcommitted with activities as their parents.

The other factor, true of most hunt clubs, was that members involved themselves in community projects: political campaigns, the
Heart Fund, Easter Seals, 10K runs to raise funds for breast cancer

research. Let there be a fund-raiser, a ball, a horse show, a trunk show to raise money for a worthy cause, and someone from the Jefferson Hunt would be there or in the chair.

Perhaps foxhunters, by their very natures, possess more animal energy. One can't fly fences in heat, rain, sleet, or snow for two to four hours without brimming with high animal spirits. This spilled over into many activities. Sister was proud of the good work her members had done for the community. She even believed in a few herself, notably the No Kill Animal Shelter, which was her pet project—her pun.

Ronnie, tough about money, punched numbers into his handheld calculator. He looked up at the faces gathered in Sister's front room. "Now look, Clay, it's not a half-pay kind of deal. You know that from your business. There's payroll, taxes, health insurance—"

"If they're contract labor, there are no payroll, taxes, or health insurance," Crawford interrupted.

Xavier folded his hands together. "Ronnie's right. In order to have someone we can trust, someone who isn't going to wreck the tractor, who will take some pride in the task, you can't go with contract labor. I mean, we can't head on down to the Salvation Army and pluck up one of the winos before a horse show. Either we keep going as we are or—"

"It's the 'or' that worries me," Walter spoke up. "Right now, the showgrounds are under my umbrella since I'm head of the Building and Grounds Committee. This is our first year, and we've been keeping everything together. For instance, the Lions Club left the grounds immaculate. The Antique Auto Club left the grounds immaculate, but grease was everywhere. Jimmy Chirios and I had to scrape down the ring, haul off the oil-soaked sand and bring in a thousand dollars' worth of twice-washed sand. And we told them not to drive cars in the ring. It's a sharp learning curve. Much as I'd like a full-time person, we can hold off for another year. Let's see if the rentals hold up. Right now we're a novelty in the county."

Betty Franklin, the newsletter editor, spoke up. "I agree. Actually, I think we're going to have more and more activity there. The grounds are more beautiful than I expected, and the county has nothing like this. We've saved the county commissioners a headache. Not having a showgrounds or fairgrounds has been a sore spot since the old fairgrounds burned down twenty years ago. Every year since then the commissioners would say, 'Costs too much to build.' Every year construction costs went up and up. Nothing got done. That we did it is thanks to the Bancrofts for the land and thanks to Crawford."

"Hear! Hear!" Everyone sang Crawford's and the Bancrofts' praises.

Golly, having disgraced herself during dinner before the meeting, perched behind Sister on the wing chair, and cackled. *"There! There!"*

"I move we table the employee issue, showgrounds, for a year." Ron moved.

This was seconded and passed.

"Now let me bring up an idea." Sister smiled. "Actually, it was Ronnie's idea. You tell them."

"Why don't we ask each member to buy a lottery ticket once a month? One dollar. If the ticket wins, they split with the club."

"Great idea!" Betty Franklin clapped her hands together.

"Who can argue with a dollar?" Her husband, Bobby, president of the club, smiled.

"How do you know they'll be honest about the winning ticket?" Crawford tilted his head slightly to one side.

For a moment, no one spoke. Then Sorrel Buruss, social chair, always the diplomat, quietly said, "It is hoped that anyone who is a member of this hunt has integrity, honesty, humor, and courage. Naturally, we also have feet of clay, but let's hope for the best."

"Why can't members buy a ticket, write their names on the back, and turn it in to the treasurer?" Crawford nodded to Ronnie.

"It would remove temptation if someone hit Lotto South's big jackpot."

Another silence followed.

"That makes work for Ronnie. It might work, but let's start with a little trust," Betty remonstrated.

"Trust is a wonderful thing—" Crawford's light voice filled the room. "—but removing temptation will yield more results."

After wasting too much time on this issue, the board voted to trust to luck and the membership.

Bobby Franklin checked off another item on the agenda. Two remained: the election of a president and the election of the master, which was announced on February 14. Whatever board meeting was closest to February 14 before that date was the elective meeting. It usually fell in January. If the membership did not accept the board's recommendation, people could be proposed from the floor.

The board did not elect new members until the start of cubbing season. Each year three members cycled off the twelve-person board, after having served three years. This provided continuity and also avoided the stress of too much change all at one time. None of the members present, with the exception of Sister and Edward Bancroft, had lived through an upheaval of masterships. The disarray for those two years before Jane Arnold became master left such a bitterness at the time that a huge effort had been made to unite behind Jane. It worked because over time she demonstrated not just knowledge of hounds, game, territory, and wooing landowners, she could get people to work together. She always said she had more patience with animals than people, but being a master forced her to develop patience with people, and to examine other points of view. She felt becoming an MFH was one of the best things that had ever happened to her.

"We are now come to the election of a president and a master." Bobby's eyes swept over the gathering. "As you know, I am stepping down as your president after serving seven years—seven years that I wouldn't change for anything in the world. But it's time for new blood and time for me to make a big decision in my life about whether to expand my business or sell it. Betty and I really need to think about all that. I am grateful to you for allowing me to serve."

"You'll still lead the Hilltoppers, won't you?" Sorrel asked. "You're so good at it."

Bobby smiled. "Flattery will get you everywhere, Sorrel. Yes, I will." He paused a moment, getting even Golly's attention. "It is customary for the outgoing president to name his successor after convening with the master and to give the reasons why he thinks this individual will be a good president. Of course, nominations will be entertained from the board, too." He paused again. The gathering sat still; the only ones in the room who knew what was coming next were his wife and Sister. "I have given the matter of who should follow me a lot of thought. One of the greatest things about Jefferson Hunt is that I think any member of this board would be a good president. That says a lot about the depth of our leadership and commitment. But the more I thought about it, the more I kept coming back to one man: Crawford Howard."

As he said this, eyes widened. No one expected Bobby Franklin to pass the torch to a man he loathed.

"This is more interesting than I thought it would be," Golly purred.

"Crawford has drive, experience in the world of business. He also has a vision. He's not afraid to express himself directly and—" Bobby held up his hand and smiled. "—we Virginians can't always do that. Or at least this Virginian can't. And I don't pretend I always like that, but I have learned that when Crawford says something, he believes it. He doesn't try to ruffle feathers; he tries to get the job done. At this point in our club's history, I believe that Crawford Howard is the president we need." He turned to the surprised Crawford. "Do you accept my nomination of you as president?"

Crawford understood that this meant he would not be joint-master, at least not for a while. What a disappointment. On the other hand, this was a chance to prove himself as a leader.

"I accept. And I want to pay tribute to a president with whom I have come to blows, physical blows. Much as we have disagreed, and violently, I have never doubted your commitment to what you believe is best for the Jefferson Hunt. Over time, I have learned to somewhat temper my ways, thanks to your example. Yours are big shoes to fill."

"Hear, hear!" all spoke.

Bobby patted his ample girth. "Big pants, too." He laughed at himself. "Do I have a second?"

Edward Bancroft, himself no fan of Crawford's, who also had learned to work with him and appreciate his acumen, said, "I second the nomination."

"Are there nominations from the floor?" Bobby waited an appropriate time. "If there are no further nominations, then I move we vote on our candidate for president. Because there is only one, we can do this with a voice vote. All in favor, say 'Aye.' "

"Aye," came the unanimous chorus.

"Crawford Howard is our new president, term effective as of the February board meeting. Congratulations, Crawford."

"Thank you." Crawford stood up. "Thank you all for your confidence in me." He sat down.

"One last item: the election of our master."

Before Bobby could continue, Ronnie called out, "I nominate Jane Arnold."

"Second," Clay said.

"Any nominations from the floor?" Bobby waited. "All in favor of Jane Arnold continuing in her duties as master, signify by saying 'Aye.' "

Everyone said "Aye."

Sister smiled. "Well, I guess you're not tired of me yet. Thank you." She waited a moment. "As you know, I have been your master since 1957. I hope I die in the saddle, literally. I have never done anything I love as much as being master of the Jefferson Hunt Club, proudly wearing our colors of Continental blue piped in buff, what our forefathers wore when they beat back the British in the Revolutionary War." She took a deep breath. "And I am sure for some of our younger members, they must think I've been master since the Revolutionary War. It's time to bring along a joint-master, dear friends. It's time for me to ensure when my day has ended that this club will have a master who knows our hounds, cherishes our heritage, and ensures that our grandchildren and great-grandchildren have available to them what we have had available to us: open land, a respect for all living creatures, an understanding of our place in nature, and a love for the fox, our most worthy adversary." People held their breath as she then said, voice firm, "I would be grateful to this board if you would elect Dr. Walter Lungrun to serve as our joint-master."

Silence followed. Then Edward, in his patrician accent, said, "Janie, that is an inspired choice. Walter is young, vigorous, dedicated to foxhunting, and eager to learn. I believe you two will make a wonderful team. I wholeheartedly support this idea."

"Walter?" Bobby realized the handsome man needed to indicate his willingness to serve, even though Bobby knew what was afoot.

"This is an honor I could never have imagined." Walter meant it, too.

Betty spoke up. "Yes. Yes."

Her simple affirmation allowed everyone else to speak at once, but the consensus was favorable, despite the twofold shock. The assembled thought Sister would go through one or two more terms alone, and many feared Crawford's ambition to be master would, in time, split the club.

"Can we have a vote on this?" Bobby asked.

"I second the nomination," Ronnie said.

"All in favor—"

Everyone said "Aye" before Bobby could finish his Robert's Rules of Order drill.

"Congratulations." Bobby got up and shook Walter's hand, then walked over and shook Crawford's hand. "Oh, I forgot," he said as the board members got up, "any unfinished business?"

"Meeting's adjourned," Sorrel called out.

Betty hugged Sister. One by one other board members also hugged and thanked her.

Then they all hastened to the bar or the coffeepot in the kitchen, breaking up into small groups. Everyone congratulated the new joint-master and the new president.

Neatly stacked on her desk were the proofs Jim Meads had sent of all the photographs he had taken at Mill Ruins. Sister had put them out for board members to peruse. Order forms were next to the proofs.

She had prudently taken the eight-by-ten glossies of the fight at Chapel Cross up to her bedroom. She'd glanced at them briefly and thought she'd look at them more closely later.

When the gathering finally broke up, Walter, the last to leave, hugged and kissed Sister.

"Any words of advice, Master?"

She kissed him back. "Produce the pumpkins. Pies will follow."

Later, snuggled in bed, Golly at her elbow, she congratulated herself on how smoothly the meeting had run. She sighed with relief. Walter would make a fine master. She felt as if a weight had been lifted off her shoulders; broad though they were, she had felt the weight of ensuring a proper succession.

She opened the nightstand drawer, bringing out the photos.

"Roll over!" Golly yelled as Rooster snored.

"Golly, you'll split my eardrums." Sister petted the spoiled cat with her left hand as she flipped over the photographs with her right. "Those boys meant business." She studied the scenes of Xavier and Sam. "Hmm." She peered at one photograph in particular. Dalton and Izzy sat side by side, looking at each other. It did not appear to be the social eye contact of acquaintances. There was heat in that gaze. She rushed through the other photos to see if any more contained a clue to Dalton and Izzy. They didn't.

"*Shut up, Rooster,*" Golly again complained.

"Maybe I am reading too much into this." Sister ignored the cat's yowl. "But, Golly, I've been around long enough to know a carnal look when I see one."

CHAPTER 21

Turning slowly, the water wheel fed a stream of clear water from the upper pond into the lower pond. Buried beneath the frost line, the pipes stayed clear. That portion above the frost line was wrapped in heat tape. Cindy Chandler hated draining pipes in winter. Her expensive solution worked. It worked for the fish, too; as a constant source of oxygen, freshening water poured into the hole in the ice.

Another warming trend sent fissure throughout the ice in the pond, looking like dark veins. The creeks, running strong, had ice crystals embedded along the sides. Thicker ice, melting, raised the water level.

The earth at ten that Thursday morning had a thin, slick coating as the frost turned to dew. Ground was softening.

Dana and Diddy, eager to make a good showing, opened when they caught scent of Grace. She frequented the ponds nightly, and sometimes even in broad daylight.

Cora chided the two young ones for being overeager. Grace's line, old, would lead only to her den. Patience might yield a better scent. Cora hoped they'd hop Uncle Yancy. He liked to dash to the rehabilitated old schoolhouse at the edge of Foxglove Farm.

"Isn't any scent as good as any other?" Diddy inquired, disappointed.

"No," Cora, nose to the ground, told the first-year entry emphatically. *"If this were a difficult scenting day, I'd advise you to keep on that line, but look, youngster, look."* Cora lifted her head and stared at the lovely house visible about half a mile away.

"I don't see anything." Diddy was puzzled.

"Smoke from the chimney. It's held down and flattening out instead of rising straight up. See? Like a big paw is pushing it back. That's good. Then look at the sky." As the young hound did, Cora continued, *"Low gray clouds, a kind of dove gray. They'll hold the scent down for us. And the temperature is just about right."* Cora inhaled deeply, the pungent odor of the earth filling her nostrils as the frost melted away. *"Forty degrees or close. We will find a hotter line than Grace's."*

Dana, impressed, asked, *"How did you know that line was Grace's?"*

Cora chuckled. *"Well, it's like being a catcher in baseball. You remember pitchers. And if Asa, Arden, Diana, Dasher, or I pick up a fox scent that we don't recognize, we are extra attentive. This fox will run in a different pattern. When you're excited, when scent is scorching, it's easy to overrun the line of a strange fox. Now that doesn't sound so bad, and on a day like today, we'd find it again in a jif."* She puffed out her deep chest. *"But on a spotty day, if we overrun, we could blow the whole hunt. Shaker and Sister would know, too. They don't have good noses—they can't help that— but they have very good eyes, and they know their quarry and know us. We have to be on top of our game."*

Diddy's soft brown eyes welled up as she put her nose down again. *"Oh, I don't want to get drafted out. I want to be a good hound."*

Ardent, behind the girls, hearing the entire exchange, encouraged the two D girls, *"Now, now, that won't happen. You'll be just fine.*

Takes a year or two to learn the ropes. And hounds get drafted for different reasons. You'll be fine.

Dana, nervous about this drafting concept, whispered, *"Like what?"*

"Too fast. Too slow. Doesn't get along with others. Not the right nose for our conditions," Ardent explained. *"But Sister and Shaker are very careful where they draft a Jefferson Hunt hound. We get sent only to good places, and sometimes she'll send a hound to help another hunt's breeding program and then the hound comes back. Usually she'll send one of the girls for that, but once she lent Archie to a pack in Missouri for a summer."*

"I don't want to leave here." Diddy lifted her ears up.

"Chances are, you won't." Cora noticed Dragon on her right. His stern stood still, then he began to move vigorously. *"We may be in business."*

"Uncle Yancy!" Dragon called out.

Diana, better able than most to deal with her brother's outrageous ego, loped over, put her nose down, and seconded his call. *"Yancy!"*

Dragon, already running, pulled the pack with him, all eighteen couple on this promising January morning.

Shaker blew the three short doubled notes in succession three times. When the rest of the pack dropped on the line, he blew "Gone Away"—a long blast followed by two or three short toots, short notes doubled three or four times in succession.

Sister, with the field of twenty-nine, large for a Thursday, felt her heart pound. No matter how many times over the years she heard "Gone Away," it gave her chills.

She squeezed Rickyroo, a lovely rangy thoroughbred with a big heart who was still learning the ropes. They trotted away from the ponds, down a slick crease in the meadows. Once off that, she moved up to a canter, but before she knew it, speed accelerated.

One of Cindy's stonewall jumps with a telephone pole on top of the stones loomed ahead. Horses take solid jumps seriously, often sailing over a stiff solid obstacle better than a lower, airy one. Ricky-roo, feeling he could jump the moon, pricked his ears forward, lifted off, and landed, sliding slightly. Sister wondered how that footing was going to be for the last riders in the field.

Hilltoppers, only six today, cantered behind Tedi Bancroft. She never minded leading Second Flight if Bobby couldn't come out that day. She always said she had more views in Second Flight than she did in First Flight.

Edward Bancroft rode in Sister's pocket today, with Walter behind him; Xavier, Clay, Ronnie, Tommy, Sam, Gray, Marty, Crawford, Dalton, Alexander Vajay, and the rest of the field fanned out behind them.

Once over the stone wall, they cut into the edge of a parked-out woods—meaning the underbrush had been cleared at least fifty feet in. Pretty as it was, Sister deplored the practice. Thick underbrush brought in game, especially rabbits, who are edge feeders. No self-respecting rabbit will sit out in the middle of a big field or parked-out woods unless there aren't any predators for a great distance.

Once in the parked-out woods, they hit on a farm trail that petered out into a deer trail. The underbrush, even in winter, tangled on both sides. Old creeper vines, pricker bushes, and endless mountain laurel kept Uncle Yancy from view. Not far off, he was running flat out. He had fallen asleep, awakening only when he heard Cora talking to Diddy. Age was catching up with Yancy, and he had a habit of dozing off on a warm rock, or in a big rolled-up bale or even a stall.

Dragon, quick as Mercury, flew not five minutes behind Yancy. Dragon was determined to catch the old fox, snap his neck, and throw his carcass over his head. Dragon dreamed of such glories.

Yancy at this moment wondered if he could make it to his den underneath the schoolhouse. He zigzagged through the brush, knowing it would slow down the larger, heavier hounds, then he slid into the creek that fed into Broad Creek. Once in the creek, he stayed there for one hundred yards, trotting over the stones, moving downstream, swimming when he had to swim. A fallen log up ahead beckoned. He clambered up, ran along the log, and then landed on the opposite bank.

The hounds moved on both sides of the creek, with Dragon beside himself, foolishly splashing in the creek. Yancy nearly got away with it, but Asa, wise in his years, saw the log, made for it, jumped on it, put his nose down, and sang out a deep resonant note. Then he jumped off and picked up the line, bringing the whole pack right with him.

Diana, steady, anchored the hounds. Dana and Diddy would glance up front to her, or Cora, for guidance.

Bitsy, visiting Cindy's barn, shadowed the pack when she heard them. The screech owl flew silently ahead. Almost noiseless in the air, prey doesn't hear an owl until it glances up and those fearsome talons, even on a little owl like Bitsy, reach down and grab it. Bitsy adored Uncle Yancy since both enjoyed gossip.

"Yancy, Yancy, duck into the overgrown springhouse up ahead. A quarter of a mile. Hit the turbo."

The springhouse, once used for the schoolhouse, had fallen into disuse. Its stone intact, the sluice of cold water still ran through, capable of keeping milk, cheeses, and meats cool for a day or two even in the hottest weather. Those children attending the school in the 1870s through the 1940s could put their bottles of milk and lunches in tins in the springhouse or even in the sluice and they would be fresh for lunchtime.

Dragon, gaining on Yancy, surged faster and faster, driven by the idea that he would make a kill.

Yancy tripped on a gnarly tree root pushed up between stones; he rolled over and over. Dragon drew close enough to see him roll. Bitsy drove down, fluttering in front of the sleek hound, baffling him for a moment, just enough time for Yancy to recover.

The old fox ducked into the springhouse, a tidy little hidey-hole in the corner.

Dragon howled at the shut door, the big old hinges black, powdered with a slight coating of rust, holding the heavy oaken door in place. He spun around to the side where the water ran through, flattened and wriggled, tried to get in through the sluice. He was too large. The small den, made by an industrious fox generations past, was well placed. Yancy had sucked way back into the living quarters. He blinked, wondering how many exits there were. If Dragon started digging, would Yancy choose the right exit or wind up in the middle of the pack?

Shaker, up with his forward hounds, swung off Showboat. He couldn't open the door, so he blew "Gone to Ground" as the slimmer members of the pack crawled in the sluice. Once inside the springhouse, the din was phenomenal. Shaker, pure frustration, was outside with the larger hounds and an irate Dragon.

Betty, riding hard, came in, hopped off Magellan, and the two of them sweated over the big old door, creaking on its hinges.

"Damn. I hope Yancy is okay."

"Yancy can take care of himself." Betty had learned to admire the senior citizen over the years. He had a big bag of tricks.

They still couldn't get the rusted door open.

Walter rode up. "Master, may I help?"

"Of course."

As Walter was the strongest man in the field, Sister readily gave him permission to move ahead of her.

Walter jumped down, put his shoulder to it. The door gave way, the sound of old iron grating on iron eerie in the deepening gray.

Yancy slithered down a pathway underground that hooked right, in the direction of the schoolhouse. He hoped so anyway.

He popped out. Yes, there they all were: the humans, their sides to him, and no one was looking. He didn't trust Dragon. He knew the hound might not obey the huntsman. He took a deep breath. Bitsy watched with apprehension. Yancy crept up out of the exit hole, slinking, belly to the ground, toward the schoolhouse. He'd be able to use the woods and then he'd come out into the open pastures where he knew he'd have to use every ounce of speed left within him.

Sister, catching movement out of the corner of her eye, saw him. She counted to twenty, considered the circumstances, counted twenty more, then said, "Tallyho."

Shaker, blowing "Gone to Ground" in the springhouse, didn't hear. Betty did and put a hand on his shoulder.

"Tallyho. Sister."

Without a word, Shaker bolted out of there, his hounds following. He vaulted into the saddle, touching the horn to his lips, then thought better of it. "Come along."

Once the hounds cleared the springhouse, Walter struggled with the door. Shaker blew the hounds to where Sister sighted Yancy. She stood still, horse's head pointed in the direction in which Yancy was traveling. Her cap was off her head, arm outstretched in the direction, also, the tails fluttering in the strengthening wind.

"Yes!" Diddy caught a scent so fresh it nearly knocked her over.

Within seconds, all were on. A dark coop was nestled in the old fence line between the woods and the pastures. Shaker cleared it first, Sister twenty yards behind. Once in the pasture, they saw Yancy streaking for the schoolhouse, Dragon leading the hounds thirty yards behind him, and the rest of the pack moving up, the young entry showing more speed than Sister had anticipated.

But Yancy had enough of a head start just to make it. He dove into his spacious den, the biggest entrance along the basement of the old clapboard structure. Once there, he flopped on his side, trying to catch his breath. That was a close call. He hated to admit that he was slowing down, his judgment getting sloppy, but it was true.

Overhead, Bitsy shadowed. Sister looked up to see the sturdy little screech owl intently watching the pack. The owl emitted an earsplitting shriek when she landed on the cupola of the roof.

Later Sister reflected on that. There was so much humans don't know about species cooperating with one another. Just why, she couldn't say, but that made her think again about the Jim Meads photograph, the one showing a hot glance between Izzy Berry and Dalton Hill.

CHAPTER 22

Snowflakes fluttered down, illuminated by the four large curved lights bending over the long white sign reading "Roger's Corner." This convenience store supplied everything from beer to rat-shot to Swiss chocolate. Its prime product, however, was gossip.

Located at the intersection of Soldier Road, which ran east to west, and White Cat Road, which ran north to south, the store had run in the black from the year it was founded, 1913. White Cat Road was the last decent north-to-south road before one crossed the Blue Ridge Mountains. Other roads running in that direction were potted or dirt or both.

Roger, a contemporary of Ronnie and Xavier, studied the business under his father. He was the fourth generation to own this store, and was named for its founder. He liked being at the county nerve center.

This Saturday evening, the Prussian blue of the clouds, the falling snow, the gas pumps wearing snowcaps, the light from the sign washing over Roger's Corner—all combined to resemble an Edward Hopper painting.

Inside Shaker, Sister, Xavier, Tedi, Lorraine, and Sari had each purchased what they needed. They lingered at the counter.

Affable Roger provided hot coffee. "So, good hunt this morning?"

"Ask the boss." Shaker nodded at Sister, then looked out the window at the snow-covered windshield of the old but strong 1974 Chevy truck with the 454 engine, a real beast.

"Pretty good, thank you for asking, Roger. We hunted at Dueling Grounds, on the flat by the river. Had a large field this Thursday and an even bigger one today: sixty people. By the time we finished, we were blue, but hey, the foxes ran, the hounds did well, and, when we returned to the trailers, we thought we'd done something."

Tedi, sneaking a cigarette because Edward hated for her to smoke, puffed. "Oh, tell Roger about the lady from where was it?" She paused a moment, a plume of blue smoke curling upwards. "Ah, she was visiting from Wabash Hounds outside of Omaha, Nebraska. Well, she couldn't have been nicer or better turned out, but they don't have the kind of thick woods we do. Takes their trees longer to grow, I guess. Our first blast through tight quarters, she feared for her kneecaps. She was a good sport. Took her fences in style, too."

"When people from the Midwest or the West hunt Virginia, they're often surprised at how thick the cover is here even in winter. Some of those places are pretty flat, too," Shaker added to the conversation. "Boss and I drove out one year for the Western Challenge. The terrain ranged from low desert to high desert to plains. Mostly coyote."

"What's the Western Challenge?" Lorraine asked.

"All these hunts in the West get together for two weeks. Each day, unless it's a travel day, you hunt with them and watch their hounds work in their territory. At the end, the best pack gets a cup," Sister explained.

"You can drive nine hours before you get to another hunt," Xavier said. "The spaces are incredible. Course the Bureau of Land Management owns most of it, which is to say the federal government."

"Is that good or bad?" Young Sari felt comfortable enough to speak with the adults. Since she had proven herself in the hunt field, the adults no longer thought of her as a teenager, but simply a young foxhunter.

"Depends. In some places the BLM preserves and protects the land. In other states, it's a struggle. If you get a warden on a power trip, he can make life miserable for everyone out there," Xavier told her. "Now I've never attended the Western Challenge, which I really want to do, but Dee and I go out to Wyoming and Montana for two weeks in August. I love it out there." He paused. "Ronnie and I are going to try and do the challenge this year."

"God, you and Ronnie in the trailer for two weeks." Tedi rolled her eyes. "Strains credulity."

"Strain more than that." Shaker laughed.

"I know." Xavier laughed. "We're the odd couple. He is so fastidious and I'm, well, I'm not as sloppy as Ronnie says, but let's just say I'm not anal." He winced. "Wrong choice of words."

Everyone laughed except Sari, who didn't get it.

"Can't wait to tell Ronnie you said that." Roger leaned on the counter with one elbow.

"You will, too." Xavier feigned mock horror.

Roger put his other elbow on the counter. "When we played football in high school, Ronnie was fast and tough. Always had the girls around him. Dressed better than the rest of us." Roger shrugged. "Guess you just are what you are, but Ronnie has made me ask a lot of questions. Funny, I'm grateful to him."

Shaker simply said, "I don't get it."

"You wouldn't." Sister raised an eyebrow.

He raised the palm of one hand. "I'm not looking to pick a fight. I just don't get it. How can any man not go crazy for a woman? Look, Xavier, I like the heck out of you, but I don't want to kiss you."

Xavier laughed. "Dee says I'm a good kisser."

"Braggart." Sister now laughed.

Tedi stubbed out her cigarette, feeling mellow from that delightful hit of nicotine.

"Gentlemen, I'm old enough to be your mother. By virtue of that, I can say what I think. What I conclude from my long and eventful life is that our knowledge is constricted by ideology and religion. We don't know why anyone is heterosexual, much less homosexual. But I know this: to deny love is to deny life."

Everyone looked at her.

"You're right." Lorraine smiled at her.

"Tedi, I've never heard you speak like that." Xavier put his arm around the lovely lady.

"Well, for one thing, Edward isn't here—not that he reins me in, but let's just say he guides me away from controversy. Oh, when we first married, and he was running the company, we'd have to entertain, and, well, I was raised a Prescott. Prescotts speak their minds. Poor Edward. He'd say after one of those affairs, 'Honey, I don't think they're ready for you.' " She grinned. "I just smoked a cigarette and now I feel glorious. Glorious!"

They laughed.

"Shorten your life." Roger winked.

"Aren't you sick of it?" Xavier smacked his hand against the counter. "Everyone tells you what to do and how to do it! Bad enough the government robs us at every turn, but now we have the health Nazis."

Lorraine, a more serious type and not a foxhunter, demurred. "But Xavier, it has been proven that cigarette smoking can cause lung cancer."

"And caffeine will put you over the edge," Xavier replied. "Sugar rots your teeth. I could go on. Given Sari's young years, I'll leave out all the sexual fears and propaganda. I mean, bad enough we got off on Ronnie."

"What was that?" Roger cocked his eyebrow. "Got off?"

"You are twisted." Xavier punched him.

Roger shied away from the second punch. "Hey, who's twisted? But I'm with you, X. People gotta do what they do. If smoking eases the nerves, hey, smoke. If bourbon at six takes the edge off a rough day, sip with pleasure. We all need a little help."

"Foxhunting," Sister firmly spoke.

"That's her answer to everything." Shaker laughed.

"But it's true." Color flushed her cheeks. "When are you most alive? Hunting."

"That's true," Tedi agreed.

"For us," Xavier amended the sentiment.

"Everyone needs something that pushes them physically and mentally. Safety numbs people." Shaker, having seen a fair amount of danger in his work, believed this.

"That's why you see people in their eighties and even nineties in the hunt field. Not only did they stay healthy from the sport, they get up in the morning and can't wait to get out there. Unless the good Lord jerks my chain, I intend to go to my nineties." Xavier patted his girth. "Better lose a little weight first. Dee keeps reminding me. She works out. I intend to, but, well, those donuts look so good. You know the rest." Xavier laughed.

The phone rang. "Roger's Corner." His head came up; he looked at the gathering. "Thanks." Roger hung up the phone. "Clay Berry's warehouse is on fire. That was Bobby Franklin."

"Jeez," Xavier's mouth dropped. "The water will turn to ice. Oh, Jesus. Guys, I've got to get down there."

"Is he insured with you?" Shaker asked.

"Yes. Maybe we can help get stuff out of the warehouse."

Shaker turned to Lorraine. He had planned to make supper for her and Sari, just to prove he could. "Lorraine, I'd better go." Then he asked Sister, "Will you take Lorraine and Sari home?"

"Of course. Then I'll come down."

"No." Shaker's voice deepened. "I mean it, boss. We need you in one piece. I'll call you."

Tedi called Edward on her cell, then she, too, left.

Driving down the snowy road, Lorraine asked, "Sister, would you mind taking me back to the farm? Alice is home, so she'll be able to feed her cats and chickens. Shaker will be exhausted when he gets back. I'll fix supper."

"I don't mind a bit. It's a wonderful idea." She was grateful Clay had brought her her silver fox fur coat. In the great scheme of life, that coat was a paltry thing, but she loved it. It's funny how one becomes attached to objects. Big Ray bought her that coat for her fiftieth birthday.

"I hope they can stop the fire. There's so much in those warehouses," Lorraine fretted.

"Let's hope it's in one of the small satellite buildings. Poor Clay." Sister felt a creeping dread, but she attributed it to the fact that she'd just driven past Hangman's Ridge. In this tempestuous weather, she thought she heard a howling from atop the ridge. The wind plays tricks on you like that sometimes.

CHAPTER 23

Flames shot into the night sky, an eerie sight with snow falling. The heat was so intense that Shaker and Xavier couldn't get within fifty yards of the small brick building.

As the firemen worked in both bitter cold and searing heat, Shaker found Sheriff Ben Sidell. "Sheriff, anything I can do?"

"No. They've contained it. Thanks to George's quick thinking, they saved the big warehouse," Ben said, referring to Fire Chief George Murtagh.

"Bad night for it."

Ben pulled the collar of his coat up higher around his neck. "Don't guess there's ever a good one. They keep coating the big warehouse with water on this side; ices right up and then melts again. Weird."

"Any idea?"

"No, George said he won't know much of anything until he can get the fire out. The building passed inspection, but the wiring is old. All it takes is one mouse to bite the wrong set of wires." Ben stared at the men holding the hose. "You know, it's warmer nights I dread the most. There are more fights, stabbings, and murders in summer when it's so bloody hot out. I know if I get a call on a bitterly cold night, someone's kerosene stove blew up or someone hit a patch of black ice." He sighed. "Either way, usually someone's dead."

"You can smell the furniture burning." Shaker wrinkled his nose.

"This one closest to the railroad tracks has furniture being shipped out. Clay said it was loaded. Next shipment was Tuesday."

"Anything I can do for you?"

Ben's eyebrows rose for a moment. "No. Thanks for asking."

Shaker walked over to Clay and Xavier.

"Sorry, Clay."

"Shaker." Clay's eyes welled up. "Thank you for coming on down."

"X and I kind of hoped we could pull stuff out."

Clay shook his head. "Wooden crates, wooden furniture, upholstery, *pffft*." He threw up his gloved hands. The furniture and valuables had been packed in wooden crates.

"Sister wanted to come down, but I told her to go home."

This made Clay's eyes tear up again. "God bless her."

"Is there anything I can do?" Shaker asked.

"No." Clay shook his head. "This stuff will smolder for days."

"Izzy okay?" X asked.

"Crying her eyes out. I told her we'd be fine."

X's deep voice deepened more. "There will be a lot of upset people, but we'll do all we can. As soon as I can, I will cut a check to replace the building. I don't anticipate problems with the carrier. They'll send someone down, but that's protocol these days."

"You know, I'm not there yet." Clay bit his lip. "I'm glad you are, but I can't think that far ahead."

"Don't worry." X meant it. He was a successful man because he backed up his word. He really did care about the people who insured through him.

As Shaker walked back to the truck, the wind shifted slightly in his direction. Tiny red and gold sparks flew upwards as white flakes fell down. He inhaled smoke carrying the unmistakable odor of flesh. He'd smelled that once before as a young man. An old house had burned down, its owner having fallen asleep in bed with a lit cigarette.

He returned to Ben.

"Ben, there's meat in that building."

Ben raised his eyebrows. "Come with me." Shaker led Ben to where he had picked up the scent; the wind was still blowing in that direction. "Take a deep breath and you'll cough. Smoke burns the hell out of your throat."

Ben inhaled, coughed, but he smelled it. "Wonder if Clay had any kind of refrigeration unit in there."

"Talk to George first. I mean, that's what I'd do."

Ben nodded. "You're right."

Ben headed toward the busy fire chief as Shaker climbed into the old Chevy, turned over the motor and sat to let the engine run a minute. If anyone was in there, he or she were burned to a crisp. Who would be in the storage house? He hoped it was a raccoon. A big one might give off a powerful odor if killed or burned.

Shaker headed out of town. He called Sister on his phone, installed in the truck.

Sister asked, "You okay?"

"Nothing for me to do. Clay's holding up. X's real calm. That helps him, I guess. Ben sent me home." Shaker listened to the crackle on the phone as he drove through a patch of bad reception.

"Strange. When I drove by Hangman's Ridge, I—" She stopped herself. "Well, that place sometimes presages bad tidings."

"See another ghost?" This was not said in jest, for once she had seen a ghost there. A year later, he had, too, even though he hated to admit it.

The souls who had been hanged on the huge oak on top of the ridge, sent to justice since the early eighteenth century, were unquiet. Many had seen or heard them; even Inky skirted the place if she could. Being a fox, her senses were far keener than a human's. She had seen more than one ghost—all men—necks unnaturally stretched.

"I just heard howling, but it's windy. Picking up."

"Yeah."

"Oh, uh, forgot what I was going to say." She hadn't actually, merely changed her mind.

"Alzheimer's?"

"Halfzimers," she fired back as she hung up.

She had been going to ask him if he wanted her to bring Sari up to the main house so he could be alone with Lorraine. Then she realized the supper was a surprise, and, also, Sari looked up to Shaker. Removing her from the picture wouldn't be fair. If romance was going to blossom, there was time for that. Sister didn't have to put a log on the fire. She repented of that image the moment she thought it.

C H A P T E R   2 4

After that Sunday's church service many hunt club members gathered at the grand, modern Berry residence. Clay's wife, Izzy, graciously met everyone at the door and invited them in. Despite their travails, she served coffee, tea, cakes, and cookies.

Betty, who used to think Izzy was nothing but a gold digger, actually warmed to her thanks to this ordeal.

The dreadful news, depressing everyone, concerned the charred body found in the burned storage unit. Shaker spared people the details of his picking up the scent. Ben Sidell also kept his cards close to his chest.

The situation was distressful enough without people hearing what a burned corpse looks and smells like. The corpse at the morgue would be, they hoped, identified through dental records. Dr. Larry Hund was usually called to solve any mysteries involving teeth.

Marty, balancing cup and saucer, leaned over to whisper to Tedi, "Does Clay have enemies who hate him enough to commit arson?"

"It would appear he does," the elegant Tedi responded, the Hapsburg sapphire gleaming on her third finger.

"Awful." Marty shook her head.

Sam Lorillard briefly paid his respects. Knowing how close Clay and Xavier were, he didn't stay more than fifteen minutes.

Gray, always a calming presence, brought the hostess a mimosa. So busy tending her guests, she'd forgotten herself. Sister watched him, blushing slightly when he smiled at her.

Dr. Dalton Hill was there, which made Sister warm a little to him. As he was getting to know people better, he became less stiff. The fact that he expressed sympathy for a hunt member, new though he was, impressed her. Foxhunters should stick together.

Walter, five inches taller than Ben Sidell, leaned on the fireplace mantel to the right of the fire screen. He asked the sheriff, "Gaston working?"

"Mmm." Ben nodded that the county coroner was on the case, then took a step away from the fireplace to get away from the heat.

"Pathologists always have the right answer—a day late," Walter said with a rueful smile, stepping away with Ben.

"Not your thing, Doc?"

"No. I like contact with people. I want to help. We live in such a cynical age, probably, it sounds corny, but I genuinely want to help and heal."

Ben smiled up at him. "Me, too."

"Neither of us will ever run out of business," Walter replied.

"Gentlemen, may I intrude?" Sorrel Buruss joined them.

"You're anything but an intrusion." Walter bowed slightly to the lovely widow, now cresting over that forty-year barrier.

"Xavier's been so tireless. On the phones half the night, this morning. The investigation for the carrier, Worldwide Security, is flying down from Hartford tomorrow. X wants Clay to get up and running as fast as he can."

"X is a good man to have in your corner," Ben agreed. His cell phone beeped. "Excuse me." He walked away from the group and listened intently. "Thanks, Gaston. I'll be right down." Then he returned to Walter and Sorrel. "Walter, would you like to come on down to the lab with me?"

Walter knew what he meant. "Of course."

Sorrel knew, too. Prudently, she asked no questions but observed the reactions of others as the sheriff and Walter left together.

One by one, the well-wishers left.

Sister—Rooster and Raleigh in the truck front seat—drove home. The plowed roads remained slick in spots. The sun shone, and the whiteness dazzled.

Not a churchgoer, although she grew up an Episcopalian, nature was Sister's church. Looking at the mirrored ponds, ice overtop, the dancing tiny rainbows glittering on snow- and frost-covered hills, the churning clear beauty of Broad Creek as it swept under Soldier Road—these things gave her a deep faith, an unshakeable belief in a Higher Power, or Powers. Sister wasn't fussy about monotheism or the intellectual comforts of dogma. To see such beauty, to observe a fox in winter coat, to inhale the sharp tang of pine as one rode fast underneath, to listen to Athena call in the night, to feel the earth tight underneath giving way to a bog festooned with silver, black, and beige shrubs shorn of raiment, such things convinced her that life was divine.

Even later when Walter called to inform her that the still unidentified corpse had not died of smoke inhalation, her faith in God's work remained undiminished. Of all God's creations, the human was the failure. Still, she hoped, in good moments, that with effort and a dismantling of grotesque ego, we might join the rest of nature in a chorus of appreciation for life itself.

She fed the dogs and put a bowl of flakey tuna on the counter for Golly.

"Pussycat, would you kill another cat for tuna?"

Golly, purring, lifted her head, small bits of red tuna in her whiskers. *"No. I'd box his ears though."*

Sister stroked Golly's silken fur as the cat devoured the treat.

Then she slipped on her old Barbour coat over a down vest and walked outside. The sun set so early in the winter, the long red slanting rays reaching from west to east over the rolling meadows. Her horses nickered as she passed. She looked at the broodmare, Secretary's Shorthand, wishing the animal had caught. Secretary looked bigger than usual, but the vet had done an ultrasound two weeks after breeding, and again five weeks after the breeding. It seemed she was not in foal. But sometimes ultrasound doesn't give the right information. Horses can fool people. Secretary was a muscular, good-looking chestnut, and Sister desperately wanted a foal from her.

She rapped on Shaker's door.

"I know it's you," he called.

" 'Tis."

"I don't want any. I gave at the church today." He opened the door, then noticed her face. "What?"

"Shaker, the burned body's cause of death was not smoke inhalation. He was dead before the flames got him but they aren't certain yet just what happened."

"Come on in."

The two sat. Neither could imagine what was going on. After exhausting all theories, Sister brought up Tuesday's hunt. It was to be held at Melton, a charming old farm.

"If the wind is up, I say we make a beeline for the hollow. If not, let's draw counterclockwise. What do you think?"

He stretched his muscular legs. "If I draw counterclockwise, from the house, you mean from the house, right?"

"Right."

"We'll go down the farm road and then turn right. Well, that meadow is pretty open, gets the morning sun. Could get lucky. Courting time." He loved fox breeding season.

"I noticed."

"Don't start. We're just friends."

"That's what they all say." Her voice was warm. "I'm glad you have someone you can talk to, enjoy."

"Sari's a great kid. Wants to learn everything about the hounds." This was the way to Shaker's heart, as well as Sister's. "And Lorraine knows some of the girls by name now. At first, Lorraine wouldn't touch a hound. She was too timid, but now she goes right in. Too bad Peter Wheeler's not still with us. If she could have gotten in the truck with Peter, I think she would have learned more than if she was riding."

"Boy, that's the truth."

"Oh, that ass Crawford called me. Says we need a fly-spray system in the kennels for summer and he'll pay for it. Jesus, boss, why'd you let him be president?"

"Because if I didn't, the club would split into two factions concerning a joint-master. The larger faction would be against him, the smaller one for him, and you and I would be well acquainted with the misery." She paused. "Leave the politics to me, Shaker. My job is to kiss toads and turn them into princes."

He wrinkled his nose. "You're right. You're right. I would never do it."

"What you do, you do better than anyone else. So what did you say? I hope you were civil."

"You'd have been proud of me. I said, word for word, 'Crawford, thank you for the offer. You do so much for the club. But the chemicals will be bad for the hounds' noses. That's why we have those big ceiling fans everywhere, keeps turning the air, and we don't have too much of a fly problem.' That's it, verbatim. How can people hunt and not know anything about a hound's nose?" He clapped his hands together.

"Because they hunt for other reasons, and that's fine. In any hunt field, and I don't give a damn what hunt it is, you can count on your fingers the people who have hound sense. Those are the ones who get the most out of hunting, I'm convinced."

He dropped his arms over the overstuffed chair arms. "I was worried when Sybil came on board that she wouldn't have hound sense, even though she can ride like a demon. But she's stepped up to the plate. Give her one more year. Still makes some stupid mistakes out there. I've got to break her of going after one hound if the hound splits off, which thankfully doesn't happen too often. I don't know why it's so hard for someone to recognize the pack comes first."

"She'll get it. On the other hand, there's Betty Franklin, a natural. And who would have thought years ago when, in desperation, we asked her to help us just because she had the time? Betty wasn't even that good a rider, but by God, she worked on it."

His eyes lit up. "I thought you were crazy. But you know, I watched her in the summer on hound walks. We were lucky we had that summer together. We knew Big Ray wasn't going to be with us much longer, and he was a damned good whipper-in, despite his ego." Shaker crossed one leg over the other. "Gave Betty time, and she really showed me a lot. She knew to get around them instead of going after them if a puppy squirted out, and the thing that impressed me the most, the most," he slapped the chair arms, "she could read their body language."

"You're born with it. I believe that. Like a sense of direction. You're born with it. One can be taught the basics, but some people come into this world with more. I don't know what we'd do without Betty."

"Rock solid."

"Well, you know how I feel about whippers-in. If I have to hear them, something's wrong. Nothing worse than hearing some fool rate hounds, crack whips, and charge around like a bronc rider." She grimaced.

"Boss, sometimes you have to hear them."

"Not much."

He smiled. "We're on the same page. The best staff work is like the best team in any sport. They make it look easy."

These two friends and coworkers talked for two more hours about hunting, hounds, other great hunts they admired. Left alone, their shared passion ignited and reignited ideas, thoughts, and much laughter.

CHAPTER 25

Plan your hunt, then hunt your plan. Every master and huntsman has heard this advice. Of course, the fox could care less. A good huntsman adjusts to the curves thrown by that prescient fox. An even better master doesn't criticize when the hunt is over.

Tuesday, a small field followed hounds at Melton, a new fixture southwest of what the Jefferson Hunt called the "home territory." Wealthy new people, eager to make a good showing, spent a great deal of money rehabbing the old place. Many jokingly called Melton "Meltdown" behind their backs. The attractive owners, Anatole and Beryle Green, in their late thirties, rode today with Hilltoppers.

The small field kept moving.

Shaker knew he'd drawn over a fox in heavy covert, but he couldn't push the creature out. When first hunting hounds as a young man, he would have wasted far too much time trying to bolt the fox. Wise in the ways of his quarry and hunting, he now kept moving.

Half the D young entry hunted this morning. The other young entry stayed at home. They'd go on Thursday if conditions looked promising.

Sister, Tedi, Edward, Walter, Crawford, Marty, Sam, Gray, Dalton, and Ronnie composed First Flight. Bobby Franklin had only three people. Izzy Berry rode with Bobby to give herself a break from the crisis. Clay would be out next hunt, she said.

The temperature hovered in the low forties, the footing—slick on top, still frozen underneath—kept the riders alert and wary. What made this Tuesday difficult, apart from footing, was the strange stillness. Not a flicker of breeze moved bare tree limbs. As frost melted on the branches, the droplets hung like teardrops.

St. Just, the large crow, flew overhead. His hunting range covered half the county, less to do with the food supply than his relentless nosiness. Unlike Athena and Bitsy, St. Just rarely swooped down on prey. He would alight and walk on the ground, his gait rocking him from side to side. He'd pick up in his long beak anything that looked delicious. If taste disappointed, he'd drop the offending item. Most country people put out seed for birds in winter. He visited those feeders that he felt contained the better grade of seeds, thistle, tiny bits of dried fruit. One kind soul even put out desiccated grasshoppers.

One of St. Just's distinguishing features, apart from his vibrantly blue-black coat, was his burning hatred of foxes, and of all those foxes, Target had earned his special venom after killing St. Just's mate.

The crow alighted on a drooping, naked, weeping cherry branch, an ornamental tree flourishing at the edge of the covert, thanks to a bird eating the seeds of another cherry tree miles away, then depositing them here.

"*Cora, Cora,*" he cawed. "*Visiting red heading back to Mill Ruins. He crossed the old retaining walls at the pump house.*" Having said that, he lifted to higher altitudes.

Diana, hearing this, asked Cora, *"If we don't get there soon, the scent will be gone."*

Young Diddy asked, *"Why can't we just run over there?"*

"Because Shaker, Betty, Sybil, and Sister will think we're rioting. We have to find a way to swing Shaker to our right," Cora informed her.

"Oh." Diddy now had another rule to remember. This hunting stuff was complicated.

"Well, we can feather, but not open and move that way," Diana sensibly suggested. *"We aren't lying. We aren't rioting. We haven't opened. Once we pick up the scent, then we can open. Shaker will never know. Humans can't smell a thing."*

"Hmm." Cora considered this, then spoke, low, to the pack. *"Follow Diana and me. Feather. St. Just swears a red isn't far, moving east from the pump house. I think this is our only hope of a run today. Don't open unless you really smell fox. Dragon, did you hear me?"*

Indignant, Dragon snapped, *"I do not babble."*

"Well, you do everything else," Cora snapped right back, then put her nose down. *"Follow me. We have to move quickly. Noses down, of course, and feather. It will give Sister and Shaker confidence."*

Darby, nose down, whispered to Asa, *"Is it true, really true, that humans can't smell?"*

" 'Fraid it is, son. Can't run either. Now if the scent is strong, mating scent, and it's a warm day, the scent can rise up, then even a human can catch it. Of course, by then it's over our head, so it won't be a good day's hunting."

Doughboy, ears slightly lifted, questioned, *"But if they can't smell, how do they survive?"*

Ardent supplied the answer. *"Totally dependent on their eyes. Their ears used to be okay, but the last two generations of humans, according to Shaker, have lost thirty percent of their hearing or worse before forty, which is like six or seven years for us."*

"Why?" Delight couldn't imagine such a thing: no nose and bum ears.

"Decibel levels. They've destroyed their hearing by turning up rock music, rap music. Just fritzes 'em right out." Delia could see they were nearly out of the heavy covert. The pump house was up ahead. *"Don't worry about humans. Worry about getting a line. If we can run a fox on a day like today, young one, we'll be covered in glory."*

Dragon bumped Dasher. His brother, outraged, snarled and bumped him hard right back. Dragon bared his teeth.

"Settle!" Cora commanded.

Neither dog hound would be so foolish as to cross the queen of the pack. She wouldn't hesitate to take them down, and Asa and Ardent would be right with her. The two angry brothers would then sport more holes than Swiss cheese.

Diddy, hearing the snarls, swerved to the right. Although young, she couldn't help but push up front with her marvelous drive and good speed. Heartening as this was to observe, Cora kept her eye on the gyp. In her first year, it would be easy for her to make mistakes. But Diddy couldn't keep herself in the middle of the pack where she'd be carried along by the tried and true hounds.

However, at this moment, Diddy's drive and position saved the day. She moved forty yards from the pack. Sybil on the right noticed this, carefully moving ahead of the hound in case she needed to push Diddy back. Anticipation is half the game. If you can prevent a hound from squirting out, it's far better than searching for the hound if she doesn't come back to the horn. And it's a foolish whipper-in who abandons the whole pack to turn one errant hound. Sybil also read Diddy's body language; the youngster wasn't going to bolt.

Suddenly Diddy stopped, rigid, her stern straight up in the air, nose glued to the ground not five yards from the crumbling stone retaining wall.

"What do I do? What do I do?" Diddy thought to herself. *"If I'm wrong, Cora will let me have it, but . . . but fox, this is a fox!"* She took a deep breath, her nostrils filling with the fading but unmistakable

scent of a red dog fox pungent in courting perfume. Working up her courage, she said in a faltering voice, *"Fox."* Then she spoke with a bit more authority. *"Fox, fading line."*

Cora lifted her head, raced to the young hound, put her nose down. Under her breath she praised Diddy, *"Good work. It's Clement, a young red."* Then she kept her nose down and spoke in her sonorous voice, *"Get on it. Fading fast!"*

The pack flew to Cora, opening as they trotted on the line. They crossed the other retaining wall, found the line again, and kept moving, not running flat out as scent was too thin. Better to keep it under nose than pick up speed, overrun, or lose it altogether. The hounds understood scent.

Sister might not be able to smell squat, but she knew to trust her hounds. Aztec pricked his ears, his own nostrils widening. He wanted to run.

"Steady," Sister said in a low voice.

"But I know they're on!" Aztec trembled.

Sam, on the new timber horse, Cloud Nine, realized he was going to need a tight seat if they took off. Tedi, hearing the snorting behind her, and possessing a keen sense of self-preservation, reined in for a second as Sam passed. No point in getting run over. She just hoped Sam wouldn't be on a runaway. Even the best of jockeys endure that at one time or another.

Once on the far side of an overgrown meadow, not yet tidied up by the Greens because it was far from the house, Nellie paused. Two scent trails crossed. Both were fox. If she called out, the youngsters might come up, get confused. She made an executive decision, pushed straight ahead on the stronger line, believing it was Clement's. If not, the humans would never know the difference.

A few yards from the convergence of scents, she let out a deep, deep holler. *"Heating up. Come on!"* Then she moved up from a brisk trot to a long, loping ground-covering run.

Sister and Aztec, happy to be moving out, kept the hounds in sight. Usually Sister would be a tad closer, but the footing was going from bad to worse.

A simple in and out, two coops placed across from each other in parallel fence lines, beckoned. Aztec hit the first perfectly, which meant the second was effortless. He didn't have to add a stride or take off early. Sister loved this young thoroughbred's sense of balance; he knew where his hooves were, which can't be said of every horse. He might do something a little stupid because he was still green, but he was smooth and careful.

Everyone made it over the coops, while Bobby Franklin lost ground opening two red metal farm gates, one crooked on the hinges.

Clement, hearing hounds, knew he was still a long way from his den. He'd been so intent on visiting the vixen, he hadn't paid attention to potential hiding places should trouble appear. He put on the afterburners, hoping to put as much distance between himself and the lead hounds as he could. That would give him time to think. St. Just shadowed his every move, signaling to Cora what was going on ahead. His cawing brought out other crows, themselves no friend to foxes. Soon the sky, dotted with fourteen crows, added to the panorama of startled deer, disturbed blue jays, and extremely put-out squirrels, chattering filth as hounds, horses, and humans roared under their trees.

When a run becomes this good, the pace this fast, the hell with footing. Sister moved her hands forward, crouched down, and hoped Aztec wouldn't lose his hind end on an icy patch.

On occasion it occurred to her that she could die in the hunt field. She didn't much mind, though she hoped it wouldn't be until she'd cleared her one hundredth birthday, which she envisioned as a five-foot log jump.

From the corner of her eye, she saw Sam Lorillard struggling with Cloud Nine. He finally got the big gelding straightened out, prudently pulling him back, forcing him to follow the others. The horse, accustomed to conventional trainers, wanted to be first. If he was going to win races, he needed to be rated. This was a good time to learn.

Tedi, Edward, Walter, Dalton, and Gray kept snug in Sister's pocket. Crawford, Marty, and Sam fell farther behind with Ronnie in the middle between the two groups.

Ronnie saw Clement charge over the next hill. Hounds were far enough in front he need not worry about lifting their heads.

"Tallyho!" He hollered, taking his cap off and pointing in the direction in which the fox was traveling.

Sybil saw him, too. Sister did not, but she knew Ronnie knew his business. She pushed a little closer to the tail hounds, Delia and Asa, perhaps five yards from the main pack.

A large fallen walnut, as luck would have it, had crashed into the old coop in the next fence line. The branches fell forward of the coop so the massive trunk, its distinctive blackish bark, added a new look and height to the coop. Sister saw Shaker practically vault over it.

Aztec sucked back for an instant. Sister hit him with the spurs and clucked. Aztec knew if he refused it made for trouble behind him, but this jump might bite. *Well, it looks funny,* the horse grumbled before sailing over.

Behind, Cora and Dragon with Dasher and Diana couldn't see the fox.

"You'll chop him!" St. Just screamed with triumph.

Clement's normal arrogance evaporated. He now ran for his life, running for the covert up ahead. Maybe he could foul his scent in there somehow.

He made it, flying by a pile of dirt about eighteen inches high. Farther into the underbrush, thinned by the weight of the snows and frosts now, he smelled a cache of deer meat.

He was smack in the home territory of a female mountain lion. A cave or rock den had to be close by. If he could find it, he'd duck in. Better to face one lone female than a pack of hounds.

He didn't worry about young. Usually lion cubs are born midsummer.

As luck would have it, a huge rock formation in a slight swale of forest jutted out ahead. He leapt into the opening, large enough for the mountain lion and therefore large enough for hounds, one by one.

Awakened by the cry of the pack, the mature lioness weighed a well-fed two hundred pounds. She was just rising when the medium-size red fellow, all of seven pounds, invaded her home.

Panting, he looked up at her, crooning in his best voice, *"How beautiful you are!"*

Vanity is not limited to the human species. She blinked. *"And who are you?"*

"Clement of Mill Ruin, son of Target and Charlene, their second litter from last year. I confess, I've ducked in here to save my skin, but I had no idea I would find such a beautiful mountain lion. How could I have missed you? I thought I knew everyone."

"My hunting range doesn't overlap yours. Game is so good down here, I and some of my relatives came down out of the mountains. And . . ." She stopped a moment; the fur on her neck rose slightly. *"Impertinent slaves!"* she said of the barking hounds.

Before the words were out of her mouth, Dragon blasted into the cave. He skidded to a halt as both the lioness and Clement stared at him.

The rest of the pack piled in after Dragon, except for Cora, Diana, Dasher, Asa, and Delia. They knew what was in there.

Even Cora couldn't stop the young entry.

Enraged at this trespassing, the lioness stood. She could leap twenty feet without undue effort. She bared her fangs, emitting a hiss. *"Get out!"*

Clement, too, bared his fangs, puffing himself up as best he could.

Shaker dismounted, handing Hojo's reins to Betty. Sister didn't know if a bear was in there or a mountain lion. She'd been running so hard she'd missed the telltale signs, the piles of dirt kicked up by the big cat's hind legs to mark her boundaries, the slash marks on the trees much higher than those of a bobcat.

She couldn't hear the hiss because the hounds were bellowing.

Shaker pulled out his .38. He didn't want to kill any animal, but he had to protect his pack.

He put his horn to his mouth and blew the three long blasts. The smarter hounds turned to emerge from the opening, one by one. Shaker quieted them. Dragon, alone, remained inside. The hissing could now be plainly heard followed by a terrifying growl.

Hojo was brave, but shaking like a leaf. Mountain lions and horses rarely formed friendships. Hojo wanted out of there.

Outlaw, a little older and a quarter horse, said, *"Hojo, Shaker's a good shot. If he has to, he'll kill the lion. We're safe."*

Hojo rolled his eyes. *"They're so quick."*

"Dragon, come to me." Shaker called outside the opening.

Hackles up, Dragon slowly, without taking his eyes off the mountain lion, backed out. She advanced. As Dragon made it out, the big cat stuck her head out, beheld the audience, and emitted a growl that turned blood to ice water.

"Tedi, get the field back," Shaker said calmly.

"Janie, come on," Tedi firmly ordered her old friend.

"I'm not leaving my huntsman, Betty, or the hounds. Now, go on."

Reluctantly, Tedi moved the field back.

Shaker quickly mounted, not taking his eyes off the lion, who seemed content to scare the bejesus out of them.

In a steady voice, "Come on, come on, foxhounds. Good hounds." Shaker turned, trotting off.

Betty, back on Outlaw, kept on his left side. Sybil was on the right. She'd stayed a short distance from the den in case hounds bolted. As Shaker and Betty had been on foot, this was a prudent decision.

Sister watched the mountain lion, whom she faced at a distance of thirty yards. She wanted to make certain the animal wasn't going to chase them. She cursed herself for not carrying a gun. A mountain lion can bring down a deer at a full run. If the deer has enough of a head start, it will outrun the lion, but for a short distance, the speed of the mountain lion is startling. This powerful animal could easily bound up to one of the staff horses and attack. Sweat ran down her back and between her breasts.

"Let's get out of here." Sister turned Aztec as the pack drew alongside her. They continued to trot. She glanced over her shoulder to see the beautiful cat still standing in her doorway, now a red fox sitting next to her.

Dragon, not a scratch on him, bragged, *"I denned the fox. I stared down the mountain lion."*

"Idiot!" Cora cursed. *"You could have killed half this pack."*

"But I didn't," he sassed.

That fast Cora turned, seized Dragon by the throat, sank her fangs into him, and threw him down hard. He fought back.

"Leave it! Leave it!" Shaker commanded.

Cora leapt up. Dragon, too, quickly got to his feet, blood trickling down his white bib.

"I will kill you one day if you don't listen," Cora growled low, almost a whisper.

The young entry, frightened of the lioness and blindly following Dragon, were now scared to death of Cora. They avoided eye contact with the head bitch.

"The fox was in the den!" Dragon coughed.

"Yes, he was," Asa sagely replied. *"Scent was hot, so hot none of us paid attention to the other scent. But, Dragon, when we reached those rocks, even a human could smell the lion. You were wrong."*

"My job is to chase foxes, put them to ground, kill them if I catch them." Dragon coughed again. Cora had hurt his throat.

Cora whirled on the handsome dog hound. *"Do you want me to shred you right now? I don't care if I do get the butt end of a whip!"*

Dragon shut up.

The pack trotted all the way back to Melton. Everyone had had quite enough for one day.

As Sister dismounted, she noticed Dalton, on the ground already, holding the reins of his horse as well as the reins of Izzy's horse. She properly dismounted, stepping high a few times as her cold feet stung when she touched the earth.

Dalton slipped a halter over Izzy's mount, then over his own horse's head. There was nothing improper in their exchange, yet there was a tension, an electricity.

Later, propped up on three large pillows, down comforter drawn up, a fire crackling in the bedroom fireplace, Sister had two American Kennel Club dog books, one from 1935 with the breed standards corrected to 1941 and the latest from 1997.

Few foxhunters showed their hounds at AKC events. Foxhunting was a life's work. Showing bench dogs was, too. Who had time for both? A foxhunter must breed a *pack* of solid, intelligent, good hounds. The show dog person need breed only *one* outstanding specimen, though as any show dog person can tell you, that's a life's work, too. The show people load their charges in minivans or big SUVs to travel around the country securing points toward their dog's championship.

Sister didn't consider bench shows empty beauty contests unless the breed, any breed, had fallen away dramatically from its original purpose. Irish setters came to mind. Today's gorgeous mahogany creatures striding in front of judges often diverged sharply from the Irish setters used in the field.

Fortunately, English and American foxhounds never achieved the popularity in the bench show world that cocker spaniels, German shepherds, collies, Labradors, and others did. Foxhounds remained relatively consistent. The breed standard in her revised 1941 book proved no different from the one in 1997, except she thought the 1941 version easier to read.

The first American foxhound registered with the American

Kennel Club was Lady Stewart in 1886. The photographs in each AKC volume displaying the American foxhound further confirmed the consistency in the breed standard. Hounds from her kennel looked like the two examples except they had scars from thorns; some, her D's, had a broader skull than was deemed just right.

For a foxhunter, their shows, none of them associated with the AKC, took place all over the country, culminating in the Virginia Hound Show at Morven Park, Leesburg, the last weekend in May. Over a thousand hounds were shown, the ultimate for many being the pack class, a test unimaginable in the show bench world. A pack of hounds, led on foot by their huntsman, usually with two whippers-in, negotiated a course. The pack that operated as a pack, exemplifying the old expression "You could throw a blanket over them," usually won. And beauty counted. Those packs where the individuals most resembled one another had a better chance than those where a small lemon-and-white hound worked with a big tricolor and some Talbot tans. Nonetheless, a good pack was a good pack even if Goliath and David ran together. If David could keep up and Goliath didn't poop out early, a master could be very proud. But even to a casual observer, a pack of uniform size and conformation had a better chance of hanging together than one with variety.

Sister knew, as did all who breed seriously, that it ultimately comes down to their minds. The most beautiful hound in the world is worthless if he or she won't hunt. The hound with the most drive in the world is useless if he or she won't listen, if he or she wasn't "biddable."

Sister's task was to breed an entire team of such outstanding individuals. Each year, this team would change: old hounds needed to retire, young hounds needed to learn the business and settle into their position. She could never rest on her laurels, but she could take justifiable pride in her pack.

Which is why she continued to study AKC shows, read and reread the standards, hunt behind other packs, whether American,

English, Crossbred, or Penn-Marydels, as well as enjoy the deep music of the night hunters, casting their Walker, Trigg, Maupin, or Birdsong hounds.

A good hound was a good hound.

She loved hunting with Ashland bassets, learning each time that pack pushed out its quarry, each time a whipper-in quietly melted nearer to a covert to keep an eye on a young entry.

Virginia abounded in beagle packs: from Mrs. Fout's pack, where one must be mounted and escorted by a child, to the more common type of packs, where one followed on foot.

When the opportunity arose, Sister was there, following, boots often squishing with mud, face torn by thorns. She didn't feel a thing. The sounds of a pack in full cry spiked her adrenaline to such a pitch that she usually didn't know she was bleeding until someone pointed it out to her back at the trailers.

Anyone who knew Jane Arnold knew she loved hounds. She'd go out with coon hunters and adored the sleek black-and-tan coonhounds, redbone hounds, even the ponderous bloodhound, king of all dogdom in terms of scenting ability. There was no hound on earth from which a foxhunter couldn't profit by observing. Even dachshunds left to their own devices will return to their original purpose, which was to hunt quarry in dens. The dachshund packed a great deal of courage in that elongated body.

Sister, every three years or so, would make the pilgrimage to the Westminster Dog Show in New York City. Much as she liked watching all the breeds, her heart having a special place for Irish terriers and corgis—dogs she had had as pets in her lifetime—it was the hounds that enraptured her. Every year, like other hound people, she would pray it wouldn't be one more prancing poodle, one more adorable terrier that this year would carry off the coveted Best in Show, that it would be a hound.

But hounds aren't bred to show and prance. They're bred to hunt. The qualities that appeal to show judges are rather insulting to a hound. His or her job is to put that nose to the ground and find the quarry, or, if a sight hound, to catch a glimpse of quarry and give rousing chase. Intelligence, determination, a beautiful stride, and marvelous lung capacity—such treasures may be overlooked by the judges as yet another fetching cairn, jaunty Scottie, or Standard poodle in full French cut paraded out like an actor greedy for applause. The hound doesn't want applause; it wants the fox, the rabbit, the otter, the raccoon.

Year after year, Sister, like so many other devoted hound people, watched unbelievable specimens in the hound category be overlooked in the final showdown. Disappointed, angry, she'd return to the Carlyle Hotel, vowing never again to waste her money by coming back to Westminster. Of course, she didn't outwardly display this anger, but to see once again the best of the hound group—a group now of twenty-two breeds—get passed by was too much!

The hound group in 1941 contained seventeen breeds. It had expanded over the decades, although not as much as other groups. That didn't bother her. After all, each time a new breed is accepted by the AKC, it's more money for them. She didn't begrudge them that, even though some of the groups were so large one needed a No-Doz to sit through them.

No, she begrudged the prejudice against hounds.

"Godammit!" She threw the 1997 book on the floor. She picked up the older edition, much thumbed over the years, smoothing down the old spine before placing it on the nightstand.

Rooster, startled, barked, *"What's the matter with her?"*

"Westminster's coming up, first week of February, I think." Raleigh chortled. *"We'll watch it on TV together. You won't believe what will come out of her mouth. She gets so exercised, we can't let anyone else watch it with her, except for Betty and Tedi. They know her so well and love her so much, if she loses her temper and cusses a blue streak, they'll laugh. Most people have no idea how passionate our mother is."*

"She has to keep a lid on it because she's the Big Cheese," Golly, on her back next to Sister, added.

"True," Rooster agreed.

"Golly, Sister doesn't go to cat shows. That's proof she likes dogs better than cats," Raleigh slyly said.

"Balls. Why go to a cat show? Every single cat is perfect, the crown of creation. The fun of a dog show is seeing the imperfections in you miserable canines."

"How do you stand her?" Rooster whispered.

"By tormenting her." Raleigh giggled.

"Furthermore, no cat in the universe is going to walk down a green carpet, stand on a table, and let some stranger inspect her fangs. Ridiculous. Why, I'd sink my fangs in the fat part of that silly judge's thumb in a skinny minute."

"Oh, you scare me." Raleigh rolled his brown eyes. *"I've got your catnip mousie, the one covered with rabbit fur. Thought I'd swallow it."* Raleigh put the little mousie in his mouth, fake tail dangling out.

"Thief!" Golly vaulted off the bed.

Raleigh just turned his head from side to side as Golly tried to get her mousie. Her stream of abuse reached such a pitch that Sister put down the more calming book she was reading, a reexamination of the Punic Wars.

"All right, Raleigh, give her the toy. Don't be ugly." She turned on her side, opened the drawer in the nightstand, and took out two greenies: little green bones made in Missouri. "Here." She tossed one to Raleigh and one to Rooster.

Raleigh dropped the mousie to grab the greenie. Golly snatched up the soggy toy, leapt back up on the bed, and batted it around for good measure.

"You know, Golly, today is Mozart's birthday in Salzburg, 1756." Sister could remember dates. "Hmm, also the day of the cease-fire in Vietnam, 1972. A good day, I would suppose, January twenty-seventh." She noticed the cat taking the toy, pulling back a corner of the pillow, and shoving it underneath.

"He won't find it there, the big creep."

Sister laughed, watching the cat. She abruptly stopped. "A

cache. I didn't notice the caches today. Like you, Golly, the big cat kept a kind of pantry. Don't see too many of the mountain lions. I wasn't looking for the signs, but foxes do the same thing, smaller scale." She picked up the book, then let it fall in her lap. "My God, I'm a dolt."

"Now what?" Rooster's voice was garbled as he was chewing.

"A cache. The storage unit is a cache. Storage houses like that don't just burn down. People don't set fires to them to see the flames." She looked at the animals, who were now looking at her. "But I don't get it. What's being hidden in that cache? What could be worth that kind of violence? And to whom? Clay? Xavier? Both? Who was found burned? I don't get it."

"Well, you'd better keep your mouth shut until you do," Golly rudely but wisely said.

CHAPTER 26

In small towns, people notice one another. Tedi Bancroft would have lunch with Marty Howard. Someone would notice. Word would spread. Not that this is a bad thing, but it can lead to that great Olympic sport: people jumping to conclusions.

Then, too, there is a certain type of personality who lives by the motto "There is no problem that can't be blown out of proportion." The media is filled with just such personalities, but they thrive even among other segments of the population.

Knowing that, Sister asked Ben Sidell to swing by the farm sometime Wednesday. If seen together in town, any number of scenarios would have been bandied about.

The two sat chatting in the library.

"That was my first thought," Ben confessed, after hearing Sister's conjecture. "Berry Storage would be the obvious place." He reached for a sandwich. "Fortunately, most people who own good silver and jewelry keep an inventory. Many now mark the items themselves in some unobtrusive spot, a number, a series of letters. If they haven't catalogued their goods, they have photographs with duplicates to the insurance agency. It's fairly easy to rip off a car and sell it. With something as unique as George II silver, it's not easy to fence. Something like that usually is going out of the country."

"What about a ritzy shop on Madison Avenue, a high-class fence?"

"We'd track it down, most likely. Now if the goods are presold, if you will, the items go directly to, say, a buyer in Seattle, we probably wouldn't find them. Sometimes you get lucky, though."

"After reading the papers about the silver thefts in Richmond, I thought . . . well, you know what I thought."

"Logical." Ben appreciated her concern. "Quite logical that antique furniture and silver could be crated and hidden at Berry Storage, shipped out, and it would all look like business as usual. Worth millions of pure profit, no taxes."

"I see." She crossed her legs. "And everything in the burned building is accounted for?"

"No. The insurance investigator from Worldwide Security is still working through what she can. What we did when we could get in there without melting the bottom of our shoes was to open the crates. The ones in the back were intact. Nothing was burned, although everything smells like smoke. We checked to see if anything was on the list of items stolen from Richmond. Nothing. Naturally, we'll work with the insurance investigator—her examination will be detailed—but I don't think Berry Storage has been a way station for this high-class theft ring."

"For the sake of argument," she uncrossed her legs, leaning forward, "if remnants of stolen silver or Chippendale chairs are found, is it possible that something like this could be done without Clay knowing about it?"

"Unlikely, but yes, it is possible."

"Or they could both be in on it . . . Clay and X. Selling stolen goods, collecting insurance on the fire."

He shrugged. "That's possible, too."

"I've wasted your time with my ideas. I was so sure I was onto something with the theft ring," she paused, "because of yesterday's hunt."

"Heard it was wild." He smiled.

"That it was, but what set my mind in motion was how my attention was so focused on the chase that I missed the danger signals, the signs of the mountain lion. I rather thought this might be the same sort of thing." She blushed.

"It might. When I get an I.D. on the body, that should help."

"I would think it would. And no one locally has been reported missing?"

He looked at her intently. "No. Think how many people live alone. If our victim was a loner, I might not get a missing-person call until his coworkers report it. If the victim doesn't have a regular job . . ." He threw up his hands. "But I'm confident we'll get a dental match soon."

"Baffling."

"Yes, it is," he agreed.

"Do you think this has anything to do with the deaths of Mitch and Tony?"

"I don't know. At this point, I don't see a connection."

"Nor do I." She put her forefingers on the sides of her temples for a second. "And yet, the warehouses aren't far from where those men lived the last part of their lives. They were throwaway labor, for lack of a better term. Perhaps they were literally thrown away."

"It's a stretch."

"I know. And I'm just running on. I don't have an ounce of evidence, but I do feel something, something disquieting, and I'm probably making too much of missing the signs after yesterday's lion hunt." She smiled slightly.

"I like having you on my team," he reassured her.

CHAPTER 27

Cold though it was, Crawford kept up with his riding. He'd go out with Fairy Thatcher, though he was beginning to prefer riding with Sam. Fairy demurred giving him advice. Sam offered guidance to him as they rode, paying special attention to Crawford's hands over a jump.

Ambition burned in the Indiana native. He desperately wanted to be a good rider. He was surrounded by people who had been riding while still in their mother's bellies. It made him all the more determined.

He and Sam entered the stables after a cold ride. They'd been going over Crawford's farm, digressing into personalities in the hunt field.

"Sam, Virginia's full of damned snobs."

"Sure it is. You can see them coming a mile away. You don't have to buy into it."

"How'd you get so smart?" Crawford had a hint of humor in his voice.

"By nearly drinking myself to death. I had to be that stupid to get smart."

Crawford's eyes narrowed. He picked up the riding crop. "Why'd you do it, if you don't mind my asking?"

"I don't. I suppose there are a lot of reasons for drinking, but no excuses. I thought I'd fill up the hollows in my life with bourbon. I wasn't a prince among men."

"Who is?"

"Peter Wheeler came pretty close. And there's my brother."

"I underestimated you, Sam. There's more to you than I thought."

"Maybe that makes two of us."

Crawford grunted. He slapped the smaller, slighter man on the back, and left for the big house. He had a lot to think about as he strode through the brisk air.

The phone rang in the tack room.

"Sam."

"Rory, how are you doing?"

"I'm doing." His voice thickened. "It's hard, man. How'd you do it?"

"One day at a time."

"But how do you live with all the shit you've done?"

"That's a bitch. Rory, you ask the people you've hurt to forgive you. If they don't, there's not much you can do about it. The hard part is forgiving yourself. And no matter what you do, there are people who will never trust you. You just go on."

"Yeah." A long pause followed. "I called to thank you for dragging my sorry ass down here."

"I was glad to do it. Hey, Rory, you hear about Berry Storage burning?"

"Don't hear nothing from home in here."

"One of the smaller buildings caught fire. Arson. Found a body inside."

"Jesus."

"I thought one of our guys might have figured out how to get in."

"Well, that's another reason I called. About Mitch and Tony. I don't know where they got what they drank, but funny you should mention Berry Storage. Sometimes Clay or Donnie Sweigert would come down and get us to help make deliveries. You did some of that?"

"Yeah, a little. We'd tote chairs to a house. About broke my back."

Well, we'd go to Lynchburg or Roanoke, even Newport News. Cities all over. I remember once we delivered an expensive desk down to Bristol."

"Yeah."

"Well, here's what I remembered. All of those odd jobs where they needed an extra pair of hands were deliveries to coaches. You know, like sports."

"I don't remember that."

"Christ, all you cared about was horses. Yeah, we'd deliver a chair to a football coach at this high school or a sofa to a college basketball coach or maybe the trainer."

"Odd."

"I might have been drunk as a skunk, but, hey, the Orioles are the world, and Tech football, bro, awesome. I pay attention to those things."

"What do you make of it?"

"I don't. Just crossed my mind."

"What about other deliveries?"

"None. Just coaches and trainers. And here's one other thing, on those runs, the ones where us scumbags were used, always the same driver: Donnie Sweigert."

"Donnie works for Berry Storage. Nothing unusual in that."

"Maybe not, but you'd think sometimes we'd pull another driver. Always Donnie."

"Huh." Sam couldn't make heads nor tails of this.

"I gotta go. They keep us pretty structured."

"Yeah, I remember."

Rory's voice, heavy with emotion, simply said, "I guess I gotta grow up."

"Grow or die."

CHAPTER 28

A thin cloud cover, like a white fishnet, covered the sky on Thursday morning. The mercury stalled out at thirty-eight degrees.

Hounds checked down by a man-made lake at Orchard Hill, the day's fixture.

As Sister waited on a rise above the lake, a froth rising off the still waters, she reflected on the past. In 1585, Sir Walter Raleigh founded the Lost Colony of Roanoke. What would Raleigh make of Virginia now?

She also wondered what those first Native Americans thought when they saw ships with billowing white sails. They must have felt curiosity and terror.

What would this lush rolling land be like four hundred years hence, could she return? Would the huntsman's horse still echo, rising up as the mist now rose at Rickyroo's hooves?

At least if Raleigh returned, he would recognize the hunt. Back then, though, they hunted in far more colorful clothing, knee-high boots turned down, revealing a soft champagne color inside. Over time, these evolved into the tan-topped formal hunt boots worn by men and some lady staff members, if the master allows the ladies to wear scarlet—still a topic of dispute among foxhunters. The flowing lace at the neck became the stock tie by the early eighteenth century. But apart from the clothing, those seventeenth-century men would know hound work, good hounds, good horses and, from all accounts, good women, as well as a surfeit of existing bad ones.

Tedi, Edward, Xavier, Ron, Gray, Jennifer, and Sari made up First Flight, the two girls allowed to ride on Thursdays. Sister had petitioned their science teacher at the high school, citing environmental studies. The teacher, an old friend, Greg Windom, agreed. After each hunt, the two students had to write up what they had observed.

This morning they observed a huge blue heron lift off from the lake when he heard the hounds, cawing raucously as he ascended.

A slow-moving creek lurched into the lake on high ground; an overflow pipe at the other end of the built-up lake flowed into that same creek some four feet below. In warmer weather, the creek was filled with five-inch stinkpot turtles: little devils, aggressive and long-necked. They'd snap at you, steal your bait if you were fishing for rockfish or even crawdaddies. Catch one and the odor made your eyes water.

Sister had taught geology at Mary Baldwin College before marrying, although her major had been what was then called the natural sciences. But Mary Baldwin had needed a geology teacher, so she voraciously read anything she could and was smart enough to go out with the guys from the U.S. Geological Survey in the area. They taught her more than anything she found in the books.

She passed on what she could to Jennifer and Sari when they asked questions, but she didn't push them. As years rolled on, Sister had ample opportunity to be thankful for her study of rock strata, soil, erosion, and such. It helped her foxhunt. People would remark that Sister had uncanny game sense. Yes and no. She had never stopped studying soils, plants, and other animals. While she realized she would never know what the fox knew, she was determined to get as close as she could.

She'd hunted most of her seven decades, starting at six on an unruly pony. She still didn't know how a fox could turn scent on and off, even though she had seen it with her own eyes. She'd seen hounds go right over a fox. Days later that same fox might put down a scorching trail for hounds.

In her wildest dreams, she prayed to Artemis to allow her to be a fox for one day and then return to her human form. Since this prayer went unanswered, she continued to read, learn from other notable foxhunters, and study her quarry. She knew her hounds, but she knew she would never truly know her foxes.

They knew her. The fox possessed a deep understanding of the human species as well as other species. The quickness of the animal's mind, its powers of judgment, and its ability continually to adapt were phenomenal. The two times a fox would lose its good judgment were when it heard the distress call of a cub, any cub, and during mating season, when the boys were lashed on by their hormones. This is not uncharacteristic of higher mammals.

One such fellow, maddened by desire, now found himself eight miles from home, smack in the middle of Orchard Hill. The hounds picked him up, then lost him at the lake.

He'd dashed around the lake, leapt straight down from the overflow pipe into the creek, and swam straight downstream until he rolled up against a newly built beaver dam. He thought about ducking under the water, coming up into the lodge, but beavers are notoriously inhospitable, even to a fox in distress. He climbed up on the dam, gathered his haunches and, soaring over to the first lodge, alighted on top. He heard the commotion inside. He hopped from lodge to lodge, finally jumping from the last one onto the land. He had outwitted everyone. Catching his breath, he enjoyed a leisurely trot home.

While the hounds cast themselves at the lake bed, Trident, an excellent nose, found a middling scent: a gray dog fox. He kept his nose down and as it warmed, he spoke very softly. Trinity, bolder than her brother and littermate, walked over.

"Line!" Trinity called out.

Cora trotted over and checked it out. *"Let's give it a try."*

The rest of the pack, eighteen couple today, joined them, although the pace was relatively slow. The American hound doesn't run with its nose stuck to the ground like glue. The animal inhales, lifts its head slightly, moves along then perhaps thirty yards later, puts its nose to the ground. As each hound is doing this, the line is well researched. And the whole point of a pack is that hounds must trust one another as well as their huntsman.

Shaker knew the line was so-so. He also knew it couldn't be the first fox they had run; the line would have been hotter, the music louder. As it was, hounds opened but never in full-throated chorus. They were more like geese, calling out flight coordinates at this moment.

But as hounds moved away from the lake, climbing to higher ground, frosty pastures still in shadows, the pace quickened. The music grew louder.

A tiger trap squatted in the three-board fence line. Shaker and Gunpowder easily popped over, the ground falling away on the landing side. They slipped a little, then the lovely thoroughbred stretched out as the hounds picked up speed. They covered the pasture, jumped a log jump into a woods filled with ancient hollies, twenty feet high, the tiny red berries enlivening the woods with endless dots of color. Called possumhaw by country people, swamp holly by newer folks, Shaker knew he'd be in a swamp soon enough. Possumhaws loved the muck.

Sister knew it, too. She also knew raccoon scent would be heavy as the coons love the berries in winter.

Hounds ran on despite the heavy odor of raccoons. The gray fox, a young one, thought the swamp would slow down his pursuers. He was right, but it also held scent. He needed to get up, get out, and fly across a meadow still untouched by the sun.

He figured this out at the end of the swamp, climbed over the slippery low banks, darted through an old pine woods, many of the Virginia pines having fallen from age, then hit the cold western meadow, revving his engine.

Gunpowder kept right up, but stumbled when he ran over flat rock in the piney woods. His right hoof skidded on the slick rock. He pitched forward, pitching Shaker with him. If a horse loses his balance or drops a shoulder, a human can rarely stay on. A cat couldn't stay perched on even with claws. Shaker shot over Gunpowder's shoulder, hitting the rock hard.

Gunpowder stopped, put his nose down on Shaker's face. *"You okay?"*

Shaker didn't move as Gunpowder stood by him.

Sister arrived within a minute. She hadn't seen the fall. Quickly she dismounted and felt for a pulse. There was one, thank God.

She lifted one eyelid. His pupil was dilated. Fearing a concussion, she hoped it wasn't worse. As for broken bones, no way to tell until he regained consciousness.

The other riders halted, watching with apprehension.

"Ron, give me your flask."

Ronnie quickly dismounted, handing his reins to Gray, and brought her his flask. He knelt beside her. She poured out a little alcohol in her hand and touched Shaker's lips with it, then rubbed it on his cheeks. Blood rushed to his face, and he flushed.

His eyes fluttered. He started to sit up, but she held him down. "Not yet."

Ronnie moved behind his head, holding it.

"Shaker, can you feel your feet?"

"Uh."

"What day is it?"

"Uh, hunting . . ."

"Can you feel your toes?"

His mind cleared a bit. He wriggled his toes in their scratched boots, polished many times. "Uh-huh."

"Can you feel your fingers?"

He wiggled his fingers in his white string gloves. "Yeah." He took a deep breath. "Ronnie, don't kiss me."

"You asshole." Ronnie laughed.

"What day is it?"

"Hunting day."

"No. What day of the week?"

"Uh . . . what happened?" He started to sit up. Ronnie and Sister let him, since nothing seemed to be broken. He winced when he took a deep breath. "Ahhh."

"Lucky it's not worse." Sister continued to kneel next to him.

"Cracked a few." His breath was a little ragged when he inhaled. "I'll tape them up."

"It will only hurt when you breathe." Ronnie stood up.

"You're a big help." Shaker wrapped his arms around his chest.

"And if you were the last man on earth, I wouldn't kiss you." Ronnie figured the best way to help him was to torment him. He was right.

"Jerk."

"Asshole."

"Gentlemen." Sister shook her head.

"Sorry," Ronnie said.

"Look, honey, you've cracked some ribs, maybe broken them. If you'd punctured a lung, we'd know; you can hear that plain as a tire hissing. But I think you've suffered a mild concussion."

"Got no brains anyway." He smiled his crooked grin, all the more appealing, given the circumstances.

"At least you admit it." Ronnie leaned over, putting his hands under Shaker's right armpit.

Sister did the same for his left. "One, two, upsy daisy."

Shaker stood up unsteadily. Both friends kept hold. He rubbed his head, the horn still in his right hand. "Jesus."

"Sister, I can call an ambulance." Xavier carried a tiny cell phone inside his frock coat.

"I'm not riding in any goddamn ambulance. I fell off. Big deal." Shaker's head throbbed. He reached for Gunpowder's reins.

"Don't even think of it." Sister took the reins instead.

"Well, someone's got to stay up with the hounds."

"Betty is there and so is Sybil. You are going to stay right here. Sari, I want you to stick with Shaker. Jennifer, ride back to the trailer, tie up your horse, drive my truck here, and then drive Shaker to Walter."

"I'm fine."

"Yes, and I'm the boss." Her words had bite. "If you don't go to Walter, as a precaution, and your damned bullheadedness costs us the season, you'll have a lot more pain from me than what this fall has caused."

"Hard boot," he grumbled.

"You'll call me worse than that." She looked up. "Jennifer, move."

"Yes, ma'am." Jennifer turned her horse, galloping back toward the trailers, which fortunately weren't but a mile away.

Xavier said, "Sister, let me go back with her, and I'll tie my horse next to hers. Just in case the horse gets silly by himself."

"That's a good idea, and X, go with her to Walter, will you? She's only a kid, and I should have thought of that. John Wayne here might feel compelled to give her orders, such as to forget it. I've put her in a bad spot. I know he can't do a thing with you."

Xavier touched his crop to his derby and cantered off.

Shaker wanted to say something back, but he was foggier than he realized. Ronnie continued to hold him up. He blinked, then handed the horn to Sister. "Better kick on."

She took the horn. "Jesus H. Christ on a raft," is what she wanted to say. She'd hunted all her life, but she'd never carried the horn. She was the master. Her field, small though it was today, looked to her. It was her responsibility to provide sport. "Okay, I'll give you a full report later."

Ronnie stayed back with Sari and Shaker.

Sister walked away, not wishing to make Gunpowder or their horses fret. Once away from the three, she turned. "Edward, take the field, will you?"

"Delighted." He nodded in assent.

The field now consisted of Tedi and Gray.

Sister moved out; she could hear hounds way in the distance. Rickyroo had speed to burn. Unless footing got trappy, she could get up with them in five or ten minutes. She trusted her two whippers-in and knew they'd be on either side.

Luck was with her. She had no heavy covert to negotiate, just open meadows, thin dividers of woods and trees on either side. She caught sight of her tail hounds climbing up a rolling meadow. Rickyroo opened his stride even more, and within minutes she was right behind Delia, Nellie, Asa, and Ardent, who were fifteen yards behind the rest of the pack.

She put the horn to her lips. A strangled sound slid out of the short horn.

"Oh, God," she said.

"Just talk to us," Asa advised.

She stuck the horn between her first and second coat buttons. "Whoop, whoop, whoop."

Cora heard this, slightly turned her head. *"Sister's hunting us."*

"No joke." Dasher smiled. *"Guess we'd better be right."*

Diana, moving fast, literally leapt, turning in midair. *"To the right!"* As anchor, and in her second season at this demanding position, she had to keep everyone on the line, correct line at that. The fox executed a 90-degree cut, smack in the middle of the pastures.

Sister watched this. The other hounds came to Diana. Cora put her nose down, confirming the shift.

When hounds are doing their job, Sister thought to keep quiet. If she'd been in heavy covert, she would have tooted as best she could, so Betty and Sybil would know where she was. Not a good thing for the whippers-in to get thrown out.

Her questioning of why the fox would head straight north into another pasture was quickly answered when she galloped well into the pasture, having taken the coop, and saw the herd of Angus on the far side. He'd made a beeline for them.

Sure enough, hounds checked. How many times had she watched this? But now it was in her hands.

"Good foxhounds," she called out to them, her voice encouraging. "Get 'em up."

Hounds circled the cattle; Dasher moved right through them. Young Tinsel found the line on the other side, and off they ran. This side of Orchard Hill was divided into ten- to twenty-acre pastures that the owner used to rotate stock. Every fence contained jumps, which made it great fun, except that Sister was so intent on staying with hounds she never saw the jumps. She cleared them, eyes always on her hounds. Rickyroo was in his glory. He lived to run and jump.

Finally, they blasted into fifty acres of apple orchard on the right side of the farm road. On the south side, where there was more protection from sharp north winds, were fifty acres of peaches.

Orchards draw deer, raccoons, possums, and all manner of birds. Even rabbit feed on the edges. The place reeked of competing scents, which the temperature kept down.

But Cora, Diana, Asa, Ardent, Delia, and Nellie untangled the scents. The younger ones, while momentarily overwhelmed, quickly imitated their leaders. They kept on the fox.

He had put distance between them when he used the cattle. Try as they might, they couldn't close it, but scent held.

Sister caught sight of Betty down on the farm road. She figured Sybil to be outside the orchard.

Edward, Tedi, and Gray were getting one hell of a hunt. They glided through the apple orchard, flattening grass soft underfoot, a welcome change from some of the footing they'd recently been over.

Sister, well up with her hounds, kept a sharp eye in case she might see her quarry. She'd see him before the hounds would.

On the other side of the orchard, a stout coop divided it from the hayfield. Rickyroo took it with ease, and Sister glimpsed the smallish gray.

"Yip, yip, yoo!"

Hounds knew what this meant from their master. Their adrenaline, already high, shot higher. They pressed.

Young though he was, the gray had some tricks in his bag. He looped around the hayfield, dipped into the narrow creek, came out, turned toward the peach orchard, which had a fire stand at the edge: a tower with a roof and ladder.

He climbed up the ladder and flopped on the lookout stand.

Hounds skidded to a halt underneath.

"*He's up there!*" Trinity screamed in frustration. "*No fair.*"

Rickyroo halted. Sister, not entirely sure that the gray had climbed, dismounted. "Ricky, hold the fort."

Hounds milled under his legs, their excitement bubbling over. Trudy tried to climb the ladder, made it up three foot holds, only to fall flat on her back.

"*Nitwit,*" Cora said.

The hounds sang and sang. Edward, Tedi, and Gray arrived in time to see Sister's small butt, covered by her buckskin breeches, moving up the ladder.

She peeped her head up and almost fell back as the small gray walked right up to her, putting his nose close to hers. Cowering wasn't his style.

"*If you throw me down, I'll bite.*"

"Well done, little fellow, well done." She smiled at him and backed down. Then she plucked the horn from her first and second buttons and tried blowing "Gone to Ground."

Blowing the horn proved easier if she wasn't moving, but she needed work. Laughing, she took the mouthpiece from her lips, "Okay, so it doesn't sound like 'Gone to Ground.' How about 'Up in the Air'?"

Everyone had a good laugh, including the fox.

"Sister, that was thrilling," Tedi enthused.

"You're being very, very kind."

Betty and Sybil came in just as Sister was blowing her mightiest.

"This is one for the books." Betty smiled broadly.

"I don't know about that." Sister swung back up on Rickyroo, who was having the best day. "But I think it's time to go in. We've sure had some big days, haven't we?"

"And the reds have just started breeding," Betty mentioned, knowing the grays had been at it for two or three weeks.

"I always said the best hunting is late January through February." Sister, high from the chase, and having managed a few warbles, laughed.

"*Grays cheat,*" Trinity complained.

"*No, that's the way they do,*" Asa reminded her.

"*Not as bad as the time three years ago when a gray jumped in the back-seat of Tedi's car. He'd foiled his scent. She drove him home!*" Cora giggled.

Since Jennifer and X had taken her truck, Sister, Betty, and Sybil loaded up hounds. Sari and Ronnie heard the whole story. They stayed back, waiting for Jennifer and Xavier to return.

Sister, using Betty's cell phone, reached Jennifer on the truck phone as she pulled out from the hospital.

Shaker grabbed the phone. "Three cracked ribs, two separated, a mild concussion. I'm fine."

Xavier took the phone from Shaker. "And he's bald. Walter had his chest shaved before they taped him so it wouldn't hurt when he took the bandages off. Such a manly chest."

Sister heard Shaker laughing, then wince. She said, "We could sell tickets. Raise a little money for the club. You know, help your huntsman change his bandages, see his naked chest."

"Wouldn't get a dime," X replied.

Once off the phone, Sister told the others, "He's okay. Cracked ribs, two separated."

Tedi and Edward both said, "Good news." Tedi added, "And you did great!"

"All I had to do was keep up, that was enough. Let's be honest, it was a pretty good day for scent."

"Janie, you did great." Tedi patted her arm. "Take the compliment."

Sister smiled. "You're right."

Gray walked over. "Are we still on for tomorrow night at the club?"

"You know, dinner there is like taking an ad on local TV."

"Exactly right." Gray reached for her hand. "I'm serving notice on all other men."

"Flatterer." She laughed.

Betty, Sybil, Jennifer, and Sari, once back at Roughneck Farm, all helped get the hounds fed, cleaned, checked over. Then the girls took care of the horses.

Shaker kept trying to do chores until Sister finally lost her temper with him, banishing him to his cottage.

"He's worse than a child," she said to Betty and Sybil.

"They all are." Betty kept working. "Overgrown boys."

"But isn't that what makes them fun?" Sybil, lonely for male companionship, winked.

"You're right," Sister agreed.

The phone rang in the office.

Betty hurried in to answer, then called for Sister.

After listening to Ben Sidell, Sister rejoined the others as they washed down the feed room. "Girls, they've identified the burned body. Donnie Sweigert."

"Oh, no!" Sybil exclaimed.

Betty, too, exclaimed, "This is awful. What in God's name was Donnie doing there?"

"Said he had a high alcohol content in his blood." Sister thought Donnie not a very intelligent man, but how could he be dumb enough to be dead drunk, literally, in the middle of a fire?

"God, I hope there wasn't hemlock in it," Betty gasped.

"No." Sister clasped her hands together.

"Well, he worked at the warehouse for years. Maybe he got drunk and fell asleep," Sybil thought out loud.

"With a can of gasoline next to him?"

"Jesus." Betty whistled.

"Before this is over, we're all going to be calling for Jesus," Sister said. "What is going on down there?"

"Doesn't make any sense." Sybil, too, was upset.

"It makes sense to somebody," Betty rejoined.

"Yes—that's what scares me," Sister half whispered.

CHAPTER 29

"Old-fashioned," Sister said, walking through the freshly washed-down kennels, water squishing under her ancient green Wellies.

Walter, having a light day this Friday, used the afternoon to check in on Shaker and to begin his hound education. "What do you mean by old-fashioned?"

"Oh, a little heavy boned in the foreleg, a bigger barrel than gets pinned in the ring these days, and a somewhat broader skull than is currently finding favor." She closed and double-latched the heavy chain-link gate leading to the young-entry run. "You breed for the territory, Walter. You'll get sick of hearing that from me, and truthfully, you breed the kind of hound you or your huntsman can handle. A lot of people can't handle American hounds; the animal is too sensitive, too up for them."

"Like house dogs? Some people like terriers; other people like golden retrievers."

"In a sense, yes. But I swear there are more born liars in the foxhound world than anywhere else but golf and fishing." She moved along to the hot bitch pen.

Sweetpea, having recently been bred, was already in the special girls' pen, as Sister called it, the hot bitch pen and whelping area. A steady hound, not brilliant, Sweetpea, when crossed to Sister's A line or Jill Summers's J line, produced marvelous hounds. Mrs. Paul Summers Jr. was the long-serving master at Farmington Hunt. She'd bred a consistently fine pack for over thirty-five years.

"*Hello.*" Sweetpea wagged her tail.

"Sweetpea, you remember Walter." Sister reached down and smoothed her lovely head, the eyes expressive, filled with intelligence.

"*I do.*" Sweetpea touched Walter with her nose.

Wanda, more advanced in her pregnancy, hearing voices, padded in from outside, where she'd been taking her constitutional. "*I'm here.*"

"This is Wanda: great drive, okay nose, strong back end, as you can see. That gives her a lot of power. Her shoulder angle could be better, but at least it's not straight as a stick. So in breeding Wanda, I want to keep her good features, but see if I can't improve the shoulder a bit and maybe refine her head just a wee bit. Again, I'm not too much into looks, but conformation is the key, as well as attitude. Same as with horses, of course. Both these girls are so easy to work with, eager to please and keen to hunt. And their offspring are even better. Wanda is bred to a Piedmont hound who actually goes back to Fred Duncan's incredible Clyde—oh, that was back in the early seventies. That hound could follow scent on a hot asphalt road. Never saw anything like Warrenton Clyde."

Walter, overwhelmed, sighed. "Sister, how am I going to remember all this? It's Greek to me."

Sister, who had a few years of Greek in college, smiled. "If you mastered organic chemistry, bloodlines will be a snap."

"Can I read up on this?"

"The books start in the early eighteenth century. Well, actually, I think Xenophon even mentioned hound breeding, but don't fret, Walter. I'll give you a list of the classics. The MFHA has FoxDog: their computer software. I struggle with it, but Shaker's got the hang of it. I'm not exactly a computer whiz, but I can send e-mail."

"FoxDog?" He bent his tall frame over to pat both Wanda and Sweetpea.

"All the bloodlines for every hunt for each of the main types of foxhounds are on FoxDog. I can't imagine sitting down and entering all that information. God bless the MFHA." She paused. "But I'll tell you, the best way to learn about hounds and breeding is to hunt, hunt, hunt, and watch. Go to any hunt you can, mounted or on foot, and observe. The great ones stay in your mind just like the great horses or movie stars."

"That makes sense."

"And you'll soon know what I'm talking about when I say that Piedmont Righteous '71 was bred to Warrenton Star, which gave us a bitch, Piedmont Daybreak '79, and she produced Piedmont Hopeful '83, a very great bitch. A lot of people will say they want Hopeful in the tail female line, and all that sounds impressive, but I just watch hounds. I don't give a damn if the nick is on top or on bottom—"

Walter held up his hand. "Sister, what's a nick? You've lost me."

"Nick is a bad hound who hunts coons." Wanda was referring to a neighbor's hound, whom she didn't much like. Although Nick was a good coonhound, he didn't pay his proper respects to Wanda—a girl with a big ego.

"I think of a nick as a lucky cross. Funny Cide, terrific racing horse, a gelding, you know whom I'm talking about?"

"Yes."

"Okay, he won't be retired to stud, but people will study his pedigree and try the same or similar cross if they can. Nothing wrong with that, but I think you can get a good result playing with the template, if you will. Instead of just copying something that in the thoroughbred world would mean hundred of thousands of dollars, reverse the nick or go back to the grandparent generation. If you study, Walter, there's always a way. I study pedigree. I study hounds, study horses, too. And one of the great things about foxhunting is I can call another master in order to take a bitch to his dog; he or she is flattered. Of course, masters allow this and everyone benefits. You don't pay for it. The opportunity is freely given. Foxhunting operates on generosity. We improve the animal if we're careful. The operative word is 'careful.' "

"What's tail line and all that?"

"Oh. The tail line is the bottom of a breeding chart, the dam or bitch's side. The top belongs to the dog hound or stallion. I'll show you when we go in to the office, but you'll see right what I mean when you check a pedigree. It's a good thing to study and research pedigrees. It's a better thing to see performance in the field and to talk to those who know the antecedents of a good hound."

"I've got my work cut out for me." He whistled. "Can't wait. And Sweetpea and Wanda, I can't wait to see the babies."

"Mine will be better," Wanda bragged.

Sweetpea, easygoing, just licked Sister's hand. *"I love you, Sister. I'll give you good puppies."*

"Precious." Sister kissed her head, then patted Wanda.

They left, closing the gate behind them, and walked the long outdoor corridor to the main kennel building. Once inside, she showed him Sweetpea's pedigree of this year's entry from Sweetpea and Ardent. Walter realized the format was exactly the same as a horse pedigree. He felt better.

The door opened, and Shaker stepped through. "Draw list for tomorrow?"

"Haven't done it yet. Did you do yours?"

"Yes." He placed his list on the desk then spoke to Walker. "I'm not sitting around."

"Give it another day, Shaker. Really. I'm not worried about your

— 253 —

Office Use RECEIVED:	PEDIGREE FOR REGISTRATION OF ONE HOUND OR TWO OR MORE LITTERMATES	Office Use REGISTERED:

MASTERS OF FOXHOUNDS ASSOCIATION OF AMERICA

Bred By __Jefferson Hunt Club__ Breed __American__ Year of Entry __2003__

Place of Birth __Afton, VA__ From Whom Acquired _____

Date of Birth __April 23, 2003__ Date When Acquired _____

If you are the breeder, list ALL living and drafted hounds of the litter. For EACH hound, indicate in the first column, if entered by you (your HUNT name), if drafted UNENTERED to another pack (their name), or if not yet entered.

DRAFTED UNENTERED TO OR ENTERED BY	NAME OF HOUND	SEX	TATTOO	COMMENTS
Jefferson Hunt	Darby	M		J01 - L
	Doughboy	M		J02 - L
	Dreamboat	M		J03 - L
	Dana	F		J04 - L
	Delight	F		J05 - L
	Diddy	F		J06 - L

SIRE Third column (below) need not be complete if sire and dam have been registered		
	JHC Archie, 1992	
Prefix **Jefferson Hunt**		
Name **Ardent, 1999** & Year		
Volume & Page	JHC Cymbel, 1990	
Prefix **Jefferson Hunt**	Keswick Predator, 1994	
Name **Delia, 1996** & Year		
Volume & Page		
	JHC Dimple, 1991	
DAM Give prefix, name and year of entry for all sires and dams		

I HEREBY CERTIFY that the information and pedigree given above are correct to the best of my knowledge and belief

Jane Overdorf Arnold
Signature   MFH   Jefferson Hunt   20 December 2003
                                          Name of Hunt   Date

ribs. The concussion worried me even though it wasn't bad. But give it another day."

"Who's going to hunt hounds tomorrow? I need to go out."

"You and Lorraine can be wheel whips. I'm not taking any chances with you. If you miss tomorrow, well, it's not great, but if you miss the rest of the season, the best part of the season, I'll be one step ahead of a fit," Sister reminded him.

Shaker sat on the edge of the desk. "For Chrissakes, people get their bell rung all the time."

"They aren't fabulous huntsmen. And how do you blow the horn when you're galloping?" Sister hoped the compliment would somewhat mollify him.

"Practice. It's a good idea to go out with an empty bladder, too."

"I figured that out." She laughed. "I'll hunt the hounds tomorrow. God willing, nothing awful will happen. Let's take steady eddies, no young entry. Make it easy for me. Tuesday, you'll be back in the saddle and all will be well."

"No, what's going to happen is you'll love hunting hounds, and we'll have a fight," Shaker grumbled.

"I will love hunting them. I loved yesterday even though I had butterflies, but you're the huntsman and huntsman you'll stay." She swiftly ran her eyes down the draw list, dogs on the left side of the page, bitches on the right, first-year entry, young entry, and even some second year with a different-colored mark before the animal's name. It was a good system. "I'll get back to you on this."

Up at the house, Sister asked Walter about Shaker's injuries as she heated water for tea.

"This is the third time you've asked since yesterday."

"I'm sorry. He's very dear to me, even if we fuss."

"He hit hard. He can wrap up his ribs. I want a few more days for his head. By the time I saw him, he was in pretty good shape from the concussion, but you always want to be careful with a head injury."

"Thank you again for seeing him. I guess we could have sent him to the ER, but I trust you; I don't know who's in the ER."

Walter smiled. "Thank you for your confidence, but the team down at the hospital is very good."

She poured tea. Walter liked dark teas, as did she. "You don't know much about foxhounds; I don't know diddly about medicine. What really is an endocrinologist?"

"Someone in the right field at the right time. It's the study of ductless glands. So it's really the study of the thyroid, the pituitary, and the adrenal glands, basic human chemistry."

"Lucrative?"

"Very. If you have a child whose growth is stunted, you'd go to an endocrinologist. Menopause—think of the money there with the boomer generation. It's a growing field that will benefit from the constant advancements just in thyroid studies alone. Pretty amazing."

"Would an endocrinologist have more ways to make illegal money than, say, yourself?"

"From medicine?" Walter's blond eyebrows rose. "Uh, well, Sister, any crooked doctor can make a fortune. Prescribe unnecessary painkillers, OxyContin, mood elevators, Percodan, Prozac. If you're less than honest, it's easy, because, of course, the patient wants the drugs."

"What about cocaine or heroin?"

Walter couldn't help but laugh. "You don't need a doctor. You can get that on the street."

"It's really easy to get coke or marijuana?"

"As pie. Easy as pie." Walter sipped the restorative brew. "Our government, the FDA, I could list agencies as long as my arm, and I've got long arms, make the mess bigger and bigger. Some drugs are classified as dangerous; others aren't. I could kill you with caffeine. There's a hit of caffeine in this tea. Sister, I could kill you with sugar or salt. Americans are literally killing themselves every day with salt and sugar. We are so hypocritical when it comes to—what's the term?—illegal substances. You've got people making policy based on their version of morals instead of, well, endocrinology. And I'm serious: I could kill someone with caffeine. I'm a doctor; in order to save lives, you have to know what takes those lives. Any doctor worth his salt, forgive the pun, can kill and make it look perfectly natural. But as I said, why bother? Americans are killing themselves."

She drummed her fingers on the kitchen table. "Mmm."

"Why this sudden interest in endocrinology?"

"Dalton Hill's speciality. He's paid his associate membership; he's been hunting pretty consistently. Good rider."

"Bought that Cleveland bay."

"Yes." She frowned a moment. "Obviously, he has money."

"Right." Walter smiled. "He's an endocrinologist."

She smiled back. "What do you know about him?"

Walter shrugged. "Leave of absence from the Toronto hospital, teaching this semester, and he's brilliant. That's what I hear."

"Do you like him?"

A long pause followed her question. Walter cleared his throat. "Not really."

"Cold."

"More or less. He's thawing a bit, thanks to your geniality and the hospitality of Virginians in general." Walter thanked her as she refreshed his tea. "He's recently divorced, which is why I think he's teaching this semester. A chance to get away. Clear the head."

"I've been curious about him." She smiled again. "Can't have too many doctors in the field. Wish we could get the entire hospital staff to hunt."

"You wouldn't want that. We've got some first-class fruitcakes."

"And the hunt doesn't?"

They laughed.

"Back to hounds," Walter said. "Can you breed for the task? By that I mean, can you breed an anchor hound?"

"We could be here for weeks on that one. Well . . . yes and no. I have noticed certain characteristics passing in certain of my lines. For example, Delia, mother of Diddy and those first-year entry, comes from my D line. D hounds are consistently steady, and they enter and learn fairly quickly. On the other hand, I've observed that my R line can be brilliant, but it seems to skip a generation. Rassle, Ruthie, and Ribot are brilliant. Their mother wasn't; she was just there. Her mother was outstanding. Like I said, the answer to your question is yes and no."

"It's fascinating."

"And highly addictive." She reached for a sugar cookie. "The more you breed, the more you want to breed, and you drive yourself onward with the dream of perfection." She sighed. "Well, humility goes a long way. And even in the great crosses, the golden nicks, you still must cull."

"The hard part."

"God, yes. I think a youngster won't work for us, I draft him to a good pack, he's terrific. Now some of that can be because he's in, say, a newer pack. He's not overshadowed by Diana or an upcoming Trident. He becomes a star. But you never truly know until they hunt for you or for someone else."

"This is going to make me think." Walter laughed.

"You think plenty. Now you'll be hunting, watching in a new way. You'll be singling out hounds, observing young entry, seeing who contributes. The slow days are the best days to learn about the hounds. You see who really works. Might be dull for the run-and-jump crowd, but those slow days offer the best lessons a foxhunter can get."

"I've never had a bad day hunting."

"A bad day's hunting is a good day's work." They laughed again and she changed the subject. "I've learned to trust my instincts hunting on and off a horse as well. I'm unsettled about Donnie's death. And the deaths of Mitch and Tony."

"Do you think Donnie wanted to burn out Clay?"

"Sure looks like he did." Sister glanced out the window. "It's like drawing through a heavy covert: you know the fox is in there, but you can't get him up and running. I've seen days when hounds, my hounds and other packs, too, have drawn right over a fox. I feel that's what's going on."

"What do you do on a day like that?"

"Keep moving, but," she paused dramatically, "later you can come back and draw in the opposite direction. Sometimes you can get him up that way because he didn't expect it."

Walter tapped his spoon on the side of the mug, then stopped. "Sorry."

"Is that how you think?"

"I have to do something rhythmic," he replied.

"I do my best thinking working outside or sometimes in bed just before I fall asleep. But do you see what I mean about drawing over the fox? We're drawing over those deaths, over information."

"I'd put it another way. You're on the right track, but the train's not in the station."

"Not yet."

CHAPTER 30

The burnt orange of Betadine stained Dragon's white fur. Aggressive and domineering as he could be with other hounds, he was an uncommonly sweet hound to people.

He stood on the stainless steel examining table as Sister and Gray sponged his wounds with antiseptic.

Lifting sixty- to eighty-pound hounds tested Sister after the sixth hound. Shaker had wanted to help, but his ribs needed to heal, so Sister threw him out of the med room. She had realized that her planned date with Gray at the club would either have to be canceled or pushed back too late, so she had called him to cancel. Since tomorrow was Saturday, the biggest hunting day of the week, she didn't want to stay out late, plus she was nervous about hunting the hounds. To Sister's surprise, Gray volunteered to help with her chores.

Riding, resplendent in perfectly fitting attire, pleases any foxhunter. Hearing "Gone Away" on the horn, hounds in full cry, is a thrill beyond compare. Few foxhunters, however, evidence any desire to be in the kennels picking up poop, feeding and watering, washing down the feed room and the runs, birthing puppies, or tending to sick or injured hounds in the med room.

The blood still seeped from Dragon's wounds. Sister's old lab coat bore testimony to that. Gray, too, wore a lab coat smeared with mud and bloodstains.

Dragon was the third hound they worked on. Two hounds had run under barbed wire Thursday, slicing their backs, although they had bled very little.

The fact that Gray was willing to forgo a fancy dinner and, on top of that, to lift hounds, get dirty, and dab wounds gave him an added luster in Sister's eyes.

Gray was the same height as Sister. He was fit and uncommonly strong, as was his wiry, much shorter brother.

Carrying a beloved red ball, Raleigh padded in to watch, as did Rooster. Golly heard there were mice in the office, so she, too, accompanied the humans and dogs. "Death to mice" was Golly's motto.

"Bon sang ne sait mentir" was Sister's motto, archaic French, which meant, "Good blood doesn't lie." This was fitting for a foxhound breeder, but equally fitting for the human animal. Blood tells.

"There you go, big fella. Guess you won't cross Cora again." Sister gave Dragon a cookie for his good behavior before Gray lifted him down.

"Handsome."

"That he is. Diana and Dasher turned out quite good-looking, too, but with a better temperament in the field. Dragon is hardheaded when hunting, and yet such a love the rest of the time."

"My nose is the best. I get sick of Cora double-checking everything. I don't care if she is the strike hound and the head bitch," Dragon explained himself.

"Kennel up." Sister pointed to the sick bay kennel, a series of separate pens with cozy boxes off the med room. Each of these rooms had a small outside run that could be shut off. Each room contained its own wall heater, high on the wall so the hound couldn't get on its hind legs to chew it. Since hounds curl up together in cold weather, they are able to keep warm; but a hound alone could use a little help in winter, especially if he or she has been injured or isn't feeling well.

Dragon obediently walked into his place. Sister closed the door behind him, dropping the latch. The other two hounds were already asleep in their pens.

Fortunately, none of these hounds had suffered severe wounds. They'd most likely be back hunting within a week. If the wounds didn't close up to Sister's satisfaction, she'd keep the hound out of hunting, although not out of hound walk. No point in reopening wounds and delaying healing, but if a hound can be exercised, that's good for him mentally. If the animal wasn't ready to rejoin the pack, Sister would hand walk him. Each of these hounds pulled his weight in the pack, so she wanted them up and running.

Gray washed his hands in the big stainless steel sink. "I never realized how much work there is."

"All day, every day." She hung up her lab coat, inspected it, then took it off the hook. "Laundry time."

"Ever get tired of this? It's a lot of physical labor, plus the actual hunting."

"I love it." Her face shone. "I couldn't live without it. Everyone needs a paradigm for life, and hunting is mine. Hunting *is* life. The way a person foxhunts is the way he or she lives."

"True." He wiped his hands on a thick terry cloth towel. "I think that's true about any sport, the way someone plays tennis or golf." He thought for a second. "Maybe a little less true of the team sports because you have help, but still: character will out."

"Hand me your lab coat." She took the coat and draped it over her arm. "It is funny, isn't it, how we spend our childhood and adolescence constructing our social masks with the help of our parents, family, friends, and school, and then something unmasks us? Usually sports, love. People are always unwittingly revealing themselves. Me, too." She opened the door to the laundry room, tossing the coats, plus other odds and ends, into the industrial-size washer. "This thing's about to go. Can't complain. It's been chugging along eight years. You wouldn't believe the dog hair we pull out of here. Same with the horse blankets. Sometimes I envy those critters their fur. No clothing bills."

"Oh, but you look so good in warm colors—peach, pink, red. Now if you had the same old fur coat, that wouldn't be the case." He handed her the detergent.

"You look good in every color of the rainbow," she countered.

"Uh-uh," he disagreed. "Not gray or beige."

"Didn't think about that. Blond colors. Walter colors."

"*Kill!*" Golly screamed from the office.

Sister and Gray looked at each other as the house dogs ran to the closed office door. "I'm afraid to look," she said.

"I'll go first," Gray said in a mock-manly tone. He walked out, peeped in the inside office door, which had a window in it, then came back. "Biggest mouse in the county, maybe in all of America."

"Good cat." Sister turned on the washer as Raleigh hurried back into the med room to retrieve his ball before Rooster snatched it.

The five friends walked back up to the house, darkness deep on this cloud-covered early evening. Golly, mouse firmly in jaws, tail hoisted as high as possible, pupils huge, ran ahead of everyone.

"*She's the only cat in the world who has killed a mouse.*" Rooster watched the fluffy tail swaying in triumph.

"*The trick will be getting her to deposit it outside. She's going to want to bring it in the mudroom and then into the house. She'll be parading that damned mouse for days.*"

"*Why doesn't she just eat it?*" Rooster asked.

"*Look at her.*" Raleigh laughed out loud, which sounded like a healthy snort.

Although Golly usually acquired a bit of a potbelly in winter, this winter she had acquired enough for two. As the dogs giggled, Golly laid her ears flat back, then swept them forward.

She couldn't open her mouth. The mouse would drop out, and one of the dogs, those lowlifes, would steal it. Something as valuable as a freshly killed mouse, neck neatly snapped, would bring out the worst, especially in the harrier; she knew it. But she thought to herself, *Go ahead, laugh. I don't see either of you worthless canines ridding this farm of vermin. At least the hounds hunt. You two do nothing, nothing.*

Once inside the mudroom, a tussle broke out between Golly and Rooster.

"All right, Rooster, leave her," Sister ordered the dog, who obeyed but not without a telling glare at the cat. "Golly, what a big mouse. What a great hunter you are. Give me your mouse."

Puffed with pride, Golly opened her jaws, the limp, gray-brown body thumping to the slate floor.

"Protein," Gray said.

Sister picked up the mouse, stroked Golly's head. "Right. Mouse pie as opposed to shepherd's pie. Hope you like shepherd's pie because that's what we're having for dinner."

"Is there time to dice the mouse?" He hung up his full-length Australian raincoat.

"No." She patted Golly again and wondered just what to do with this prize. "Gray, I'm going to put this out by my gardening shed in case Inky comes in tonight. Why don't you go inside and fix yourself a drink if you're in the mood?"

"Sure you can tote that heavy mouse by yourself?"

"With effort." She grinned.

"Can I fix you a drink?"

"Hot tea. I need a pick-me-up."

When she returned, steam curled out of the Brown Betty teapot. Before she reached the oven to check on the shepherd's pie, Gray poured her a bracing mug of orange pekoe and Ceylon mix.

"You know how to make real tea." She lifted the lid, the mesh tea ball floating inside the pot, emitting even more of the delightful fragrance.

"The English taught me."

"Really?"

"I lived there for five years when I worked for Barclays Bank."

"I didn't know you did that."

"Well, I got my law degree then my accounting. I did it backwards, I suppose. I thought if I had a strong background in banking before finding the right firm, I'd be a triple threat. And when I graduated, I had a choice between Atlanta—where my color would actually help me at that time, remember those were the days of Andrew Young and Maynard Jackson; they put Atlanta on the map in terms of banking and investing—or London. Well, I wanted to experience other cultures, and I thought England would be easier than if I tried to crash Germany."

"Aren't you the smart one?" Another ten minutes and the pie would be ready. The crust was browning up.

He smiled. "In some ways. People think tax law is boring. Not me. The power to tax is the power to destroy. I learned a lot about taxation in England. Here I was, a kid really, negotiating a culture mentioned by Roman writers, finally subdued by Agricola in A.D. 84, wasn't it? I soaked it all up. Haunted Hatcher's." He mentioned the venerable bookstore. "Didn't have enough money to shop at Harrod's but I liked to stroll through. And on weekends for pennies I could go to France, Germany, Spain. Loved Spain and the Spanish. Couldn't get into what were then Soviet satellite countries, but I met people, high-level types, visiting Barclays. You know, it was just the right time, the right place."

"Sounds fabulous. What are you drinking?"

"A perfect Manhattan. I make a mean Manhattan—a good dry Manhattan or Manhattan South. Name your poison."

A sudden memory of the drunks guzzling hemlock shot through her. "Tea. I'm not much of a drinker, although my flask has port in it."

"I drank a lot. Not as much as Sam, but a lot. Especially when my marriage tanked." He helped her set the table. "One day I realized I needed to slow down. I didn't want to wind up like Sam. Alcoholism floods both sides of the family." He folded a white linen napkin in thirds. "One drink in the evening, even if it's a party. One."

"Good rule."

"You never drink?"

"Champagne to celebrate, but I don't have a thirst for it. It's a true physical drive, and I don't have it."

"Sam said even when he was in high school, he'd be plotting how to get liquor, where to hide it. When he rode competitively, he would secrete a bottle in the trailer. He stashed booze in the tack trunks. Carried a thin flask in his barn jacket. Controlled his entire life. Still does. He has to fight it every day."

"Insidious."

Golly sauntered through, warbling, *"A Mighty Fortress Is Our Puss."* The cat had no sense of religious decorum.

"Still crowing." Sister laughed at her friend.

The dogs, chewing greenies, ignored her. The problem was that Golly wouldn't ignore them. Their scratched noses bore testimony to her relentless need for attention.

"When did you have time to make shepherd's pie?"

"I just slaved over this stove." She giggled. "Lorraine brought it by. She'd made them for Shaker and me. Those two are getting along, but he's close-mouthed. They're inching toward each other, and, truth is, he's scared to death. The divorce took a big chunk out of him."

"Always does."

As they enjoyed their meal, Sister asked, "You don't speak of your first wife, your only wife, I assume." When he nodded in affirmation, she continued. "That bad?"

"No. Few romantic relationships can last a lifetime. We'd probably be better off with different people at different times in our lives. The person you marry changes. That can be good, but for me those changes were filled with resentment, anger, feelings of abandonment. Nothing too original."

"Who changed?"

"We both did. The focus of our relationship was our children and my career. We lost sight of each other. Theresa and I get along better today than when we were married. We see each other once or twice a year, usually something involving our kids. I expect in the next few years, we'll be dealing with grandchildren." He stopped for a moment. "I talk to her once a week. After the first year of the divorce was over, we both calmed down. I kept telling myself, even in the worst of it, 'Whatever you saw in her in the beginning is still there.' And I went into therapy. That helped."

"You did?"

"You didn't?"

"I foxhunt three times a week, and attend other hunts if I can. Does it for me. I figure things out. I may not use the same language a therapist does, but I really do figure things out."

"You're smarter than I am."

"Not at all. It takes a lot of courage, especially for a man, to ask for emotional help. Actually, I don't know if I could do it. Too big an ego."

"You?" His voice lifted upwards.

"Me. I think I can fix anything, including myself."

"Whatever you do, it works."

"Well, I hope so. Lately the truth jumps up at me like a jack-in-the-box. I wonder how I missed it."

"Unhappy?"

She shook her head. "No. Actually, I love my life, and I suppose, for lack of a better way to put it, I love myself, but I'm blind to things, inside things."

"Everyone is."

"I know, but Gray, I think I'm smarter than anyone else. Isn't that awful to say? But I do. I'm not supposed to be blind. I'm supposed to be the master. I'm supposed to know hounds, horses, territory, people, weather, scent, the game, game trails, plants, wildlife, and I'm supposed to know myself. I surprise myself these days. Like right now. I can't believe I'm babbling all this."

"You're not babbling."

"Gray, I was raised a WASP. Grin and bear it. Stiff upper lip."

"I was raised that way, too. Not so bad. We don't need to know everyone's intimate details, but it's good to know your own."

"Yes."

"It's a rare woman who will admit she has a big ego."

"Gargantuan. I hide it well. In fact, I've hidden it pretty effectively for close to six decades. My first decade I gave my mother hives. With a great effort on her part, she taught me how to cover it all up. She harbored a pretty big ego herself."

"Funny."

"What?"

"What we're told as children. It may be damaging, on the one hand, but it's the truth. Our parents, family, older friends tell us what the world is like."

"They tell us what the world was like for them. They don't know what it will be like for us because we will change the world."

He put down his fork. "Sister, no wonder you take your fences as you do."

She laughed. "Every generation changes the world. You hear what went before you: your parents' victories, miseries, and fears as well as hopes for you. They tell you their truth. You've got to find your own."

"But remember the past."

"I do."

"I don't think I've ever met anyone like you. I'm sure I haven't."

"I've never met anyone like you. Maybe we've reached a point in our lives when we molt. We shed our feathers. But this time, instead of growing the same feathers, we grow different ones: the feathers we've always wanted."

"Your metaphors come from nature."

"Nature is what I know. Now if you speak in metaphors, do I have to get a law library? Do I have to study *Marbury* versus *Madison* or the *Dred Scott* case?" She knew her history, those being landmark American cases.

He laughed. "No."

"Tell me about those Manhattans you mentioned. I thought a Manhattan was some blended whiskey and a bit of sweet vermouth."

"The basic Manhattan." He leaned back in the chair. "Well, a dry Manhattan is the same, only you use one-fourth ounce of dry vermouth instead of sweet. Easy. A perfect Manhattan is one and one-fourth ounces of blended whiskey, one-eighth ounce of dry vermouth, and one-eighth ounce of sweet vermouth, and you garnish it with a twist of lemon. The dry Manhattan you garnish with an olive, the standard Manhattan, use a cherry."

"What about a Manhattan South. Such mysteries."

"One ounce dry gin, half ounce dry vermouth, half ounce Southern Comfort, and a dash of Angostura bitters, no garnish, and it's not served on the rocks as the others can be. You always mix it in a glass filled with ice, stir, then pour it into a chilled cocktail glass."

"You know, the first party I gave after Ray died, a year and a half after he died, I never even thought about mixing drinks. When one of my guests asked for a vodka stinger, I had no idea what to do. My throat went dry, my heart pounded. I missed Ray and I had learned once more how dependent I was on him for so many things, the small courtesies, the minutiae of masculinity, for lack of a better term. I no more know how to make a vodka stinger than how to fly. Thank God, Xavier was there. I asked him if he would mind, and he graciously tended bar. Ever since, if I give a party or if the hunt club has a real do, I hire a bartender."

"For me, it was fabric. Theresa knew all this stuff about fabrics, for shirtings, for sheets, for towels. She wasn't dead, of course, but that was my first big clue that there was another side to the moon that I needed to explore."

"Well said. You know, earlier we were talking about sports, about how the way a person foxhunts or plays a game shows who they are. I don't know, it crossed my mind, do you think the pressures of high-level competition drove Sam toward more drinking?"

"Yes, but he had it in him already. He could just as easily have become a drunk without that career. I learned a lot about alcoholism, thanks to my brother. I thought for the first years that Sam drank a lot, but he wasn't an alcoholic. The bums at the railway station were alcoholics. Well, they represent about five percent of alcoholics. Most alcoholics sit next to you in church, stand next to you at the supermarket, work next to you at the office. They function quite well for years and years, and then one day, it's like the straw that broke the camel's back. All those years of hiding, lying, performing even while hung over, just collapse. I think Sam would have become a drunk no matter what. He's full of fear. Drunks, basically, are afraid of life. I learned that much."

"Then it is possible that Mitch and Anthony wanted to end it all?"

Gray thought about this for a long time. "Yes."

"Do you think they committed suicide?"

"No."

"I don't either, and I wish I could stop thinking about them, especially. All three of them were part of our community. To see familiar faces year in and year out is a great comfort; ties that bind, even if you don't know someone well."

"Some people realize that quite early, but for most of us, it doesn't come until middle age."

"We're pack animals. We need a community. Giant cities, where are the communities? Maybe the neighborhood, maybe not. It might be a shared interest like dancing or professional associations. We need to be part of one another."

"Hard to imagine Anthony Tolliver and Mitch Banachek being part of a community. I guess the drunks at the station are their own little world. Sam doesn't talk about it. Winding up there is really the bottom of the barrel."

"We couldn't reach those men. But we saw them. They saw us. And maybe, in the darker corners of our souls, they made us feel better about ourselves. At least I'm not as useless as Mitch Banachek. I've still got my teeth unlike Anthony Tolliver. They allowed us the secret thrill of superiority."

He watched her mobile features, listened to her, and found himself completely engaged by this forthright woman. "You don't flinch, do you?"

"Oh, I do. I don't like knowing those things about myself."

"It's human. I think the entire media industry is built on just that emotion."

They both laughed so hard that Golly returned from her post in the library to see if she'd missed anything.

"What's doing?"

"High-tone talk," Raleigh replied.

"Why don't they just go to bed and get it over with?" Golly rubbed her face against Raleigh's long nose while Rooster wrinkled his.

"Because they're human," Raleigh said.

"They complicate everything," Rooster said without rancor, a simple observation.

"She was reading this book on sex in ancient Greece and Rome. When you guys were asleep. She woke up, started reading this book. I can't sleep when she turns the light on, so I watched over her shoulder. And you know what she said? She said, 'Life must have been heaven before guilt.' And then she went on one of her tears. 'How clever of Judeo-Christians to put the cop inside instead of outside.' You know, that's guilt. In Rome, you tried not to get caught if you were fooling around. In America, you catch yourself. She has these odd insights. I wish, for her sake, she weren't human. She'd be so much happier." Golly truly loved Sister.

"She's happy enough for a human." Raleigh, too, loved her.

As the animals discussed their weighty issues, Sister and Gray cleared the table, did the dishes, talked some more. Eventually, Gray got up to leave. He put on his coat, walked with Sister to the door, and kissed her good night. This kiss led to another then another. Finally he took his coat off, and they went upstairs.

They removed their clothes. Considering their ages, they looked pretty good.

Gray in a soft voice said, "Sister . . ."

Laughing, she interrupted him, "Under the circumstances, I think you'd better call me Jane."

CHAPTER 31

S ound travels approximately one mile every five seconds. Sister believed it traveled faster in a hunt club. Not that she was ashamed of bedding Gray, far from it, but neither of them was quite ready for public proclamations. Nor did either know if this was the beginning of a relationship or simply a matter of physical comfort.

When she walked out to the kennels at four forty-five, she noticed Lorraine's car parked in Shaker's driveway. Maybe the moon, sun, and stars had been aligned for romance. She smiled and walked in the office. The hounds slept, though a few raised their heads. Most humans need clocks. The hounds knew it wasn't time yet to be called into the draw yard, so they continued to snore, curled up with one another, dreaming of large red foxes. She dropped her amended draw list on the desk, a neon orange line drawn across the top of it, indicating this was the final draw. She'd discovered neon gel ink pens and gone wild with them months ago. Every color now had a special meaning.

Back in the kitchen by five, she checked the outside thermometer: twenty-seven degrees. She clicked on the Weather Channel. The day, according to radar and a host of experts, should warm to the low forties, high pressure overhead. High pressure, theoretically, made scenting more difficult.

Golly leapt onto the counter. *"I'd like salmon today. And you certainly look happy, happy, happy."*

Sister grabbed a can of cat food, which happened to be a seafood mix, and dumped it in the ceramic bowl—"The Queen" emblazoned on its side—then ground up a small vitamin. Golly stuck her face in the food as Sister finished sprinkling the vitamin powder over it.

Raleigh and Rooster patiently waited for their kibble mixed with a can of beef.

Sister made herself oatmeal. Today's fixture was at Tedi and Edward's, parking at the covered bridge. She thought about the draw. Then she realized she had to plan for the wind shift. She wanted to draw north, but if the wind wasn't coming out of the northwest as was usual, she'd better produce a backup plan.

"God, this takes every brain cell I have," she said aloud.

"You can do it!" Raleigh encouraged her. *"Think of all that good energy you got last night."*

"Yeah, sex is energy," Golly agreed.

"Why do people do it under covers?" Rooster cocked an ear.

"No hair, they get cold," said Golly, who thought of herself as a feline in possession of important facts.

"Oh." Satisfied, Rooster returned to his breakfast.

"If all else fails, I bet I can pick up a line if I head toward Target's den." Sister was drawing a rough outline on a pad. "But usually I'll get Aunt Netty just above the bridge. Well, I'll see what Shaker thinks." Then she smiled. "Bet he's in a good mood. Making love with cracked ribs might test his mettle, if indeed he did." She smiled, twirling her pencil.

By the time she and Shaker filled the draw pen, he was whistling, and she was singing. They looked at each other and laughed.

Lorraine's car was still there.

Sister didn't refer to it, but she peppered him with questions on the first draw, the wind, how quickly did he think the mercury would climb today?

Finally, Shaker slapped her on the back. "Cast your hounds. Be alert. The best advice I can give you is what Fred Duncan gave me when I was a kid, 'Hunt your hounds and don't look back.' "

"If Fred said it, must be true." She had greatly admired the former huntsman and his wife, Doris.

Being a huntsman's wife called for tact, patience, and humor. Doris had all three, plus creativity of her own. She would sit in the kitchen and write novels. Fred would read them and wonder how he had won such a talented woman.

Successful marriages mean the two main participants enjoy each other. Sister and Big Ray had. That foundation of truly liking one another saw them through many a trial.

"So, Gray left at four-thirty." Shaker's lips curled up at the corners, a twinkle in his eye.

"What were you doing up at four-thirty?"

"Had to take four Motrin and two extra-strength Tylenols. Breakfast of champions. Couldn't go back to sleep. Saw the light on in your kitchen."

"I didn't see your light on."

"Got one of those little book lights, so I can read some."

"Lorraine still asleep?"

"Guess we both got lucky, huh?" He thought a minute. "The man is supposed to be lucky. What do women say to each other?"

"If they're smart, nothing."

He laughed. "Good point."

"You . . . happy?"

He draped his arm around her broad shoulders, kissing her on one smooth cool cheek. "Yes. I'm a little nervous, too."

"She's a good woman from what I can tell."

"Solid. Shy, but solid." He kissed her again. "You?"

"Too early to tell, but I'm—" She stopped. "—I'm waking up. I thought I was too old for all this." She laughed at herself.

"Not you."

"You haven't said one word about Gray being African American, black, colored, a person of color, take your pick."

"I'd like to think those days are over."

"I do, too. For us maybe they are, except the fact that I brought it up means the worries are still in me. Not like they would have been thirty years ago." She paused, then spoke with a controlled vengeance. "God, we're stupid. So bloody stupid. Do you think any of those beautiful hounds cares if another one is tricolor or red or black and tan? I hate it."

"Ever wonder what it would be like if the situation were reversed? Wake up one morning and you're black?"

"I'd slap the first silly bastard who mistreated me. Guess I wouldn't get far in this life."

Shaker, a thoughtful man, a deeply feeling man, softly replied, "If I was born that way, I would have been shaped, pruned, restrained to hold the anger in, you know, hold it in. All that negative shit, excuse my French, must be like a drop of acid on your soul each time you feel it. The only thing I can liken it to is sexual desire. For men anyway, we are taught to rein it in, control, control, control. One day you let go, and you feel like you're flying."

"I thought women were the ones who had to deny their sexuality."

"Mmm. We both do in different ways. Takes its toll, and you don't know it until you let it go. But I think about what it's like to be black in this country. It's better, but we still have work to do."

"The work of generations . . . about lots of stuff." She smiled a small, sweet smile. "I think that's why I like foxhunters. Half of us are stone stupid and can talk only about hounds, horses, and hunting, or worse; the other half of us are the most interesting people I have ever met. Like you, for instance."

"Go on." He squeezed her tight, then released her. "Let's load these babies up."

Once at the fixture, Shaker handed her his horn, a symbolic gesture with the significance of a scepter being handed to a ruler.

"Still can't blow this thing worth a damn, despite your quick lesson."

"Do the best you can and use your voice. They know you. I'll get in the truck. I'm on foot, it might confuse them. Their impulse will be to follow me. But you have to use the horn when you move off. They will go to the horn, and they'll go to you if you encourage them. We didn't put all those years into this pack to have them fizzle out because I'm on the mend. This is a great pack of hounds, Sister. You love them, and you're going to do just great."

She smiled down at him from her mount on Lafayette. "Shaker, you can tell the best fibs, but I love you for it."

"I mean it." He did, too. "You can hunt these hounds. Remember, hunt your hounds and don't look back."

She rode Lafayette to the assembled field, Edward, the logical choice, acting as field master. Tedi, who knew hunting and the territory, could have just as easily led, but the field was large for this time of year; she didn't want to tangle with Crawford or other shaky riders. Edward possessed a quiet sense of command. She readily deferred to him. Tedi thought to herself that it was better someone get mad at Edward than at herself.

"Gather round." Sister called in the faithful. As she scanned the field, she couldn't help but linger on Gray, who winked. She blushed, smiled, then said, "Our hosts, the Bancrofts, will again spoil us with their hospitality. Breakfast follows. Shaker is mending quickly. He'll be back Thursday. Edward is your field master, so you're riding behind the best. Edward will never tell you, but he won Virginia Field Hunter of the Year in 1987. The hounds of the Jefferson Hunt want you to know they are going to get up a fox for you. And I'm so glad they're smarter than I am. Let's go."

The small thermometer in the dash on Sister's truck had read thirty-four degrees when she had first pulled into After All Farm. Now, as she and Lafayette walked north with hounds alongside the strong-running Snake Creek, the temperature remained close to that. She could feel it on her skin. The bright blue winter skies were cloudless. The frost sparkled on the earth. All pointed to a tough day for scent. But a light northwesterly breeze, a tang of moisture coming in, hinted that maybe in two hours or less, conditions would improve.

In the meantime, she needed to do all she could to flush out a fox. She walked for five minutes, quietly talking to the pack. Settling them, especially with young entry in tow, helped them and helped her. After a long discussion, she and Shaker had decided to include some young entry. Shaker was already on his way, Lorraine as a passenger, to the sunken farm road close to the westernmost border of the Bancroft estate, a border shared with Roughneck Farm.

Knowing she had Shaker as a wheel whip bolstered her confidence. Knowing Betty rode on her left and Sybil on her right also gave her a lift.

"Girl power," she whispered.

Diana looked up at the human she adored. *"You'd better believe it."*

"Ha," Asa said.

"Bet you one of us finds scent first," Diana challenged him.

"I'll take that bet. What about the rest of you boys?" Asa sang out, but not too loudly or Sister would chide him for babbling.

Dasher, Ardent, Trident, Darby, Doughboy, Dreamboat, Rassle, and Ribot quickly picked up the gauntlet.

Cora, up front, smiled, a puff of breath coming from her slightly opened mouth. *"Girls, even if we run on rocks all day, we are going to find a fox!"*

The girls agreed, then all turned their faces up to their master and now huntsman.

Sister smiled down at them. "Good hounds."

A powerful emotion burst through her. She was of this pack. She was one of them, the least of them in many ways, and yet the leader. The only love she had ever felt that was this deep was when Ray Jr. used to wrap his arms around her neck and say, "Love ya, Mom."

She whispered, "Ride with me today, Junior," then turned her full attention to drawing up the creek bed.

The grade rose by degrees, until Sister and the pack were walking six feet above the creek. The drop into the creek was now sheer. Where eddies slowly swirled, a crust of ice gathered next to the banks.

The smooth pasture containing Nola Bancroft's grave soon gave way to woodlands.

Behind her, Edward led a field of sixty-five people. Everyone came out today because the snows had made them stir-crazy. This was the first good day since then. Before the first cast, Sister noted that Xavier and Sam kept a careful distance between them. Clay, Walter, Crawford, Dalton, Marty, Jennifer, Sari, Ron, plus visitors, all came out.

She also noted, walking a distance behind them, were Jason Farley with Jimmy Chirios. Bless Tedi and Edward, they found someone to guide a newcomer who couldn't ride but showed interest.

A warm air current fluttered across her face, a welcoming sign.

"Get 'em up. Get 'em up."

The hounds, also feeling wind current, a lingering deer scent sliding along with it, put their noses down, fanned out, moving forward at a brisk walk. Raccoons, turkeys, bobcat, deer, and more deer had traipsed through in the predawn hours. Rabbits abounded, now safely tucked in their little grass hutches or hunkered down as flat as they could get. Foxhounds might chase a rabbit for a few bounds if the animal hopped up in front of them, but otherwise the scent offered scant appeal.

Tinsel got a snootful of badger scent. *"Cora."*

Cora came over. *"Must be more moving in. Strange, strange."*

Young Ruthie, wonderful nose, inhaled, then sputtered a moment. *"A heavy fox, a heavy fox."*

Heavy meant pregnant. Dasher and Asa hurried over. Both sniffed, sniffed some more, and then jerked their heads up. Ruthie, in her youth, had made the wrong call.

Cora came over. She inhaled deeply. *"Coyote."*

"Dammit!" Asa swore. He knew how ruinous coyotes were to livestock, house pets, and foxes. In his mind, the foxes' welfare outweighed the others.

Sister noticed, stopped Lafayette. Both human and horse carefully watched.

"Can we run coyote?" Rassle, Ruthie's littermate, asked.

Cora hesitated for a second. *"Yes. They're fair game, but,"* she raised her alto voice, *"young ones, they run straight, they run no faster than they must; occasionally one will double back, but this is really a foot race. Don't forget that. If anywhere along the way, any of you finds fox scent, stop. Stop and tell me. The fox is our primary quarry, understand?"*

"Yes," all responded.

Diana, her voice low, said to Asa, *"Thank God, Dragon's still back in the kennel."*

Asa chuckled. *"Right."*

"Ruthie, you found, sing out." Cora encouraged the youngster.

"Rock and roll." Ruthie lifted her head a bit then all joined her.

Hounds went from zero to sixty in less than three seconds. Sister, eyes widened, at first didn't know they were on coyote. Could be fresh fox scent.

Hounds threaded through the woods, pads touching lightly down on the narrow cleared trail. They clambered over a fallen tree, kept on, then burst out of the woods, leaping over the hog's back jump in the fence line separating After All Farm from Roughneck Farm. They'd covered two miles in minutes.

The electrifying pace only increased as they charged through the meadows, blasted along the edges of the wide wildflower field, the stalks of the odd wisps of broom sage bent with winter's woes, the earth beginning to slightly soften, releasing ever more scent on this crisp day.

As Sister flew along behind her hounds, she noticed they headed straight for the bottom of Hangman's Ridge. A large dark gray cloud peeped over the uppermost edge of this long formidable ridge.

Hounds circled the bottom of the ridge. On the Soldier Road side, they abruptly cut up the ridge on an old deer trail.

Lafayette effortlessly followed, his long stride making the ride comfortable.

Sister blew a few strangled notes when hounds first took off. Now she relied on her voice. She whooped and hollered, shouting as she and Lafayette began to climb to the top of the ridge.

Halfway up, they were enshrouded in a thick veil of white mist. By the time they reached the top, she could barely see fifty yards ahead of her. The heavy moisture in the low cloud felt clammy.

Onward and upward hounds roared. As they passed the hanging tree, they ignored the mournful spirits there. The wind rustled that strange low howl, whistling at a varying pitch just as Sister rode by. The hair on the back of her neck stood up. She thought she saw, out of the corner of her eye, the specter of a well-dressed eighteenth-century gentleman standing next to a Confederate veteran in full uniform.

"Balls," she said out loud, and heard a ghostly snicker.

She loathed this place. Lafayette snorted. They galloped, clods of thawing turf flying up behind his hooves, to the end of the ridge, down the wide dirt road, the last road the convicted ever trod.

Then along the farm road—faster and faster, farther and farther—past the turn into her farm, hounds in the kennel making one hell of a racket, down the farm road, out to the tertiary road, the briefest of checks.

Sister dropped her head, then tipped it back, gulping air. She turned her head, looking back. Behind her, the clouds slid from the ridge, some fingering down the Blue Ridge Mountains as well. Weather was not just making its way in from the west, it was coming full throttle.

She saw Edward emerge at the bottom of the ridge, a dot in bright red.

"Cross the road," Ardent sounded.

The others picked up the line where he'd found it, and on they flew on a southeast line. They shot through the tiny graveyard, marked only by an upright stone. Legend was this was the last stop for suicides who could not be buried in consecrated ground. No one knew for certain. Hounds kept running again, coming out on another tertiary road, the gravel spitting up beneath their claws as they dug in for purchase. The top of the road darkened as dew sank into the bluestone. Lafayette thundered across it, plunging into the rows of cornstalks, leaves making an eerie rustle as the wind picked up.

They were at Alice Ramy's northernmost border. She left the corn up for wildlife every winter. Hounds reached the end of the cornfield, hooked left, and forded an old drainage ditch, snow filling the bottom.

Sister and Lafayette didn't even look down. They flew over the wide ditch as though at the Grand National. A soft thud on the other side as they landed, Lafayette reached out with his forelegs and on they ran, now turning northward, then northeast. Again, they crossed the dirt road, over the meadows, into another wooded area, land mines of rock everywhere, tough soil.

Hounds stopped. Searched.

Sister stopped, hearing the hooves behind her about a quarter of a mile. She figured the drainage ditch held some of them up. God knew, Edward would fly over it.

Hounds moved at a slow, deliberate pace, trying to pick up the scent. The coyote, pausing for a breather on the rim of a ravine a half mile away, heard them, judged the distance between himself and the pack, then trotted toward After All Farm.

He crossed the paved highway, a two-way road with a painted center line, walked down a steep embankment, and then loped toward his den at the southern edge of After All Farm, not a third of a mile away.

Hounds found his line. By the time they reached the den, he was safely inside.

Sister dismounted, blew "Gone to Ground" with what wind she had left. She studied the tracks. "Knew it, goddammit."

"Well, we knew they were here." Betty, who had swung in, looked down.

"What a pity." Sybil, also joining the pack, face cherry red, mourned.

"If we're very lucky, they won't run off our foxes. Still, I think we should shoot every damned one of them." Sister bore no love for the coyote.

"Yeah," Betty agreed.

Edward, top hat firmly in place, red hat cord ensuring it wouldn't be lost, relaxed his shoulders a moment.

"What a run," Crawford enthused.

Coyote did give glorious runs, but the play by play was much simpler. It was the difference between high school football and the pros. The coyote didn't use the ruses the fox did, and most dyed-in-the-wool foxhunters wanted to pit themselves against the cleverest of creatures. The coyote might be wily, but he wasn't sporting like the fox.

Hounds, jubilant at putting their game to ground, sterns upright, eyes clear and happy, pranced as they packed in back to After All Farm.

"Girls won." Cora laughed.

Asa, generous, conceded, then said, *"After a go like that, I'd say we all won."*

"Yes, well done, youngsters," Diana praised the first-year entry, who beamed.

As the field walked back, clouds filling half the western sky, a little spit could be seen coming from them: more snow.

"Mercury's taking a nose dive," Betty mentioned.

Sybil hunched up her shoulders. "What a winter we're having."

"Was Gabriel Daniel Fahrenheit who first put mercury in a thermometer. Born in Poland in 1686. Just think how every day we are enriched by someone who went before us," Sister mused.

"It is pretty wonderful." Betty smiled.

"Bet you by the time we get to the covered bridge, snow will be falling there." Sybil furrowed her brow.

Sister studied the western sky. "Yep."

Shaker and Lorraine waited at the turnoff to After All Farm. He rolled down the window of the truck, stuck his thumb up.

Sister stuck hers up, too.

He rolled up his window and drove down to the trailers, less than a mile away. He wanted to be at the party wagon when hounds arrived.

Sam, on Cloud Nine, chatted with Gray and Tommy Cullhain.

His horse, the timber horse, has a long stride, but he wasn't paying attention.

The horse bumped Xavier's paint horse, Picasso.

Xavier turned around, beheld Sam, and snarled, "Drop dead."

"You first," Sam fired back.

C H A P T E R   3 2

A towering bouquet, winter greens interspersed with rich red and creamy white roses, stood majestically on Sister's front hall table, a long narrow Louis XVI, its gold ormolu gleaming against the deep black lacquer.

Sister opened the note, which read, "Who says flowers don't bloom in winter? Beautiful. Gray."

Her right hand touched her heart for a second.

Golly sat behind them, a feline part of the display. *"Patterson's delivered."*

"Spectacular!" Sister exclaimed.

She loved flowers—what woman doesn't? One of the small disappointments of age was that men did not seem to send them as regularly as they once did.

She took the stairs two at a time, stripped off her clothing. She always took off her boots in the stable, and the girls would clean them. She'd slip into her Wellies, cold in the winter, finish the chores, then come into the house.

She hopped in the shower, Raleigh and Rooster pressing their noses to the glass doors. Then she toweled off, fixed her hair, threw on makeup, opened the closet door, and uttered those immortal words, "I have nothing to wear."

"How can she say that?" Rooster, having lived with a man, was just learning that women were different in some respects. He was only in his second year with Sister.

Raleigh, nosing a soft pair of leather shoes, answered, *"Color, season, fabric, she has to worry about all of that and then when she picks the right thing, the shoes."* He rolled his eyes. *"The downfall of women!"*

"Peter would shower, shave, put on a suit or a navy blazer with some kind of pants, a tie, and off he'd go. Twenty minutes, tops," Rooster informed Raleigh.

A red ball rolled into the large closet as Golly giggled. *"Look what I have."*

"That's not yours." Raleigh snatched the ball.

"Pig." Golly sat on a forest green pair of high-heel shoes, squashing them.

Finally Sister settled on a tailored suit, doubled breasted, with a magenta pinstripe. She wore a pale pink blouse and a deep teal silk scarf. She was always putting together colors in odd ways, but they worked. After much deliberation, she wore shoes the color of the suit.

"Can you imagine wearing panty hose?" Golly wanted to snag the nylons.

"No." Rooster wrinkled his nose. *"Where's she going, anyway?"*

"Special party for Reading for the Blind. Kind of a fund-raiser, but more low-key than the dance stuff." Raleigh knew his mother's charities and special interests.

Golly shot out of the closet, cut in front of the dogs, and walked into the bathroom where Sister performed a last-minute makeup check. Golly hit the wall with all fours, bounced off, and turned to face the dogs.

"King of the hill!"

The two canines stopped, then Rooster said, *"Golly, you're mental."*

"I'm a killer. I can bring down bunnies twice my size. I can face off a . . . a bobcat. I can terrify a cow. I am Kong!" She spun on her paws, flew the entire length of the upper hallway, hit the wall there, bounced off, and flew back, running right under the dogs' bellies.

"She is mental," Rooster repeated.

"I think she has to go to the bathroom," Raleigh said. *"She gets that way if she has to do Number Two."*

"I do not!" Golly was outraged. *"But if I have to go, I'll go in your bed because you have mortally offended me."* She turned in a huff, jumping onto the counter where the makeup sat.

"I don't know how you've stood it for all these years," Rooster consoled Raleigh. *"At least when I lived with Peter, he didn't keep cats. They're horrible."*

"Oh, ignore her, Rooster. She just wants attention. Think of her as a tiny woman in a fur coat."

Golly, purring for all she was worth, watched as Sister put on lipstick, considered it, wiped it off, put on a more pinkish, subdued color, considered it, threw the tube in the trash in disgust. Finally Sister wiped her lips and rubbed in a little colored gloss.

"She's losing it," Golly grandly announced.

"No. She's finding it," Raleigh answered.

By the time Sister reached the gathering, darkness enveloped the town, the white church steeples contrasting against the darkness. A light snow fell.

Marty Howard, a force in the reading group, urged people also to get involved in the Committee to Promote Literacy.

Clay and Izzy Berry moved through the group. Izzy had a sister who was blind and was passionate about the work of this group. Xavier and Dee were there, as well as Dalton Hill and Ben Sidell.

"Ben, this is the first time I've seen you at one of our functions. Thank you for coming," Sister warmly greeted him.

"Marty asked me to drop by. You gave us great sport today, Master." He smiled at her.

"Thank you. Mostly I was trying to hang on and stay up with the hounds. Coyote, as I'm sure you know."

"That word filtered back to us. Bobby Franklin galloped as fast as I've ever seen him go." He nodded in the direction of the genial, plump Bobby.

The Franklins donated printing to this group.

"Big as he is, he can go." Sister smiled. "He's trying the Atkins Diet now. Let's all encourage him. Betty sure looks fabulous. She put her mind to losing weight last summer, got it off, kept it off."

"Well, you don't see too many fat whippers-in, do you?" Ben absentmindedly rattled the cubes in his glass. "Guess you heard about the brief exchange between Xavier and Sam?"

"I did," Sister tartly responded.

"Gray intervened, and Clay moved Xavier up. Lends spice to the proceedings."

"Maybe too much." As Xavier and Dee came over, Sister pecked him on the cheek, then her. "Haven't I just left you?"

"What a day." Xavier, face drawn, complimented her.

"X, thank you for your restraint."

He shrugged. "I've got bigger things on my mind than that worm."

"Honey," Dee gently chided him.

"Well, I don't mind telling you all how I feel. It's not like we don't know one another. And Ben, you're out there riding, so I count you in." Xavier inhaled. "The storage fire is turning into a nightmare."

Sister sympathized. "I'm sorry. It's got to be a strain."

"The investigator won't release the money until the situation, as she calls it, is clarified. How can I clarify Donnie Sweigert winding up as Melba toast? Melba toast that committed arson. It's crazy."

"Honey." Dee squeezed his arm.

"Sorry. I'm a little stressed."

"These investigators are good, sugar. She'll figure it out," Dee reassured her husband.

Ben glanced briefly to the floor, then looked up.

"Sorry, Ben. Dee didn't mean it that way. This is a tough situation. I know you're doing all that you can." Xavier, for all his troubles, was sensitive to the feelings of others.

Clay and Izzy joined them. Politically wise, Clay didn't want the tension between Xavier and himself to become gossip fodder. Yes, he wanted the check, but he didn't know what more to do about it either.

After a few moments of social chat, the group broke up. Ben remained with Sister. She noticed Clay moving off to talk to one group of people while Izzy moved over to another, chatted briefly, and then left the room. She noted that Dalton also left the room by another door.

"Meant to ask you, you know the high school and college coaches around here, don't you?"

"Some better than others," Sister answered.

"With the exception of the university men's basketball coach, most of these guys have been working a long time, great stability."

"Winners don't get fired," Sister replied, knowing the same applied in the hunt world.

Few people understood the pressures on a professional huntsman. He or she has to produce, just like the quarterback for a major league team. Huntsmen are professional athletes minus the endorsement, media hype, and titanic salaries. Many of these men and women could have had careers in the lucrative sports. They chose love instead of loot.

"What's the problem with men's basketball at the university?"

"Boy, it's a yo-yo, isn't it? Let's hope they've turned the corner." She touched his arm. "Look at these kids playing basketball and football now. They're hulks."

"That they are." Ben lowered his voice. "Sam Lorillard mentioned something to me at the breakfast. Mitch and Anthony did some odd jobs for Berry Storage. We knew that. Donnie Sweigert was always the driver, never any other driver."

"I don't see the significance."

"I'm not sure I do, either. Sam's friend, Rory Ackerman, who's now in rehab in Greensboro, was the one who told him this. Anyway, Sam said Mitch and Anthony only delivered furniture to coaches or trainers."

"Have you asked Clay?"

Ben nodded that he had. "Said he'd check his records. Said he couldn't trust Mitch and Anthony or any of the railroad denizens to stay sober long enough for a long haul. They only made the short runs, and Donnie drove those because he didn't like going cross-country. Also Clay said he felt Donnie could control the drunks. I think Donnie himself drank more than Clay knew."

"What a pity."

Ben shifted his weight from one foot to the other. "You know these people. Can you think of anything—no matter how far-fetched—that would tie in Mitch, Anthony, and Donnie to the delivery of expensive furniture to coaches?"

"Drugs," she replied. "These days it always seems to come down to that. We have a counter economy in America, not one tax dollar produced from it. Billions."

"I know," Ben said with feeling.

Sister replied, "I can't see that Clay or X would be involved in drugs. They don't appear to use them. But," she inhaled, "an insurance scam fits the bill, doesn't it?"

"Yes."

"Worried?"

Ben looked her right in the eyes. "Yes."

"You don't think it's over?"

"No."

She rubbed her forehead a moment. "They aren't afraid to kill."

"Selling OxyContin can yield hundreds of thousands of dollars. Prozac, Percodan, anything like that. Even Viagra." He smiled slightly. "Off market, the drugs can make one very rich very fast. As for cocaine and other party drugs, they can make you rich fast, but they're more dangerous because the other people dealing them are smart, tough, quick to kill."

"Ben, have you ruled out the furniture and silver theft entirely?"

"No. No evidence so far for linking the fire to that, *but*," he said, with emphasis, "these people are highly intelligent, very well organized. This may be a warning to someone else in the ring or to competition. They'd be stupid to burn down a warehouse full of stolen goods, wouldn't they?"

Sister agreed, then asked, "What can I do?"

"The Jefferson Hunt is one of the hubs of the county. Can you think of any one or any group who might be involved in a high-class theft organization or involved with drugs? For example, and I certainly don't mean she would do this, just as an example, can you imagine Betty Franklin buying illegal diet drugs in this country on the black market?"

"No." Then Sister chuckled. "Bobby would be thinner."

Ben smiled. "Keep your eyes open. Keep thinking. We're right next to it, Sister, but we can't see it."

When Ben walked away, she thought about the ghosts on Hangman's Ridge. She shuddered. Those ghosts appeared when someone was going to die. She used to think it was a tall tale, but over the years she had learned to believe it.

She moved around the party. Marty Howard caught up with her for a moment. "Thank you for coming. If you ever have any time, Sister, we'd love for you to read. It's not just books we need, but magazines and newspapers. It's often hard for the blind to keep up with current things."

"I never thought of that. I could read for an hour to two. Let's see how I do."

"I'll call Monday and we can check calendars."

As Marty moved away, Dalton Hill joined her. "The hunting has been very good. I'm glad I joined."

"Me, too." Sister noticed he wore an English school tie, quite expensive. "Beautiful tie."

"Eton." He blushed slightly. "Actually, I didn't attend Eton. I went to St. Andrews College, Aurora, but I liked the thin Eton blue diagonal stripe."

"I can see why. I heard you purchased the Cleveland bay."

"Yes. I'm going to have my two hunters brought down from Hamilton, too." He named the town where his horses were boarding. "I want to hunt as much as I can. One of the great things about teaching is I can set my schedule, so I have arranged all my classes to be in the late afternoon."

"Perfect." She paused, then addressed him. "Dr. Hill—"

"Do call me Dalton. I'm trying to downplay the doctor," he interrupted, a conspiratorial note in his voice. "I really don't want to hear about someone's gallbladder."

"I promise never to discuss mine." She smiled. "In Canada certain drugs are available that aren't available here, am I right?"

"Not hard drugs, of course, but yes. Canada's laws are more patient-oriented. Forgive me a bit of national pride, but in the United States, Master, everything is driven by profit, by the huge pharmaceutical companies."

"Call me Sister. But surely those mega companies—and not all of them are American, I mean the Germans and the Swiss have giant pharmaceutical companies, all those companies do business in Canada."

"They do, but we have them more in check. The whole point is to heal the patient. If you can't heal the patient, then you make him or her as comfortable as possible; it's cruel to deny a suffering person relief."

"What about performance drugs? Not drugs for illness, but drugs to enhance performance?"

"Sexual performance?" His eyebrows rose.

"Now there's the elixir of life as well as profit," she wryly exclaimed. "I wasn't thinking of that, but let's include it. I was thinking along the lines of drugs to retard aging, and yes, I would be the first in line."

"No need."

"Dalton, thank you. You're fibbing, but it falls sweetly upon the ear." She smiled broadly. "I was thinking of anti-aging drugs and athletic-performance drugs. Guess I was remembering that fabulous runner, Ben Johnson, the Canadian sprinter who set a record for the hundred-meter dash at the 1987 World Championships, and won the Gold Medal at the 1988 Olympics, and then forfeited it when he admitted to steroid use."

"Athletes are far beyond that. The coaches, the team doctors— everyone is more sophisticated now, and the drugs are more sophisticated, too."

"And some of these drugs are legal in your country?"

"Not steroids."

"Do you condone their use?"

Hesitating, he replied, "There is no way any professional athlete can make a living, can hold down his or her job, without chemical help. I find nothing wrong in trying to advance human performance. The caveat is abuse. Aspirin is a drug. Caffeine is as well. Bodybuilders routinely drink a cup of coffee before working out. Actually, I find your country's drug laws backward, repressive, opening a wide door for crime."

She sighed deeply. "I'm afraid you are right."

"The entrenched interests here, meaning those people making tax-free billions, have churches and politicians on their side. It's hypocritical. It's shocking. It's big business."

"Prohibition on a higher plane." She sighed again.

"Exactly." His lips compressed. Then he relaxed. "I apologize. Being an endocrinologist, I study human chemistry. We really can improve performance with drugs. We really can retard aging. And we really can begin to solve the riddles of some dreadful degenerative diseases with stem cell research." He threw up his hands. "I cannot for the life of me understand why any human being would deny a cure for Parkinson's to another, and yet that's exactly what's happening."

"For many people, these are complex moral issues."

"There's nothing moral in watching a human being die by inches."

"I agree, Dalton, I totally agree. But I am one lone woman in Virginia without one ounce of political clout."

"You can vote, and you are a master. Masters are members of Parliament in training." He was warm to her now. "Same skills."

"Perhaps they are."

"Why did you ask me about drugs?"

"Oh, Ben and I were talking about the university basketball team. One thing led to another. And then you said you wanted to shy away from being called a doctor. I thought I'd better ask while I could, especially about the aging stuff." She laughed as she evaded telling the truth.

"I'll tell you what. If you come to my office, I'll pull blood, run an EKG, do a few other tests. I can tell you, with accuracy, the true age of your body. Not your years but the true age of your body. In fact, you'd be a fascinating subject. Without the tests, I'd hazard a guess that internally you are between forty-five and fifty. You have never abused alcohol, drugs, or smoked. Am I correct?"

"You are."

"Come see me."

"I shall. I appreciate the offer."

"You'd be doing me a favor." He paused a moment. "I believe, no, I *know* we can live longer, stronger lives than we imagine. Aging must be recast in our minds as a slow disease that can be fought. I can envision a day when men can live to be a hundred and fifty with full productive lives."

"Women?" she asked slyly.

"Ah." He smiled. "A hundred seventy-five."

"Right answer. Can you envision a future where a woman can run the hundred-yard dash, well, I guess it's a hundred meters now, in nine seconds?"

"Yes. And a man will do it in seven and a half."

"Are you being sexist?"

"No. Men really are faster. Yes, the fastest woman in the world will be faster than eighty percent of the men but, at the top, the men are faster. That's the real difference in professional tennis. It's not upper-body muscle, which people focus on, it's speed. Men can return shots that women can't. So if a woman plays a man, she's not used to her 'winners' being fired back that fast."

"Never thought of that."

"In your favor, women have much more endurance, and, this I can't quantify scientifically, but also much more emotional strength."

She studied his earnest features. "Perhaps. But there's so much we can never know accurately because our concepts of male and female are formed in a rigid cultural grid. Even scientific research reflects unconscious bias."

"I agree. It does." He noticed a pretty woman talking to Marty Howard.

"That's Rebecca Baldwin, Tedi Bancroft's grandniece. Thirty-one, I should say. Used to hunt, but she went back to school to get her doctorate in architectural history. Lovely girl. Allow me to introduce you."

After Sister performed this service, she smiled to herself at how Dalton's demeanor changed in the presence of a pretty woman. Ah yes, though he was an endocrinologist, his hormones pumped just like in the rest of us.

She found Gray, whispered in his ear. "You are so handsome. I have no idea what I'm doing, but I'm having fun."

He slipped his arm around her waist for a moment, inhaling

her fragrance, her hair. "I'm walking on air. And I do want to take you to a proper dinner. Let's go Sunday. And sometime, too, let's go up to the Kennedy Center. I have season seats, box seats, for the opera. Do you like the opera?"

"I can learn." Sister knew nothing except she loathed recitatives.

He hugged her tighter. "We've both got a lot to learn. We'll never be bored."

Tedi noticed this exchange and prayed silently. "Dear God, let this be something special. Bring love into her life. She deserves it. And help us all get over this black/white stuff." Then she glanced across the room, filling with more people, catching sight of the man she had loved for fifty years. Her eyes misted over. When she had stood before the altar next to a black-haired Edward Bancroft, she could never have dreamed that fifty years later she would love him more deeply, more passionately, with more insight into the man than when he slipped that thin gold band on her finger. She prayed again, "Thank you."

Sister checked her watch as she made the rounds. Time to get home. She thought to herself that she didn't give Gray much of a chase. So many men love the chase. Well, seductive gamesmanship wasn't her style. Then she thought to herself, Admit it, I'm seventy-two. I haven't any time to waste. She nearly laughed out loud at the thought.

As she was ready to leave, she overheard Clay and Xavier inside the cloakroom.

". . . a real bind."

"Clay, I know. I'm doing everything I can. I can't just write a check out of my company's funds."

"It's not just the money, X. It's the suspicion. People are looking at me like I'm an arsonist, a scam artist, like I'm a murderer. Do you know what this is doing to my wife and children?"

Xavier's voice rose, almost pleading. "What can I do? Neither Ben Sidell nor the investigator can figure it out. What can I do?"

"Can't you write me a small check? Even five thousand dollars?"

"You're putting me in a terrible position. If I do that, I'm undercutting the carrier. I have hundreds of clients placed with them, and Worldwide Security has been excellent. I can't screw up that relationship for myself or my other clients."

"So you'll screw up our friendship?"

"Clay, my hands are tied."

CHAPTER 33

At five-thirty Sunday morning, the snowflakes swayed as though on invisible chains. Heavy clouds blocked the pale light of the waxing moon, this February 1.

The winter solstice was forty-one days behind this morning; roughly forty more minutes of sunlight washed over central Virginia since then. Gaining that minute of sunlight a day put more spring in Sister's step, though she wouldn't see any sun today.

She walked through the fresh snow, tracks beginning to fill even as she lifted her boots out of them. Raleigh and Rooster faithfully accompanied her, although both were loath to leave the warm house.

"Rooster, leave it," Sister softly said, for she spied Inky carefully exiting the stable. She'd been eating up the gleanings, the sweet feed being a particular favorite, as well as the little candied fruits she craved. "Morning, Inky."

Inky turned a moment, blinked, then scampered toward the

kennels where the hounds slept. Occasionally, Diana would be up walking about. Inky enjoyed speaking with her. She didn't like Rooster, though, but then he wasn't behind a chain-link fence. Being a harrier, Rooster was keen to prove his nose could follow fox scent just as readily as rabbit.

"*Bother,*" Rooster complained.

"*Can't do much in the snow anyway,*" Raleigh commented.

Although not a hound, Raleigh possessed a good nose, but his obligation was to protect Sister, her other animals, and her property. He took this charge quite seriously.

Most animals operate on an internal clock. Sister's alarm sounded between five and five-thirty every morning regardless of when she crawled into bed at night. A day's work is more easily accomplished if one has had seven or eight hours sleep, so Sister was usually in bed by ten.

She noted that Shaker's old Jeep Wagoner was gone. Scrupulous about Sister's equipment, he wouldn't use the old Chevy truck unless he asked her. As many times as she told him to take a day off, he'd be at the kennels no later than seven-thirty in the winters, usually six in the summers. He was a huntsman to the bone.

She whistled at the paddock. The horses ran up, their hoofbeats muffled in the snow. She brought Lafayette and Keepsake in, then Rickyroo and Aztec. Each had his own stall, nameplate prettily painted and fastened to its door. Then she brought in Shaker's mounts: Gunpowder, Showboat, Hojo.

Although puffs of breath came from her mouth, the temperature hung right around forty degrees in the barn. The barn, well built and well ventilated, provided enough warmth to keep the horses happy but not enough to make them ill. Each horse had his blanket on with a thin white cotton sheet underneath, sort of an equine undershirt. Too tight a barn causes respiratory problems for horses, plus they shouldn't be overly warm in cold weather.

Pawing, snorting, and whinnying filled the barn as Sister rolled the feed cart to each stall, sliding the scoop through the opening to dump the crimped oats with a bit of sweet feed into the bucket. Everyone received the amount appropriate to his weight and level of work. As all of these horses worked hard, they received as much high-quality hay as they wished and one or two scoops of food depending on their individual metabolisms. If an animal needed a special supplement, it was crumbled into the oats. Usually, the good grain and particularly the hay kept them tip-top. Of all that they consumed, hay was the most important. It kept the motility in their intestines. So many people—not horsemen, but horse owners—fed pellets or too much grain in the winter. Their poor animals would come down with blocked intestines.

Sister had grown up with horses and hounds. She didn't even know what she knew, for it was like breathing to her. However, she was still willing to learn and never minded reading about hoof studies, new medications, new exercise therapies. She noted that many horsemen were fanatically resistant to new methods. She thought a lot of the new stuff bunk, but that didn't mean she shouldn't keep abreast. Occasionally there was value in something new.

She could think in the stable better than in the kennels. With the hounds she was busy talking to them, assessing their abilities or working with them one on one. But with the horses, she could truly think. She'd adjust a blanket, check legs, listen to breathing just in case. The large animals relaxed her, their scent intoxicated her, and her love for them was unconditional. She had always loved horses, hounds, cats, and dogs more than 99 percent of the people she had met in her life. She was, however, wise enough to keep this to herself, or she thought she was. The human race is so grotesquely egocentric that any human who finds another species more worthy of affection is branded a misfit, a misanthrope, someone with intimacy issues, oh, the list went on. She paid them no mind. She knew she was closer to God when with his creatures than she ever would be with chattering people.

She needed that closeness this morning. Bouncing between elation and worry, her chores helped her concentrate.

Thinking of Gray made her smile, while the thought of the club's troubles caused distress. The hostility between Xavier and Sam upset her. She also secretly worried about working closely with Crawford. He would not easily set aside his large ambition. She hoped he wouldn't work to undermine Walter. The tension between Clay and Xavier was a new cause for concern, and this dreadful mess at Berry Storage made her sick. With the instinct of a good fox-hunter, she knew the two deaths at the railroad station were connected with Donnie's. She felt as though the snow was covered with tracks that ran in circles.

If Jennifer and Sari could get through the roads, they'd arrive after church to groom each horse, so she didn't attend to that. Instead, she walked into the tack room, dogs behind her, and sat down in the old, cracked-leather wing chair, the heady fragrance of leather, liniment, and horse filling her nostrils.

With the door closed, the tack room was pleasant. Its small gas heater looked like a wood-burning stove; a glass door in front kept the fifteen-by-fifteen room toasty. In the old days, tack rooms had real wood-burning stoves, but sparks flying out of the chimneys, in a downdraft, could swirl onto the roof or find their way into haylofts. Constant vigilance and many buckets of water were necessary.

"Could I have a bone?" Raleigh asked. He'd left the house without breakfast, as had Sister.

"Me, too," Rooster begged.

"I know, I didn't feed anyone. I'll make a good breakfast when we get back up to the house. Just let the horses eat, give it another half hour. I always like to see how much each has eaten. You know how fussy I am with them." She rose from the chair, opened a mid-size dark red plastic garbage can, almost a little art object in its own way, and handed each dog a large milkbone.

She sat down again, talking to them as they chewed. "Boys, I keep thinking about all this. There is such a thing as the criminal mind. I can't say that I understand that mind, but Ben Sidell does, I'm sure. There are people born without a conscience, psychopaths, sociopaths, I don't know all the technical terms. It boils down to a criminal brain. I don't necessarily believe a criminal mind is an insane mind, although some are. If you think about it, every single society on earth since B.C. has faced criminal behavior and destructive people. We think we've advanced in our handling of it, but I think we've backslid, abandoned our responsibility to the law-abiding. That's not what worries me at this moment. You see, boys, I'm thinking about Donnie, Mitch, and Anthony, especially Anthony. Three people who have died of unnatural causes in a short period of time. Three people loosely connected by work."

Raleigh stopped chewing a minute. *"I'm listening."*

"Are these deaths the work of a nutcase? I think not. What is this about? There's no element of passion. That shows on the corpse. This is cold murder, just getting people out of the way and trying not to make too big a mess out of it. With Mitch and Anthony, it appeared natural until the autopsy. Then, the question: Is it murder? Of course it is. I think so. They were thought out. But they weren't thought out quite well enough, were they? Could Donnie really have been stupid enough to soak the warehouse and light a match without making sure of his escape? That's pretty stupid. This mess isn't about love, lust, or revenge. It's greed. So I ask you, my two friends, where is the money? Show me the money."

CHAPTER 34

"Are you dog tired and ready to bite?"

"Tired. No biting. Not you, anyway." Walter gratefully accepted the hot soup Sister placed before him. He'd had an emergency call with a patient at four in the morning, Monday. He had finally reached home at eleven to find Sister waiting for him with food.

Tonto, a bundle of energy, ran laps in the big old kitchen as Rooster and Raleigh watched. Bessie stayed in her carpet-covered box. She didn't like Raleigh and Rooster.

"You've transformed this kitchen. I wish Peter could see it." She admired the patina of the hand-polished maple cabinets, the granite-topped counters, the built-in appliances, unobtrusive except for the huge Wolf stove, gleaming in stainless steel. A welling of lust for this stove filled her.

"Maybe he can." Walter waited for Sister to sit before putting the large spoon in the chicken rice soup. "This is exactly what I needed."

From the small bowl in front of her she tested the soup, which she made last night. "Not bad. Soups seem perfect in the winter. This has been one hell of a winter."

"The roads are bad. I sure appreciate your coming here."

"Drove slow. It's four-wheel drive, not four-wheel stop."

He broke off a bit of pumpernickel from the fresh loaf.

"Do you have a bread oven?" she asked.

"No." He pointed to a square machine, two feet high and built in flush with the wall. "I put the ingredients in, set the timer, the bread is ready. It's remarkable."

"What's remarkable is that you think of it."

"I like cooking. A transitory art form."

She smiled. "Extremely transitory. Well, I am in love with your stove. Forgive me, it's rude to ask prices, but how much is that thing? I mean, it has six gas burners, a griddle, which is perfect for me, a big oven. It's really impressive."

"That particular model was nine thousand dollars. There are less-expensive models, four burners instead of six."

"Good God."

"A lot of money, but it should last generations, and you saw how wonderful it is to work on. You can get them without griddles, but you like the griddle."

"I do." She drummed her fingers on the farm table. "Nine thousand dollars. And where does one purchase this thing?"

"You can go online or shop around, but I wasted too much time doing that. I finally went down to Ron Martin and got it. They delivered, installed it, the gas company came and hooked up the line after burying the gas tank. It wasn't nearly as big a mess as I thought it would be. Kind of like plumbing. You know, I fooled around and then woke up and went down to Maddox in Char-lottesville, bought my shower, hot tub, old restored 1930s sinks. Had some of the sinks and johns that were here rebuilt for me. They stand behind what they do. That's the problem with online shopping. The only person you can call when something goes wrong is the manufacturer, and he'll bounce you to the dealer, and, if the dealer is in Minnesota, you're cooked. Forgive the pun."

She smiled. "I agree. Always do business locally. Nothing can replace that connection to another person." She scratched Tonto's head as he bounced over, sat down, then put a paw on her thigh.

"Too cute," Raleigh sneered.

"Gag me," Rooster coughed.

"I love everyone in the world!" The half-grown Welsh terrier cocked his head as Sister scratched him.

"Terriers are mental." Rooster closed his eyes, feigning boredom.

"Born to dig. That's it. Dig." Raleigh felt his calling in life of far more importance than ridding the world of vermin.

"Tonto is a most engaging creature."

"I'm a terrier man," Walter said, then hastily added, "hounds first though, I know that."

She laughed. "Working with a pack is different. But yes, I love foxhounds. I've spent most of my life studying them, and I'll still never know as much as the late Dickie Bywaters." She looked up from the dog and beamed at Walter. "Wonder if Rooster likes being back here?"

"I do, but I miss Peter," Rooster replied.

The two humans looked at the harrier.

"Maybe he heard you," Walter said.

"I expect they know a great deal more than we give them credit for knowing. Which is one of the reasons I'm here—not about dogs, I mean." She leaned forward. "Tell me about athletes and drugs."

"How much time do you have?" He rose to ladle more soup in his bowl.

"I made it. I should have done that."

"Miss Manners isn't here." Walter pointed to the pot of soup on the stove. "More?"

"Yes." She handed him her bowl.

As they started on their second bowls of soup, Walter tried to answer her broad question. "Football, basketball, baseball, weight-lifting, and track and field would collapse without drugs. For runners or endurance sports, um, not as prevalent. Well, let me put it this way: they aren't on steroids or human growth hormone. Those are the drugs of choice."

"What about women's sports?"

"To be competitive, you've got to be strong and fast, as strong and as fast as your competition. Gender is irrelevant."

"Do these drugs really work?"

He put his spoon down. "Without a doubt."

"I see. So if you truly want to compete at the highest levels, it's better living through chemistry?"

He nodded. "If you're the defensive tackle for the Oakland Raiders, facing someone in the trenches, and you haven't taken drugs and he has, he'll beat you seven out of ten times—or more. For one thing, his ligaments will be stronger."

"Bigger muscles?"

"Yes, though that can be a disadvantage. One of the problems we're now seeing, especially in football, is the number of injuries has escalated because these men now have bodies that are so big and heavy, they slam into one another like a train wreck! Three hundred and twenty pounds of lineman beef, say, a center, crashing into two hundred and eighty-nine pounds of defensive guard. And they're quick. Big as they are, they're quick. They're slamming into each other at speed. And then if one of the linebackers really clocks a halfback, it's ugly."

"Do they take painkillers to play?"

"Yes, legal and illegal."

"And the efforts of the governing bodies are ineffective?"

He nodded. "The coaches are scientists. And then again, let's lay it on the line, Sister, the American public craves violence. If the mayhem dries up, there go the advertising revenues; there goes the ticket sales to say nothing of all those empty skyboxes. I don't think the commissioners of any of the professional sports—men's or women's—are going to try too awfully hard, although they'll talk a good game. Again, forgive the pun."

"Was that a true pun?" Her brow furrowed.

"Uh." He wondered now, too.

"No matter. Okay, next question. As profit has transformed professional sports, what about college sports?"

"College sports are nurseries for professional sports. Only baseball supports and pays for minor leagues. For the rest of them, they siphon the players right out of college without pouring money into the colleges. A good deal for the NFL and NBA."

"Why is baseball different in your opinion?"

"It's such a difficult game to play well. Apart from the phenomenal hand-eye coordination, for every situation there are maybe three possibilities. You really have to think in baseball. It's not enough to learn your position. I love baseball."

"Thought you were the halfback on Cornell's football team?"

"I was, but I played center field for the baseball team. Love baseball."

"Actually, I do, too." She sipped her tea. "So the college athletes are taking steroids and whatever?"

"You bet. The coaches are right in there with it or turning a blind eye. You can't have a kid go home during the summer of his sophomore year, return for football practice thirty pounds of muscle heavier without drugs. Just throwing hay bales on the farm isn't going to do it, although, truthfully, it will give you a better body."

"Really?"

"Sure. More flexible. Natural muscle is different than muscle enhanced by steroids. Once you get used to looking for it, you can always tell the difference."

"Why so?"

"An athlete who has taken steroids has a rounder, fuller look.

Essentially, the muscle cell has been pumped up with fluid. I won't bore you with a long explanation. You and I don't have muscles like that. Our muscles are less full but have a harder, almost shredded look."

"I thought the bodybuilders were the ones who got shredded."

"They do. Lots of purging water from their systems before a contest, but you can still see the difference. The only way I can explain it is those steroid bodies have a real roundness to the muscle."

"Dangerous?"

"Sure. In excess, the drugs can shut down the liver, shrink the testicles on a man, give men what they call 'bitch tits.' For women, we know much less. In fact, we know much less about women on so many levels of medicine that it's a sin. Man has been the measure of all things."

"This is fascinating. I had no idea."

"Sister, kids are using steroids in high school. A kid wants to make All State and then wants to play for Nebraska. He starts shooting up."

"With the help of the coach or the trainer?"

Walter shrugged. "I really hope that a high school coach knows better, acts as a father to those kids, but," he said, holding up his hands, "a high school coach is under pressure, too. Although not nearly as severe as the college coach at a PAC Ten school who makes one million dollars a year in salary and God knows how much in benefits."

"Good Lord, I picked the wrong sport."

"Far from it." He patted Tonto, who now pestered him. "One of the things I most love about foxhunting is that it can't be corrupted by money."

"But racing can. Three-day eventing. Show jumping. Drugs?"

He shrugged. "Not steroids. Not for people, anyway. You know more about the horse end of it than I do. I know some racehorses have been loaded with the stuff. Saddlebreds, too. But the drugs in the horse world for humans are almost always alcohol, cocaine, or some kind of painkiller."

"Makes sense."

"I have yet to meet a horseman without broken bones."

"Me, neither." She sat for a moment. "You haven't asked why I'm on this track."

"You're the master." He grinned, his white teeth straight, although a few had ragged edges from his playing days.

"Before I get to why, what about human growth hormone? What's the deal there?"

"It's extremely important. It may be able to dramatically slow aging. I personally think it needs to come onto the market. We have done enough testing on the stuff. But it is abused by athletes because it will grow muscle and it is theoretically safer, in large doses, than steroids. Some people react to steroid abuse with rages, 'roid rage. Taking HGH doesn't produce rages. It builds a stronger body, stronger ligaments, which are more important than bulk, as I said before. If abused, the taker will get a lantern jaw, larger hands and feet. You know the look."

"I do. Acromegaly."

"HGH is gold on the black market, pure gold."

"If HGH and steroids create better bodies, what about plain old testosterone?"

"Up to a point, that will help. The body has its limits. You can go over the limit, but you aren't going to get the kind of dramatic, rapid gain you'll get with isolated steroids—think of them as turbo testosterone. And all this stuff affects one's cholesterol levels and liver. There is no free ride."

"These drugs are on the black market, I suppose, along with mood elevators and stuff like that?"

Again, he nodded. "The odd thing is, Sister, every single person is a different cocktail. Let's throw out numbers: not real but as examples. Let's say the so-called average woman pumps out ten cc's of estrogen and one cc of testosterone. Okay? The so-called average male pumps out ten cc's of testosterone and one cc of estrogen. If I pulled blood from every member of our hunt club, I probably wouldn't find one person with an average ratio. Okay, that ratio is made up, but you know what I mean. We really don't know nearly enough about the human body as an individual unit. You pick up the newspapers or listen to TV and hear the latest scientific study," he paused, "be wary. You can't make policy or prescriptions based on tests of even ten thousand people. Yet this is done regularly and on test groups of far fewer numbers. It's insane. I'm a physician, and I'm telling you it's utterly insane."

"Why is it done?"

"Money. Mostly it's the drug company's hot desire for ever-escalating profits, but also it's from public pressure. They want instant answers and easy answers. There is nothing easy about it. One tiny example, the human heart. It's supposed to be here, right?" He tapped the left side of his chest. "Well, most of the time, it's actually here." He tapped just to the left of the breastplate. "Often it's here." He tapped his chest, dead center, a bit high. "And you'd be amazed how many times I find it over here." He tapped the right side of his chest just off center line.

"Amazing."

"Circadian rhythms. You're a hunter. You know how important the diurnal rhythms are, the seasonal rhythms, even the phases of the moon. Right?"

"Right. I live by them."

"Medicine reacts differently in the body according to the time when it is administered. But you're instructed to take a pill in the morning or three times a day. The truth is, that might not be the optimum time to administer that drug, a drug, prescribed by your physician, that you've just spent hard-earned money buying from your pharmacist. And we sure don't know enough to make the kind of outrageous pronouncements and promises you see every day in advertisements."

"Now, would you like to know why I've asked you these questions, which have nothing to do with horses, hounds, or the weather for Tuesday's hunt?"

"I would." He smiled.

"A stray fact wandered in through someone Sam Lorillard knows, one of the alcoholics who hangs around the station. Ben Sidell told me this. When Mitch and Anthony picked up odd jobs delivering furniture for Berry Storage, Donnie Sweigert always drove the truck. Nothing too strange about that, but what *is* interesting is that those men only made deliveries to coaches or trainers."

"Ah." He held his breath for a moment. "You're thinking this has to do with performance-enhancing drugs, maybe even recreational drugs. Have you said anything to Ben?"

"He's smart. I expect he's there ahead of me."

"It's deeply disturbing. Not only are three people dead, but other lives are being ruined. The chances of a high school athlete and then a college athlete making it to the pros are tiny, infinitesimal. But every kid thinks he can do it. Even more damaging, less than twenty-five percent of black male basketball players at Division 1A schools graduate. Graduate!" He exhaled loudly, which made Tonto stand up on his hind paws to make sure Walter was okay. "Here, bud." Walter gave him a small piece of pumpernickel. "I guess every one of us needs a dream. I don't mean to sound negative, but more than a dream, they need a degree."

"Not negative, just realistic. I probably have this fact wrong, but I remember reading somewhere that of all the college male basketball players, less than three percent will make it to the pros, and out of that percentage, most will wash out in five years."

"Sounds close enough to me."

"I don't know what to do. I don't want to say anything. That would be stupid, kind of showing my hand too early. This is inside our tent, I think. The finger points at Clay Berry or Xavier. Possibly Sam, because of his connection to the railroad station gang. From time to time Sam would help deliver furniture. I guess those who had any muscle power left took a job with Berry Storage from time to time. Makes me sick to think of it. I've racked my brain to see if anyone else could be doing this, using the Berry Storage as a distribution point. When you think about it, it's pretty smart. Furniture with drugs hidden inside."

His voice remained even then rose. "Hard to think of Clay or X being involved in drug sales."

"Yes. Well, I don't know anything, but I have this instinct, like when I know where my fox is."

"Your instincts have kept us all going."

"And now I know something else."

"What?"

"Professional athletes are on everything but roller skates."

CHAPTER 35

Each time he blew the horn, Shaker's ribs hurt, taped though they were. Yesterday's rare day of sunshine was followed by more gray clouds this Tuesday.

In the far distance, the grand estate of Rattle and Snap, a Georgian pile, red brick with massive white Doric pillars, reposed on a hill overlooking its snow-filled acres. While it was exquisitely beautiful, everyone who bought it lost pots of money, eventually leaving it to the next rich outsider.

Sister, back leading the field, wondered if places didn't have good spirits or bad spirits. Maybe the Chinese were correct in lining up their buildings and doorways according to their ideas of energy. Feng shui made as much sense as any other system for attracting luck.

The hunt club enjoyed a bit of luck as Alexander Vajay, owner of Chapel Cross, purchased a lottery ticket, one of the scratch kind, and won a thousand dollars. He happily gave half to the hunt club before the hounds took off this frosty morning.

Alexander, with his dark Indian skin, white teeth, and expressive eyes, delighted Sister and the members. He and his family had been members for only a year, but their exuberance, matched by their warmth and sophistication, had made the family quite popular.

Tuesday's field consisted of twelve people: Tedi, Edward, Sam, Gray, Crawford, Marty, Alexander, Xavier, Clay, Ronnie, Jennifer, and Sari. The girls lucked out with a snow day. Two flakes of snow make principals shaky, the result being kids make up snow days well into May and sometimes June. It was one way to learn that one pays for one's pleasures, but Sister always thought if a child had mastered the work, let him or her go.

They'd had a few good runs in the snow but nothing longer than fifteen minutes. It was one of those hunt-and-peck days, but still, anything beats a blank. The temperature nudged up to the midforties and then skidded right back down into the midthirties. Sister wondered what was behind it. Probably another storm, more snow. No one would be likely to forget this winter.

Shaker circled back toward the outbuildings behind the mansion. He might have a chance to pick up a line going in or out of the hay barns. The puddles in the dirt road were shining ice. The ice, close to an inch thick, could bear the weight of a hound, but not a horse.

Aztec, careful with his hooves, mistrusted the shine off the frozen puddles. He'd try to sidestep them, but too many puddles filled the road. Sister squeezed him on. He did it, but complained by flicking his ears back and tightening the muscles along his spine as though he was going to hump up.

"Don't even think about it."

"*I don't like this,*" Aztec answered.

"Oh, come on." She hit him with her spurs.

"*I'm doing it, but I still don't like it.*" He vaulted the puddle instead of going through it.

Fortunately Sister had a tight seat. "Weiner."

"I'll take any jump in anyone's hunt field, but I don't like ice." He kept going, his trot eating up the yards.

This chase, out of a trot for all of five minutes, ended a mile and a half from the mansion, the fox ducking into the abandoned mule barns. Back before World War I, Melton supported a workforce of over three hundred laborers—men, women, and children. The main crops—apples, hay, corn, and some tobacco—needed many hands to plant, nurture, then pluck. All the old tobacco barns, built of heavy stone, stood, the lingering smoky scent tangible even to the human nose.

Mindful of Shaker's ribs and his pride, Sister felt they'd been out for two hours, shown some sport on a dicey day. As he dismounted, blowing "Gone to Ground," she waited for him to finish.

Riding on Showboat, she signaled him by tapping her hat with her crop. He nodded. He hurt more than he cared to admit.

The field, feeling the precipitous temperature drop now that they weren't moving along, sighed with relief.

Gray rode with Sister as they turned back.

"What I most like about Melton is the mile-long drive lined with sugar maples."

"It's a beautiful estate," she said.

"Did you watch Westminster last night?"

"Glued to the set. Loved the English setter in the hunting dog division. Thought the corgi was fabulous in the herding group. Course tonight we see hounds, terriers, and toys. And then the Best in Show. I guarantee it won't be a hound, no matter how spectacular the hound. Just makes my teeth hurt, I hate that so much!" She laughed at herself. "I've half a mind to take my hounds to Madison Square Garden and really give the audience a show!"

Crawford joined them. "Sister, I have an idea about the staff."

Her eyebrows rose. "Love to hear it."

"What if we advertised in Horse Country's newspaper and *The*

Chronicle of the Horse for an intern? You know, someone in vet school or a college kid who rides on the show-jumping team. You and Shaker would have help in the summer, and it wouldn't cost as much as full-time help." He caught his breath, the cold air stinging his throat. "If it proved efficient, then in the fall we could organize some fund-raisers for a permanent position."

"Excellent idea," Sister replied. "Even if we couldn't hire full-time help, we'd make progress. Excellent," she repeated.

Sister turned to see how the others were coming along behind them. Sam and Marty rode well to the rear, far away from Xavier, Clay, and Ronnie, all three in an animated discussion.

Back at the trailers, Sister asked Ronnie, "What was that all about?"

"Sam Lorillard."

"Oh."

Ronnie loosened his horse's girth. "X swears he's drinking again, but X hates him so much we're taking it with a grain of salt. I don't know." He shook his head.

"Here." She took the saddle as he took off the bridle, then slipped on a high-quality leather halter from Fennell's in Lexington, Kentucky.

"You know, Ronnie, when you were a Pony Clubber with Ray, I told you to keep the saddle on the horse, but to loosen the girth. They get cold-backed in this weather if you take the saddle off."

"I know, I know," he answered as though he were still twelve, pony in hand. "But Regardless," his horse was named Regardless, "is cold-backed. I have this big gel pad." He took the saddle from her, stepped up into his trailer tack room, put the saddle on the saddle-tree and the bridle on the bridle rack, and plucked out a blue gel pad wrapped in warm towels. "Feel it."

"Still warm."

"These things are amazing. They'll stay warm for hours." He stepped down, put the pad on Regardless's back, looped a soft web overgirth over it. Then he draped on the sweat sheet, pulling a sturdy blanket over all. "This really works."

"I should have known not to chide you. You were my best Pony Clubber, even better than Ray Jr."

Ronnie beamed. "Thanks."

"Ronnie, forgive me for asking you this. I don't want to put you on the spot, but, well . . . can you in your wildest imaginings think that Clay could be part of a criminal ring, whether it's furniture or something else?"

He faced her as he stood on the other side of his horse, putting his arms over Regardless's back. "No. But having said that, do we truly know anyone? I guess we're all capable of things that aren't pretty. But no."

"He makes enough money honestly."

"Greed. It's a vice like lust. Or maybe I should say it's one of the seven deadly sins." She stood close to Ronnie. "It's irrational— obviously—and Izzy has expensive tastes."

"That she does. Wraps him around her little finger." Ronnie grimaced for a second. "Still, I can't imagine Clay as a crook. Just can't. Now," he lowered his voice as he rubbed Regardless's forehead, "I can imagine Izzy doing many out-of-the-way things."

"Yes, I can, too. Think she's faithful to Clay?"

After a long pause, Ronnie replied, "No. Do you?"

"No, but I can't judge these things." She sighed, then brightened. "Let me tell you again that your lottery ticket idea was just the best."

"How about Alex winning a thousand dollars?"

"I know. Five hundred for the club, and every dollar helps as you well know."

"Yes." He smiled sheepishly. "Obviously, I don't have the gambler's gene."

"That's why you're treasurer."

On the way back to the farm, driving slowly on roads that remained slick in some spots, while the slush turned to ice in others, Sister and Betty rehashed the day's hunt.

Betty fretted, "I hope that kid of mine is being sensible."

"She'll be at the stable. She left before we did, and she's a good driver."

"She's young. She hasn't seen as many bad roads as we have."

"Betty, there are days when I look like nine miles of bad road." Sister laughed at her. "Stop worrying."

Betty scrunched back down in the passenger side of the truck. "You could never look like nine miles of bad road."

"Aren't you sweet?"

"Ha."

They rode in silence for another mile, then Sister said, "You never know the length of a snake until it's dead."

"Huh?"

"My dad used to say that. I was thinking about the fire, all that. Might be a long snake, you know?" Sister answered.

"Whoever is behind this will screw up sooner or later. They always do." Betty crossed her arms over her chest.

"But that's just it," Sister became animated. "They already have. If everything's running smoothly, seems to me, you don't have to kill people."

"Maybe. Maybe not. Get rid of people or partners, and the money is all yours, if it's about money. And when you think of it, why two drunks and one, well, working-class guy. Doesn't seem to me much money there. Sorry to call Anthony a drunk. Seems disrespectful somehow."

"He was." Sister gripped the steering wheel tighter. "I keep remembering his laugh, the time he threw the basketball from half court when the buzzer sounded in the game against Lee High his senior year. Jesus, what happens to people?"

"Life," Betty said.

CHAPTER 36

Back at Roughneck Farm, Sister had just hung up the phone after a glowing conversation with Gray. She glanced out the kitchen window. Snow was falling heavily.

She reached across the counter to turn up the radio, 103.5. Mozart's "Turkish Rondo" played.

"Always makes me think of fat people dancing." She laughed, then performed a rumba across the uneven heart pine floor.

"Mental!" Golly giggled, but followed Sister, batting at her legs.

Raleigh and Rooster, ever attuned to Sister's emotions, jumped out of their fleece-lined dog beds to dance with her. Raleigh turned in circles as Rooster hopped on his hind legs, only to suffer a whack from Golly on his swishing tail.

"Hey!"

"Anything that moves is fair prey to Golly, Killer Queen Among All Felines!" The calico sang her own praises.

As the short musical piece continued, the four became sillier and sillier, each influencing the other until the music stopped. Sister, laughing until the tears ran down her cheeks, dropped to her knees, hugged the squirming dogs, wildly happy, then scooped up Golly as she stood up. She held the cat like a baby, burying her face in her longhaired tummy. If anyone else did this, Golly would rearrange his or her face. She purred.

"Are we nuts or what?" Sister then turned the cat over, putting her on her shoulder.

"Yeah!" Raleigh danced to the next selection on NPR, another Mozart.

"So ungainly." Two tiny streams of air from Golly's nostrils brushed Sister's hair.

"I don't think I've laughed this hard since we ran up on Donnie Sweigert drenched in fox pee! Course, I couldn't laugh then."

"Never did bag a deer," Raleigh said.

"Weather," Rooster, doing his best to dance, replied. "Messed up the last of deer season."

The phone rang again.

"Gray, did you miss me?" She insouciantly spoke into the mouthpiece.

His heavy voice lifted a second. "I did. But I called to tell you that Dalton Hill just phoned me to say he's with Sam on Garth Road in Charlottesville. He stopped when he noticed Sam's Toyota off the road right there where you turn to go back to the Barracks," he said, referring to the famous show stable, its turnoff being right after a deceptive curve in Garth Road. "He said Sam is drunk, blind drunk."

"Oh. Gray, I'm so sorry. Would you like me to come over?"

"Well, I've got to get my brother."

"I'll pick you up. One of us can drive Sam's truck back if it's not wrecked."

"Weather's bad."

"I've driven in worse."

By the time Sister and Gray had reached Sam and Dalton, Dalton had managed to dislodge the truck, which was now parked on the shoulder.

Sam, sprawled on the front seat, was out cold.

"Dalton, I don't know how to thank you."

"Dumb luck. I happened to be heading home this way. Given Sam's record, I thought if the sheriff found him, he'd lose his license for good."

"And be put in jail."

"Perhaps that's not a bad thing."

Gray took a deep ragged breath. "I know," he said as he fought back tears. "I thought he'd beat it this time. I really did."

"Gray, drive my truck. I'll drive the Toyota with Sam in it."

"No, we'll do it the other way around. If he comes to and pukes or gets belligerent, you won't have to deal with it or clean it up." He paused as snowflakes whitened his salt-and-pepper hair. "This is it. This is the last time I help him. I can no longer be my brother's keeper."

"Gray," Sister put her hand on his shoulder. "You did more than your share for him. More than your share by far."

Gray dropped his head, then looked up, "Getting worse, the storm."

"I can follow you to wherever you're taking him."

"Thanks. We'll turn left at Owensville Road, and I know you'll go straight to get home." Sister smiled. "Thank you, Dalton."

"No need." He nodded and climbed back into his Land Cruiser, a vehicle that can get through just about anything.

Sister followed Gray as he negotiated the twisty road, snow blowing across it as the winds intensified. She was sick at heart for Gray and for Sam, too.

Gray helped his brother to bed at the old home place. He and Sister took off Sam's clothes, tucked him in, and put a wastebasket by the bed in case he did get sick and couldn't make it to the john.

"I'm not staying with him. I'm afraid I'll kill him when he wakes up."

"Good decision." She looked down at Sam, oblivious to the grief he was causing, and felt a rustle of anger at him. "Come home with me. You don't have to entertain me or vice versa, but tonight's the kind of night when you need a friend."

He lightly placed his hand on the back of her neck. "You're a good woman, Jane."

That night as the winds howled, Sister held Gray as he fell asleep. She stayed awake for another hour and thought about the miseries people inflict upon others when they won't be responsible for themselves.

CHAPTER 37

China lined the two cupboards. Glasses sparkled next to them. A glass display case up front across from the checkout counter protected antique pieces. On the left side of these treasures, men's furnishings and ladies apparel stood out from the paintings and paneling. On the right side hung hunt whips, both knob end and stag horn, professional thongs—eight-plaited or twelve-plaited—and beyond, bridles and saddles, their vegetable-tanned leather emitting a satisfying fragrance.

A change of venue usually stimulated Sister's brain. So that morning she took Gray and drove the ploughed-out and ever-overcrowded ribbon of Route 29 north to Warrenton, a town she loved, where the courthouse alone was worth the two-hour drive, to visit Horse Country. Fauquier County, its rolling foothills, restrained estates, was currently braving an onslaught of Washington, D.C., money. Like lemmings, Washingtonians scurried out Route 66 West, hooking left on Route 29, down to Warrenton. This trip without heavy traffic could be accomplished in an hour or even less; with traffic, it was anyone's guess. Like Loudon County, infested with developments where verdant land used to delight the eye, Fauquier staggered and faltered. The money was too good: people sold or subdivided their estates.

Each time Sister drove up to Horse Country to visit Marion Maggiolo and her staff, like a family really, Sister felt her credit cards burning in her pocket.

Gray, spirits somewhat restored, rejoiced in Sister's company. Marion, who knew Gray from his days of hunting in Middleburg, was pleasantly surprised to see how attentive he was to Sister. The two friends caught up for a while before Marion went back to her office and Sister started shopping.

She picked out a blue tattersall vest, and a shirt off the men's pile, then she discovered a pair of gloves that had been handmade in England. A true glover put these together: it wasn't two or even four pieces stitched together, but over twenty. The stitching was done in such a way that the threads never touched the inside of the hand. Between the third and last fingers a special patch was sewn on, just where the reins rubbed. The soft inside palm also had another layer, cut to conform to the lay of the thumb. The spectacular gloves made of Capibara leather carried a spectacular price. Sister touched them, pressed them to her nose, put them back, picked them up.

"Dammit!" She cursed under her breath, picking them up for the last time and placing them with her ever-growing pile on the counter.

Gray, his own credit card in hand, perused her pile. "I thought you were just coming to visit Marion."

"People who live in glass houses shouldn't throw stones." She pointed to his mass of breeches, socks, stock ties, and shirts resting on the counter. "And I see that you, too, bought these gloves. Gloves that cost as much as a car payment."

They burst out laughing as Wendy, behind the counter and a fixture at the store, totaled up their bills.

Charlotte strolled by, and in her hand was a lovely Moroccan bound book, its rich burgundy leather soft to the touch. She ran a bookstore; gorgeous antique hunting volumes and other equine objects were her speciality. "While you're spending money." She dangled the book in front of Gray.

"*Ask Momma*," he read the title aloud, a classic from the nineteenth century. "Charlotte, you're such a temptress."

"Yes, everyone says that about her." Wendy kept ringing up items.

Gray added *Ask Momma* to his pile.

Driving back down Route 29, they laughed at their impulsiveness.

Gray took a deep breath, slapped his hands on his thighs. "I worked hard enough making it. I might as damn well spend some of it."

"Hard to resist those gloves."

"I know." He whistled appreciatively.

"We've driven all the way up; we're driving all the way back. I can't stand it. What did Sam say when he was restored to his senses?"

"When he called this morning on my cell phone," Gray paused. "First, I didn't tell him where I was. Second, I didn't tell him you and Dalton helped him. He'll find out in good time. Third, do you have your seat belt on?"

"I do."

"He swore he did not take a drink."

"What?" She was incredulous.

"Swore on our mother's soul!"

"But he was blotto. Gone."

"He swears it. I asked him what he remembered. He said he left the AA meeting with two other men, whom he couldn't name because he's not supposed to tell."

"How convenient."

"Right. And the next thing he remembers is waking up in bed, head thumping, stomach churning."

Her voice softened. "Do you believe him?"

"Jane, he's lied to me for close to thirty years. It's hard to believe him."

"That it is."

"And I didn't feel like talking about it when we left. I didn't mean to keep it from you. It's just," he rested his hands on his knees, "I'm so sick of it."

"I understand."

"I can't thank you enough."

"For what?"

"For picking me up in a snowstorm, for driving up to Garth Road, for driving back and putting Sam to bed, for putting up with me last night."

"I like your company."

He breathed in deeply, turned to her, and ran his left forefinger along her right cheek. "I like you, Jane. So much."

They drove in silence to where Route 29 and Highway 17 converge, 29 going south and 17 stretching on to Fredericksburg.

Sister finally spoke. "Can't stand it. My curiosity's getting the better of me."

She punched in Ben Sidell's number, speaking into the truck's speaker phone when he picked up. "I'm a nosy twit, but is Donnie Sweigert's autopsy complete?"

"Yes."

"Was he shot or knocked over the head or stuffed with a knock-out drug?"

"He had been in a fight shortly before his death. His neck, deep tissue, had been bruised. A deep bruise on his thigh, a cracked rib. He was most likely unconscious and then died from smoke inhalation."

"Do you think he started a fire with a gas can next to him?"

"I don't know." Ben cleared his throat. "The can, although mostly empty, blew up from the small amount of gasoline in the bottom. Maybe the fire got away from him. Granted, Donnie wasn't terribly intelligent, but he didn't appear to be that stupid."

"So now, Ben, three men are dead. They knew one another. They worked together sporadically. Maybe they were closer than anyone realizes."

"Perhaps."

"I assume you have contacted the people Donnie, Mitch, and Anthony delivered furniture to?"

"Yes."

"We have four suspects, don't we?"

Ben thought a moment. "Sister, you haven't been idle. If you count Isabelle Berry, yes."

"I do and I don't. Wives can go along for years and know not one thing about the business of their husbands. Not their bailiwick."

"True."

"Have you checked Dalton Hill's background?"

"He is what he says he is. Highly respected in his profession and in his hobby, the decorative arts of the eighteenth century. Guess that's what you call it."

"It's possible his coming here is a coincidence."

"I don't know." Ben's voice grew louder as she drove through an area of better reception. "What I do know is that you had better keep your mouth shut. Forgive me for being blunt. For one thing, I'm piecing this together, and I don't want you upsetting the apple-cart. It's tough enough as it is, and our killer or killers don't shy away from murdering people."

"Afraid he or they will fly the coop?"

"Yes. I'm worried about that and I'm worried about someone getting in the way or another murder, if this is some sort of vendetta."

"Ah." She absorbed his comment about who might become a

victim. "Can you think of anyone else in particular who might be in danger?"

"I don't know. My hunch is that this is a falling-out among thieves." He waited a moment as the reception cackled. "I beg you to be careful, please, Sister."

"We're talking about millions of dollars, aren't we?"

"Yes. And people have killed for less."

She pressed the End button. "Shit. Excuse my French."

"If this is a falling-out among thieves, I'd think that Donnie, Mitch, and Anthony would have had money."

"Donnie flashed around an expensive rifle."

"He did, but if you want to know my hunch, it's those three men who may have figured out the scam. Maybe they blackmailed the real criminals."

"Yes. I wonder if any of them knew how much money was at stake." She stopped for the light where Route 28 connects with Route 29. "It's close, this evil."

CHAPTER 38

S unny, cold, and crisp, Thursday's hunt at Orchard Hill unfolded as though Nimrod himself had written about it. Tomorrow night's full moon would illuminate the snowy fields. Predators,
hunting in full force, pursued rabbits, field mice, even ground
nesters among the avian family. Why the tempo of hunting accelerated before a full moon, Sister didn't know. She just knew it happened. Also that people's emotions swung higher and wilder; sexual
attractions heated up, too. Artemis possessed powers, as did her
twin, Apollo. His were more obvious, hers commanded study.

On that glorious February 5, as hounds streamed across the
thirty-acre hayfield, its imposing sugar maple, solemn as a sentinel
in the middle of the snowy field, Sister thought how little glory
remained in modern life. War, so technological and covered by
reporters as an entertainment, had room for heroism, but not
glory. Only sport and art retained the concept of, as foxhunters
would say, throwing your heart over the fence. Professional sport—

micromanaged, increasingly scientific—was like a salmon pulled out of the water: its colors were fading, and with it, glory. There's a heedless, sunny aspect to glory, a disdain for profit and even the applause of others that appealed to Sister. Not that she minded applause or profit, but that wasn't why she raced across the clean whiteness this morning. She wanted glory.

The field, large for a Thursday at twenty-one, looked like a nineteenth-century aquatint; the packed snow flew off hooves like large chunks of confetti. Faces, red from cold and exertion, radiated intensity and happiness.

The fox, a quarter of a mile ahead of the pack, swung round the other side of the hayfield, turning back toward his den not far from the simple Federal-style house.

Sister, in her eagerness, had gotten a bit forward of her field. She soared over the black coop, snow still tucked along the planks, then paused a moment to watch others take the obstacle.

Tedi, perfect position, arched over the coop, the sky bright blue above her. Edward followed, derby on his head, hands forward, eyes up—not as elegant as his wife, but bold. Behind Edward came Ronnie, light, smiling, another one with perfect position. Xavier followed Ronnie, lurching a bit on Picasso. Xavier really had to lose weight. It was affecting his riding. After Xavier, Clay took the jump big. That was Clay, clap your leg on the horse and devil take the hindmost. Once Clay cleared, Crawford, keen to be up front, tucked down on Czpaka and thundered over: not pretty but effective. Walter on Clemson, his tried and true, took the fence in a workmanlike manner, no muss, no fuss, all business. Sam took his fences like the professional he was, with as little interference with the horse as possible.

She heard the horn, figured she better move along. She asked Keepsake for speed, which he readily supplied despite the snow. Keepsake had a marvelous sense of balance.

Sister looked for brain first, balance second. Anyone could

pick apart a horse, a hind end a trifle weak or a shoulder slope too straight. For Sister, conformation was a map not a destination. The way the horse moved meant everything to her. As her mother used to say, "Movement is the best of conformation."

Another jump, an odd brush jump, level on top, sat in the turkey foot wire fence that enclosed the back acres. Keepsake glided over, smooth as silk. They turned toward higher ground, while a soft grade upward, given the snow, burned calories.

On top of that meadow, the 1809 house and outbuildings in clear view, Sister saw a red fox running toward the toolshed. The outermost building, its white clapboard matched all the others.

She said nothing as hounds were speaking. It's incorrect to call out "Tallyho" if the hounds are on.

Viewing the fox is as good as a twenty-minute run. The field excitedly looked in the direction of Tedi's outstretched arm, her lady's derby in her hand. Tedi did not yell out but did the proper thing when viewing a fox. She removed her derby, pointing it in the direction of the fox. She continued this for four or five strides as there was no slowing down, then she clapped the derby on her head realizing she'd snapped her hat cord in her eagerness to confirm her view.

"Bother!" she muttered under her breath as the hat cord swung from side to side on her neck, its small metal snap cold when it touched bare skin.

Within four minutes the fox popped into his den, hounds marked it, Rassle turning a somersault of delight, which made the whole field laugh. Shaker blew "Gone to Ground," praised his charges, mounted with a wince, and looked at Sister.

Like a schoolgirl bursting with eagerness, she said, "Let's hunt the back acres. If we don't pick up anything in twenty minutes, we can call it a day. I mean, unless you're hurting."

He shot her a baleful stare. "Who's hurting?" He spoke softly to the hounds, "Good hounds, good hounds, pack into me now."

"*More?*" Ruthie, sleek and fit, was as eager as Sister.

"*Yes,*" Cora happily told her.

"*Yay!*" the young entry cheered.

"*All right, now. No babbling,*" Asa gruffly instructed them, although he was as thrilled as they were. A good hound always wants to hunt. "*Discipline, young 'uns. Discipline's what makes a great foxhound and a great fox. You're a Jefferson hound, you know, not some raggle-taggle trash.*"

They obediently quieted, but Ribot, Ruthie, and Rassle couldn't help themselves. As they walked to the next cast, they'd jump up to look over the pack, to see Shaker.

"Jack-in-the-boxes." Tedi, alongside Sister, smiled.

"Isn't it wonderful?" Sister had tears in her eyes from the run, from happiness.

"Yes." Tedi rode a few paces, then said, "Pity so few people feel that way."

Sister, without rancor, replied, "Their own damn fault for the most part."

"I agree," Tedi said, thinking back to the joy she and Edward shared when both their daughters were alive, the family following the hounds, the pace like lightning. She'd had her share of happiness and her share of sorrow, and she thanked God for both. She knew Sister did, too.

Tedi wondered if this was a function of age or intelligence. She set aside age: she knew far too many immature, selfish, querulous old people. They'd been bloody bores as young people and had grown worse with the years.

Some people figured out the secret to happiness. Others didn't. The problem with the ones who didn't was they got in the way of the ones who did. Like psychic vampires, they'd swoop down on the happy. Eventually, one learns to dispense with their entreaties, manipulations, and excuses.

Tedi thought Nola, had she lived, might have become panicked in middle age as younger beauties challenged her fiefdom. Whether Nola could have gotten through it, she didn't know. She wondered, too, how young Ray would have matured. He had had an uncommon sweetness to him, far sweeter and softer emotionally than her own eldest daughter. Tedi loved Sister for many reasons, not the least because Sister was lovable. But what bound them like a steel cable was the shared loss of their children.

Hounds found another line on the southwestern side of Old Orchard, down by the remains of a railroad spur bridge, the railroad long defunct. This run, although brief, took them over hills like camel humps. When folks made it back to the trailers, they were tired but exhilarated.

Tedi, Isabelle, and Ronnie had brought a tailgate. Despite the cold, people grabbed sandwiches, hot coffee or tea, and Ronnie's signature brownies, chewy with tiny bits of bitter chocolate scattered throughout.

Sam, quiet and withdrawn, took a sandwich back to the tack room of Crawford's large trailer. He sat on an overturned bucket, sandwich in one hand, while dipping the bit of Nike's bridle in a bucket of warm water with the other hand.

He was surprised when X's large bulk loomed on the other side of the door window.

X opened the door, stepped inside, and closed it behind him. "You're one lucky bastard." Sam kept at his task. X continued, "I know you were drunk, drove off the road, and once again your brother saved your black ass."

Sam glared up at him. "You know a lot, don't you?"

"Cars passed you until you were hauled out. No one told Crawford. You're lucky."

"And are you going to tell Crawford?"

"No." X folded his arms across his broad chest. "No, I'm not."

"White of you."

X leaned down. "Listen, you worthless piece of shit. You'll

fuck up again. You'll do yourself in. Why should I get my hands dirty?"

"That why you came back here? To tell me this?"

"No, actually. I came back here to tell you that I think you know more about what's going on than you're telling. For all I know, you killed those winos and Donnie. I know Donnie was in AA but couldn't go thirty days without a drink. I know a lot more than you think I know."

"Let me tell you what I know." Sam stood up, hung the bridle over its hook, put the sandwich on the saddle seat. "I know that you and Clay Berry are old friends, right ball and left ball. I know that Clay will receive a six-figure check from the insurance company. And I wouldn't be surprised to discover you two split that check."

X grabbed Sam by the throat, choking the wind out of the small, wiry man. "I could kill you. Wouldn't bother me." He released Sam, whose hands fluttered up to his bruised neck. "You aren't worth a jail term. Tell you this, you keep your mouth shut, so shut I don't even want you to say hello to Dee. Don't even look at her. You hear?"

Sam nodded in affirmation and coughed, his windpipe searing with pain.

As X opened the door, Sam whispered hoarsely, "She's too good for you."

X spun around. "For once we agree. She would have never—" He stopped; he couldn't say it. "—if I'd paid attention to her as I should have. She would never have looked at you."

"I did you a favor," Sam replied.

"Oh?"

"I woke you up to what a self-centered bastard you are."

X took a menacing step toward Sam, who grabbed a crop. "I did wake up. I worship that woman. Worship her. I'll never make that mistake again. She's the most important thing in my life. You keep well clear of her." X turned, stepped outside on the plastic mounting block as Sam closed the door. He'd lost his taste for the sandwich.

That evening Sister and Gray dined out. Gray decided he couldn't wait until Saturday. They talked about everything under the sun. He had his perfect Manhattan; she had Earl Grey tea.

They wound up back at Roughneck Farm in bed.

Afterwards, they sat up, covers pulled around their shoulders. Even with the fire in the fireplace, the cold sneaked inside. Outdoors it was bitterly cold, a full moon bathing the world in silver.

"My nose is running." Sister wiped her nose with a Kleenex.

"Well, you better catch it," Golly, snuggled on the foot of the bed now that they were done, smarted off.

"Think it's the dust?" he said.

"Probably." She leaned against him, sliding down so her head was on his shoulder.

He wrapped his arm around her. "I feel like a teenager."

"Act like one, too." They laughed, and she asked, "Okay, give me hell if I'm rude, but isn't it true that all men will have prostate troubles sooner or later?"

"It is. Why, do you want to know if I have to get up five times in the night to go to the bathroom and not much happens?"

"Actually, I hadn't thought of that."

"Took care of it. Well, I mean I'll continue to take care of it. But all is well."

"I know that." She giggled. "Want my medical history?"

"Well." He hugged her. "I suppose at our ages that's germane."

"Broken right leg, three places, clean through, 1962. Fractured ribs, too many times to count, starting in the fourth grade. Broken toes, but that's no big deal, wrap them in vet wrap. Can't do anything else. Two discs, L4 and L5, are crumbling—enough to make me stiff if I've been sitting in one position too long. Other than childhood diseases and the occasional flu and cold, that's it."

"Impressive."

"You could play dice with my bone chips."

"Broken wrist, college basketball. Hmm, tore my anterior cruciate, left leg, must be eleven years ago. Fixed it. I'd say we've both been lucky. I take that back. We're active, so we haven't rusted out."

"What's the point of having a body if you don't use it?" Sister smiled as Golly walked over her to rest on her lap.

"*I know you've missed me,*" the cat purred.

"*Nobody misses you, Golly, you're—*" Rooster began.

"*Don't start. It's been a pleasant evening,*" Raleigh said quickly.

"Are you surprised that we're here?" Gray asked.

Sister propped on her elbow to look at him. "No. I know you. There's been a thirty-year interval from when you moved away for good, but even then, I'd see you from time to time. It's not like we're complete strangers." She paused. "Even if we were, who is to say we wouldn't wind up in bed together? The chemistry is either there or it isn't."

"It's there." He sighed deeply.

"Thank you, Jesus." She laughed. "Thought I'd never feel that rush again."

"It's a terrible loss, isn't it?"

"Yep." She changed the subject. "Had a moment to watch people take fences today. I always say people ride like they live, and you know it's true. There was Tedi, cool, elegant, in control. Edward, bold as brass, keen. Ronnie, another elegant rider, relaxed. X, getting the job done, hampered by his weight but enjoying himself. Clay, I swear sometimes I don't think he has a brain in his head. He doesn't think too much out there, just goes for it. I used to pound into Little Ray's head, 'First reckon, then risk.' Never could get that message through to Clay. Walter, improving, not a chicken."

"Did you see me?"

"Not today, but I've watched you. Good position, hands forward, you pick your spot. You reckon."

"I'm flattered. I love watching people ride in the hunt field."

"I usually can't do it unless I'm in someone else's hunt field."

"Who were the riders you admired when you were up and coming?"

"Ellie Wood Keith, Baxter now, she married a Baxter; uh, Judy Harvey; Jill Summers; Mary Robertson; Rodney Jenkins, of course, but he was a show ring rider. Sometimes I'd see him out with Keswick. The list could go on and on, but my focus was always how people rode in the hunt field. Impressive as show riders are, they're hitting fences on level ground. It's math; they count their strides, stay in that infuriating canter, in the hunter classes, I mean. I'd need a No-Doz to sit through a hunter class. In the field you and your horse encounter everything, often very fast. You grow a set of balls out there, or you don't make it. Maybe I should say ovaries, given the circumstances."

He laughed, his body shaking. "Jane, you can be wicked in your way. Too bad most people don't really know you."

"I can't very well go about saying what I think and be an effective master, now can I?"

"No." He thought a moment. "You're lovely to watch on a horse. Fearless, but not foolish."

"Thank you, but let me tell you my secret: I have fabulous horses. I just sit there."

"Don't be modest."

"I mean it. Sure I can ride a bit, but if you've got the right horse, everything is peachy. Ray, Little Ray, went through his peachy phase, and it stuck with me. Thirteen—remember when your kids were twelve and thirteen, and you endured the word play, the horrible puns, and the really dumb jokes? They get fixated on words. Peachy. Totally. What were some of his others? Used to drive me crazy until I remembered my mother still said 'swell' until the day she died. Funny." She pulled her arm from under the cover to pet

Golly. "Tomorrow would have been Ray's forty-fourth birthday. I can't imagine him as a middle-aged man."

Gray kissed her cheek. "He would have been fortunate if he looked like his mother, which he did."

"He did, didn't he? Walter looks like Big Ray." She stopped. "You knew, I mean, I didn't let the cat out of the bag?"

"Everyone knew. Even the black folks."

"Thought the black folks knew everything first."

"Pretty much do."

"Wonder if anyone knows what's going on about these deaths?"

"No. I asked around."

"Ah-ha, so you're curious, too."

"Of course. That could have been Sam, you know?"

"I do."

They lay awhile, watching the fire.

Gray spoke up as a log crackled. "Jane, have you ever felt the presence of your son or your husband?"

She sat up. Golly grumbled. "Why?"

"I don't know."

"You ask the damnedest questions. The only other people in my life who would ask something like that are Tedi or Betty. I'm not mad—don't get me wrong—just, uh, warmly surprised. I'm not accustomed to people truly wanting to know about me. They want things from me, but they don't want *me*, if you know what I mean. Tedi and Betty love me for me."

"I know exactly what you mean. And I want you for you. Of course, I also want torrential sex."

"Oh that." She sighed, a mock suffering sigh. "A sacrifice, but someone's got to do it." She waited a moment, took a deep breath. "I have felt both Big Ray and Little Ray. When my son was killed, I felt him strongly for months. I don't know, could have been some kind of wish fulfillment, a way to fight the pain. But even now, there are moments, Gray, when I feel his kindness. I feel him smiling at me. I feel Mother, too. Less so Big Ray, but every now and then, usually in the hunt field, he'll be near. I often feel Archie, my anchor hound. I know animals possess spirits. Archie is with me. And I can't tell you how loving the sensations are, how restorative, and, well, I don't know, I feel a blessing on me, a benediction."

"Good."

"You?"

He nodded. "My grandmother. Warmth, love, understanding, the same feelings you're expressing. You can't go about talking about this kind of thing, especially if you're a man. Men aren't supposed to sense ghosts, if you will, or spirits of love. But Janie, they are with us. And who is to say there aren't loving spirits with us whom we didn't know in this life but who have taken an interest in us, or whom we knew from another life? I rather believe that, past lives, I mean. I'm certain you were a queen."

"Go on!"

"A king?" He shrugged.

"One's as bad as the other." She laughed. "If there are kind spirits, there are also evil spirits."

"Like up at Hangman's Ridge?"

"Yes. I don't know if they're evil or suffering."

"Both. Lawrence Pollard, the first man hanged there, wasn't evil, just greedy. It was 1702, wasn't it? But some of the others, probably psychopaths, are evil. Or maybe some just broke bad, like Fontaine Buruss broke bad." He named a hunt club member, now deceased, the former husband of Sorrel Buruss.

Fontaine, handsome, charming, devolved into sexual self-indulgence, seducing women he should have left well alone because of their youth. He paid for it with his life.

"Fontaine, what a son of a bitch, but a fun son of a bitch. I actually miss him." She smiled. "He crumbled in middle age. I swear, what in hell are people afraid of? We are all going to get old. We are all going to die. So why does a man in his forties want to be attractive to twenty-year-old women. The women aren't any better. They go about it differently, that's all. You get old, period. In fact, Gray, I love being older."

"You're not old. You're healthy. You're beautiful."

"Oh Gray."

"You will always be beautiful. And sure, if a gorgeous twenty-year-old woman walked into a room, every man's eyes would go to her, mine included. Do I want to sleep with her? No, I already have two children. I want a woman who can keep up with me, forgive the arrogance."

"Me, too."

"You want a woman who can keep up with you?"

"Haven't tried that. Another life, perhaps. For this one, I'll stick to men."

"I'm so glad." He kissed her again.

"Gray."

"Hmm."

"I think I know who the killer is, might be two, not one. Might even be three or four, but I know the locus of greed. I just don't know how to root it out."

"Logic or instinct?"

"Both. I've used both. I don't have proof, but you asked me if I felt my son. What is that? An openness, clear channels? Whatever it is, it leads me to my best hounds, my best horses, and I usually know where my fox is laying up. A kind of sixth sense. I'm not eschewing logic. Logic, too, brings us to Clay, Isabelle, if she's in on it, X, possibly, and possibly Dalton Hill."

He sat up straighter. "Clay makes sense because of the warehouse. Isabelle, well, hard to say. Why Xavier and Dalton, unless you think this is an insurance fraud?"

"No. I think this is about illegal drugs such as steroids, HGH, OxyContin, stuff like that. Dalton has the knowledge, he can get that stuff readily."

"Then Xavier would look better." Gray half laughed.

"I don't know, but I am ninety-nine percent sure I'm on the right track. If only I could figure out a way to flush them out, get them in open territory."

"Jane," he said sternly, "this isn't a foxhunt. This is murder."

CHAPTER 39

February, although two steps closer to spring than December, feels far away from that first bright crocus. Usually the coldest month of the year in central Virginia, February dragged some folks down into a bad case of the blues. Fortunately, foxhunters usually escaped this dive in emotional fortunes because hunting reached its apogee. Only the toughest hunted, the others having retired to their fireplaces or even to Florida until spring. The foxes gave delicious sport. By now the pack worked like a well-oiled machine; the young entry were part of the pack, bringing vigor and curiosity to the hunt. The horses, hunting fit, were keen. The humans, if they hadn't eaten themselves insensate over the holidays, were also lean and mean. Truly, February was perfect.

Sister loved whatever day she was in: cold, hot, cloudy, sunny, rainy, dry, she didn't care. She was alive, healthy, and doing what she loved. This particular day, February 6, she fought off the sadness of Ray Jr.'s birth by remembering her labor. Doctors tell you, as do psychologists, that you won't recall physical pain. Clearly, they had never given birth. To this day, she could remember the contractions. For a brief period there, she would gladly have killed Big Ray for getting this upon her. Then Ray Jr. made his appearance after eight hours of nausea, heaving, and pushing. Red, wet, wrinkled, he was a shock until she held him in her arms. Mother love is the most powerful, the most irrational force on earth, even more powerful than sexual love. However, one does lead to the other, so best not to spurn the former.

She had had fourteen years with a boy of uncommon good humor and generosity. Little Ray loved animals, loved sleeping with kitties, loved falling down in the kennels as the hounds swarmed over him, licking him. He gurgled to the horses even when he was in his mother's arms. He kissed their soft noses and laughed if they blew air out of their nostrils. He held her hand when they walked, even into his fourteenth year. He kissed his father without embarrassment. He hugged his friends, boys and girls, without thinking twice about it. His path was physical, touching, connecting through flesh. He showed his love by touching your arm, smoothing a hound's head, patting a horse's hindquarters. Like all happy people, Little Ray was a magnet to others, as well as animals.

She loved him even when he committed the childhood sins we all commit—telling that first lie, stealing a candy bar from Roger's Corner, doing someone else's homework. Ray always polished off his homework in record time. When he erred, she'd discipline him, and Big Ray would back her up. Then, when the first flush of puberty showed on her son's cheeks, father and son drew much closer. The minutiae of masculinity is best taught by a loving father, which Big Ray was.

He showed his son the difference between a regular tie knot and a Prince of Wales. He instructed his son in the duties and courtesies due women. Given that they lived in central Virginia, of course, this process had really begun when the boy was a toddler.

Southern men, especially Virginians, adhere to a strict code concerning the ladies. Doesn't mean they can't keep a harem busy, but the proper tokens and forms must be observed.

Both parents worried about sex. Young Ray hadn't quite gotten to that yet; his voice was only beginning to crack when he was killed. But she and her husband wondered what would happen because he was so affectionate and loving. They worried that he'd be misunderstood, and they worried that he wouldn't understand himself. Learning about sex, love, lust, and friendship with the opposite sex takes restraint, compassion, and a wealth of common sense. There's not one of us who doesn't learn a few of those lessons the hard way. They prayed the hard way wouldn't mean a baby born out of wedlock.

One of the great things about her husband was that they could talk about anything, anything, even their affairs, if it came down to that. Usually it didn't, but on those occasions when it did, they evidenced a rare understanding of each other. They agreed if their son fathered a child before he was ready to be married, they would take care of it and make young Ray fully aware that he must provide financial assistance to the mother if she wouldn't give him the child. Big Ray summed it up, "You play, you pay."

When Little Ray's flapping T-shirt tail got caught in the tractor PTO, the power transfer axle, choking the life out of him in seconds, he had never slept with a woman. That haunted Sister. She wished he had known the richness, the power, even the fear of that connection. He died a virgin. His death caused slashing grief among his classmates and friends, among the members of the hunt club. The hounds, his horses, his beloved cats, all mourned him as deeply as his parents. Their mute suffering tore out Sister's heart. For three months after his son's death Big Ray couldn't go past Tijuana, young Ray's favorite hunter, without bursting into tears.

On Little Ray's forty-fourth birthday, gunmetal gray clouds swung down from the mountains. Athena brazenly sat in front of the stable in the big pin oak, Bitsy on the branch beneath her. The two owls made crackling cackling sounds at each other. Sister noticed them when she looked out the kennel window.

Sister remembered odd bits of information. When Ray was born, she flipped through history date books, delighted to find that Julius Caesar had beaten King Juba II in 46 B.C., J. E. B. Stuart had been born on that day in 1833. As Stuart remains the beau ideal of the cavalryman to this day, February 6 seemed a good omen.

Sister had reached the point in her life when she was able to thank God that she had fourteen years with her remarkable son. She'd learned, in her own quiet way, to trust the good Lord. It had been her son's time.

Shaker dripped in water tracks from his rubber boots as he stepped into the kennel office. "Dragon can go Saturday."

"Good."

They'd exhausted the Westminster Dog Show as a topic. The show had ended Tuesday, but being hound people, they had to discuss it in minute detail for days running. And there was a ripe disagreement about who won, who was reserve, et cetera. Needless to say, a hound did not win Best in Show.

"Boss, I know this is Ray Jr.'s birthday. Anything I can do for you?"

"Shaker, you're good to think of me. No. Just the fact that you remembered makes it a better day. I was lucky to have him."

"He was lucky to have you."

Later, when she arrived back at the house, she found a huge bouquet from Gray. The card simply read, "Love is eternal."

That brought tears to her eyes.

The biggest surprise of the day was when she took a break from chores for four o'clock tea. A new Lexus SUV pulled into the driveway, disgorging Ronnie, Xavier, and Clay.

They stamped in the mudroom door just as they had as boys. Ronnie carried champagne, Clay a hamper basket of treats, and

Xavier gingerly held an arrangement of white long-stem roses interspersed with lavender.

They burst through the door, calling, "Hi, Mom."

Each one kissed her, gave her his present, then plopped at the kitchen table.

She poured the champagne, put out sandwiches, whatever she had. They sat down as they did when they would follow behind Ray Jr., like so many railroad cars hitched to his engine.

After she cried a bit and wiped her eyes, they sat, remembering, laughing, eating.

Ronnie wistfully glanced around the country kitchen. "Where does the time go? Wasn't it Francois Villain who wrote, 'Where o where are the snows of yesteryear?' It was the 1400s when he wrote that."

"The snows of yesteryear are right here," Clay, not being poetic, replied.

"Are you going to give us a lecture about evaporation and condensation and how there might be a molecule that once belonged to George Washington in that glass of champagne?" Ronnie rolled his eyes.

"Molecule belonged to François Villain." X winked. "From France."

"Clever, these insurance agents are clever. Hey, I remember when you were *dying*, and I mean *dying*, in Algebra I. Rayray bailed you out."

X turned beet red. "No need to bore Sister with that story, Clay."

"Ah-ha!" Clay put his sandwich on his plate, thumbprint on the bread. "X sat in front, Rayray behind. Passed him the answers to the tests."

Sister feigned shock. "X!"

"Makes you wonder about having him as your insurance agent, doesn't it?" Ronnie giggled.

"If it has a dollar sign in front of it, X is Einstein," Clay said, a hint of sharpness in his voice.

"If it has a dollar sign in front of it, Dee does the work. Give me credit, I married a woman smarter than myself."

"Not hard to do." Ronnie laughed.

"I could be really ugly right now." X dismissed him with a wave of his hand.

"I'll be ugly for you, Ronnie, since we know you aren't going to marry for love, why don't you woo some rich old widow? Think of the good you could then do for the hunt club?" Clay nodded in Sister's direction.

"Yeah, Ronnie, you could always lash it to a pencil." X laughed, then realized he was sitting with Sister. "Sorry."

"Don't apologize to me, I've said worse; you just never heard it. And you all used to say the grossest things when you were kids." She put her hand on her stomach. "Makes that show *Jackass*, look tame."

"You've watched that?" X was amazed.

"I'm trying to keep current with popular culture."

"Hardly culture." Ronnie sighed.

"A phase, grossness. Girls do it, too," Clay said. "But since girls don't make movies, for the most part, or shall I say movies are made for teenage boys, we don't see it. Bet you were gross, too, Sister."

Sister replied, "You forget how much older I am than you all. It was strict when I grew up. I could have matriculated to West Point and felt right at home, course they didn't take girls then, but I thought about things gross and otherwise. Didn't show it."

"Ever wonder where Ray would have gone to school?" X asked.

"Sure." She drank some champagne. "Princeton or Stanford. But you know, he was leaning toward the fine arts, driving his father crazy. I don't know, maybe he would have gone somewhere else. What do you all think?"

"Bowdoin," Clay said. "He would have loved Maine."

"Colorado State," Ronnie pitched in. "I think he would have

gone west, but wound up in veterinary medicine or something like that. And he was a good athlete. He would have played football. Bet you."

X shook his head. "Princeton. He would have followed his father to Princeton. And he would have played football there, baseball, too. Maybe lacrosse. Do they have lacrosse at Princeton?"

"Even if they do, if you want to play lacrosse, you go to Virginia, Maryland, or Johns Hopkins." Clay spoke with certainty.

"Johns Hopkins is a good school," Sister said thoughtfully. "I wouldn't have minded that, and it's closer than Princeton or Stanford." She paused. "What a joy to have you all here."

"We never forget you." Ronnie smiled.

They always remembered Ray Jr.'s birthday in one fashion or another. They remembered his death day, too, each calling Sister to tell her he was thinking of her. Tedi and Betty always called or dropped by as well.

The boys, for Sister thought of them as "the boys," grew louder, more raucous. They argued about the NBA, dismissed the Super Bowl, which had just been played. They looked forward to baseball season. They talked horses, fixtures, other people in the hunt field.

"Think Crawford will cough up enough for you to hire someone else, really?" Clay asked.

"Um . . . if we make this a club effort, I think he'll contribute more than his share," Sister replied judiciously. "But if anyone pressures him, he'll get angry and I won't blame him. He's hit up all the time."

"True." Clay sipped the coffee that Sister had made to accompany the champagne and sandwiches. "You make the best coffee. Wish I could teach Izzy how you do it."

"Patience and good beans." She laughed.

"You know that brass coffee maker Crawford has in his tack room? That thing cost over five thousand dollars. Imported from Italy." Ronnie relayed this with amazement.

"Does his coffee taste any better than Sister's?" X's eyebrows, some gray in them now, rose.

"No," Ronnie answered firmly. "No one makes coffee as good as Sister."

"Ronnie, back to the subject of your marriage." Sister surprised them all by this. "You don't even have to marry some rich old broad to make me happy. I want to see you happy, and I know, if you'll relax and let us love you, you'll find the right man."

A silence followed.

X chuckled. "As long as it's not me."

"For Crissakes, X, you're so fat, even if I loved you and wanted you, I couldn't find it, you know?"

They roared, even X.

"Ronnie needs someone. We all need someone." Clay dabbed his mouth with the napkin. "But I don't think we have any other gay men in the club. Or at least, that we know about."

"We don't," Ronnie answered grimly.

"Well, Ron, you can't have someone in your life who isn't a fox-hunter." Sister was firm. "We'll keep our eyes open at other hunts."

"Guys, I can do this on my own."

"You've done a piss-poor job of it so far." X snorted. "I can count on the fingers of one hand the affairs I know you've had. Not counting one-night stands."

"Do we have to get into this?"

"I'm fascinated." Sister's eyes sparkled.

"Yeah, we do. If Rayray were alive, he'd be right here with us, pushing you on." Clay drained his champagne glass.

With four of them on a bottle, there was little left, even though Sister drank lightly. She got up, pulled a bottle out of the fridge, and handed it to X, who opened it. She always kept a bottle of champagne, a bottle of white wine, and a six-pack of beer in the fridge for guests.

"Okay, okay," Ronnie 'fessed up. "My walks on the wild side

were furtive and unsatisfying. It's a different day now. You all know who and what I am. I gave up hiding and lying. Maybe I will find a good man."

"A good man who rides hard," X corrected him.

"A hard man who rides good," Sister mischievously added.

They laughed.

After the boys killed the second bottle, they readied to leave. Wives waited. It was Friday night, and both X and Clay faced social obligations. Ronnie had a church vestry meeting, and then he'd join X and Dee at a small dinner the Vajays planned.

As they gathered their coats, Sister nonchalantly said to all, "Fellas, I'm no spring chicken, so I've been doing research about human growth hormone. What do you think about my asking Dalton Hill to bring me some from Canada? I can't get it here. I want to try it."

"I wouldn't mind either," Ronnie chimed in, "but you look great. You don't have to take anything."

"*The Wall Street Journal* carried an article about it June 2003, I think." X's brows furrowed. "I'm interested in it myself."

"Supposed to help you with muscle, lean muscle," Sister said.

"Don't talk to Dalton Hill." Clay held up his hands. "He is so goddamned fussy. He's the last person to talk to about something like that."

"Well, he is a doctor, and he is Canadian. He can get it up there," she insisted.

"Not him. Really. Let me think about it." Clay smiled. "It's like everything else in the world. If there's a market for it, then there's a way."

"A huge market, I'd think." Ronnie clearly had no idea what was going on or why Sister was throwing out a baited hook.

She had done her research about HGH. If she could get it, she would. That wasn't her purpose though, and she wondered if she was right to do this. Too late now.

"Clay, you think Dalton is 'prissy,' for lack of a better word? You think he'd be offended?"

"He'd go off about stuff being illegal in the United States. But maybe you could get a referral from him and fly to Toronto." Clay's voice kept even. "That's better than risking, well, you know."

"I've read where you can buy it online, out of the county, but online."

"You can," Clay spoke again, a bit more volume, "but you don't know what that is. How do you know it wasn't harvested from monkey glands? You don't want that. How do you know it wasn't taken from the pituitary gland of someone who died of AIDS? Come on, now, if you're determined to do this, you have to be careful. You have to find medical-grade HGH. None of this online stuff. You're much too valuable to us."

"I'm so glad I brought this up. I've been a little embarrassed to bring it up with Tedi or Betty."

"Well, Tedi could buy the entire laboratory," Ronnie interjected. "She'd take it if she knew about it. Even if she already looks like a million bucks."

"Never tell a billionaire she looks like a million bucks." Clay punched Ronnie.

"Now, now, Tedi doesn't have a billion dollars," Sister gently chided him.

"Triple digit millions," Clay said, pulling on his coat.

"More power to her." X bore no one the least amount of envy.

"Clay, instead of Wake Forest, you should have gone to Columbia or New York University, one of those northern schools full of rich kids," Ronnie teased him.

"Damn straight. Yankees taught me the value of money by keeping it all to themselves. But, hey, I learned a lot at Wake. I'll be a Deacon until I die."

"Actually, Clay, I think your father taught you the value of money," Sister gently inserted this observation.

"He did, he did," Clay agreed. "Sister, let me look into this. And whatever you do, don't go to Dalton."

"You're right. I knew you'd know." She kissed Clay on the cheek as he went out the mudroom door, then kissed Ronnie and X, too. Ronnie gave her a bear hug.

She watched as they drove down the snow-packed road, then she closed the door, leaning her head against it, tears falling on the floor. Corruption and greed had claimed one of the boys as surely as death had claimed her son.

CHAPTER 40

"Hear me out." Sister sat in the kitchen at Sam's house. She'd called him at work and told him she'd be there at six-thirty.

Sam shifted in the wooden kitchen chair; they sat at the old porcelain-topped table.

"I didn't take a drink. Not knowingly."

"I hope you're telling me the truth. You have got to tell me who you left the AA meeting with and where you went."

"I can't do that."

"All right then, let me tell you what I think. I think someone who we don't realize is a recovering alcoholic, like, say, Clay Berry, left with you. And you were hungry. You went to eat. I think you looked away or got up to go to the bathroom and that person spiked your drink. What was the old phrase? 'Slipped you a mickey'? And whoever did this is behind the killings of Anthony and Mitch."

Sam's face registered a flash of fear. "Why?"

"They knew something, those guys. And you were friends with them. You used to perform odd jobs with them, didn't you?"

"Sure." He shrugged.

"But you're back. I mean, your senses are restored. You've got a good job. Why would anyone want to take you down? *Think!*" she commanded.

"My memory might return." He stopped, leaned toward her. "But I didn't do that much with Anthony and Mitch. I rarely worked for the same people they did. They were big guys or bigger than I am. I wasn't going to be able to lift the stuff they could. The jobs I picked up were mostly janitorial or the odd tack cleaning and repair job. Mostly I tried to keep some horse contact going, even when I was down at the station."

"You know that, but the killers might not. They might think that Anthony and Mitch told you a lot. Did they?"

"No. Every now and then they'd get money. Seemed like a lot then. Anything over fifty dollars was a lot to us. I never asked. Hell, Sister, I was too drunk or too hungover to care."

"You're sure?"

"I'm sure. And if these people are that worried about me, why don't they just kill me?"

"Good question. I think I have the answer." She folded her hands together on the tabletop. "They've done enough damage, taken enough chances. They either need to set you up as the killer or kill you with booze."

He passed his hand over his eyes. "Christ."

"You might want to pray to him because you're in danger."

"Did you tell Gray?"

"No. He's worried enough as it is, and he thinks you're back on the bottle."

"I don't blame him," Sam's voice lowered.

"Will you help me catch them?"

"Yes," Sam said with conviction.

"It's a funny thing, Sam. Call it loyalty to an old dance partner, but tattered as Anthony's life was, no one had the right to take it away from him. He didn't deserve to die like that. None of them did."

"No. What do you want me to do?"

"I've drawn over our foxes, lying tight in a covert. They know I've drawn over them, and they think I've gone. With me?"

"Sure."

"I'm going to swing back around and draw in the opposite direction. I think I can flush them out."

"Who?"

"Dalton, Clay, and Izzy. I'm damned certain she's in on this, if not behind it."

He swallowed hard. "Oh."

"And one of them was with you at that AA meeting, am I correct?"

"Yes."

"Well, keep to your rules. I guess I don't need to know exactly which one. What I want you to do is to get into a fight with Xavier."

"That's easy enough." He laughed.

"Yes and no. It means you two must cooperate."

"Have you talked to X?"

"I've come directly from his house. He agrees."

"He likes to hit me." Sam smiled ruefully.

"With good reason, but you know what I always say. Send the past into the ocean; let the waves take it away. He can't change it, you can't, Dee can't. Done is done."

"He doesn't see it that way."

"Not now. He might later. X is a good man. I love him very much."

Sam sighed deeply. "And I once hurt him very much."

"You did, but that's over."

"Why do you want us to pick a fight?"

"A diversion and a shake up. Next hunt. I'll turn and lift my crop up over my head. I think of the three of them, Clay's the shakiest. While you two put on your show, I'll go for Clay. I think Dalton and Izzy will be mesmerized by your joint performance, and they won't look to help Clay."

"You're taking a risk."

"Life is a risk."

"You must have loved Anthony once."

She blinked, then slowly said, "He was the first man I ever slept with, and at eighteen, I thought it was love. Perhaps it was."

"You're something, Sister."

"Know something? So are you."

CHAPTER 41

W hat's the difference?" Xavier angrily countered Marty Howard.

"The difference is your life, the quality of your life," she fired right back, secure in the righteousness of her cause.

"Marty, I like you. Understand that. I do." Picasso's reins were draped over his shoulder. "But I'm going to do as I damn well please. I'm smoking and that's that. And don't give me crap about filtered cigarettes or low tar. All that crap. All you do is inhale the tiny fibers from the filters or whatever they treat the tobacco with. I'm better off smoking straight cigarettes. The others are for wimps anyway." Defiantly, he blew a puff of blue smoke.

"Then at least smoke good tobacco." Crawford emerged from the trailer's tack room. "Addictive personalities. You know. If they don't do drugs, they turn to God. Forgive the cynicism. If they drink and give it up, they smoke. You're an addictive personality." He handed Xavier a pack of Dunhill Reds. Same cigarettes he bought for Sam, now lurking on the other side of the trailer since he didn't want to get into a run-in with Xavier.

"Thanks." X didn't think he was an addictive personality.

"How could you?" Marty felt undermined.

"Honey, people will live as they see fit, and you can't improve them. Besides, I'd rather have him or Sam smoothed out by nicotine than not, wouldn't you? Life is too short to put up with other people's irritations. Seems to me our efforts should be directed toward steering young people away from smoking. I don't think you can do much to change older ones. X is my witness."

"Lung cancer is hardly an irritation," she snapped.

"His lungs." Crawford shrugged.

"What's Sam got to do with this?" Xavier was now irritated, edgy.

"I buy him a carton of Dunhill Reds each week. A bonus. Keeps him happy. Rather have him smoking than drinking."

Xavier opened his mouth to say once a drunk, always a drunk, but he shut it, then opened it again. "I'm smoking again to lose weight."

"There are better ways." Marty was persistent.

"Tried them all." He paused. "Although last night Sister mentioned HGH. I went home and looked it up on the Internet. Might work. I'm not going to the gym. Christ, I hardly have a minute to myself now. Foxhunting is my solace, and if I have time for only one sport, this is it."

Crawford, familiar with strategies to stay young, had his HGH flown in from England, and no one was the wiser for it. "Xavier, get a stationary bike and ride it while you watch the news. Better than nothing. And try the Atkins Diet. I'm serious."

A rustle from the kennel alerted them to the hounds walking out in an orderly manner.

"Damn." Crawford tightened his girth.

As Crawford and Marty hurried to pull themselves together

with Sam's help, Xavier walked Picasso back to his trailer, mounting block by the side, and heaved up just as Clay and Izzy rode by.

"Didn't hear you grunt that time," Clay said.

"Shut up," said X.

"What's the matter with you?"

"If I hear one more lecture from Marty Howard about cigarettes or women's rights or sugar or Free Tibet, I'll spit in her face, so help me God."

"Umm," Izzy murmured as if in agreement, furtively looking for Dalton. She caught his eye. He smiled, then looked away.

Ronnie rode up. "If you all don't want to ride in the back of the field, hurry up."

"X is having a snit."

"I'm not having a snit!" He breathed deeply, petted Picasso, and said, voice low, "I'm tired of being middle-aged and fat."

"Nothing we can do about the middle-aged part, but fat, that's fixable." Ronnie walked on toward the kennels.

"Come on." Clay rode next to Xavier. Izzy rode a little behind them.

This Saturday's fixture was Roughneck Farm. Apart from being full of foxes, Sister and Shaker enjoyed hunting from home because they could luxuriate in an extra hour of sleep. Also, they could load up the pack with the young entry, since, if someone did take a notion, the young ones knew the way back to the kennel. This year's class had made great progress since September's opening day of cubbing. The fact that it had been a moist fall greatly helped them enter properly.

Sister figured the day would be start and stop, hunt and peck, since last night was a full moon. Contented, stuffed, most foxes were curled up in their dens, a tidy pile of bones and fur outside the opening. Inky had buried her debris, not an unusual habit, though most foxes kept their own open garbage pit.

A field of fifty-nine showed up, formal attire creating a timeless tableaux of elegance. Bobby counted twenty-three Hilltoppers. He asked Ben Sidell if he would mind riding tail along with Sari Rasmussen, who volunteered for gate duty today. Jennifer rode tail with First Flight. Sister liked having someone to close the back door, as she put it. Also, if the field straggled; it wasn't good. They might turn a fox or, if the pack turned, hounds would have to run through horses. So Sari pushed up the Hilltoppers while Jennifer pushed up First Flight. Much as the girls liked being in First Flight, as close to the front as they could get without offending the adults, these days doing tail duty led to squeals of laughter back in the barn when they recounted what occurred. The tail rider sees everything: the misdeeds, the bobble in the saddle, the split britches, the bad fences.

When the field walks out, a hierarchy lines up behind the field master. For the Jefferson Hunt, this meant that Tedi and Edward rode in the master's pocket. As the oldest members with colors, they were entitled to pride of place. Also, they rode divine horses, so they could keep up. As the hunt unfolded, this hierarchy altered. Whoever could really ride, whoever was well mounted, could move up without censure, although few ever passed the Bancrofts. Occasionally Tedi would pull back if she sensed someone behind her who was antsy or who couldn't control his or her horse.

During joint meets, the visiting master, if that master did not hunt hounds, rode with Sister. Guests then rode forward as Jefferson members graciously fell back for them. Again, once the hunt unfolded, if some guests weren't well mounted, the Jefferson Hunt members could pass them without being considered rude.

The American way of hunting, most particularly in the South, involved manners, hospitality, and strict attention to the pleasure of one's guests. Hunts in other parts of the country could be equally as welcoming, but the southern hunts believed they performed these services better than anyone. And of course, the Virginia hunts took it as an article of faith that they towered over all other hunts, a fact not lost on other states, nor especially admired.

Many was the time that Sister repented being a Virginia master when she hunted, say, in Kentucky. So keen were those masters to show their mettle that they gleefully rode out in twelve-degree snowstorms, taking three- or four-foot stone fences.

The "By God, I'll show these Virginia snobs" attitude meant that the Virginians had to ride quite well in order to survive. Yet it was all in good fun. There is not a sport as companionable as foxhunting.

Sister looked over her shoulder at the line of well-turned-out riders snaking behind her as they briskly walked toward the peach orchard next to the farm road.

She remembered hunting in Ireland one fall after she and Ray had been married four years. The Irish rode right over them. She never forgot her first hedgerow jump with the yawning ditch on the other side. That night she thanked God for two things: One, she was an American. Two, she had rented a superb horse who took care of her.

Clay and Xavier whispered between themselves as hounds were not yet cast. Ronnie, riding just ahead, paid no attention. He'd listened to Xavier's wails of frustration over his poundage every day. Just because X was his best friend didn't mean there weren't times when X bored him to tears. He always thought that Dee was a saint, and he envied X his partner in life. Funny, too, for of all the original four friends, X, average-looking, would have seemed to be the last one to attract a marvelous woman.

Ronnie liked Izzy well enough, but she was impressed with her beauty and impressed with money a bit too much for him. His eyes darted over the field today. He'd known some of these people all his life. The newer ones brought fresh ideas and energy, and he had to admit that he learned from them. Pretty much he liked everyone out there, although Crawford irritated him. He wasn't overfond of Dalton Hill either.

Hounds reached the field across from the peach orchard, the low gray clouds offering hope of moisture and scent. The temperature clung to a steady thirty-nine degrees. The layer of fresh snow had had enough time to settle in, pack down a bit. The going might be icy in spots but mostly, if the horses had borium on their shoes, they should be okay.

A blacksmith charged $105 to shoe with borium, a bit of metal powder put onto the shoes. Some people put caulks in their horses' shoes, a kind of stud. Some could even be screwed in and then screwed out. Sister hated studs, refusing to use them. Like most horsemen, she had strong likes and dislikes. She had visions of her horse tearing the hell out of himself with studs if he overreached or stumbled, then scrambled, hitting his forefeet with his hind or catching the back of his foreleg. It wouldn't do.

As she watched Shaker cast hounds into the field, a wave of envy swept over her. Shaker was right. Once you hunt the hounds, you never want to go back. Still, she was a sensible woman. He was a gifted huntsman, and Jefferson Hunt was lucky to have him. She'd content herself with leading the field.

Trident picked his way over the snow. Trudy, Tinsel, and Trinity were out, along with Darby, Doughboy, Dreamboat, Dana, Delight, Diddy, Ribot, Rassle, and Ruthie.

Cora hoped the youngsters would keep it together. She, like Sister, felt good about their progress. A day like today could be tricky. The conditions seemed favorable, but the full moon last night generally made for a dull hunt. Cora hoped they could pick up a visiting red dog fox.

Nellie, Diana, Delia, Dasher, Dragon, Asa, Ardent, and the other veterans, like a scrimmage line sweeping forward, moved over the terrain.

Back in the house, Raleigh and Rooster were furious because Sister locked their dog door to the outside. Both dogs would shadow the hounds if they could, and they had no business doing that. Golly relished their misery.

"*Maybe we'll pick up Grace?*" Trident said.

"*Too far for her on a cold night like last night. She's over there at Foxglove by the water wheel.*" Asa had a fondness for the small red.

"What about Aunt Netty?" Ribot inhaled rabbit odor.

"Figure that any scent you get will most likely be dog fox," Delia instructed Ribot. *"The vixens sit because they know the dog foxes will come to them. If you do get a vixen's trail, chances are she hunted a bit; you're picking her up going back to her den, especially now."*

"Then why did we get long runs on vixens in late October?" Ruthie puzzled over this.

"The young fox entry, so to speak, left home to find their own dens. Don't you worry over that now," Delia instructed. *"I'm telling you what I've learned over the years, though if there is one thing I have learned about foxes, it's to expect the unexpected. For all I know, Ruthie, a vixen will show up and give us a ripping go today. They are peculiar creatures, foxes."*

Nellie, another old girl, giggled. *"That's what Shaker says about women: They're as peculiar as foxes."*

"Hasn't said much like that since he took a fancy to Lorraine." Ardent laughed.

The hounds laughed with him. If the humans heard, it would have sounded as though they were letting their breath out in little bursts.

Dragon, although pushing up front, was subdued. He kept half a step behind Cora, off to her right. For her part, next time he challenged her, she'd kill him. She was the head bitch as well as the strike hound, and she was in no mood to put up with any more bad behavior.

They pushed through the field heading east, toward After All Farm.

"Not much." Ardent caught a faint line. *"It's Comet."*

"Let's follow it, Ardent. Might be all we'll get today. If we're lucky, it will heat up." Cora trusted Ardent completely.

The hounds moved with Ardent as he turned northward. The scent warmed but remained faint until they crossed over the thin ice, breaking it, on a small feeder into Broad Creek.

"Better. Better," Asa called, and hounds opened.

Bare in the winter light, old silky willows, some fourteen feet high, dotted the path of the stream. Lafayette picked his way through the trappy ground, took a hop over the stream, trotting after hounds who were moving steadily but not with speed.

For twenty minutes, hounds pursued this line until they wound up at the base of Hangman's Ridge. Scent turned back along the edge of the farm road, heading back toward the peach orchard. Hounds took the half leap off the road, sunken with time and use, up into the peach orchard.

Betty, out in the open field on the left of the road, wondered if the fox might be close by. She was in a good spot to see him break cover.

Sybil, on the right, was at the edge of the peach orchard. Hounds moved through, baying stronger, moving at a faster trot. They cleared the orchard, crossed the grassy wide path separating the peach orchard from the apple orchard, then plunged into the apple orchard. They began a leisurely lope, Cora square on the line, but she no sooner reached the halfway point in the apple orchard than she turned a sharp left.

Betty intently, silently watched.

Shaker, on Showboat, followed. The scent was stronger now.

Comet, bright red, crossed the open field, glancing at Betty. He moved to the easternmost edge, jumped on the hog's back jump and from there to the fence line. Balancing himself, he carefully walked northward for one hundred yards, jumped off the fence line on the far side, and slipped into the woods.

Tempting though it was to follow the fox and have her own personal hunt, Betty patiently waited for the lead hounds to appear. Three minutes later, they broke from the apple orchard. Four minutes later, the bulk of the pack pressed behind Cora, Dragon, and Dasher. Betty could now see Shaker cantering through the snowy lane between apple rows. As the lead hounds drew even with her, she turned Outlaw and kept with them about ten o'clock off of Cora's twelve o'clock. The field, slushy in parts, demanded a tight seat.

Hounds, much lighter than a twelve-hundred-pound horse,

easily negotiated the terrain. They climbed over the hog's back, then stopped.

"Hold hard," Sister commanded.

The field reined in behind her, a few bumps here and there, a few curses muttered under someone's breath.

"I can't find him. All I have is the scent on the hog's back," Ruthie, excellent nose, barked.

"Keep calm, Ruthie. Foxes don't disappear into thin air much as they want us to think they do," Diana reassured her.

The field fanned out to get a better look, Clay and Izzy together—unusual because Izzy usually rode in the back with her gal pals. Sam Lorillard kept well to the rear and couldn't see a thing. Gray, too, couldn't see anything in the middle of the people, but he thought it unwise to go too far out in the field for a look in case the hounds turned. Those people craning their necks could be standing right on scent, ruining it for hounds if enough of them tore up the snow and the earth underneath.

Hounds milled about for two or three minutes.

Ardent suggested they move along the fence line in both directions with a splinter group going ahead from the hog's back in case the fox had managed to make a big leap of it.

"Have to be really big," Delia mumbled.

"Who is to say he didn't hitch a ride. Target once rode on Clytemnestra's back," Cora said. *"That's one story, anyway. None of us ever saw it, but he sure did lose us last season back in the apple orchard and we had him, had him fair and square."*

"We'd see tracks. We'd smell the vehicle." Dragon had no time for speculation as he moved right along the fence line.

Tinsel, moving left along the fence line, eager, got a snootful of fox scent. *"He's here!"*

Dragon, turning left in midair, raced to the young hound. *"It's Comet, all right."* Hounds opened, their voices a chorus of excitement.

Sister waited for Shaker to clear the hog's back, then she took it as the field followed.

The scent line—a magic trail of pungent delight—curled just above the snow. The temperature, forty-two degrees now, allowed it to lift off, releasing the musky aroma.

The hounds passed through the woods as Sister found the old deer trail. Moving at speed, the dips and rises in the earth barely registered in Sister's brain. Her only thought was to keep hounds in sight and not crowd Shaker, blowing as he rode, encouraging his pack.

A ravine cut crossways. The fox cleverly dipped down, using the rocks to foil his scent. He didn't go all the way down into this steep cleft in the earth. Hounds overran the line, yelped with frustration, and then began the patient process of returning to where they first lost the scent to look again.

Darby surprised everyone by examining the first bunch of rocks, some large and smooth covering twelve square feet, little crevices packed with blue ice. He picked up the line, charging up out of the ravine. He was so intent on his task, he forgot to tell the others.

Ardent watched him, ran over to the rocks, checked it out, then he, too, picked up the line. *"Here we are, buddies. Here we are."* He called up to Darby, *"Wait for the pack, Darby. Can't go off on your own like that, even when you're right. Steady there, fellow."*

Darby slowed as Ardent caught up to him. Within seconds Dragon, Dasher, and the lead hounds drew alongside.

"Good work," Cora praised him. *"Smart to wait."*

Darby, grateful to Ardent for saving him a tongue-lashing from Cora, put his nose down, lifted his head, and let out a song of happiness.

Hounds ran back through the woods, back under the fence line while the field searched for the closest jump, then back through the large snowy field, back to the base of Hangman's Ridge, where the fox disappeared. No scent. No anything. No tracks.

"This makes me crazy!" Tinsel wailed.

"He's around," Trident said with conviction.

Hounds milled about, confused. Diana noticed a thin trickle coming off the side of Hangman's Ridge, a trickle spilling over black jagged rocks. Underneath that was a mass of elongated blue ice that looked like icicles had melted a little, then refroze, creating this imposing mass. The fox had gotten under the trickle, following it down, water washing scent away.

By the time she picked up his trail Diana knew Comet had put a half-mile ahead of her. But still, scent is scent. She opened. Hounds moved around the base of the ridge, moving southward and then turning west into the long floodplain that Soldier's Road bisected.

The field became strung out, thanks to the footing, which had tired some horses more than their riders realized. They'd been pushing through the snow for an hour and a half now. Even Jennifer couldn't keep them all together; Bobby Franklin soon overlapped the rear of the First Flight, which was their problem not his.

Sister raised her crop over her head then let it fall. Cloud Nine, quite fit and with a marvelous ground-eating stride, opened up, passing stragglers, passing through the middle of the field, finally coming up behind the knot of hard riders behind Sister. He passed Izzy, who was falling behind. Came alongside Marty and Crawford, both doing quite well. Cloud Nine stretched out, and Sam figured, why fight with the horse? He was moving out, loving it, and at least there were no bottlenecks. He hoped he could rate the big thoroughbred if he needed to. They had been working on that.

But Picasso had other ideas, flattening his ears as he heard Cloud Nine come up. Clay moved out of the way and up, hearing the hooves behind him. Ronnie, better mounted and really a better rider, asked more of his horse and got it, moving up until he was next to Edward.

Walter fell back a little, figuring Rocketman didn't need to get into a race. Then, too, this was his first season with this horse, and he wanted to know him better.

As Cloud Nine came alongside X and Picasso, the paint let

out an ugly cow kick. Kicking is bad enough, but a cow kick—which is to the side—is nasty. The hooves, packed snow dislodging in a squished clump, shone dully in the cloudy light. Picasso just missed his target.

"Idiot!" X, his face dark, looked at Sam. "You're a groom. Stay to the rear!"

"You don't fool me, you fat pig. I know you and Clay will cream the insurance money. Cream it like you creamed Mitch and Anthony," Sam spat back, his voice loud.

"What the hell are you talking about?"

Sister turned, hearing the commotion. "Hark!"

This had no effect on the two as Sam bumped Picasso, like a ride off in polo, before the massive paint could kick out again. Then Sam moved ahead of Xavier, but not before X caught him around the neck with his thong, choking him, yanking him clean off his horse.

Clay, the strain too much, lost it when he heard Sam's brazen challenge to X. He didn't stop to separate the two. He blew past Tedi and Edward, came alongside Sister, reached down with his left hand, and grabbed Lafayette's reins.

"Hey!" Lafayette hollered.

Sister, cool, dropped the reins. "I'm sorry it was you, but I thought you'd take the bait."

Clay twisted in the saddle to hit her across the chest with his right hand, but he had to swing across his own chest. He couldn't get a square blow. Sister squeezed Lafayette to go faster. He was a faster horse than Clay's, but Lafayette, head turned toward Clay, couldn't lengthen his stride.

"Steady, steady," Sister spoke to her beloved horse.

Dropping her stirrup irons, she swung both legs back, then up for momentum, reached forward with her hands, using Lafayette's neck for balance. She half stood, both feet now in the middle of her saddle. Then she leapt over behind Clay.

Clay dropped Lafayette's reins, but the beautiful gray kept running alongside, calling to hounds, *"Cora! Diana! Delia, Nellie, hounds, stop, stop! Sister needs you."*

Nellie, at the back, heard him. *"Hold up, hold up!"* She bellowed for all she was worth.

The hounds slowed. Cora turned to see Sister, behind Clay, one arm around his neck, the other straining forward for the reins, which she couldn't reach.

Savagely, Clay elbowed her. Her legs were so strong she didn't weaken her grip on his horse even though she had no stirrups.

Tedi and Edward, on fast horses, moved close to the battling pair. The field watched in horror as their master clung to Clay and the horse.

She jerked Clay hard around the neck; his hands came up, and his horse skidded, hind end going out behind him, sliding along the snow. The two humans rolled off, fighting.

At six feet tall and 150 pounds of lean muscle, Sister was a formidable opponent. But Clay was six two, middle-aged, and 200 pounds. He was getting the better of her, but she refused to let him go. He reached into his pocket with his right hand, brought out a trapper jackknife, and flicked it open. He rammed his knee in her back and then brought the knife to her throat with his right hand, clasping her with his left arm.

Before he could cut into the jugular, Dragon, the strongest hound, hit him sideways. Eighty pounds of fury knocked Clay off Sister. The knife slid across her throat, blood spurting over her white stock tie, sprinkling the snow as she sank down on one knee, hand to her throat.

"Kill him!" Cora screamed. The entire pack swarmed Clay, tearing through his breeches, biting clean through his expensive Dehner boots, gouging his hands as he instinctively covered his own throat.

Shaker blew them back. They refused to obey. He galloped up, dismounted as Betty and Sybil came in. He saw blood on the snow and wanted to kill Clay himself.

"Leave him. *Leave him!*" The pack obeyed with outraged reluctance.

Clay, although badly torn, lurched for his mount, who had scrambled to his feet and was standing still. As Clay vaulted for his horse, Gray, riding faster than he had ever ridden in his life, caught up to Clay, leaned over, and knocked him down.

Walter jumped off Rocketman before his horse even stopped, tearing through the snow to Sister, blood seeping through her fingers as she clutched her throat.

Betty and Sybil took their cues from Shaker, who was standing stock-still. Walter was a doctor. If he needed them, he'd ask. Meanwhile, the pack, snarling as they watched Clay stumble toward his horse again, needed to be held in check.

Gray turned. As he did, Edward rode up. The two men got off their horses and grabbed Clay. Without a word Edward put his crop across Clay's throat, tying his hands with the long thong so that if he moved he'd choke himself.

Dalton Hill and Isabelle could be seen in the distance, riding for all they were worth to reach the trailers.

Ben Sidell didn't bother chasing them. He plucked out his cell phone, giving his officers the particulars.

Sam and Xavier stopped beating the crap out of each other. They crawled up on their horses and rode up to the debacle.

Ben arrived.

"Surface cut, thank God," Walter said to Ben as he tenderly untied Sister's stock tie, rewrapping it around her neck as a bandage.

"Jesus Christ, Sister, you a rodeo queen or something!" Ben cursed out of admiration and relief.

She nodded, and Walter put his arms around her. She couldn't speak.

Tedi, also on foot now, having handed her reins to Ronnie,

came over to see if her dearest friend needed help. She stopped a moment, the picture of Walter embracing Sister filling her with emotion. Tears spilled over her cheeks.

To herself she thought, A son has come home. To Sister she said, "Janie, Janie, let me help you home."

"I can ride back," Sister croaked. Her throat hurt from the cut and from the fight. She half whispered to X and Sam, "Thanks boys, well done."

"My God, you're a hardhead." Tedi threw back her head, laughing as the tension leached out of her, laughing because they were still alive.

"Good hounds," Shaker's voice trembled with emotion.

"We want to go to Mom," Diana implored Shaker.

The pack inched toward Sister. Shaker, knowing them as he did, walked on Showboat to his master.

"I can still kill him!" Dragon sang out.

Cora came up to Sister, looking up at the woman. *"You okay?"*

That did it. Tears flooded, and Sister knelt down as her hounds gathered around her, kissing her, rubbing up against her. Lafayette bowed his head as he, too, nudged her.

"The best friends, my best friends," Sister cried, hugging and petting each hound.

By now everyone in the field was crying, even Xavier and Sam. Xavier looked at Clay. A lifetime friendship smashed, but another saved. He sobbed. He had at that moment realized how much he loved Sister, as did Ronnie.

"Sister, why don't we walk back to the farm?" Shaker found his voice at last.

She replied in a loud whisper, "I can ride. Walter can fix me up later, right?"

"I'll ride with her. Looks worse than it is, Shaker." Walter cupped his hands for Sister's left boot. Tedi held Lafayette, who nickered happily when he felt her familiar weight on his back

Tedi turned to the field, her voice strong. "We're calling it a day. Your master is determined to ride back, so we'll ride with her." She paused, searching out each concerned face, then broke into a smile even as the tears ran down her face again. "She's bullheaded, but I love her."

Everyone started talking at once as sirens could be heard roaring down Soldier Road.

By the time they reached the kennels, four squad cars had Dalton and Isabelle penned in by the trailers.

Walter insisted that Sister sit down in her kitchen. The girls took the horses even as Sister complained in a hoarse voice that she needed to count her hounds.

"You can do that later." Walter took charge.

Betty kissed Sister on the cheek. "Shaker, Sybil, and I can handle it. I'll be up when we're done. *You* take care of *you*, Sister. There's only one Sister."

Tedi, Edward, and Gray followed Walter up as Sister grumbled that she didn't need an escort, she was fine, et cetera et cetera.

Once Sister was seated on the kitchen chair, Raleigh and Rooster, smelling her blood, whimpered and came over, sticking to her like glue.

"Go lie down," she croaked.

"If I lick you, you'll heal faster," Raleigh promised.

"Ugh." Golly jumped on Sister's lap. *"Dog licks, yuck. I can do better."* She put her paws on either side of Sister's neck as Walter unwound the stock tie.

"Golly, you need to get down," Sister told her.

When Golly wouldn't budge, Tedi reached over, picked up the cat, and placed her on the floor.

"I'll get even," Golly threatened as she joined Raleigh in his bed.

Edward, holding Sister's black frock, realized the front was sopping with blood. He put the coat in the mudroom, making a mental note to take it to the dry cleaner's.

Walter unbuttoned the front of her white shirt, also covered with blood. "Sister, you need to take this off. I want to make sure you don't have other injuries. When your adrenaline gets high like that, sometimes you won't feel a broken bone for hours."

Sister looked at Edward and Gray. "I'm not really all that modest, but I do ask you men to remember that Britney Spears doesn't have anything that I don't have; I've just had it longer."

They laughed at that, then Edward said, "Gray, why don't we go to the library? Walter, if you need us, you know where we are."

"I do." Walter waited for her to remove her blouse, then gingerly pulled off the long-sleeved silk undershirt.

Tedi watched as Walter felt her ribs, the bones in her neck and arms. "Clay landed a couple of good ones."

"Yeah, but the frock is heavy."

"Mmm, you'll have some bruises." He pointed to red marks on her chest, a large one on her back where she hit the ground.

Tedi drew closer. "They'll turn a fetching shade of black, then purple, then burgundy."

"Peachy." Sister felt her neck sting where it was cut.

"I'm going to wash this. You'll feel it," Walter warned her.

Tedi brought over a bowl of warm water, went into the downstairs bathroom and brought out a washrag and a towel. Sister closed her eyes when Walter washed it, the wound bleeding anew as the caked blood was rinsed off.

"Stitches?" Tedi inquired.

"No." Walter checked to see how deep the cut was. "She was lucky. Keep it clean. It's going to continue to seep blood. Wrap a soft gauze around your neck. You clot up quickly enough, but every time you take the gauze off it will seep a little. I'll bring over some antiseptic."

"What about Neosporin?" Tedi asked. "She's got that upstairs."

"It will help."

"Oh, just slap Betadine on me," Sister suggested.

"If you want to walk around with an orange neck, that's okay by me." Walter squeezed her shoulder. "Take a long hot bath once we're all out of here. The sooner you get in the bathtub, the better. It will help the thumps and bumps," Walter ordered. "And when you're finished put some ice on that chest bruise."

"I'll stay with her," Tedi offered.

"I'm not crippled."

"Not yet," Tedi replied slyly. "And while I'm here, we can indulge in girl talk. You can tell me why Clay attacked you. I'm assuming you knew more about that fire than the rest of us."

"Couldn't prove a thing. Clay just flipped his switch."

"With your help, I'm sure," Tedi replied. "I'm going upstairs to draw your bath."

CHAPTER 42

She hurt in places she didn't even know she had. Moving stiffly, Sister walked through the boys' run at the kennels. They had been turned back out after eating in the feed room.

"Boys, thank you." Sister touched each head, knelt down with a pang to rub their broad chests.

"I was ready to kill him." Dragon pushed his head under her hand, moving his brother out of the way.

"You're a bold fellow, Dragon." She reached over the handsome tricolor to smooth the pate of Dasher. "Boys," she addressed all her dog hounds, "you're the loves of my life."

She then returned to the feed room, where the girls were. She told them they were wonderful, but didn't bother them as they were eating. Diana kept leaving the long orange metal feeder to touch Sister with her nose.

"Good girl, now go eat or Delia and Nellie will eat your share."

"Delia's the porker, not me," Nellie replied.

"Thanks for washing my kennel coat. Must have done that last night," Shaker said.

"Tedi stayed over, so we banged out a few chores. She tried to keep me in the tub, but I was turning into a white prune. Anyway, I can't sit around."

"I wish I'd seen you jump on Clay's horse. I was up with hounds and didn't know what was going on until the pack turned. Damnedest thing, the pack turning like that. Just left off the scent and came to you."

"Thank God, they did. Lafayette whinnied, the tail hounds turned." She leaned against the wall; her back hurt. "They communicate with one another. Once we could, too. Once we were part of nature's grand conversation, but we got about our raisins. We lord it over all, but we're alone, desperately alone."

He folded his arms over his broad chest. "One way to put it. Mostly, I think we're sick."

"Sick and savage or sick and cowardly. Not much in between." She ruefully nodded. "Tedi thinks more deeply than I do. Always has. We were talking last night, and she said people's emotions were stronger in the Middle Ages. People expressed them. We're muted. The farther we move away from nature, from our animal selves and from other animals, the more we vitiate our emotions. Actually, she was more eloquent than that; I'm recalling it as best I can."

Shaker smiled. "Bet Gray would have gladly taken care of you last night."

She quickly returned the smile. "Lucky me, but it was a night to be with my oldest friend, a night of two souls, if you know what I mean. I think that comes with deep friendship. Once sex gets into the picture, there's a blast of lust, desire, magic. But that quiet, eternal love between best friends," she said, looking into his eyes, "there is nothing like it in the world."

"My brother," Shaker replied. "Have that with my brother. Don't get to see him much, though."

"We're lucky. We both have a strong circle of dear friends, and now it looks like we might have a bit of the other." He blushed, and she continued. "The people who don't have that love become bitter, or they dry out. Hateful. I think that's what happened to Clay."

"He had friends. Had a wife."

"He was never honest. He lied since the time he was a kid. Always wanting to be something he wasn't. Married for show not for a deep emotional connection."

"There's no excuse for him."

"No. But it's funny some folks aren't satisfied. More, always want more."

"Ben call?"

"Briefly. Clay won't confess to anything. Declaring mental anguish, breakdown." She drew in her breath. "Some truth to it. Izzy's clammed up, too, but Ben said the good Dr. Hill is singing like a canary."

"And?"

"Drugs. Performance drugs. Like I suspected."

"Too bad we didn't get any." Shaker stifled a guffaw.

"I know." She laughed with him. "Course it's one thing if someone my age takes HGH. Quite another if a fifteen-year-old high school kid shoots up, you know? And Dalton said their network covered the entire mid-South."

"What did Mitch and Anthony have to do with it?"

"Delivered the drugs in the furniture. They never made the long runs out of state because Clay figured they'd go on a bender somewhere between here and Tennessee. Mitch figured it out and told Anthony. They decided to blackmail Clay. Remember, Shaker, those two might have had moments of lucidity, but they'd killed a lot of brain cells. Like dopes, they threatened Clay directly. He paid them, and they'd immediately drink it up. It was easy after a few months of this to put hemlock in two bottles of whiskey. Clay was a Pony Clubber, took the nature courses with me as a kid; he knew cowbane as well as I did. He could dig it up and not get sick. And there's cowbane all over. We can't get rid of it. That part wasn't too hard for Clay. Jesus, it's so bloody stupid."

"Yeah, it is."

"And Izzy sat down in the lap of luxury and didn't want to get up again."

"She was sleeping with Dalton, too. No surprise. She was perfectly ready to ditch Clay when the going got rough. Made me think of the hunt at Foxglove when Bitsy shadowed Uncle Yancy. Izzy and Dalton were sure looking out for each other. Poor Clay loved being rich. He loved it so much, he set aside right from wrong."

"What happened to Donnie?"

"Made a dumb move. He saw Anthony and Mitch get extra money here and there. Anthony told him what they were doing, getting money out of Clay. Donnie wouldn't have figured it out for himself. So Donnie got in the act, demanding a lot more once Anthony and Mitch were out of the way."

"You'd think he'd know he was next."

"You would, wouldn't you? The human mind has a fabulous capacity for denial. Clay lured him to the warehouse; they had a brief struggle. Donnie lost consciousness, although not by a blow to the head. Gaston Marshall thinks Clay shut off Donnie's air, hence the bruised windpipe."

"He's a good coroner. Had to be to figure anything out from that charred corpse."

"And it was Clay who set the fire. The tip-off was the gas can being so close to Donnie. He wasn't that woefully stupid, at least not about physical things."

Yeah. Makes sense." Shaker wiped his hand on his kennel coat. "Three people dead. For what? Three more will go to jail."

"They lived high on the hog for a while."

"Trinity." Shaker walked over to the young hound. "Over here." He moved her to a less-crowded feeder. "Always wants to be next to her sisters, and they eat faster than she does."

"She's a lady about her table manners."

"She's the only one." Shaker laughed.

"Well, I'm glad we switched to the higher-fat-content feed when we did, high protein, too. With this cold and the incredible runs we've been having, the children would have gotten down in weight quickly. I hate to see a weedy pack."

"Once it goes off, it's hard to get it back on until season's over. They're like people; some incline to weight and some do not. Most of our pack inclines to being lean."

"Yes, they do. And I never praise you enough for your kennel practices and your attention to nutrition. Look at the shine on those coats."

"That's my job," he modestly replied.

"Hey, there's people out there doing the same job, 'cept they don't know what they're doing. Boy, if you get a master who doesn't know hounds and the huntsman's not worth squat, the poor pack suffers. Another reason why we need the MFHA and district reps." She mentioned the Master of the Foxhounds Association of America, which divided Canada and the United States into districts, each one with a chosen representative.

One of the duties of that representative was to make sure every hound pack in his or her jurisdiction was properly kept.

"They're getting like the government, sending paperwork."

"To me."

"Then you give it to me!"

"Some of it." She poked him with her forefinger.

"Think Clay could have gotten away with it?" asked Shaker, returning to the dramatic events.

"He snapped. But he was sloppy, too. Wouldn't it have been smarter to keep paying off Mitch and Anthony and then dispose of them later, somewhere far away? Makes me believe the pressure was already getting to him. Maybe Izzy was greedier than we know, or maybe Dalton got cold feet. Sounds like Dalton's the type."

Shaker's eyes twinkled. "Committing perfect murders now, are you?"

"Me?"

"You said Clay could have handled this better than he did."

Her face reddened. "You're right."

"Maybe it's easy," he said.

"What?"

"Murder. Stealing, other stuff. Maybe you think about what's right for you, and you don't think about what's right for the rest of us. What's the difference between Clay Berry and Kenneth Lay? Sure, boss, Kenneth Lay didn't kill anyone, but is the impulse different?"

"It's tricky, Shaker. I break rules. I go over the speed limit if I think I can get away with it. Maybe that's the same impulse you're talking about: a self-centeredness."

"Not the same," he replied.

"Okay, take another kind of rule: sexual behavior. I broke the rules when I was younger. Maybe I'm breaking them now. What's the difference between that, and, say, thinking you'll sell OxyContin because people want it? Is it a fixed set of morals? Are they written in stone? Is sexual behavior on a different plane than financial behavior? If you start to think about it, you'll run yourself crazy."

"No, you won't." His voice was firm. "Sex is about our animal self. That's nature. Money, that's man-made. Animals defend their turf, but we've created elaborate ownerships that pass from generation to generation. In nature, each animal has to be strong enough to defend his or her territory, like the mountain lion we ran up or the badger. We've bent the natural rules and we keep bending them. It's one thing to have an affair, it's another to kill three people."

"You're right, but when I think about this stuff, I get dizzy. And when I started to figure out this really was Clay's doing, it made me sick. It was under my nose, but I didn't want to see it. I finally did, though."

"Hard to look at an old friend in a new way."

They chattered until all hounds were fed, yards picked up, runs cleaned and washed down.

Then they left the kennels, passing the paddocks, including the mare paddocks.

Secretary's Shorthand stood in the snow, nuzzling a light bay foal who was wobbly, but nursing.

"Boss, what's that foal doing in there?"

Sister, despite her bruises, climbed over the fence, Shaker right behind her. They walked up to the contented mare.

"She didn't show!" Sister was amazed and thrilled.

"Hardly bagged up either." He reached over and squeezed one of Secretary's nipples; a stream of rich milk oozed out. "She's producing okay."

"Delivered the baby herself!"

Shaker laughed, face radiant. "They do it in the wild all the time, but I didn't think she was in foal either. Sometimes they fool you."

Sister nodded, slipping her arm around his waist. "Life. New life!"

SOME USEFUL TERMS

AWAY—A fox has "gone away" when he has left the covert. Hounds are "away" when they have left the covert on the line of the fox.

BRUSH—The fox's tail.

BURNING SCENT—Scent so strong or hot that hounds pursue the line without hesitation.

BYE DAY—A day not regularly on the fixture card.

CAP—The fee nonmembers pay to a hunt for that day's sport.

CARRY A GOOD HEAD—When hounds run well together to a good scent, a scent spread wide enough for the whole pack to feel it.

CARRY A LINE—When hounds follow the scent. This is also called "working a line."

CAST—Hounds spread out in search of scent. They may cast themselves or be cast by the huntsman.

CHARLIE—A term for a fox. A fox may also be called Reynard.

CHECK—When hounds lose the scent and stop. The field must wait quietly while the hounds search for scent.

COLORS—A distinguishing color—usually worn on the collar but sometimes on the facings of a coat—that identifies a hunt. Colors can be awarded only by the master and can be won only in the field.

COUPLE STRAPS—Two-strap hound collars connected by a swivel link. Some members of staff will carry these on the right rear of the saddle. Since the Middle Ages hounds had been brought to the meets coupled. Hounds are always spoken of, counted, in couples. Today hounds walk or are driven to the meets. Rarely, if ever, are they coupled, but a whipper-in still carries couple straps should a hound need assistance.

COVERT—A patch of woods or bushes where a fox might hide. Pronounced *cover*.

CRY—How one hound tells another what is happening. The sound will differ according to the various stages of the chase. It's also called "giving tongue" and should occur when a hound is working a line.

CUB HUNTING—The informal hunting of young foxes in the late summer and early fall, before formal hunting. The main purpose is to enter young hounds into the pack. Until recently only the most knowledgeable members were invited to cub hunt since they would not interfere with young hounds.

DOG FOX—The male fox.

DOG HOUND—The male hound.

DOUBLE—A series of short, sharp notes blown on the horn to alert all that a fox is afoot. The "gone away" series of notes are a form of doubling the horn.

DRAFT—To acquire hounds from another hunt is to draft them.

DRAW—The plan by which a fox is hunted or searched for in a certain area, like a covert.

DRIVE—The desire to push the fox, to get up with the line. It's a very desirable trait in a hound, so long as they remain obedient.

DWELL—To hunt without getting forward. A hound that dwells is a bit of a putterer.

ENTER—Hounds are entered into the pack when they first hunt, usually during cubbing season.

FIELD—The group of people riding to hounds, exclusive of the master and hunt staff.

FIELD MASTER—The person appointed by the master to control the field. Often it is the master him- or herself.

FIXTURE—A card sent to all dues-paying members, stating when and where the hounds will meet. A fixture card properly received is an invitation to hunt. This means the card would be mailed or handed to you by the master.

GONE AWAY—The call on the horn when the fox leaves the covert.

GONE TO GROUND—A fox who has ducked into his den or some other refuge has gone to ground.

GOOD NIGHT—The traditional farewell to the master after the hunt, regardless of the time of day.

HILLTOPPER—A rider who follows the hunt but who does not jump. Hilltoppers are also called the "second field." The jumpers are called the "first flight."

HOICK—The huntsman's cheer to the hounds. It is derived from the Latin *hic haec hoc*, which means "here."

HOLD HARD—To stop immediately.

HUNTSMAN—The person in charge of the hounds in the field and in the kennel.

KENNELMAN—A hunt staff member who feeds the hounds and cleans the kennels. In wealthy hunts there may be a number of kennelmen. In hunts with a modest budget, the huntsman or even the master cleans the kennels and feeds hounds.

LARK—To jump fences unnecessarily when hounds aren't running. Masters frown on this since it is often an invitation to an accident.

LIFT—To take the hounds from a lost scent in the hopes of finding a better scent farther on.

LINE—The scent trail of the fox.

LIVERY—The uniform worn by the professional members of the

hunt staff. Usually it is scarlet, but blue, yellow, brown, or gray are also used. The recent dominance of scarlet has to do with people buying coats off the rack as opposed to having tailors cut them. (When anything is mass-produced the choices usually dwindle, and such is the case with livery.)

MASK—The fox's head.

MEET—The site where the day's hunting begins.

MFH—The master of foxhounds; the individual in charge of the hunt: hiring, firing, landowner relations, opening territory (in large hunts this is the job of the hunt secretary), developing the pack of hounds, determining the first cast of each meet. As in any leadership position, the master is also the lightning rod for criticism. The master may hunt the hounds, although this is usually done by a professional huntsman, who is also responsible for the hounds in the field, at the kennels. A long relationship between a master and a huntsman allows the hunt to develop and grow.

NOSE—The scenting ability of a hound.

OVERRIDE—To press hounds too closely.

OVERRUN—When hounds shoot past the line of scent. Often the scent has been diverted or foiled by a clever fox.

RATCATCHER—The informal dress worn during cubbing season and bye days.

STERN—A hound's tail.

STIFF-NECKED FOX—One that runs in a straight line.

STRIKE HOUNDS—Those hounds who through keenness, nose, and often higher intelligence find the scent first and who press it.

TAIL HOUNDS—Those hounds running at the rear of the pack. This is not necessarily because they aren't keen; they may be older hounds.

TALLYHO—The cheer when the fox is viewed. Derived from the Norman *ty a hillaut,* thus coming into our language in 1066.

TONGUE—To vocally pursue the fox.

VIEW HALLOO (HALLOA)—The cry given by a staff member who views a fox. Staff may also say tallyho or tally back should the fox turn back. One reason a different cry may be used by staff, especially in territory where the huntsman can't see the staff, is that the field in their enthusiasm may cheer something other than a fox.

VIXEN—The female fox.

WALK—Puppies are "walked out" in the summer and fall of their first year. It's part of their education and a delight for puppies and staff.

WHIPPERS-IN—Also called whips, these are the staff members who assist the huntsman, who make sure the hounds "do right."

About the Author

Rita Mae Brown is the bestselling author of (among others) *Rubyfruit Jungle, Six of One, Southern Discomfort, Outfoxed, Hotspur,* and a memoir, *Rita Will.* She also collaborates with her tiger cat, Sneaky Pie, on the *New York Times* bestselling Mrs. Murphy mystery series. An Emmy-nominated screenwriter and a poet, she lives in Charlottesville, Virginia. She is master and huntsman of the Oak Ridge Foxhunt Club.